ARCANA

A HISTORICAL FANTASY

JESSICA LEAKE

Talos Press

Talos Press books may be purchased in bulk at special discounts for sales promotion, corporate gifts, fund-raising, or educational purposes. Special editions can also be created to specifications. For details, contact the Special Sales Department, Talos Press, 307 West 36th Street, 11th Floor, New York, NY 10018 or info@skyhorsepublishing.com.

Talos® and Talos Press® are registered trademarks of Skyhorse Publishing, Inc.®, a Delaware corporation.

Visit our website at www.skyhorsepublishing.com.

10 9 8 7 6 5 4 3 2 1

Library of Congress Cataloging-in-Publication Data

Leake, Jessica. Arcana : a novel /
Jessica Leake.
        pages cm ISBN 978-1-940456-14-0 (hardback)
        I. Title. PS3612.
        E216A73 2014 813'.6--dc23

Cover design by Jason Snair

Print ISBN: 978-1-940456-34-8
Ebook ISBN: 978-1-940456-57-7

Printed in the United States of America

For my best friend and love of my life, who also
happens to be my husband

ONE

Bransfield Estate, Gloucestershire, England 1905

THE horse's hooves thunder across the hillside, and my heart pounds with each bunching of his muscles. My hair breaks free of its pins, pale strands sweeping across my cheek. Though the wind breaks through the thin barrier of my breeches and tall boots, the smile never leaves my face. Mild discomfort is a small price to pay for a journey unhindered by the heavy skirts of my riding habit.

I glance at Robert, who is keeping easy pace with me.

"Careful, dear sister," Robert calls out, the wind snatching at his words, "I'm gaining on you."

I laugh. "Serenity will refuse to jump this next bank, just as she always does."

I press my booted heels to Orion's sides, and a little thrill jolts through me as he charges forward. His excitement bubbles over my skin, making his buoyant joy hard to distinguish from my own. Arcana, derived from the warmth of the sun, cloaks us both, its invisible golden bands connecting us until we are nearly one creature. He floods my mind with his every thought: the way the light layer of snow gives way beneath his hooves, how crisp the air smells when he takes deep breaths, the light pressure of my weight on his back. The mare behind him is on his mind, too, a speck of awareness I take advantage of; it tells me how close I am to reaching the creek before my brother, therefore winning our little race.

The bank jump approaches. It's nothing but a fallen log on a hilltop, but from this direction, the horses will have to jump down nearly four feet. Orion's ears prick forward as he notices the log, and his strides increase. I loosen the reins and let him have his head.

One heartbeat, two, and then he arcs over it. I follow his center of balance, lifting up slightly from the saddle as his legs stretch toward the snowy ground beneath us. His front hooves land, the rest of his body follows, and his long strides cover the ground until we are at the creek. I spin him around to face the bank.

The teasing smirk on my face disappears as Robert's horse jumps the log. "Well done," I say, pride blooming in my chest.

But then Robert's mare slips on the landing.

Too fast, her legs fold beneath her weight, dragging my brother down with her. I drop the reins and sit up straight in the saddle. My arms reach toward Robert as though I am trying to catch him. A deep tug at the core of me, and my power unfurls, sliding over my skin like silk. The familiar smell of energy releasing washes over me, like the refreshing scent of the earth right after it rains.

Golden light pours from my fingertips and bathes Robert and his horse in brightness. Robert squints as the light glitters around him, illuminating his mop of unruly blond hair. The arcana stops Serenity's fall and suspends her inches above the ground.

I wince as more energy siphons away; it becomes more difficult to concentrate. There are times when drawing from the sun as a source of power is not always convenient; a heavily clouded sky, one which renders the sun's rays essentially useless, is one of those times. With each beat of my heart, more energy leaves me. Pain radiates from my chest as Serenity treads the air in slow motion. When she finally straightens out her legs, the light fades, leaving them safe at the bottom of the hill.

As though I've just surfaced from the depths of the ocean, I take gulping breaths of air. My heart flutters wildly while my hands fall to my lap as the rest of me goes limp. The power of arcana leaves me, and Orion tosses his head at the loss of connection. Like a room suddenly plunged into darkness,

Orion's images disappear from my mind, and I can no longer guide him by my thoughts alone.

Robert walks his mare toward me. My lips part in surprise when I see his wide grin. "Wren," he says, "beautiful save with the light. I would have been a broken wreck for sure."

I try to smile back, but the image of Robert twisted beneath his horse at the bottom of a hill makes it impossible. I force some tension back into my limbs, since I refuse to let him know how much using arcana has cost me.

When I fail to respond, he tilts his head, the smile falling. "Are you alright? You look pale."

Fatigue threatens to take over, but I fight it. My heart beats sluggishly in my chest. *Don't lose consciousness. Don't lose consciousness.* As if the sky hears my prayer, the clouds part, and a slice of sunshine falls across my arm. I soak up its energy greedily. It fills my body like partaking of a banquet after days of no food. In a few heartbeats, my strength is almost restored, my brother none the wiser.

"Of course I'm pale," I say. "I just watched my brother nearly break his neck."

"Come now, you can't still be fretting over that little mishap. I'm well." He gives his horse a pat on the neck. "Serenity is well."

"You're incorrigible. Next you'll be crowing you got the silly thing to jump it in the first place."

His grin returns. "Of course. I'm only sorry I didn't make it to the creek in time."

I give the smallest shake of my head. "Let's rest here for a few moments, since I'm in no hurry to return home. Father will have our heads for racing the horses again."

Robert chuckles. "My head, perhaps. Yours he will dote over and continue to ignore every wild thing you do."

I give a shrug of my shoulders. "It's the least he can do when one considers how much time and energy goes into keeping my darling older brother alive."

He opens his mouth to retort, but shuts it immediately after, a look of concern flashing across his face. I follow his line of sight to Margaret, one of the maids. Her shawl has slipped unheeded to the ground, and an overturned basket of bread lies at her feet.

Though she is too far for me to make out her precise expression, I can tell by her stiff posture that something is very wrong. My heart pounds a warning inside my chest.

"Margaret!" I call out, my voice wavering despite my best effort to appear calm. "Are you alright?"

My voice seems to rouse her, and she takes one small step backward. Robert and I—even our horses—stand frozen, awaiting her response. Instead of answering, she turns and flees. I watch slushy footprints form ahead of us as cold dread fills my stomach.

"She saw everything," Robert says, his face tight.

I manage a single nod. Our father will not be pleased.

Charles, our footman, greets us as we enter the manor. His eyes are quick to avoid mine, and the snake pit of nerves within me returns. Does the whole house know already?

"Begging your pardon, milady," he says while Robert kicks the dirt and snow from his boots. "Your father would like to see you in his study."

"Thank you, Charles," I say, and he responds with a short bow. I give him a harried smile before pulling Robert into one of the nearby sitting rooms.

The room's cheerful yellow chintz print on the walls does nothing to calm me. I close the door and lean against it. "I told you we should've questioned Margaret."

Unflappable as usual, Robert flips on the lamp beside his favorite chair and sits down. "What would you have me do? Run her down on horseback? I'm sure *that* wouldn't have frightened her at all."

"She's obviously told everyone she encountered."

"Margaret is as kind and timid as a mouse. I very much doubt she told everyone. We didn't give her that much of a head start."

I shake my head. "Charles knows. He could barely stand to look at me."

Robert's expression turns skeptical. "You mean the way he always looks at you when you're dressed as a gentleman instead of a lady? Truly, Wren, you're reading too much into everything. This has happened before," Robert says in his infuriatingly nonchalant way, "and it will happen again."

"I was seven the last time it happened," I say, my voice coming out as more of a screech. "Everything's different now."

Robert crosses his arms over his chest. "Do you regret saving me?"

I shoot him an exasperated look. "Of course not."

"And I very much doubt Father will be angry with you for saving his only son."

"Yes, but—"

"Father hand-picked each of the servants here to be loyal and to hold their tongues. Most of them have been here since we were children." His lips curve in a half-grin. "And, honestly, who will believe such an impossible tale?"

I rub my forehead, trying to ease the tension amassed there. "Mr. Baxter will." As butler, he was head of the servants. He knew all.

Robert snorts. "I'm sure he already does. He's probably the first person she went to, and you should be thankful since he'll put a stop to the spread of it."

My shoulders relaxed marginally. Robert was right, of course. Mr. Baxter had been with our family since before even Robert had been born. He was unfailingly loyal and would tolerate nothing less from the others. Unfortunately, he had no doubt already talked to Margaret, and Papa would know we'd disobeyed him in every possible way—again. "We shouldn't have raced again today."

"If I recall correctly, you were the one to suggest such an outing in the first place."

I blow a lock of hair out of my face. "Did I? Well, even if that were true—"

"It is true."

I narrow my eyes. "Even if it were true, I still think you should accompany me to explain."

He shakes his head. "I'm sure Father will want to meet with me as well, but I'd rather send you in first to appraise his mood."

"What kind of an older brother are you?" I demand.

Robert lets out a loud bark of laughter. "The kind who knows his father has a soft spot for his silly younger sisters. I will walk you to the door, but no farther."

"Very well." I glance down at my mud-splattered breeches. "Perhaps I should change?"

"It's too late now," Robert says with some sympathy. "I'm sure he already knows. You'll only make it worse to keep him waiting."

We leave the cheery room and make our way down the long hall, our boots echoing on the wood.

Outside the white panel door, I take a deep breath, and Robert pats me on the back. I knock once, and Mr. Baxter opens the door.

His ruddy face holds very little emotion, but he gives my arm a squeeze as I walk by. I have the urge to throw my arms around his generous middle as I used to do when I was younger and had done something wrong. He would always comfort me with a kind word and a scone stolen from the kitchen. Today, however, I straighten my spine and walk over to Papa.

My father sits in his favorite brocade chair by the fire, a book in one hand, and a cup of tea in the other—but only because it's daytime. Were it evening, the tea cup would be replaced by a glass of scotch. He is surrounded by books—some so old the binding struggles to retain their hold on the pages within—all in piles that threaten to topple at any moment. Papers and pens littered on the top of the mahogany desk obscure its beauty, and if it weren't for the servants, the whole room would likely be covered in dust.

Even still, the room is cozily familiar, lit only by a small lamp and the fire.

He lowers his book to the little side table and gestures for me to sit in the matching chair across from him.

"You wanted to speak to me, Papa?" I ask. I search his face for a sign of his mood, but if the tired lines around his mouth and eyes are any indication, he is more exhausted than angry.

"Indeed, my dear." He leans back in his chair, and I try to take comfort from the relaxed position. "I find I'm at my wit's end."

I clasp my hands together in my lap, but I cannot prevent my eyebrow from arching.

"This is your eighteenth year, is it not?"

"Yes, Papa." The tiniest hint of where this conversation is going enters my mind, and I grip the arms of my chair.

"Ah." His eyebrows furrow. "And yet you still insist on deliberately disobeying every social edict you've learned from both your governess and myself?"

"I'm not sure I understand—"

He cuts me off with a gesture toward my clothes. A small clump of snow drips off my boot incriminatingly. "Your manner of dress. Riding astride. Racing with your brother. Shall I continue?"

I bite my tongue to keep from arguing. The color rises in his cheeks, and I know he is past listening to my excuses. I shake my head.

"Indeed, I feel I must. For I've just spoken with Mr. Baxter." He eyes me with his bushy eyebrows raised. "Seems Margaret witnessed an unusual event this afternoon." He turns to the butler. "Mr. Baxter, would you be so kind as to repeat to Katherine what Margaret said?"

"Of course, my lord," Mr. Baxter says. "Margaret returned from a trip to town this afternoon and saw Katherine using arcana to save Robert from a terrible fall. Apparently his horse tried to take a jump but slipped at the last moment." He pauses to look at me with more than a hint of admiration. "Margaret was frightened but very willing to keep the family secret—once she realized no harm would come to her."

"Thank you, Baxter, that will be all," Papa says, and Mr. Baxter bows and leaves us.

"Papa, I had no choice," I say as soon as the door closes behind him. "Robert would have . . ." I choke on the thought of what might have happened, swallow, and try again. "He would have been gravely injured had I not intervened."

"No one is contesting that fact, my dear. But it's because of your poor choices that you were forced into such a dangerous situation." He points at the snow falling lightly outside. "The slush is no condition for a race—especially for a lady."

Guilt and a strong urge to defend my right to enjoy a ride in the countryside battled within me. "I regret I had to use arcana," I say, unwilling at the moment to apologize for much else.

He gives me a long, appraising look. I resist the urge to squirm in my chair. "With any luck, Margaret will not reveal what she saw to anyone from town. But of course, you needn't worry about that."

My eyes dart to his. I don't like the hint of warning in his tone.

"You've left me with no choice, Katherine. I've decided you will travel to London to have your debut at the start of the season."

I jump to my feet. "So soon! You said I could wait until I turned nineteen."

"That was before you continually ignored good sense." His expression softens. "My darling, you know I love you, but I feel I have been remiss in my fatherly duties. Your dear mother would have wanted you to be a proper lady, to be as comfortable in the bosom of Society as you are on the back of a horse." He rubs his mustache with his thumb and forefinger. "You'll never find a suitable husband holed up in the country—especially if what happened today spreads around town. As difficult as it will be, the season will enable you to be introduced to gentlemen who are worthy of you."

I try to keep the disgust off my face. The season is a subject I tend to avoid. Nothing is more displeasing to me than the silly, pointless marriage mart. I pace in front of my chair, hating he brought Mama into this. Respecting her wishes and honoring her memory are important to me, but what my father suggests is intolerable. I thought I would have another year, one to either convince Papa I will never make a good wife and would be better off as a spinster—even in spite of the abject horror with which Society greets such a position—or to resign myself to my fate. Either way, I thought there was more time.

"But where will I stay? Who will help me debut?"

"Mother has agreed to let you and Lucy stay with her. She has even brought in a rather accomplished London governess to continue Lucy's studies for the duration of your stay."

I think of the cheerful, though somewhat dowdy governess who instructed my siblings and me. No doubt my grandmother had found her wanting. "And what of Miss Taylor?"

Papa flashes a wry smile. "Not up to the London standard, I'm afraid. Those are Mother's words, of course, not mine."

I sit back in my chair with a huff. We aren't able to visit with my father's mother often, but I know she will expect me to be debut-ready. I picture the thinly veiled horror on her face if she could see me now, my white-blonde hair tangled from the wind, clad in muddy breeches and boots.

"Papa, I know you think this is what's best for me, but I'm happy here at Bransfield with you and Lucy. I find it difficult enough to enjoy myself at the country balls much less grand ones in London."

"And what of a husband? Will you find one who is worthy of a viscount's daughter here in the countryside?"

A husband—someone to tell me what to do, what to think, how to live. I'd seen fine men at some of the balls, but none who would ever make me want to risk telling him the truth about my abilities. There is also a part of me, a rather large part, that believes there will never be such a man. Why would London be any different?

I steel my spine. "Perhaps it would be better if I never married."

My father nearly spits out his tea. "Katherine! What has gotten into you?"

The warmth of a blush creeps up my neck. "I'm just not certain I will ever meet a man who will find me . . . agreeable."

My father shakes his head, lets out a soft chuckle. "How utterly ridiculous. You have your mother's striking beauty and a wit and sensibility all your own. Any man who would think otherwise is the worst sort of fool and should be beneath your notice."

I glance out the window at the snow swirling in the breeze. Mama and I do share some similarities, with our willowy frames, large eyes, and high cheekbones. The older I get, the more I recognize her in the mirror. But it is not my appearance that concerns me. "And what if he realizes what I truly am—what I can do?" I whisper.

He reaches over and clasps my hand in his. "It never prevented me from marrying your mother."

I meet his kind hazel eyes. "Perhaps you're the only one."

"Nonsense. There is a man out there who is your perfect match, and I will do everything in my power to put you in the path of such a suitor." He fumbles in his coat pocket for a moment before pulling out a folded letter. "It is for this reason I have shamelessly asked a favor of someone whose very presence at your side will draw the attention of every eligible bachelor in England."

My eyebrows wing up, for I cannot help but be curious. My father rarely leaves the estate save for business, and I can't imagine who he means.

"The Earl of Thornewood."

"The earl?" I repeat a bit breathlessly. My father never made mention of him before, but it is of little consequence. Having such a lofty member of the peerage in my favor would make my coming out noteworthy indeed.

I cannot imagine anything more horrible.

My father nods. "Your dear Grandmama believes him to be a rake, but I know better. Colin is the mirror image of his late father, who received the very same label. Utter rubbish."

My hands are gripped so tightly in my lap that my knuckles turn white. The late earl's *son*. This would be no father-like figure to ease me into Society. This would be a highly sought after London bachelor. Any other girl would be in raptures, but a cold fear grips me. An earl's patronage will assure I will be the center of attention at every ball and party—more scrutiny and censure than I will ever be comfortable with.

"Katherine, are you well?" my father asks, his eyes full of concern. "You look rather distraught."

I take a few steadying breaths and nod.

"Shall I call for some smelling salts?"

"No," I say, finally finding my voice again. "That won't be necessary. I was just surprised at such an illustrious person offering me aid."

My father grins. "It may be true I love the lifestyle I have now, but before your mother made an honest man of me, I ran with a different sort. Colin's father and I were close growing up and were never far from White's." I draw my eyebrows together as I try to place the name. "The gambling house," he says when he notices my confusion. "Though we were always careful not to risk too much. Robert Thornewood always said we would need money for dowries one day."

I nod but don't meet his eyes. I loathe the subject of dowries almost as much I hate speaking of the marriage mart. They go hand-in-hand, and I always feel like ladies are a commodity to be sold to the highest bidder. Even in this modern age, with our electricity and railway carriages, women still have shockingly few rights. But such thoughts go against everything high Society says on the subject of marriage, and I would be much happier if I could tear them from my mind.

"When will I leave for London?" I ask.

"Your train will leave in two days. Your brother will accompany you on his way back to Oxford."

"If I am to leave in so short a time, I must get my things in order." I stand and bend at the waist to give my father a kiss on the cheek, and he pats my shoulder.

"Katherine," he says when I reach the door. I stop and turn back to him. "Your mother and I protected you the last time this happened, and though I no longer have her wisdom to guide me, I will keep you safe."

"Yes, Papa," I murmur, already caught in the snare of my own memories.

I leave his study in a daze, and I am powerless to stop my mind from returning me to the last time I was caught using arcana.

TWO

ASIDE from my siblings, I had one close friend growing up.

Henry and I were inseparable as children. He lived in the village just down the road from Bransfield, and he came every day to fish with me in our creek or walk through the woods. The day my secret was revealed, we were both around seven years old. We went to the stables to check on the barn cat that had her litter of kittens the week before. For whatever reason, the cat foolishly decided to situate her litter in the hayloft, close to the edge. It was only a matter of time before one of the kittens fell.

That day, we walked into the cool stables, happy to be out of the hot summer sun.

"I'll climb up and see how the mama is doing," Henry said. "You wait here."

Before he could shimmy up the narrow ladder, one of the runts of the litter wandered too close to the edge.

"She'll fall!" I cried, pointing to the fluffy white kitten.

Henry climbed faster, but he didn't make it in time.

The kitten fell, breaking her neck instantly upon impact. I scooped her up, tears streaming down my face. I can still remember the feel of her in my hands, her light body limp but not yet stiff.

Henry jumped the last few rungs of the ladder and rushed over to me. "Is she dead?" he asked, his own eyes shiny with tears.

I nodded sadly. Then I felt it, that little spark of life. It was there, but faint. I knew I had only seconds. I held my hands over her and closed my eyes. She was such a little thing, barely bigger than a mouse. The amount of energy I needed was small, but I still had to borrow it from living things around me. I had nowhere near the stores of energy I have now.

Luckily, the stables were full of horses. I siphoned minuscule amounts of their considerable energy, filling the kitten with it.

"What are you doing?" Henry asked, his voice wavering with fear and unshed tears.

My hands were glowing, imparting life back into the cat. And then her chest started to rise and fall with her breaths.

When I opened my eyes, a relieved smile on my face, Henry was looking at me with huge eyes and a pale face.

"Henry, it's okay," I whispered. "She's alive." I held the now-squirming kitten toward him as proof. My seven-year-old self didn't understand that Henry's hesitancy wasn't due to disbelief the kitten was alive but rather horror I had brought her back. He had heard the rumors about my family that had circulated around the village ever since my mother had come to Bransfield. He just hadn't had reason to believe them—until I gave him one.

He shook his head, coming shakily to his feet. "What did you do?" he demanded.

"I helped her," I said, holding the little cat close to my chest. She purred, but I could take no comfort from it.

"She was dead," Henry said. "I saw her."

"Yes, but I helped her."

He shook his head again. "No."

"Henry, please," I said and reached for him.

He pushed me away. "No! Stay away from me. You're a—a witch."

I barely understood his words, but I understood his meaning. Henry fled from the barn like I'd taken a life instead of resurrecting one. His story of my abilities spread throughout the village not long after. None of the adults believed him, of course. But the children did. Because of my lofty social status, I could not be obviously shunned, but I could be avoided. Children averted their eyes as they curtsied or bowed when they met me in the village, treating me as though I truly was a witch to be feared and hated. No one would dare come anywhere near Bransfield.

In time, the children's memories of that terrible day faded, and I was treated with vague suspicion instead of outward disdain. My friendship with Henry, though, was destroyed for good.

My mother comforted me over my loss of a friend, but she also told me resurrection arcana was the most dangerous form. She said I was to never attempt anything like it again.

I stand before my open wardrobe and stare, biting my lower lip in dismay. The vast majority of it consists of skirts and blouses suitable for any number of leisurely pursuits but which fail miserably as an appropriate wardrobe for the season. Most are only appropriate for long country walks as they are certainly not the latest Parisian fashion, being rather plain with not a single bit of lace or even ornate buttons. Some of the skirts are meant to be worn with matching jackets, but I have long since ruined them—too often I visit the horses in the stables and end up so filthy, no amount of washing will repair the damage.

The wardrobe contains several hats, but they are like my surviving shirts and skirts: too plain and practical for London. I do have one hat, a nightmare gifted to me by a distant aunt, with no less than five plumes of ostrich feathers. It was buried at the very bottom and is hopelessly crushed.

I have two tea-gowns that I quite like, but as they have no boning in the bodices, they would be shameful presented at a dinner or ball in London. Composed of light and airy chiffon, they are dresses meant to be worn around the house only. My shoulders slump.

The assembly at Mrs. Quinn's tonight will be difficult enough. If it weren't for the music, I would feign a headache. But of course I must go—if only to ease my mind that Margaret really hasn't told anyone else. I pray only our servants know.

I hear a soft shoe scrape the floor, and then my younger sister throws her arms around me in a tight hug.

"Oh, Wren," she says in her breathy voice, "I am so excited about London."

I give her a little squeeze back. "I'm glad you are."

Her hazel eyes widen. "How could you not be? This will be your coming out!"

"Oh yes, all my dreams are finally coming true," I deadpan.

She laughs. "Maybe not *all*. But I'm sure it could be delightfully fun if you'll let it. I can't tell you how happy I am Papa is allowing me to accompany you." She reaches out and touches the skirt of my tea-gown, and a stab of guilt goes through me. If this was Lucy's debut, she would be excited and thankful. Not resentful and resistant as I am. Her smile loses some of its brilliance when she catches sight of my expression. "You truly do not wish to go?"

I pick up a framed painting of Mama, her dark blue eyes smiling back at me. She was beautiful in a way that was not quite human. Though I share some of her physical traits, I could never emulate that otherness she possessed, that natural grace she had just from being Sylvani. "If there were a way to escape to Mama's land and never go to London, I would do so in an instant."

Lucy's eyes, the mirror images of Mama's, widen. "You wouldn't really, would you? We know almost nothing about it."

A sad smile touches my lips as I replace the painting. "It doesn't matter if I would or wouldn't. Mama never told us where to find the entrance to her realm." Relief wars with regret on my sister's face. I recognize it because it's what I always felt when Mama spoke of her homeland. There has always been a part of me that has longed to see my mother's homeland, if only to feel closer to her.

Most children heard fairytales in the nursery. My siblings and I had our mother's stories of Sylvania. Late into the night, she would enthrall us with accounts of the many ways her world differed from ours: forests with trees so old they had a language of their own, sparkling cities carved into the mountains, and what I liked to hear of most of all, immortal people who could use arcana freely.

My mother's soft voice flickers in my mind. "Sylvania was where all the magic from the human world escaped when humans decided they had outgrown such fantasy," she said. "Dragons guarded caves high in the mountains, while faeries and unicorns maintained the forests. Every creature could communicate, if you only knew its language."

I had told her I wanted to go there, to see the dragons and unicorns for myself.

"It wasn't all perfect, darling," she said. "Just as in this world, there was a struggle for power. My family was in the thick of it, and I'm only glad I was able to escape."

As a child, I couldn't understand what she meant. She never elaborated, and I am still at a loss. Was she as bound by the whims of Sylvania's Society as I am by London's?

"Perhaps we should be thankful Mama never told us where to find the entrance," Lucy says, as if she has shared the same memory. "She said she could never return."

"Perhaps," I say to appease her. "It would take a monumental catastrophe to make me leave our family, in any case. How could I possibly survive without Rob's teasing? Or your kindness?"

"You wouldn't," Lucy says, "and neither would we. Oh, but I'm sure you will find London agreeable if you let yourself. Think of the dancing!"

"You are the one who loves dancing, but you're right. I should at least try to enjoy myself, though I'm sure Grandmama will keep me so busy I won't have time for homesickness."

"What do you think she'll be like?" she asks quietly.

I hesitate. "You don't remember her?" I think of Grandmama's cold indifference while our mother lay dying of an illness no doctor could cure. Blessedly, Lucy's memory of that time has always seemed foggy.

"Only a little."

I reach out and smooth one of her blond curls. "She will adore you."

Lucy turns to me with humble doubt in her eyes. "Truly?"

"How could you doubt it? Everyone is instantly charmed by you." I smile because I mean it.

"Perhaps, but I haven't seen Grandmama since I was very small. And I know she can be . . ." I watch with amusement as my kind sister tries to find a way of politely describing our curmudgeonly grandmother. "Discerning," she says after a moment.

"That's one way to describe her. I'm hoping she will be so taken with you that she will overlook how much work it will require to turn me into a proper debutante."

"Nonsense, you'll be the talk of Society."

"That's what I'm afraid of," I say to myself, and she shakes her head.

"Are you afraid she will find out about your gifts?"

"You have them, too," I say, almost defensively. I know they don't mean to, but Robert and Lucy often make me feel as if I'm something else entirely.

Lucy touches her hand to my arm. "I only meant yours are more powerful than mine and harder to keep secret."

I stride over to my vanity and glance at my tangled hair in the mirror. I frown back at myself. My more obvious abilities are the sole reason Grandmama barely tolerates me. I remind her too much of Mama, and Mama scared her.

Lucy walks up behind me.

"I'm not afraid of her finding out," I say. "She already knows." I meet Lucy's eyes in the mirror. "It's why we haven't seen her since you were small."

Her face falls, and guilt twists in my stomach like a serpent. Still, she needs to know what to expect. This won't be a tearful reunion with a beloved grandmother. It will be nothing more than business, myself the merchandise.

"Oh, I see," Lucy says, and I turn and give her a brief embrace.

"She will still love you, Luce. It's me she cannot stand."

The room is stuffy from the number of people in such a small space. The lit fireplace at the other end of the room isn't helping matters, its added heat causing me to flush before I've even set foot on the dance floor. I glance at the wall lined with windows, the golden curtains drawn back so that we may admire the view of the gardens beyond, and wonder if anyone would stop me from opening them. Hemmed in as I am by people on all sides, I can do nothing at the moment but stare at the lovely painting of some ancient nobleman astride a white charger. The air smells of cloying perfume and whiskey—the latter because the gentleman behind me keeps sneaking a nip from his flask.

"Remind me why we're here again," Robert says. He takes a sip of his wine and peers around the room with a bored look on his face.

"For the simple reason that Mrs. Quinn cornered me in town the other day, and I was too distracted to come up with a proper excuse."

"Hm. Well, as inconvenient as this is, I suppose it's a good opportunity to make sure Margaret's testimony hasn't spread throughout town."

"Yes, I suppose we should watch for anyone who treats me as more of a pariah than usual," I say with a bitter edge.

Robert snorts a laugh into his wine glass. "Lord, I'd forgotten how melodramatic you could be. No one treats you as a pariah. They have a healthy fear of you, perhaps, but that's to be expected with such a biting wit."

I try to glare at him but end up grinning instead. "Because I know you are only teasing, I shall refrain from feigning a headache and leaving you to fend for yourself."

"Robert!" a nasally voice calls, and we both turn our heads in the direction of a girl around my age, sashaying her way over in a gaudy pink dress, the corset so tight I'm surprised she can breathe at all. The crowd parts, and I hear my brother groan.

"Robert, I thought it was you," the girl says. She practically bounces on her toes. "No one told me you'd be here." She shoots me an accusing look before remembering her manners and smiling instead. Her family is new to Gloucestershire, new enough not to know our family history. This would be a wonderful thing—possibly even a chance for me to have a friend again, at last—only her character is so obnoxious I can hardly stand to be civil.

"Good evening to you, Harriet," I say.

"Evening, Harriet," Robert says, hardly more than a mumble. Harriet looks at him with naked admiration.

"Oh, good evening," she says. "I am so very happy you could come." Her eyes are still on Robert, but she shifts them to me briefly. "You look lovely tonight, Wren."

"You are too kind," I say, glancing over her person to find something I can compliment in turn. Her hair is frizzy, her dress is cut much too low and seems to feature entirely too much lace, but then I spot the pretty pearls around her neck. "I adore your necklace."

She smiles brightly at me, and I'm glad I took the time to be kind. "Thank you." She turns back to Robert. "What do you think of my dress? It's new. Mother bought it especially for this ball. They say it's the latest London fashion."

I take a sip of my lemonade to hide my grin as my brother fidgets with the cuffs of his shirt.

"Ah, yes. It's very fine," he says after a moment. Though it doesn't seem possible, her smile grows even wider, and I decide to finally give in and rescue my brother before the determined girl attaches herself to him for the rest of the evening.

I swallow the rest of my drink in an un-ladylike gulp and thrust my glass at him. "Robert, would you be a dear and fetch me more lemonade? I'm terribly parched."

Any other time, he would roll his eyes at my proffered cup and tell me to get it myself, but he smiles at me like I've offered him a gift of gold. "Certainly, dear sister. Do excuse me, Harriet."

She stares after him forlornly for a moment before turning to me, but as I offer no marriage potential, she moves on to a young soldier. My good deed done for the evening, I glance around for Lucy, who was asked to dance soon after we first arrived. At fifteen, she will be too young to accompany me to the London balls, but I am glad she can enjoy herself tonight.

I watch and sigh as Mrs. Quinn makes her way toward me. She is dressed in a shocking red dress with a strange ostrich feather turban. I glance at the refreshment table where Robert carries on a lively conversation with one of father's friends. No one will come to my rescue, it seems.

"Katherine," she says before she's close enough to talk at a comfortable level. "I simply must have you play for us." I watch as everyone around us glances our way. Wonderful. Now everyone heard. At least I see nothing but normal curiosity in their expressions.

"Oh, I wouldn't want to intrude," I say and groan inwardly. I always come up with the worst excuses.

She loops her arm through mine and speaks at the same loud level. "Nonsense. It wouldn't be an intrusion in the least. Come, you must see my new piano."

She points to the gleaming instrument in the next room, and my fingers itch to play it. I shouldn't play, but I can't resist her offer.

The crowd parts for me as I walk to the piano and sit on the bench before it. I take a moment to arrange my skirt, the satin rustling as it settles. She hands me sheets of music, but I don't even glance at them. I know which song I will play, though part of me whispers I would be foolish to release even a small amount of arcana. But there are times when I am unable to resist the lure of power inside me. This is one of those times.

Hauntingly beautiful music plays in my head before I've even touched the keys. My eyelids flutter closed for a moment as I listen to notes only I can hear.

This arcana is different from the kind I used to save Robert. I've always thought of it as part of Mama, as it is gentle like her but also strong, like the unexpected strength of silk. Ever since Papa and I spoke of Mama's wishes, I haven't been able to stop thinking of her.

I touch the tips of my fingers to the keys, and then I am swept away like a petal in the current of a river. My fingers know the song, one of a series my mother used to play—her music, the songs from her land. Music is the only remnant I have left of her homeland, as my mother gave up her immortality and ability to return to that land when she married my father.

"How can you lose your immortality, Mama?" I had asked when I was old enough to understand the meaning of the word.

It was the only time I'd seen her eyes dim with loss. "I was forced to leave my spirit behind, darling."

I'd pictured a ghost at the time, but she explained later that all the Sylvani had spirit animals. Made entirely of energy, they provided the Sylvani a never-ending source of power.

The melody is slow and dark at first, weaving threads of sadness around each heart in the room. I don't have to look at them to know; I can feel the emotion it's evoking—I feel it in my own heart. The room seems to disappear until all I can see is the cool ivory keys beneath my fingers.

The music, more than her stories, would remind her of her lost realm. One night, when I was only five years old, I found her sitting at our piano. With her hair loose around her shoulders, she played the same haunting melody I play now. Her eyes were red-rimmed, but not a single tear shone in them.

"I'm sorry you miss your home, Mama," I said.

She drew me close to her side and pressed a kiss to my forehead. "This *is* my home, darling."

The melancholy of the beginning has given way to a sound so angelic it breathes hope into the darkness created with the first few bars. The tempo increases, building tension, and as one, each person in the room draws a deep breath. This music tells a story, though of what, I've never been able to determine. Images of a pristine forest always come to my mind, at the center of which is a silvery waterfall cascading over white rocks.

Tears slide down my cheeks, but I can't stop playing. I'm glad I'm turned away from the crowd. This always happens when I play my mother's music.

It reaches its crescendo, and I picture white birds, as big as eagles, taking flight amongst the trees. I finish with a flourish, my cheeks warm, and hastily wipe away the tears. I turn to the crowd, and they erupt with applause, their eyes shiny and wet.

Every man save my father and brother looks at me as if I'm the famed Helen of Troy, and every female save Lucy looks at me as though I am her goddess and she my priestess. I make a quick bow and dart from the room.

I had let the arcana free again.

The pillow is cool against my warm cheek. Why did I give in to my inner desires and play my mother's music? Now I will have to avoid everyone who was there—at least until the enchantment has worn off.

I curl into a ball around another pillow. I wasn't consciously weaving a spell, but my music always has that effect on people. They become enamored—not truly with me—but with the feeling the arcana gives them. Only my siblings are totally immune. My father gets teary-eyed, but only because it reminds him of Mama.

I close my eyes and picture her—I rarely let myself do so since it only stirs up my grief, but tonight the music conjures her memory. I think of her voice, so bright and clear, and the way she always knew exactly what to say. She was so kind and loving—Lucy inherited that gene. And, of course, she had the power in her.

In light of what happened this evening, I'm more wary than ever of going to London. So many more people, more eyes upon me. I'll have to be careful of letting my power influence others.

I push the pillow away and get out of bed, tugging my nightgown down until it brushes the tops of my feet. The air is cool, so I pull a wrap around my shoulders. It's very early in the morning. Still, I know Papa will be awake. He's hardly slept since my mother died ten years ago.

When I enter his study, the warmth from the fire envelopes me like a wool coat.

"Come sit by the fire with me, Wren," he says without looking up from his book. I sit, and he reaches over and pats my hand. "I miss her, too."

A wan smile touches my lips. "I know. I'm sorry for playing tonight. I hope it won't make things more trying for you."

"No, I was glad to hear your mother's music. It has been far too long." He leans over to his side table and retrieves a small leather-bound book. "Since your mother is on both our minds, now is the time to give you this."

I take the book from him, marveling at how buttery the leather is and at the beautiful silver tree tooled on the front. "Was this Mama's?" I ask in hushed tones.

He nods. "She wanted you to have it before your coming out."

I open the book eagerly—what if it will reveal more about her world?—but my eyebrows furrow when I see the pages. "They're all blank."

"It's part of your mother's arcana. It will prevent you from reading the whole thing at once. Only a page or two will reveal itself to you at a time."

"How frustrating," I say.

He smiles. "It was in your mother's very nature to be frustrating. She was more mysterious than the stars. We are lucky she let me in on the secret to that little book, else we'd both be left staring at each other dumbly."

"Mysterious indeed. Was this her journal?" I run my hands over the blank pages, imagining my mother's slender fingers and feminine script.

As if she writes them before my eyes, words appear on the page. I gasp. "Papa, look."

We watch as a letter to me forms.

My dearest Katherine,

I have asked your father to keep this journal safe until you come of age. I know you will be reluctant about finding a suitable husband, but believe me, it's for your own protection.

Two gentlemen will present themselves to you as potential suitors. They will be two sides of the same coin, one dark, one light. Only you will be able to discern which is which, and this will be your greatest challenge. Guard your heart, my darling, for one of these men will be drawn to your power and will seek to ruin you.

There are those who know the truth of our abilities, those who will use their power and influence to have you for their own. In a city as large as London, you must be on your guard at all times.

I am so sorry I cannot be there to see you come into your own, my darling, but it is my hope that this journal will provide a semblance of comfort.

With much love and tender affection,
Mama

I read and reread the words, but I cannot make the letter any longer. Her first letter to me, and it's about potential suitors? I know it's wrong, but I find my ire rising as I think on my mother's words. I have no intention of falling in love in the first place. Perhaps if I do not give a man my heart, he will be unable to hurt me—or worse, control me.

I glance over at my father, but his eyebrows are drawn low over his eyes and his mouth is tight.

"This is very worrisome," he says. "Your mother had a gift for knowing things before they came to pass, so we must take her words seriously."

"Perhaps I shouldn't tempt fate by going to London, Papa."

He tilts his head, as if considering my words, and my heart beats faster in my chest. "No, that's not the answer either. Your mother wanted you to be presented at court, so you will leave on the morrow as planned." His eyes scan Mama's words again. "This line here—about others who know the truth—should encourage the utmost caution."

"Have you heard of such people before?"

"No, indeed. Your mother never told me, but then, she often kept things from me she deemed 'upsetting.'" He shakes his head and lets out a soft laugh. He pats his rounded belly. "As if I'm of such a delicate constitution I cannot handle troublesome news."

Not for the first time, I think of how my mother never would admit to us whether other Sylvani could be found in this world. *Not all of our kind are like me, my darling,* she would say. But now her journal entry had admitted as much.

I close the book. "So there could be those who know the truth about what I am, but you would still have me go to London?"

He reaches over and takes my hand. "My darling, there are wolves in sheep's clothing everywhere we look. It's the world we live in. It's the darker side of human nature. Do I want to protect you from that? Of course. But I also want you to have the life you deserve—with someone who deserves and respects you—and you cannot live caged up like a canary."

I bite the inside of my lip to keep it from quivering. I have the strongest urge to burst into tears, but I swallow them down. As often happens in the dark of night, when fear reigns over common sense, I can't help but succumb to the belief I've held since I was seven years old: no suitor will ever be able to accept the truth of my power. Even at that young age, I learned that to be absolute.

THREE

THE train leaves the station with a puff of steam and a short whistle. We settle into one of the opulent first-class carriages, the lighting comfortably dim, the dining tables already set with crystal and china. Lucy sits beside me on a plush velvet sofa, with Robert across from us in a tufted leather chair. We have the railway carriage to ourselves, which comes as a pleasant surprise since I had hoped to have the chance to share Mama's journal with my siblings.

Before I can retrieve the book from my reticule, Lucy loops her arm around mine. "I was awake all night dreaming up the perfect dress for Court."

Her eyes dance so merrily, I have to humor her though my interest in fashion is small. "Did you? I hope you have managed to keep it looking like a wedding dress."

She grins. "Well, it is white, of course. There is no helping that. But I took some liberties with the silhouette and fabrics."

"That does sound lovely. Perhaps you could draw it," I say.

She smiles as she unfolds a piece of paper. "I already did."

I can weave enchantment with the piano, but my sister can make even a simple drawing a work of art. In perfect detail, she has created a rendering of a dress with a heart-shaped bodice, intricate lace flowers blooming across the skirt, and delicate sleeves hanging just off the shoulder.

After a surreptitious glance around to be sure we are alone, she leans over me and touches the tip of her finger to the dress. "I thought you'd like to see the whole thing."

The dress rises from the page, flat at first like a paper doll. As I watch, it fills out, like a miniature version of the real thing. The skirt rustles softly though there is no breeze. I laugh as it makes a slow pirouette so I can see it from every angle.

"Oh, Luce," I say, "it's beautiful. I'll give this to Grandmama's dress-maker as soon as we arrive."

Her hands are clasped against her chest. "Nothing would give me greater pleasure." She touches her finger to the rotating gown and it deflates before returning to a simple drawing.

"What say you, Robert?" I ask my brother, who has paid us very little attention. Instead, his focus is on Virgil's *Aeneid*.

"Lovely. You'll be the belle of the ball," he says without looking up from his book.

"You really should pay more attention to this, considering my entire future relies upon it," I say with a wry smile.

"All the more reason I should *not* give my opinion. I would loathe myself if I were the sole reason my sister did not immediately secure the highest earning suitor in London." He grins at me, and I shake my head.

I lean toward Lucy. "I think he's simply jealous because his only arcana is an unnatural amount of charm. Perhaps that is why he always manages to escape his headmaster's censure."

"What nonsense," Robert says, and Lucy giggles. "I cannot help the fact that the lion's share of Mama's abilities passed down to the females in the family any more than I can help the blue of my eyes."

"It *is* true about your charm though, Rob," Lucy says. "Everyone hangs on your every word."

"Everyone but my silly sisters. They *never* heed my advice."

"I'm sure you're exaggerating," I say.

"You think so, do you?" Robert asks, a mischievous glint in his eyes. "Name a single instance where you've followed my advice."

"Wren," Lucy says, her hand on my arm. "Your reticule is glowing."

I look at her with furrowed brows before glancing down at the bag at my feet. Belatedly, I realize Mama's journal is within. I pull it out and find that it is indeed shimmering with a soft white light.

"I didn't want to wake you last night," I say to my siblings, whose eyes are riveted by the small leather book in my hand. "This was Mama's. Papa gave it to me last night when neither of us could sleep."

Lucy reaches out and touches the cover gently, a look of wonder on her face, as if she's touching our mother's skin instead of a journal. "What does it say?" she asks.

"It only reveals a page at a time, so it may not say anything," I warn as I open it. For an instant, the light shines as brightly as the sun reflecting off water and then it fades away.

My mother's familiar script appears, and Lucy and Robert crowd closer to me to see.

My dearest Katherine,

When I realized I would never recover from the strange disease taking over my body, I knew I had to find a way to reach out to my children even when I was no longer with them. You were so young I never had the chance to explain some of my abilities. One of them is the gift of premonition, though it is by no means exact. I see so many versions of the future, it's difficult to determine which will actually come to pass. But I feel I must warn you of the most dangerous scenario.

There is a brotherhood of both men and women who have their own power. Instead of arcana derived from the sun as we use, they wield the power of knowledge and societal influence. You may think this is nothing compared to what we can do, but always remember, we live in their world and follow their rules.

Your father and I sheltered you from so many things, and maybe we were wrong to do so, but I hope you will take my warning of this brotherhood seriously. They call themselves The Order of the Eternal Sun, and I am afraid to think of what they might do if any of them discovered who you really were. Don't underestimate their power and influence.

There were whispers of a certain ability some of the members possessed that allowed them to steal away our energy. We have never been able to determine what it is they do with our power, but it is a dark art, one which should be avoided at all costs.

I very much doubt I need to do so, but as your mother, I feel I must caution you about the use of your arcana while in London. Any use is a danger to you as it draws upon your own energy, but in the bosom of Society, you have the added worry of unfriendly eyes discovering the truth.

Remember this, my darling. Be cautious of gentlemen and ladies alike.

With much love,
Mama

We fall into a hushed awe, our eyes scanning and rescanning her words as if she might at any moment appear before us.

"Well, that was ominous," Robert says, frowning.

I squeeze Lucy's hand as a tear spills onto her cheek. "It's like she's right here speaking to us, isn't it?" I whisper, and she nods.

"I know caution is a foreign concept to you," Robert says, "but I think for the first time, I must encourage you exercise it."

"She said there's no guarantee any of that will happen," I say, and he gives me an exasperated look. "But of course I will be on my guard."

Lucy leans forward and examines the journal entry. "Is that a rune?"

She points at a small mark near the bottom of the page. Shaped almost like a human eye is a rune with delicate swirls. It's so faint, I never would have noticed if not for her.

"Where?" Robert asks, evidently having as much difficulty as I did in seeing it.

"Here," I say. I press my finger to the rune. A little spark of energy, and then the train carriage fades away. In its place is crystal-clear water cascading over rock, filling a shimmering pool. A dark forest surrounds the water. I know this place. I see it every time I play my mother's music. Something about it whispers to me, and a longing so strong wraps itself around my heart in a painful vise. Could this be a vision of Mama's realm?

As if in answer, a creature that is like a deer, but not quite, takes a drink from the water. Its pelt is as white as the rocks with silver dappling. Leaves sprout from its antlers, and it's as though it doesn't have antlers at all, but tree branches instead. It's joined by a creature that looks like a snow fox, but for the silver tips at the ends of its fur. It turns and appears to look right at me, its turquoise-colored eyes piercing me.

Katherine, it whispers in my mind.

With a jerk, I take my finger from the rune, and the lovely vision fades.

"Oh yes, I see it now," Robert says, as though no time has passed at all. The vision, it would seem, only appeared in my own mind.

"Lucy," I say, "do you recognize that rune?"

She tilts her head as she examines it again. "I do, actually. Mama had an entire book of runes, and I used to love looking at them. They're just so beautiful. This one means 'homeland.'"

So that *was* my mother's realm. Excitement and that painful longing war with each other in the center of my chest. "When I touched the rune, it showed me a vision of Sylvania."

Lucy's face brightens with awe. "May I try?"

"Of course," I say and hand her the journal. She touches her finger to the rune and closes her eyes.

After a moment, her face falls. "I don't see anything."

I touch the rune again, but this time, nothing happens. "I don't understand. It worked just a moment ago."

"Wren, you shouldn't tease Lucy," Robert says. I glare at him.

"No, I'm sure she was being truthful," Lucy says, examining the rune. "I think it may be a bit like my own arcana. The rune has only a single charge of energy stored. After that, it's only a drawing on paper."

"Then I am sorry I used its only charge."

"Don't be," Lucy says. "I believe it was meant for you."

The water so clear I can almost taste it, the cool shade of the forest, the beautiful creatures, all of these images run through my mind until I'm gripped by the desperation to see more. Why would Mama show me something I can never see outside of my own dreams? I think of what Papa said: that Mama was more mysterious than the stars. Though this was true, she never did anything without purpose.

A hiss of steam and a small jolt signals we've arrived at Oxford, and Lucy and I disembark with Robert, reluctant to part.

John, Robert's valet, walks toward us from one of the rear railway carriages. His cheeks are flushed, his eyes bright. "I shall have your luggage brought to the coach straight away," he says, and I cannot help but return his wide smile.

With her hand on Robert's arm, Lucy points to the skyline just beyond the station. "Is that the university?"

We can just make out the taller spires from our vantage point. The sand-colored stone and gothic architecture makes it seem more like a monastery or cathedral than a place of study, though I suppose there are some who do see it as a place of worship. It's the type of place that inspires a hushed sort of awe, and I wish with a sudden intensity that I could go with Robert.

A twinge of jealousy causes me to blush. I shouldn't be jealous of my brother, but I cannot help but compare the freedom of his life at university to mine. How I would love to trade dresses and ballrooms for books and the classroom. But even in this modern age of electricity, new ideas, and advances beyond our imagining, the expectations for ladies still remain firmly planted in the Middle Ages. As a gentleman, Robert's potential is limitless. For now, all he need do is concentrate on his studies.

I glance over to find Robert watching me with a grin. I return his smile. "I could stand here and stare at this architecture for ages."

"I am of the same opinion," Lucy says, her artist's eyes wide, as if taking in every detail.

"I'm glad someone finds the old place impressive," Robert says. "The only thing it inspires in me is a sense of dread for the essays I must write."

"For shame," I admonish. "Think of all the things you can learn here, and in such stately beauty."

"We could trade places if you'd like. I will suffer through the frivolous balls, and you can stay here amidst ancient professors and moldy tomes."

"I would gladly do so. Anything to avoid the season." I grimace, and he laughs.

"It won't be as bad as all that," he says and pulls me in for a firm embrace.

"Will you be coming to town in a week for my coming out?" I ask. "I cannot think how Lucy and I will endure it all without you."

"I shall check with the headmaster, but I'm sure it would be no hardship." He signals John to bring the carriage 'round before turning back to me. "Good luck, dear sister. I know you will do extraordinarily well."

He embraces Lucy, and we return to the train, a short ride ahead of us.

By the time we arrive in London, I've gone so quiet I can no longer carry on a decent conversation with Lucy. She, on the other hand, is flushed and has been chattering nonstop from the moment we disembarked from the train and found the coach Grandmama sent to meet us.

"Oh, London is simply incredible," Lucy exclaims. "Look at the number of carriages on the road; there's scarce room for ours."

I give a brief nod as I struggle not to beg the driver to take us home at once.

London is everything I expected and more. It's large, overly crowded, full of a curious mix of animals, pedestrians, elegant carriages carrying fashionable people, bicycles, and even a few motorcars. The size of the buildings towering over our carriage as we drive by causes me to feel closed in, restrained. A desperate need builds in me for the open space of the country, and I fear it will be a very long time indeed before I will feel free again.

Lucy presses her face closer to the window. "Wren, just look at those exquisite dresses. And the hats," she says in an almost childlike squeal. "I've never seen such beauty. Do you not agree?"

I glance at a pair of ladies talking outside a stylish little shop. Their stiffly tailored dresses are of vibrant hues, a lovely contrast to the dreariness of the city. Both wear wide-brimmed hats with enormous feather plumes, and they carry color-coordinating parasols. I look around at all the mess left by the animals, the refuse and dirt on the streets, and it almost seems as though they are overdressed.

"Beautiful indeed," I say.

"We must be close; these seem to be a row of houses. Which one do you suppose is hers? I hope we haven't missed tea, though I don't know if I could eat anything at the moment."

My mind scrambles for a response, but all I keep thinking is, *Will Grandmama hate me?*

The carriage rolls to a stop in front of a red brick terrace house with a black door. I stare at it with much trepidation as the coachman helps us out.

We thank him and move toward the door. With a shaky hand, I reach for the brass door knocker and let it fall with a hollow-sounding *thunk*. My heart beats faster as a servant in a perfectly pressed tailcoat shows us inside.

I glimpse an abundance of lovely things—richly colored paintings, vibrant red and gold carpet, marble pillars—before we are led up to the first floor by way of a sweeping marble staircase. My grandmother waits for us in the drawing room, and it is just as elegant as the entrance hall—but with a much more feminine feel. The walls are done in pretty robin's egg blue hues with floral silk wall hangings, while the floor-to-ceiling windows admit the afternoon sun.

Grandmama stands in the middle of the room, her hands folded in front of her violet-hued tailored dress. Her hair has not yet gone gray, and is still a rich auburn. Another lady catches my eye; she waits behind my grandmother with her hands clasped, dressed in a smart tailor-made suit done in somber shades of charcoal. This must be the governess Grandmama brought in for Lucy. Her expression is one of polite interest, but her eyes seem kind.

After a brief hesitation, Grandmama steps forward and presses a dry kiss on my cheek. "Katherine, you're as beautiful as your mother."

She turns to Lucy and kisses both her cheeks. "Lucy, darling," she says, gazing at her with a warm smile, "you look so grown up."

"Thank you, Grandmama," I say. "We're delighted to see you. You were so kind to invite us here for the season."

"Your home is exquisite," Lucy adds, her smile brightening her eyes.

"I'm thrilled your father could spare you." She holds her hand out toward the lady behind her. "If I may introduce Miss Coraline Watts, Lucy's governess."

"Pleased to make your acquaintance," Miss Watts says with a reserved smile.

"Lucy, dear, I was just horrified when I discovered your father had not graduated you to a finishing governess. Miss Watts is extremely accomplished in all the things a young lady will need to truly shine: fine arts, piano, dancing, proper etiquette . . ." Her eyes briefly meet mine. "She will have you ready for your own debut in no time at all."

Lucy smiles brightly at the mention of her own future debut, but the slight against Papa has me gritting my teeth. *Where were you, then, Grandmama,* I think, *if you believe him so incompetent?*

"I thank you for such a glowing recommendation," Miss Watts says, not quite meeting Grandmama's eyes. "Miss Sinclair, we will begin your instruction tomorrow after breakfast."

"Thank you, Miss Watts," Grandmama says, and the governess shares a brief smile with Lucy before taking her leave. Grandmama gestures toward an ivory sofa. "Come, sit and have some tea with me. You must be parched after traveling all day."

Another liveried servant appears to pour our tea and returns to his place against the wall.

"Now then," Grandmama says, "we'll have a brief chat, and then you must retire to your rooms. Rest is in order so you will both be fresh for the small assembly we shall attend this evening."

I take a sip of tea to hide my disappointment. Going somewhere tonight is the last thing I want to do after traveling all day. At least she's taken into account our need for rest. "What will this assembly entail?"

Her dark eyes narrow at me ever so slightly. "We have been invited to dine at Lady Hasting's this evening." She turns to Lucy. "Because it will be such a small affair with no dancing, you will be allowed to attend."

Lucy smiles at her graciously. "Oh, how exciting. I only hope the gowns we brought with us will be fashionable enough."

"You'll find your wardrobes are already well-stocked," she says in a self-satisfied way.

I think of the beautiful drawing Lucy did and frown. "Our gowns have already been chosen for us?"

"Naturally." Her eyes scan my wrinkled and travel-worn skirt. "I thought you'd much rather have a new wardrobe for the season."

What she means is: "I knew your own wardrobes would be unfit for London Society." It was true, but I find my defenses rising. Will we have no say in what we wear?

"I'm very grateful you've anticipated our need, but I hope we will have a chance to speak with your dressmaker while we're here." Her eyes widen, like she can't believe I'm being so forward, but I press on—for Lucy. "Lucy has a talent for designing gowns, you see, and we'd hoped to show her drawing and have a dress made."

I nod at Lucy, and she pulls out her drawing from her small reticule. She hands it to Grandmama, a hesitant smile on her face.

"What a fascinating skill," Grandmama says, after glancing at the paper. "I'll send for the dressmaker on the morrow."

"Thank you, Grandmama," Lucy says.

"Now then. We must discuss how important tonight will be," my grandmother says. "As I'm sure your dear father has told you, the Earl of Thornewood has agreed to ease your debut into Society."

I nod, a prickle of worry tensing my shoulders. It's a curious thing. Part of me is very much afraid I will embarrass myself in front of this man, and the other is nervous he will be just the thing to make my debut successful.

Unfortunately, the only thing my father and grandmother will consider a success is marriage.

"He will be there tonight, so I've had your lady's maid lay out a gown for the evening that will best showcase your fair coloring."

"You make it sound as though the earl is a potential suitor," I say, the tensing of my shoulders now spreading to my spine.

She raises her delicately arched eyebrows. "But of course, darling. What else would he be?"

"Someone to ease my debut into Society?" Had she not said these very words to me? As had my father.

"He is that, but he is also an earl, and an earl is a potential suitor—no matter his original purpose."

Nightmare images of my grandmother dragging me determinedly from potential suitor to potential suitor flash before my eyes.

"Tonight will also be a chance for me to examine your social graces and determine whether they are up to par," she says.

"Our father has provided us with such tutelage," I say. Lucy glances at me and raises her eyebrows. I'm sure she disagrees with the edge in my voice, but I do not heed her warning.

Grandmama waves her hand as if shooing a fly. "Country manners are quite different. Here your every move will be judged. You must be above reproach." I open my mouth to let out another retort, but she gestures for one of the servants. "I'm sure you are both fatigued. Allow Mary to show you to your rooms."

I'm torn between wanting to have my say and take my rest, but I know when I've been dismissed.

FOUR

A small gathering for dinner clearly does not mean the same thing to my grandmother as it does to me. I pictured perhaps ten people at most, including Lucy, Grandmama, and me. But more than twenty faces stare at me as we enter the room and a servant takes our coats. After a brief impression of the narrow, but well-lit, entryway, we are led to the drawing room.

As I take in the room, it seems the owner is rather fond of garish décor. Every wall is covered in crimson satin, and a tapestry hangs atop the satin on more than one wall. Though the room is of a modest size, it has two crystal chandeliers and so many light bulbs and lamps it appears as if it is the middle of the afternoon.

"Lucille," a short round woman says with her arms open wide. She and my grandmother embrace, and she gives her a kiss on either cheek. "How lovely to see you." Her owlish eyes turn to Lucy and me. "These must be your granddaughters."

"If you'd give me a moment, Claudia," my grandmother says with a touch of annoyance, "I shall introduce them."

"Ah, yes," Claudia says without a shred of remorse.

"This is Katherine, my eldest granddaughter," she says, "and Lucy, my youngest. I have a grandson, too, but he is away at Oxford. Girls, this is Lady Claudia Hasting, the hostess to whom you owe your thanks for this nice party."

Our first introduction to a member of the upper crust of Society, and she is nothing like I expected. I'd imagined someone with stiff manners and cold demeanor, but she is neither. As a baroness, she is technically of a lower station than Grandmama, but as Grandmama so kindly explained to us in the carriage, Lady Hasting is a great deal wealthier. And as the Americans have taught us, wealth can often overcome title.

We smile politely, and Lady Hasting says, "You see my youngest daughter, Penelope, there on the piano. Does she not play beautifully? She has a great love for music and has become rather accomplished."

I look over at a girl with Lady Hasting's same large eyes and silky brown hair pulled into an intricate style. A gentleman with rather severe-looking features watches from a nearby table as she plays a lilting Irish tune. Her mother didn't exaggerate, though—she does play beautifully.

"My dear husband is there," Lady Hasting says, indicating the man watching his daughter with a critical eye. "Of course you know you're horribly late," Lady Hasting says to Grandmama, "but I shall forgive you since we are awaiting the earl with bated breath, and your entrance was of little consequence."

I stiffen in response to her slight, but my grandmother laughs her off good-naturedly. "Claudia, dinner hasn't even been served yet."

"Very well then. I shall make introductions later. No one will pay me the least bit of attention until Lord Thornewood has arrived—and perhaps not even then."

Lucy and I seat ourselves upon the closest sofa—which happens to be the only one facing the drawing room door.

Lucy leans toward me. "So the earl isn't here yet?"

"It would appear not."

"Well, we have quite a nice vantage of the door," she says with a grin.

I glance at two other girls about my age who watch the door like a cat watches for a mouse. "Yes, but they will certainly beat us there," I say, and she laughs. "Not that I'm any more interested in the earl than I am in this sofa."

"Even if he is very fine?"

A smile touches my lips. "Perhaps I could be persuaded to care a bit more if that were so."

A commotion at the door draws my attention. The two watchful girls are tittering excitedly, but a wide woman with an even larger hat blocks my view. She shifts to the right, and then I see him. Dressed almost entirely in black, in an elegantly cut tailcoat and top hat, stands a man I can only assume to be the earl.

I'm staring. Every bit as rudely as the two girls who waited so eagerly for him. He is handsome in the same way the sea crashing against rock or snow-capped mountains are beautiful: in a way you can't help but stare at. I need to look down, look anywhere but at him before he catches me.

I glance at Lucy, and her eyebrows rise. Something draws my eyes back to him, and now that he's closer, I get a better look. Thick, dark hair, even darker eyes, and a strong jaw. Heat flushes my cheeks and my heart pounds as though I am in mortal danger.

Evidently the wide woman with the hat is related to the two girls, because she is quick to shoo them over to make introductions. But instead of waiting for her to do so, the earl continues forward as if he doesn't see her. I cringe with vicarious embarrassment as the woman follows him.

"My lord," she says to his back, "please allow me to introduce my daughters, Misses Jane and Mary Everley."

He stops and turns toward the woman, and her whole face lights up. For one horrible moment, I fear he means to ignore them, but then he bows stiffly. "How do you do."

The mother immediately recounts every one of her daughters' accomplishments in nearly one breath. Lord Thornewood watches her with an expression that is not unlike Robert's when he's been cornered by Harriet—only the earl's is more exasperated and less pained.

The lady is either one of those unfortunate breed of people who are blissfully unaware of social cues, or she is so determined she chooses to ignore the earl's obvious disinterest.

When she finally stops to draw breath, Lord Thornewood bows to her girls and says, "You must excuse me."

Before anyone else can set upon him, Lady Hasting draws our attention. "My dear guests, the first course will be served if you would be so good as to follow me to the dining room."

She leads us to an adjacent room, one decorated in shades of gold and red. An ornate crystal chandelier hovers above the table, its light creating lovely prisms upon the walls. The table itself is covered with more crystal, fine china, and silverware than I have ever seen. At regular intervals is an ornate floral arrangement bursting with fresh flowers, greens, and fruit. Our names are written elegantly upon small cards, and Lucy and I find to our mutual relief that we have been seated together.

"My lord," Lady Hasting says to Lord Thornewood, "We've saved you the seat of honor at the head of the table, just there." She points to the seat next to mine, and I widen my eyes at Lucy.

His face lacks expression as he takes in the room. I try to avert my gaze as his eyes rove over me, but I'm too late. We lock eyes, and I feel the pulse in my neck throb. Why must he be so handsome? He turns back to Lady Hasting. "Yes, that will do. Thank you."

She beams like he's told her this was the best assembly of his life and leads him to his chair.

He sits beside me, and I don't dare look at him. My physical reaction is much too worrisome.

Grandmama, though, has other plans. "My lord," she says, materializing at his side, "I believe your late father was good friends with my son, the Viscount of Bransfield." A pause, and then she adds, "Allow me to introduce his daughter, the Honorable Katherine Sinclair."

My heart is pounding as if I've just returned from riding. I meet his hooded gaze. "How do you do."

"Pleased to make your acquaintance," he says, his voice deep and rich as red wine. Something stirs inside me at the sound.

"And his youngest daughter, the Honorable Lucy Sinclair," she says, and his eyes slide over to my little sister. When they quickly return to me, I feel a blush creep up my neck.

The footmen bring steaming bowls of soup with fresh bread, and though the tendrils of steam bring the smell of cream and mushrooms to my nose, I find I have little appetite. All eyes are on the earl as he lifts his spoon to his mouth. With a nod, he says to Lady Hasting, "It's very good."

A collective sigh, and then everyone returns to their own meal, chattering excitedly.

I lean toward Lucy. "How utterly absurd." My quiet tone is drowned out by the sounds of laughter, silverware clinking against porcelain, and music. "You'd think King Edward himself walked in."

Lucy giggles behind her hand, and I take a sip of soup.

"I am afraid only a mere earl would attend such a dull affair as this," Lord Thornewood says, and a sick feeling washes over me. A glance at his face reveals nothing.

I should apologize profusely, but instead, my mouth runs away with me. "My lord could not possibly have ascertained my meaning, especially as I was speaking only to my sister."

His spoon pauses on its way to his mouth, and he puts it back in his bowl. "Perhaps you would do well not to speak to your sister about the person sitting close enough to smell your perfume."

"You are exaggerating. I am not even wearing perfume." I should stop talking now. Why am I still talking?

He takes a sip of his soup, his eyes on me. "Do you mean to tell me you naturally smell of such an enticing scent?"

My eyes widen. Surely he couldn't be flirting with me. But then why does my pulse suddenly jump as he looks at me with his dark eyes? "Is it not true the fairer sex, by their very nature, should smell pleasantly?"

"You answer a question with a question. How very diplomatic of you. But you are lucky tonight, Miss Sinclair. I feel very generous." He grins, and the look is so rakish, I remember the words of my mother's letter.

I stiffen. How easily I let myself be taken in by him. He is exactly the sort of man my mother warned me about, of this I am sure.

"Have I offended you?" he asks, but his face reveals not a shred of contrition. "I shouldn't be surprised. You young debutantes are all just a bundle of emotions in pretty packaging."

"Are we indeed? I dare say it's assertions like that which result in ambitious mamas parading their carefully groomed daughters before unappreciative men."

A spark of amusement appears in his dark eyes. "You seek to prove me wrong then?"

"Perhaps if I had any interest in the game, I would trouble myself to take on such an endeavor. Unfortunately, I do not."

Before he can respond, a footman leans in to clear away our soup. This break in our conversation is all the beautifully dressed lady seated to Lord Thornewood's right has been waiting for, and she deftly draws him into the discussion she and the other ladies seated across from us have been having on their recent trip to Bath.

I look over at Lucy, who is engaged in a discussion of her own with the young girl seated next to her. They are good-naturedly arguing the merits of oil versus water-color painting, and since I know very little about either, I return my attention to the rich food before me.

So determined are the other ladies to keep Lord Thornewood's attention, I manage to avoid talking with him for the rest of dinner, though every so often, I see his eyes drift in my direction.

Once dessert has been cleared away, Lady Hasting stands. "Since there are so few gentlemen in attendance here tonight, I thought we would all retire to the drawing room."

Everyone nods happily at this, for they wouldn't want to miss the chance to remain in the earl's presence. Lucy and I stand, and Lord Thornewood offers an arm to us both. Lucy accepts with a shy smile, and after only a moment of hesitation, I take it as well.

I look up to find Lord Thornewood watching me with amusement. "You needn't worry. Offering you my arm is merely polite—not part of the game you mentioned earlier."

I flush, chagrined and already half-regretting my waspish words.

He leads us to a lovely cream-colored sofa closest to the grand piano. "If you'll excuse me," he says once we're seated, "I believe I will need a cocktail before this evening is over. May I ask the servants to bring you anything?"

We both shake our heads no, and I try rather unsuccessfully to prevent my eyes from following his broad back as he seeks out a footman.

"He is unbelievably handsome," Lucy says with almost a sigh.

Guard your heart, my darling, Mama's words warn in my mind.

"Dangerously so," I say, and Lucy gives me a sharp look.

"Do you think he is . . ." her words trail away, but her meaning is clear. *Is he one of them?*

"I have no reason to believe he is, but then, I know no more of what to look for than you do."

"But surely a friend of Papa's can be trusted," Lucy says, her expression hopeful.

"I hope so, too, Luce," I say. "It's a pity they do not wear some sort of identifying mark—a name badge, perhaps?"

She grins. "A garish pin of the sun upon their bow ties?"

"Miss Sinclair," Lady Hasting calls, "your grandmother tells me you are rather skilled at the piano. Would you be so kind as to play something for us?"

I glance at the gleaming instrument longingly. I know I shouldn't, but as it so often does, the music calls to me. "She has most likely exaggerated my talents, madam, but I will be glad to play for you."

My mother's music is, once again, itching to be played, but I cannot—not here. Instead, I play an Irish ballad I've always loved. It's a bold and dramatic song, and I play with intense focus, my eyes never leaving the keys.

I'm halfway through when the wide woman who greeted Lord Thornewood calls out to me. "My dear Miss Sinclair, do you not sing? That song you play is quite nice, but it needs a strong voice to complement it." She turns to the somber lady beside her. "Both my girls sing and play beautifully."

"Yes, madam," I say when she returns her gaze to me, "but I—"

"Then by all means, sing. It will greatly liven our little party here." She gives me a knowing smile. She must think me an incompetent singer.

With an acidic smile in her direction, I let the movement I'm on blur into the first before singing the opening lyrics. I know it's wrong to let a stranger goad me into this, but my pride often overshadows my good sense. As I move into the verses, I allow myself to glance up.

Everyone is watching me. Some, with narrowed eyes. Others, with wide smiles. I close my eyes once in relief. They seem to be enjoying the music, but not in a way which would suggest they've fallen under my power's influence. Lucy smiles at me sweetly, and Grandmama watches me with approval. Lord Thornewood, though, watches me with an intense fascination, as if he cannot believe the sound is truly coming from my mouth. When my heart races in response, I close my eyes again to block out his mesmerizing face.

My reaction is worrisome enough without taking into account my mother's warning of gentlemen who prey on people with abilities. What if he watches me because he can somehow sense the truth? I almost wish I'd never read that entry. Now I will jump at every shadow.

My voice soars with the song's crescendo, and then I let it fall, soft and gentle through the final bars. With the last notes humming in the air, I rise and give a brief bow of my head to the polite applause. Before anyone—especially Lord Thornewood—can say a word to me, I make my excuses and escape to the retiring room.

My grandmother breezes into the room, her eyes landing on my face. "Katherine, what ever could you be doing? Do you intend to remain here for the rest of the evening?"

I think of the way he watched me with such intensity while I played the piano, a love for music obvious in the brightness of his eyes. "I'm sorry, Grandmama, a sudden headache came over me," I lie.

She tilts her head like she can see right through my words, but she doesn't contradict me. "I must say I am very pleased with your musical talents. You play as well as your mother."

My grandmother may not have had any love for Mama, but she did respect her. I smile, but not too brightly, since I'm still keeping up the façade. "That's a compliment indeed."

"You've done extraordinarily well tonight." She holds her arm out to me. "But we mustn't keep Lord Thornewood waiting any longer." She leans close to my ear as I move toward the door. "You've done a wonderful job of piquing his interest."

That's what I was afraid of.

The smart thing to do would be to simper, bat my eyelashes, and fawn over him as soon as I enter the room. Nothing would deter him faster, but I find I am incapable of such duplicity.

A footman holds the door for us, and I walk in, my head held high. If I cannot deter him with foolishness, perhaps a cold demeanor will.

I scan the room for Lucy, but almost everyone has left the tables, so I can't find her before my grandmother leads me to Lord Thornewood.

"My lord," she says, and he turns toward us. Now that we're both standing so close to one another, I realize how tall he is. He must stand at least a head taller than every other person in the room.

Grandmama abandons me with a polite little bow of her head. I glare at her retreating back.

"Ah, there you are, Miss Sinclair," he says, his left hand in the pocket of his trousers. "I'd thought for a moment you were only a figment of my admittedly over-active imagination."

"My apologies. I was unaware you sought my attention."

He takes his hand from his pocket, and he loses some of his prideful stance. "I was overcome by your talent. I've never heard a voice so beautiful." The look he gives me is so sincere that an answering warmth spreads in my chest. But no, I mustn't be taken in by him.

"You flatter me, my lord."

"I do not. It was well-deserved."

I resist the urge to look away from his dark eyes, suddenly uncomfortable with his attention. "I thank you for the compliment."

He smiles then, and it takes everything in me *not* to bat my eyelashes like a simpering fool. Oh, how painfully handsome he is. Frustration twists in me at the apparent lack of control I have over my own body.

He leans in close as if to speak to me in confidence. "You did well to play the piano so beautifully. No doubt you have been told how much of a music enthusiast I am and sought to snare my attention."

"Ah, but that would be playing the game, my lord, and I already assured you I have no intention of doing so."

He grins at my teasing tone, but his eyes hold a more serious expression. "You did say that, yes. And I'm surprised to admit I'm actually disappointed."

His words rob me of mine, and for many moments, we only stare at one another.

Our brief staring contest is interrupted by Lady Hasting, who, as all superior hostesses are, is skilled at sensing when any of her guests have stumbled into an awkward moment. In this case, her mission seems to have benefits for other guests as she leads over yet another fashionably dressed lady with daughters in tow. Their tailored corseted dresses are of complementary jewel tones, as though the mother wanted to present her daughters as a package of marriage potential to Lord Thornewood.

"My lord," Lady Hasting says, "you must allow me to introduce you to Lady Marie Belleview, Countess of Dirkshire."

The countess embodies my expectations for nobility with sharp features and haughty air, down to her elaborate dress. The dress is a rich shade of crimson trimmed in gold embroidery, befitting someone who outranks nearly everyone here—save for the earl.

The earl's expression never changes from one of indifference, but he dips his head politely at least.

"And her daughters," Lady Hasting continues, "Hyacinth and Rose."

They execute perfect curtsies, though I notice Rose bites her bottom lip to mask her nervousness. This endears them to me more than anything else, since I now know what it feels like to be carefully groomed for the sole purpose of securing a gentleman's interest. My eyes narrow at the earl when he continues to look unimpressed.

"Pleasure to make your acquaintance," the earl says, his tone polite and nothing more.

Rose's fair complexion hides nothing, and her cheeks flare pink.

"And have you met the granddaughter of my dear friend, Lady Sinclair?" Lady Hasting asks the countess.

The countess turns to look at me, her eyes appraising me in an instant. As her nose remains high in the air, I can only assume she finds me lacking. "Lovely to meet you," she says.

I curtsy, smiling in a more genuine way when I look at Hyacinth and Rose. They return the gesture, Hyacinth's timid smile not quite as bright as her sister's.

I glance at Grandmama, who stands only a few feet away, and I am ready to leave before my words come ahead of my thoughts again. "I do hope you'll excuse me," I say. "I believe my grandmother and sister are ready to leave."

Before I can take more than a few steps in the direction of Grandmama, the earl easily falls into step beside me. "Leaving already?" he asks, his voice low.

I have to force myself to take a breath before I speak, else I know I will stutter. The man knows how to set one on edge. "I'm afraid we must, my lord. My sister and I only just arrived in town, and we crave rest after our trip."

"Understandable. I'm only sorry our conversation was interrupted." He glances back at Lady Hasting and the countess, who are thankfully having a discussion of their own.

I think of how nervous Hyacinth and Rose were. "Yes, I'm sure it's exhausting to be forced to make the acquaintance of so many young ladies."

The corners of his lips twitch as if he is suppressing a grin. "You cannot imagine."

If he was Robert, I'd roll my eyes at him. As he is the earl, I can do nothing but smile tightly.

He bends low over my hand. As he barely brushes a kiss over the sensitive skin, his eyes lock onto mine. "However, I was very pleased to make your acquaintance, Miss Sinclair. Perhaps escorting you will not be such a hardship after all."

FIVE

I awake at dawn, as I do every morning, and find I'm the only one up. The servants are quick to inform me the others don't leave their rooms before eight o'clock in the morning, and breakfast would not be served until nine.

I would love to go riding, but I also know I cannot go unchaperoned. A book in hand, I curl up on the window seat, though it's difficult to rein in my wandering mind. I usually only stay indoors and read at night or when the weather is adverse, and I long to be outside.

I read the same sentence five times before I give up and shut the book. The earl's face keeps appearing in my mind, and I resent that he has taken over my thoughts without even being present.

I walk over to my trunk and retrieve my mother's journal. Perhaps an entry will appear that will serve as a distraction from the earl's overbearing presence in my mind.

The leather is smooth in my hands, and I let the book fall open to a page somewhere in the middle. It's blank, and I almost close it again, but then the words appear. I lean back with a contented sigh and pray Mama will have some words of advice.

My dearest Katherine,

I hope it will not be too much of an imposition for you to stay with your grandmother. She is such a well-connected figure in high Society your father and I always knew it would be for the best if she were the one to help ease your debut. Though, of course, I believed I would be there with you.

I'm sure, as a young lady, you are well aware your grandmother and I were never close. I pray she will not let this color her relationship with you, but I fear she will only see my eyes when she gazes upon your face. Your grandmother is not a bad person, but she is one of those who, like others I tried to shield you from, was never able to accept the truth of our lineage.

There is so much I wish I could teach you about Society: how there are so many rules it sometimes feels as though you are suffocating, or how everything from your manner of dress to the type of carriage in which you arrive is picked apart. Or, most importantly, how a single rumor can have the destructive power of a criminal offense. And yet, the rules of English Society pale in comparison to those of Sylvania.

Just as the English nobles marry for wealth and titles, the Sylvan nobility married for the most powerful arcana bloodlines. Our family has many abilities, not least of all manipulating the elements, healing, and premonitions, but even these were not enough. Your grandfather desired one of the rarest arcana: the ability to harness our energy and use it for destructive force. The Sylvani who could perform this terrible arcana could level whole cities with a wave of power. And for the first time in thousands of years, a Sylvan male recently manifested this ability. Political battles broke out over which family would be joined in marriage to the Sylvani who would now rule us all.

Your grandfather won that battle, and my marriage was arranged to Lord Elric without my consent. After I fell in love with your father, it was only because of my mother's unwavering love for me that I was able to leave my realm. She braved my father's wrath, though in the end, not even she could prevent my exile. She was beautifully strong and steadfast. You have always reminded me of her.

*I know navigating Society will be difficult for you, as outspoken
as you are. It's practically a requirement for nobility to be obtuse; they
never say what they mean. But neither must you become caught up
in their petty games.*

Never lose sight of who you are.

With great love and tender affection,
Mama

I read and reread my mother's words. She very rarely spoke of my Sylvan grandparents when she was alive, and now I know why. How terribly painful to have a father who thought only of the advancement of his family's blood-lines—and how blessed my siblings and I were to have such a loving father. Just the thought of being forced into a marriage with a man I have never met makes my stomach twist in disgust.

I think of the small glimpse of Society I encountered last night. If I learned anything from my interaction with the earl—and the almost palpable desperation of the ambitious mamas in attendance—it was that social status trumps all else. Though even that rule seemed to depend upon the wealth of the noble in question, since Lady Hasting was able to practically insult my grandmother without consequence.

My mother was certainly right about Grandmama, though I suppose her treatment of me hasn't been quite as cold as I expected. I still remember a time when I was only four or five years old, and my grandmother was visiting Bransfield for the last time. My grandfather had still been alive. Mama worked for weeks to prepare the house for their stay; she wanted it all just so, and she let me tag along with her while she spoke with the servants to choose everything from linens to which dishes would be served when.

My grandparents arrived a day later than planned. From the moment Grandmama entered our home, she radiated a sort of cold indifference. She greeted her room with a critical eye, she found the meals bland, and she reduced two of the maids to tears. When Robert and I were brought down from the nursery to see her, she sneered at us like we were lepers. "Their manner of dress leaves much to be desired," she told Mama and walked away without another word.

It was the last time Mama ever made an effort to reach out to Grandmama. Though I've never been able to discuss it with her, now that I am older, I know it was the insult to her own children that hardened Mama's heart.

One of the maids interrupts my anger-provoking memories to call me for breakfast, and I try rather unsuccessfully to bury the dislike I have for my own grandmother before entering the dining room.

"Good morning," Lucy says and sits in the chair beside me. She glances around the room for a moment and lowers her voice, "Were you able to find any garish sun pins upon Lord Thornewood's bow tie?"

I laugh. "No, he was quite free of any identifying marks."

"Either that, or you gave up the search."

I take a sip of tea to hide my smile, but Lucy is perceptive as ever.

"I knew it," she says. "I saw the way the two of you were staring at one another—like you rather wished no one else was there."

"He is intriguing, I'll grant you that. Though I think he may be charming in the way many dangerous men are—the better to draw unsuspecting ladies in."

She gives me a look much too wise for her years and takes a bite of her toast. "You are hardly unsuspecting. He was reserved, perhaps, maybe even aloof at times, but not dangerous."

"How can you be sure? You cannot, of course," I say when she flounders for a retort. "Rob was right to say I should be cautious." Unbidden, thoughts of the earl's gaze intent on mine rise to the forefront of my mind.

Annoyed with my thoughts, I press down too hard with my knife, and it skitters across my plate.

Lucy smiles. "You're blushing again."

Grandmama walks into the room, effectively ending any further talk on the subject. When she joins us at the table, I have to force myself to take a bite of food else I'll pepper her with questions. Am I to spend each day in such mind-numbing boredom as this morning?

My booted foot taps beneath the table as she takes her time buttering her toast and fixing her tea. She takes a sip, nods, and then turns to me. "Mary tells me you were up before even she was this morning."

"Yes, mum, I—"

"A lady in town for the season does not rise with the servants. It's just not done."

My mouth tightens. "Well, I cannot simply tell my body when to sleep. I'm used to rising early, and it will not be an easy habit to change."

"That's an easy way to wear yourself out. With the late suppers and balls, you won't be fit to be seen the next morning."

Lucy nudges me with her foot, so I press my lips together and stare at my plate. I cannot believe she is telling me when to wake now.

Grandmama pulls out a slip of paper and passes it to me. "While we're on the subject of your schedule, here is your itinerary for the week."

My eyes scan back and forth over my grandmother's neat handwriting. For the next week, I'm scheduled to do everything from letter-writing to a carriage ride in the park each day. She has my entire day planned, so I will scarcely be able to draw breath before going on to the next thing.

She points to tomorrow's schedule. "You see I have added a visit with the dressmaker." She smiles at Lucy. "We shall show her your drawing and see how well she can replicate it."

"How wonderful," Lucy says, her eyes bright.

"So I am to go to the park today?" I ask. That is one good thing.

Grandmama glances at the paper. "Yes, and I dare say, you'd best get ready. We'll leave in an hour."

Just before I leave the room, she says, "Oh, and Katherine? Wear the violet carriage outfit. I know for a fact Lord Thornewood will be there."

"Yes, Grandmama," I say.

Let the parade begin.

Hyde Park. The place where Society goes to gossip and husband hunt with exercise as a thin excuse. Even worse, it's just Grandmama and me. Lucy remained behind with Miss Watts, studying art from the Renaissance period.

It's unseasonably warm today, and I long to remove my coat, lovely as it is.

"Do not even think of removing your coat," Grandmama says with a little glance my way. "It is meant to be worn over your blouse and skirt." I close my eyes to keep from rolling them.

She guides the horses through the park's entrance and slows them to a sedate trot. I fret with the edge of my coat as I take in the number of people already here. Ladies dressed in elaborate hats perch in high open carriages, elegant men ride by on their sleek horses and tip their hats to us, while others stroll down the paths for promenade.

Grandmama greets each person by name as we pass, and my face soon becomes tired of holding a smile. I stare longingly at the river that runs parallel to the driving path, and when the horses slow even more, I have to fight the urge to simply jump down.

"Grandmama, do you mind if I go for a walk?"

She doesn't answer me right away, and I fidget the entire time. "Yes, I think that would be a good idea. You will be able to meet far more people that way. I'll drive the horses around once and come back for you."

She guides the phaeton off to the side, and I climb down as gracefully as possible in my long skirt with its sturdy fabric. I stride off before she can change her mind.

Many people smile and nod at me as I make my way to the shining lake, and I return the smile briefly but avoid making eye contact for long. I would rather not be caught in a dull conversation on the weather or how I'm enjoying my stay in London.

As soon as I reach the water's edge, I let out a breath and relax my tense shoulders. Though it's only been a day, I can already feel the gilded cage of the city closing in around me. I miss the fresh, open air of the country. Even in this park, with its open fields, trees, and idyllic lake, there are more people than I would see in a week at Bransfield.

The water rushing past me is cold, but I long to dip my feet in. I step closer to the bank and tilt my head up to the warm sun. A breeze teases a few tendrils of hair loose from my chignon, and I smile at its caress. My skin soaks up the sunlight, replenishing my lost energy. Yet another reason I feel so restricted in the city. Without regular time spent outdoors, my stores of power reduce drastically. And as they are irrevocably tied to the energy that keeps my heart beating, I'd rather not find out what happens when I am denied my time in the sun.

The trod of horse hooves alerts me to someone's presence, but I am loath to turn around.

"You would do well not to get too close to the water," a man's voice says behind me. "Many have drowned before."

I turn and shield my eyes with my hand. I have to look up to see him as he is astride a lovely bay mount. "My lord," I say and drop into a curtsy. "You are concerned for my safety?"

That came out more flirtatious than I intended, and I watch a grin bloom across his face. In one smooth movement, he dismounts from his horse. His gaze rakes over my appearance; I try to ignore the effect it has coupled with his equally dark hair and eyes, but it still accelerates my heart more than I would like. I frown up at him.

"Well imagine how horrifying it would be if I were to witness such a thing," he says. "I would undoubtedly have to go in and save you. We'd both catch cold, and then it would all be for naught."

"How morbid you are. Can I not enjoy the view?"

He ignores my question and peers around. "Where is your mount? Or carriage?"

"Perhaps I walked here," I say, my voice betraying my irritation at his abrupt subject change.

"Don't play coy, Miss Sinclair." His grip must tighten on the reins because his horse tosses his head in protest. "Do you need an escort? This park is well attended, but there are areas that can be rather . . . unsavory."

"No, I came with my grandmother." I look back at the shimmering water. "I just wanted a chance to walk."

His horse lets out a loud snort and stamps his hoof, and out of reflex, I reach out to stroke his neck.

"Don't—" the earl calls out, but cuts himself off when his horse drops his head and allows me to stroke his velvety nose.

I meet the earl's look of surprise.

"I was going to say he has a temper," he says, "but I can see it was an unnecessary warning."

I withdraw my hand and laugh when his horse seeks it out again with his nose. "I'm just used to my own horses. They can be temperamental, too. I wish I had one or two here with me. My grandmother's are too sedate for my tastes."

Lord Thornewood's eyebrows raise and he smirks at me. "Indeed? You like a mount with more fire?"

"I wouldn't describe them so, but I do like a horse that enjoys a faster pace than a trot."

"I cannot believe I'm discussing horses with a lady. You haven't yet learned the infuriating female art of small talk, I take it."

I tilt my head at him. "Does my having an opinion on something other than the weather or the latest fashion intimidate you, my lord? If so, I apologize. I shall endeavor to dumb down my conversation posthaste."

As soon as the words leave my mouth, I drop my eyes to the horse's nose. What is wrong with me? How could I speak in such a thoughtless manner to an earl of all people?

To my surprise, he laughs, the sound delightfully rich. "You have a fascinating manner of speaking, Miss Sinclair. I cannot wait for your coming out. Society won't know what to make of you."

"I was under the impression Society does not look kindly upon those who do not follow their rules."

"They *say* that, yes." He leans closer to me. "But secretly, it fascinates them."

"That is very good to know since I would like to avoid excessive attention."

And I've said too much again. What debutante wants to *avoid* attention? Preposterous. I shouldn't be allowed to speak.

His eyes appraise me. "I very much doubt you will be able to avoid it. Perhaps if you avoid singing, playing the piano, or speaking."

Before I can answer, two ladies call out to Lord Thornewood on their way down to the river. They are both dressed in crisp white blouses, dark skirts, and corresponding embroidered jackets. They walk with mincing ladylike steps, and though I am wearing an equally expensive outfit, I still feel out of place.

"My lord," the one with hair nearly the same color as my own says, "how fortuitous of us to stumble upon you here. I don't believe I have ever seen you at Hyde Park." Her eyes dart from his face to mine, and I can see she very much wants to ask who I am and why we are alone talking by the river, but to do so would be impolite. In any case, it's hardly my fault no one else is around.

"Good morning, Miss Gray. Miss Uppington." He holds a gloved hand toward me. "Allow me to do the honor of presenting the Honorable Katherine Sinclair, here in town for her debut."

We face each other and sink into curtsies. As we are all around the same age, they give me their first names as well: Miss Eliza Gray and Miss Amelia Uppington.

"Did you just come to town?" Eliza, the one who first addressed the earl, asks.

"Yes, my grandmother was kind enough to invite me here for the season."

"I know of Lady Sinclair," Amelia says with a smile. She has a heart-shaped face and dark hair, and she seems the more approachable of the two. "She is a very dear friend of my aunt's."

"And when will you have your debut?" Eliza asks, though it seems she has a difficult time keeping her eyes on my face when Lord Thornewood is much more interesting to look at.

"Wednesday next," I say, and her eyes dart to mine.

"Where did you say you were from?" she asks, sharply.

"I didn't," I say.

Her friend giggles nervously. "We will both be debuting then as well."

Eliza puts a gloved finger to her chin. "I seem to remember a Lady Sinclair who is a rather upstanding member of the peerage."

"She's her grandmother," Amelia says.

"Ah," Eliza says, "she must have arranged for your debut then."

I open my mouth to retort, but she turns to Lord Thornewood. "My lord, I hope you will be in attendance at Duchess Cecily's ball next Wednesday."

He looks at me when he answers. "Yes."

Her eyes narrow, and I find myself stiffening in response. "Now that I think of it," she says, "I believe I heard talk about town of a Miss Sinclair from Gloucestershire."

I don't like the idea of anyone in London talking about me, especially after what poor Margaret witnessed just a few days ago. "My father's estate is located in Gloucestershire," I say in as neutral a tone as I can manage.

"Indeed? Well, then, you must be the country beauty I heard talk of." She casts her eyes over my dress as though appraising whether this is true.

"How very kind," I say.

Eliza turns to Amelia. "But what else did we hear? Something about a girl who has become so headstrong, her father sent her to London because not even the country gentlemen would have her." She laughs humorlessly, her eyes trained on mine. "But that must have been a different girl from Gloucestershire as the one who stands before us is so well-turned out, there can be no doubt of her gentle upbringing."

If I were one of my father's hounds, my hackles would be standing on end. I cannot imagine what I did to deserve such animosity from this perfect stranger. I glance at the earl, whose mouth is turned down in an irritated frown, though whether it is directed at Eliza or the gossip she deposited at our feet, I'm not sure.

I smile as though she's said something amusing. "Perhaps. Though I'm not sure *headstrong* would be such a terrible insult. I find it is much preferred to that of a vapid gossipmonger."

The earl lets out a noise somewhere between a snort and a cough. His frown has been replaced with bright amusement in his eyes, but I cannot even enjoy it. My body thrums with nervous energy. I've wielded my tongue like a sword, and I know I have yet to pay the consequences.

Eliza makes a sniffing sound and turns to Amelia. "We should continue our walk. I believe we have trespassed on his lordship and Katherine's private conversation."

"We weren't—" I start.

"It was nice to make your acquaintance, Katherine," Eliza says. "I look forward to seeing you again soon."

My eyes narrow at her back as she walks away. If anyone I've met so far is a member of the Order, it's Eliza. Why else would she hate me on sight? Though if that's the caliber of its members, I fear my mother worried herself for nothing.

"My dear Miss Sinclair," the earl says, his tone steeped with regret, "as amusing as that was, I do believe you've made yourself your first enemy."

SIX

THE rest of the week is unbearably dull, and yet busy at the same time. After that day in the park, I haven't seen Lord Thornewood, even at the evening suppers. The fact that he has disappeared from Society is worrisome. It seems just the thing someone would do if he were from the Order my mother warned me of. A sickening feeling of dread fills me. Not only is the success of my debut dependent upon his good name, but I also cannot deny the attraction I have for him. Surely fate would not be so cruel as to curse me with an irrepressible fascination with the man.

"Pardon me, milady," Mary says as she enters the room. "A letter just arrived from Oxford."

"Oh, it must be from Robert," I say and reach eagerly for the letter. "Thank you."

She bobs a curtsy and leaves me at the desk to read. My eyes scan through it first. I want to be sure he is coming for my debut. Once I see he is and will be arriving later today, I read it again, slowly. The letter is short, mostly well-wishes and tales of outings with his friends, and it only makes me miss him more.

I carry the letter upstairs and glance in Lucy's room, but she must still be with Miss Watts. As I walk into my room, I see my mother's journal glowing softly on a chair near my bed.

I rush over and open it with such eagerness I nearly drop it.

My dearest Katherine,

By now your debut will be upon you. Though I never made a formal debut before the Court, I remember the first ball I ever attended: a glowing night of dancing, music, and most importantly, meeting your father. I know you think finding a suitor is silly or inconsequential, but for our kind, it is important—at least if we want to remain part of this world.

Perhaps you have already met some of the other girls who will debut with you. While some can be trusted, beware those who are blinded by jealousy. You have been given a gift that draws others to you, and many will hate you for it. Your more unusual gifts you must keep hidden, for there is no greater scandal than the one fueled by fear.

I wish I could be there with you, my darling. I know you will be breathtaking.

With much love,
Mama

Tears fill my eyes, and I slam the book closed. Her words are so beautiful. The pain cuts through me like a dagger. At least I know to whom this letter refers—Eliza and girls like her.

I've seen her once or twice since that day in the park, and though she was careful not to shun me in front of Grandmama, her demeanor was undoubtedly cold. Though I watched her carefully, she never gave a hint of knowing the truth about me. But of course, I'm not entirely sure what to watch for. I can only imagine what it will be like when we are in each other's company every night at the balls.

The soft glow of the journal draws my attention once again. Strange, since it usually fades once I've read the entry.

I open it and reread my mother's words. When I get to the bottom of the page, I find the reason for the glow. Another rune. My finger hovers over it. I should run and find Lucy; she could tell me its meaning. It's shaped like an hourglass tipped on its side, but I know it must represent something else. In the end, I cannot resist the possibility of seeing more of Mama's realm.

I touch the rune.

A surge of energy, and then my room in London disappears. In its place is a rocky countryside. The sky is gray overhead, with still darker clouds threatening to release a tumult of rain. In the distance, a rock formation looms.

Katherine, a voice whispers in my mind.

The fox with the turquoise eyes moves into view. It starts to move away, only to stop and look back again. I make the decision to follow, and once I do, I'm transported forward until a pile of jagged rock stands overhead. The rocks form a bridge of sort, cut by centuries of wind and rain.

Here, the voice says.

Where is this? I want to ask, but cannot. I am formless in this vision; I can only see what is before me with no other power over my environment.

The fox looks at me again, innate intelligence in its gaze.

The vision fades as quickly as it came.

A commotion by the stairs draws my attention, and I get to my feet just as my grandmother sweeps into my room, her eyes brighter than I've ever seen them.

"My dear, you must get dressed," she says, even her words hurried.

My mind still transported to another place, I can only blink at her. What was that place? Was it in this realm or my mother's? What is she trying to tell me?

"Katherine, for goodness sake, girl, did you not hear me?" my grandmother says. "Get dressed."

Before I can ask why, she walks back into the hall and calls for my maid. When Mary enters and bobs a curtsy to my grandmother, she looks just as confused by Grandmama's distressed look as I do.

"Yes, milady?" she asks, her thick eyebrows drawn inward.

"I need you to dress Katherine in her nicest day gown—perhaps the gold one."

"Yes, milady."

"Are we going out?" I try but fail to keep the exasperation from my voice.

"No, child. The earl has come to see you," Grandmama says, matching my tone.

I freeze, and my stomach twists in surprise.

"I'd like her hair done in the same style as the night she first came," she continues.

Mary efficiently secures my thick hair into a pompadour of which the Gibson Girl herself would be proud. She turns to my grandmother for approval.

"Yes, that's it," she says.

As Grandmama watches Mary help me into my dress and dictates every nuance of my look, I begin to feel more and more like a show pony groomed for a country parade.

"What would you have me say to him?" I ask, my tone sarcastic.

"Be sure to mention your father's connection with his. Also, make sure he will be in attendance at your debut. Oh, and your brother's connection to him through Oxford."

"Speaking of Robert—"

"Mary, not the silver comb. Use the gold. There, see how well it complements her dress?"

I blow a strand of hair out of my eyes, and Grandmama narrows her eyes at me. She places her hand on my arm. "Lord Thornewood is paying you the highest honor by calling on you today. You must be above reproach."

So many snide responses jump to the tip of my tongue, begging to be unleashed, but I force my lips into a closed-mouth smile instead. "Yes, Grandmama."

I follow her downstairs to the parlor, thankful my irritation masks the shivery feeling in my stomach.

He waits by the window, his back to us. My anxiety intensifies as I gaze upon his perfectly tailored coat and riding breeches.

"Lord Thornewood," my grandmother says, "how good of you to visit."

He turns, and those dark eyes seek me out immediately. "I came to ask you to accompany me to the park this afternoon, Miss Sinclair."

It is abominably rude for him to ignore my grandmother and address me instead, but the smile never leaves Grandmama's face.

"It is the first time the weather has been agreeable," he adds. "I thought we could go riding."

"I would love to," I say before I have even thought it through. I simply cannot resist any opportunity to get out of the house. It's possible I'm joining a member of the Order for a ride in the park, but I would sell my soul for the chance to escape my grandmother for an hour.

He smiles as if he had no doubt I'd say yes. "I brought along one of my horses for you to ride. I've heard you enjoy more of a challenging mount."

The smile overtakes my face. "This is a surprise, indeed. And a welcome diversion. I have been in need of a challenge for quite some time."

His brows rise ever so slightly, and I shake my head inwardly at myself. Why does everything I say to this man come out coy?

"I am very glad to provide you with one. My groom has saddled the mare with a sidesaddle that I hope you will find comfortable."

My excitement dims. A sidesaddle? Heavens, when was the last time I rode as a lady? How can I be expected to keep my balance with both legs on one side of the horse?

"If you'll excuse me, I'll change into something more appropriate," I say. *And figure out how to do this without embarrassment.*

"Katherine," my grandmother says, "aren't you forgetting something?"

I halt on my way out the door. Does she know of my admittedly scandalous behavior?

"Madame?"

"I have not given you permission to go," she says, her face tight.

My cheeks flame red. I should have asked her first, but I can't believe she'd call me out in front of Lord Thornewood. "My apologies, Grandmama. I'm afraid the excitement of the moment overtook me."

Her face relaxes but her smile remains tight. "I understand, dear. Our schedule is open for the day, so you may go."

"How generous of you," Lord Thornewood drawls.

"My lord, the invitation is greatly appreciated," she says, and I'm not sure if she deliberately mistook his tone or simply didn't notice.

His eyes seek out mine. "It's my pleasure."

"Mary," she calls, and my maid appears in the doorway. The poor girl must know to hover nearby should Grandmama need her—which is often. "Katherine will need assistance changing for a ride with Lord Thornewood."

Mary curtsies. "Yes, mum."

I start for the door, but my grandmother leans in close. "Perhaps the navy blue riding habit?"

Heavens, a riding habit, too? I have never understood why I must wear a skirt atop breeches instead of wearing them alone, which would be infinitely cooler and more comfortable. And combined with a shirt, jacket, cravat, top hat, and veil, it may be hours before I am ready. I nod in agreement, though, and follow Mary back to my room, gathering my energy for the day ahead. As unskilled as I am in riding sidesaddle, it will take a considerable amount of power to keep me from looking like I've never ridden this way a day in my life.

As promised, the mare is a challenge. Oh, she's sweet-tempered enough, but very green. It seems as though she has very little training under the saddle, and I am certain the earl is testing me. Probably to see if I am nothing but a braggart.

I adjust my seat in the saddle to better balance the awkward way I am forced to ride. A pommel supports my right thigh, which sits slightly higher than my left leg. The majority of my weight is centered over the left side of the horse, which I know doesn't help the mare's balance either.

"Is the saddle comfortable?" Lord Thornewood asks as we guide our horses onto the well-worn path in Hyde Park.

"Yes, my lord, very comfortable." I squeeze the reins when the mare tries again to break into a trot. Her frustration washes over me again and again. She wishes I would sit properly like every other rider or allow her to go faster than a walk. But she is sweet enough to fret I am about to slip off her back, for that is what it feels like to her.

"And the mare, you find her agreeable, as well?"

The mare in question tosses her head as I once again restrain her from trotting. "Yes, very agreeable."

I risk a glance at him though I have been staring straight ahead this entire time, and he smirks at me. "You seem very tense, Miss Sinclair. Perhaps this mare was not the right choice for you?"

"Oh, no, my lord. I like her. She has spirit."

He grins. "A good match for you then."

I feel heat creep up my neck. I cannot tell if his comment is meant to be teasing or insulting. "I suppose you mean to say I am spirited as well. I only wonder if you join other gentlemen in thinking this is a serious character flaw in a lady."

He guides his horse closer to mine until I can make out the flecks of amber in his dark eyes. "On the contrary," he says in low tones that elicit a shiver from me, "I find a lady with a mind of her own intriguing."

My inner temperature rises as I glance away from his captivating stare. "How refreshing," I mumble.

His grin is back. "Shall we move to a faster gait? I'm sure this has become a tedious pace for you."

"As you wish," I say, and glance down at the mare's long gray mane for a moment. The day is too overcast to provide me with much energy from the sun. I center myself, focusing on the stores of power I have bubbling just beneath the surface. When I release it, it tingles over my body as if I've submerged myself in a hot spring. I will need its energy to stay on this horse. I refuse to embarrass myself in front of Lord Thornewood. The warmth feeds every muscle in my body, strengthening them past normal human limits. I bind myself to the saddle, so the mare and I are more like one being than separate horse and rider.

I know it works when the mare's ears shoot back, and emotions of surprise replace her earlier frustration.

Lord Thornewood's bay gelding transitions into a smooth canter, and I ask my mare to do the same. She responds instantly, and I let the tense muscles in my neck and shoulders relax. My body moves with her, and she relaxes, too.

I shoot him a sly grin. "Care to race?"

He gives me a look of surprise but quickly recovers. "How can I ignore such a challenge? Where to?"

"The bridge?"

He gives one short nod. "Ladies first. You'll need a head start."

I let out a very unladylike snort and ask my mare to gallop. She surges forward, and even though I know I will pay for the amount of energy it takes to keep me in the saddle, I cannot keep the smile from my face.

It isn't long before the earl's horse and mine are neck and neck, and I shake out the reins to encourage her to take longer strides. A bead of sweat slips down my spine beneath my warm riding jacket despite the cool weather. As my mother always taught me, arcana has its limits. Anything that enhances my abilities as a mortal drains energy faster than small acts of arcana, like small manipulations of nature or the enchantment of my music. The more I use this type of power to stay in the saddle, the more it draws from my life energy. When it becomes more difficult to draw a breath, I know I'm approaching my limit, but I'm having too much fun to slow.

His horse overtakes mine at the last second, and I pull my mare to a halt beside the river.

"Good race," he says with an almost boyish grin.

"A very good race indeed," I say. "I can hardly catch my breath." As though noticing my short breaths, the clouds move aside for the sun. With its light, I breathe a little easier.

Lord Thornewood reaches out and pats my mare on the neck. He glances up at me, eyes still bright from the exercise. "You handled her well."

I smile back. "I'm not entirely incompetent on a horse."

He opens his mouth to reply, but the shrill cry of a woman's voice stops him. We both turn toward the river, seeking the source.

A woman not much older than me runs frantically in the direction of a small child toddling toward the water on the opposite bank. He stumbles, rights himself, and continues toward the gray water, heedless of the danger it presents.

"Good God, she'll never make it," Lord Thornewood says and wheels his horse around toward the bridge. I watch them gallop away for a moment before returning my attention to the boy.

Apprehension grips me as all my mother's warnings resound in my mind. But I cannot stand by and watch this child drown. Lord Thornewood and the woman are closing fast, but not nearly fast enough.

I walk my mare forward until her front hooves are in the water. "Easy there," I murmur to her as I send my power traveling down the length of her legs. She twitches, but doesn't move. As it did the day I saved Robert, the power tugs at the very core of me, pulling energy out of me like the spindle of a spinning wheel. It shimmers over the water, and I concentrate on the mud of the opposite bank. I picture what I want: for the mud to cover the boy's feet and create suction he cannot escape. The earth shifts in obedience to my arcana's request. I feel it deep inside me; a force as powerful as gravity.

The boy comes to a stop inches from the water's edge. His face takes on a look of intense concentration, and I know he's struggling against the mud. When at last he realizes he will not be able to free himself and continue to the water, he lets out a frustrated wail. The woman reaches him, and at the moment she scoops him into her arms, I release the arcana. His feet come free, and mud flies in every direction. She spins him around, kissing his fat cheeks.

Lord Thornewood arrives a moment later and says a few words to her. She nods, still holding the boy tightly to her breast.

A flash of emerald green velvet catches my attention just to the right of where the boy was. Eliza's eyes meet mine over the river. I can feel her cold stare from even this distance, and anxious fear snakes down my spine. How much did she see? The power rippling across the water? The mud drawing up around the boy's ankles? I shake my head. Perhaps I'm merely being paranoid.

I back the mare out of the water as Lord Thornewood returns to my side. I feel as feverish as I did when I saved Robert, so I release its hold before it saps all my strength. The lovely support disappears, and my horse tosses her head, nearly knocking me off balance.

"Whoa there," Lord Thornewood calls out to my mare sternly. He looks at me with some concern. "Are you alright, Miss Sinclair?"

"She just surprised me. I'm fine," I say. My breathing is rapid, though, and I force myself to take deep breaths. I glance up at the sky, but the sun is now hidden away by thick clouds. My only other option is to draw strength from the river. "Actually, my lord, I wonder if you might help me dismount for a moment?"

"Of course," he says, throwing his leg over the side of his gelding and landing lightly on his feet. He strides over to me and holds my mare steady. "You look so pale. Are you sure you're alright?"

I cannot even answer him. It takes all I have to force my leg over the pommel so I may slide down into his arms. Shakily, I do so. His hands are firm but gentle on my waist, holding me steady.

My knees threaten to buckle, and I beg them to hold out just a moment longer. "Could you help me to the water? I just believe I've become overheated."

His jaw flexes once, but he nods and helps me to the water's edge. With wooden movements, I yank off my gloves. I let the cold water rush over my bare hands. The clouds part again, the sunlight restoring my energy even as the water cools my feverish skin. I gasp as I'm able to catch my breath again.

"Better?" Lord Thornewood asks when I straighten. "I don't scare easily, Miss Sinclair, but I have to admit, the prospect of you fainting has me a little nervous."

"I won't faint," I say, my voice much stronger. I tug at the jacket of my riding habit and give him a wry smile. "Perhaps I shouldn't have worn wool today. I almost felt as though I was suffocating."

"Ah, well you wouldn't hurt my feelings if you removed your coat," he says, a teasing light entering his eyes.

This brings up the image of undressing in front of him, and my face flames. A rakish thing to say if ever I heard one.

The sound of another horse draws our attention, and I frown when I see it is Eliza. Her eyes have a glint of malice in them, which sets my teeth on edge.

"Lord Thornewood, Katherine," she says when she is closer. "I find you deep in conversation by the water once again. Why, it must be your favorite place to meet."

She is dressed in a riding habit as well, but the deep green sets off her pale hair and green eyes wonderfully. Not a single hair is out of place, and she looks much more comfortable in the sidesaddle than I do.

"Good morning, Miss Gray," the earl says.

She smiles at him, even bats her long eyelashes a bit, and I stifle a groan.

"It's lovely to see you again, Eliza," I say, and she drags her eyes to my face.

"And you as well. But Katherine, you look so fatigued. And you're no longer mounted. Did you have a tumble?"

She couldn't be any less sincere. I know she is commenting on the fact my hair is in disarray and my cheeks are no doubt flushed from the exercise.

"No, just a tad overheated."

"Hm," she says, still watching me with a knowing smile. Again I wonder just how much she saw—and more importantly, if she knew what it implied. "A terrible business with that little boy just now."

I stiffen, and my eyes dart to Lord Thornewood.

He nods somberly. "Yes, it was lucky indeed the banks are so muddy this time of year. He was unable to make it to the water. His nanny and I wouldn't have made it in time otherwise."

"Oh," I say, "is that who she was? I wasn't sure if she was his mother or a nanny."

"A nanny, which I suppose is in some ways worse. I cannot imagine having to inform the parents if anything had happened to him." He gazes out over the water, the current rushing by us. "I asked her if she needed any assistance, but she declined. I think she was just overcome with relief."

Eliza puts her hand to her chest. "Oh, you are too kind, my lord. When you galloped across the bridge to help, I thought surely I'd never seen anything so chivalrous in my life." Just as I'm about to gag on her saccharine words, she adds, "I was on the other side of the bank, you see, and I saw everything."

My eyes snap to hers, but she is wearing the same catty look she always does. Again I wonder if she truly knows I wielded arcana, or if she is merely playing with me.

My mare stamps her hoof in boredom, ready to be moving again. As I give her neck a pat in reassurance, I notice a familiar chestnut mare approaching. My brother lifts his hand in greeting and trots his horse over to us.

"Robert," I say, my face taken over by an enormous smile. "I wasn't expecting you to arrive so soon. I am delighted to see you."

His expression is equally as bright. "Grandmama insisted I seek you out. Naturally I wanted to see you right away." His eyes land on the earl's face. "But I see you are with company."

"Oh, forgive me. May I present Lord Colin Thornewood, and Miss Eliza Gray. This is my brother, the Honorable Robert Sinclair."

"Charmed, I'm sure," Eliza says, her eyes traveling the length of him. I tighten my grip on the reins.

"Robert is in town for my debut. He's on leave from Oxford." There, let her realize he is too young to be thinking of marriage yet.

"Ah, I see. Welcome to London, Mr. Sinclair," she says.

"Thank you, I'm very glad to be here." He turns his attention back to me. "Father has a wonderful surprise for you. He sent a couple of our horses here for you to ride."

"Oh, which?" Finally, my own horses. Now maybe I won't be so unsteady.

"The chestnut gelding and the gray stallion."

"Stallion?" Lord Thornewood asks, his brows drawn low over his eyes. "Your father would send a stallion for your sister to ride?"

"My sister is a very talented equestrian. She can easily handle the horse, and indeed, does so all the time." My brother answers calmly, but I see the telltale tightness in his jaw that suggests he's annoyed by Lord Thornewood's criticism.

"She's riding a mare now and seems very fatigued," Eliza says. "I commented on it just a few moments ago."

"Yes, well, she's not used to riding sidesaddle."

A silence descends upon us, and I hold my breath. Foolish Robert! How could he say something like that? Doesn't he realize what a scandal it is for a lady to ride astride?

Eliza lets out a mean little laugh. "You cannot be suggesting your own sister is fast. Or do you fancy yourself a man, Katherine?"

I'm too stunned to reply. Anger and humiliation churn in my stomach. I cannot believe she'd say such an insulting thing.

Robert finally catches on he's made a terrible blunder and stumbles over his words. "Oh, I—no. No, of course not. I misspoke. I meant to say she's not used to so modern a sidesaddle."

"Ah, I see," Eliza says, but her eyes squint in a calculating way.

"Miss Sinclair," Lord Thornewood says, "you seem to have done well with the mare I brought along today. You are welcome to ride her anytime you wish."

Clearly he doesn't approve of my choice of horses. So what would he think if he knew I really don't ride sidesaddle? Or did he see through my brother's attempt to cover his candid words? Either way, I am sick of people who insist upon imposing their will on me.

"How very kind of you," I say, and even I can tell my tone has gone cold. "My apologies, but I must beg to return to the house. I am more tired than I thought."

"Of course," the earl says, concern turning his mouth down at the corners. "Will you excuse us, Miss Gray?"

"By all means," Eliza says. "It was so lovely to make your acquaintance, Mr. Sinclair."

"And yours," Robert says with an irritated frown.

"May I assist you in mounting again?" Lord Thornewood asks.

I hesitate, wishing I could ask Robert to help me instead. "Thank you. Yes."

I turn to face the mare, gripping the saddle with both hands. Lifting my left leg slightly, he takes hold and boosts me up in one smooth movement. Once I'm settled back in the saddle, he mounts his own horse.

He and Robert turn their horses back toward the path. Before I can follow, Eliza says, "Oh, and Katherine? Good luck with your debut."

Her cruel smile is clue enough I can consider her words a threat.

SEVEN

THE day of my debut, the weather refuses to cooperate despite my grandmother's constant complaints. Rain streaks down the windows of the sitting room where Lucy and I take tea and thunder rumbles ominously in the distance. Since Grandmama is finally preparing herself for the ball we will attend afterward, I enjoy the precious few moments of peace—at least as much as I can since my stomach has transformed into a snake pit of nerves.

"The dressmaker did a superb job making the gown," Lucy says and reaches out to feel the heavy satin.

"Thanks to your drawing," I say with a smile.

"What do you think of the color?"

I glance down at the creamy ivory and touch the veil covering my hair. "I look like a bride."

She laughs. "I knew you'd feel that way."

"It's an embarrassing tradition. I can't think of a single way to make it more obvious what the true purpose of a debut is." I can only hope the lace flowers on my dress are enough to set it apart from an actual bridal gown.

"Well, take comfort. Robert will be there, and I'm sure he'll be just as miserable as you."

I heave a sigh. "It's little consolation. He will only be able to accompany me to the ball afterward. I must face the court—and the queen—alone."

"You will be brilliant, I'm sure of it. I so wish I could be there, but I shall have to make do with your faithful recounting of the evening."

"I will not leave out a single detail. Oh, and lest I should forget," I say and withdraw Mama's journal from my reticule. "I thought we could see if Mama has any words of advice."

Lucy lets out a breathy sound of excitement and moves closer. "I do hope so."

I let the journal fall open, hoping for my mother's guidance on this of all nights. The creamy pages stare up at us, frustratingly blank.

Lucy puts on a forced smile, as if hiding her disappointment. "I'm sure an entry will appear later—perhaps after you return?"

"Perhaps," I murmur, still watching the pages for any hint of words—or runes. "There was another rune at the bottom of the last entry."

"Did it show you another vision? Was it Mama's realm?" Lucy asks, her speech rapid with her excitement.

"I'm not sure. It was a rock formation, almost like a bridge." I think of the fox, but for some reason, I cannot bring myself to speak of it.

"What did the rune look like?"

"Like an hourglass, only it was on its side."

"An hourglass . . . Oh! That rune represents a threshold or gateway."

"A gateway. But to where?" First the vision of her realm, and then a rock formation under the gateway rune. Could she be showing me the way?

We both look up when Robert enters the room, dressed in his most formal tailcoat and white bow tie.

"Robert, you look very dashing," I say and he grimaces.

"I look nothing of the sort." He pauses as he takes in our melancholy expressions. "But why do you both look as though you've lost your favorite puppy?"

I hold up Mama's journal before returning it to my reticule. "We were hoping for a little encouragement."

"Ah, that is disappointing indeed. I cannot offer anything by way of advice, but I will certainly provide as much encouragement tonight as you can stand." He smiles at me with his usual hint of mischief shining in his eyes. "You do look exquisite in that gown. What an improvement over riding breeches."

"When will you learn to keep quiet? Grandmama might hear you."

He at least looks moderately apologetic. "I suppose we shall find out tonight what damage I may have inadvertently caused."

I cover my face. "Oh, do not remind me of that day. In front of Eliza of all people."

"She did seem to delight in my mistake. Have you made an enemy so soon, Wren?"

"She's been cold and jealous from the start," I say with a glare. "Enough to suggest I was fast—how ludicrous."

"She would do well to keep quiet," Robert says. "If only they knew what powers you have."

"Stop making it sound as if I could cause someone harm," I say with a glare. "You make me feel monstrous indeed. It's bad enough I'm not sure how much Eliza saw that day."

Robert's teasing look fades. "What do you mean?"

I glance down at my hands. "She may have seen me use a little arcana."

"Oh no," Lucy says while Robert shakes his head at me. "What happened?"

"A little boy was running for the river, so I manipulated the mud into holding him captive." I widen my eyes at Robert's disappointed look. "If I hadn't, he would've been swept away by the current."

"Well what is it you think Eliza saw? Surely she couldn't have seen such a small amount of arcana," he says.

"I looked up to find her watching me with . . . this *look* in her eyes. Oh, but I cannot be sure," I say and rub my brow in frustration. I'm so overly sensitive to everything around me because of Mama's warnings. Though I know I'm not imagining her dislike of me.

"Wren, honestly, you need to start telling us about these things," Robert says. "We're here to help."

"You've been away at school, busy with your studies," I say with a bit of an irritated edge to my voice. "And Lucy needn't be burdened with every little thing that goes on."

"I don't mind," Lucy says. "It'll give me something to puzzle over while I'm cooped up in this house all day."

I give her arm a squeeze. "I'm sorry Grandmama has kept you under lock and key."

"What was the rumor she heard about you?" Robert asks.

"It's not what you think," I say just so he'll stop glowering. "She just mentioned hearing about a girl from Gloucestershire who was so rebellious her father had to send her to London."

"Seems the girl has some reputable sources then."

I glare at him. "I wouldn't laugh at someone spreading rumors about you."

He holds up his hands. "My apologies, dear sister. I can see you are not in the mood for teasing." He looks at Lucy with a mischievous grin. "Dare I ask, then, why she has feathers in her hair?"

I reach up and feel one of the two white ostrich feathers. "It's another ridiculous debutante tradition. Grandmama ignored my pleas for a simple comb."

"Ah, I see." He pats the single line of braid on his trousers with his pair of white gloves as if eager to leave. "Well, come along then. Grandmama sent me to tell you the carriage has been pulled 'round."

"Why didn't you say so in the first place?" I say and struggle to my feet, balling the gown's long train into my left hand.

"Don't bunch it so," Lucy says and straightens it out. "You'll wrinkle it."

I roll my eyes at her and follow Robert out the door.

Instead of my grandmother's elegant barouche, a hired hackney waits in its place. Confusion furrows my brows as I glance at the awaiting footman. I would think tonight of all nights she would want to flaunt her considerable position in Society with her own carriage.

"Katherine, hurry into the carriage before you ruin your gown," Grandmama says, her tone sharp. She glares at the sky for a moment before pulling her velvet cape tighter around her.

"Grandmama, where is your barouche?" I ask.

She turns her glare from the sky to me. "What concern is it of yours where my carriage is? We have transportation for the evening. Kindly save your ridiculous questions for a time when we are not standing in cold, pouring rain."

"Forgive me for asking the question anyone would in my position," I snap. Surely I will not be able to take much more of her acerbic character.

She signals to the footman to help me into the carriage, pointedly ignoring my jibe.

"Oh, and lest I should forget," she says once we are inside, "there has been a change in plans. Instead of Robert escorting you to the ball after your debut at Court, Lord Thornewood will meet us there to take his place."

I gape at her. I knew the earl was to aid in my debut, but I thought we would share a dance or two. I never imagined I would enter a ballroom on his arm. I hate the thrill that runs up my spine almost as much as I resent the nervousness curled in my stomach.

"What about Robert?" I ask Grandmama. "He came all this way—"

"He's here to support his sister, but your brother has not the social pull of an earl to make Society take notice." She waves her hand dismissively. "Surely you see that."

Robert puts his hand over mine and gives a gentle squeeze. "Everything will be fine, Wren."

I shoot him a dark look. It's easy for him to say; he isn't about to be an object of intense scrutiny.

After waiting for an hour in a crush of carriages, our coach is finally allowed through the imposing gates of Buckingham Palace. The palace beyond is so large and formidable, I suddenly feel quite ill-prepared, as though even the creamy-beige stones of its neoclassical architecture have judged me and found me wanting. My eyes are drawn up to the wide stone balcony, and even farther up, to the Royal Standard flying limply in the rain.

"Remember to curtsy to not only the queen, but the princesses as well," Grandmama says as I am unceremoniously pushed out the door of the carriage. Men in palace livery move forward immediately to assist me.

"No one is to accompany me?" I ask, my eyes pleading with Rob for help.

"Do not be daft, child," Grandmama snaps. "It is your debut, not ours. Just follow the others, do exactly as I instructed you, and you will do splendidly. We will await you at the ball."

With these dubious words of wisdom, the door is shut behind me, and the carriage rolls away.

I join the queue of other debutantes entering the palace. They titter excitedly like ostentatious white peacocks, but I can only gape about like the country girl that I am. Lucy would absolutely love the majesty of the palace, with its color scheme of cream and gold, as rich as its sovereign. These colors are broken up by vibrant crimson in the carpeting and wall coverings, until the interior of the palace resembles a room of jewels: pearls and rubies all encased in gold.

One of the palace officials halts our procession in the antechamber outside of the Throne Room in Buckingham Palace. A buffet table laden with petit fours, biscuits, and other sweets along with refreshments has thoughtfully been provided for us—most likely to keep us from fainting beneath the weight of our gowns. A photographer holding a large, square camera takes photos of us, a parade of debutantes falling upon the golden buffet table like a flock of seagulls, and I cannot stop myself from enjoying the delicious treats laid out for us.

I choose a variety of petit fours as light as air and take a bite.

"Careful, dear," a familiarly snide voice calls out, "you wouldn't want to spill anything on your lovely gown."

Eliza trills a laugh as she bumps into my elbow, nearly causing me to spill my tea all over the front of my dress. I down the rest of my drink to prevent her from repeating her little trick, since I am fairly sure such a horrible stain would bar my entrance to the Throne Room. I glare at her back as she makes her way to the front of the queue and poses with her ridiculous bouquet of flowers for the photographer.

"You do well to ignore her. She has always been rather cruel," a soft voice says beside me. I turn to see Lady Hasting's daughter, the girl who had played the piano so beautifully at the supper we attended. She holds out her gloved hand, and I shake it. "I believe we've already met. Miss Sinclair, is it? I'm Penelope Hasting."

I smile. "It is a pleasure to see you again, Penelope. And please, call me Katherine."

She leans in closer. "Are we not a lovely bunch of brides . . . er, debutantes?"

A sort of joyful relief at the rareness of our shared way of thinking bursts through me like a firework. "Do you think it is the veil or the train that most gives away the true purpose of this tradition?"

"It's difficult to say, though I think you shouldn't forget the bouquet when creating your list of evidence."

"Indeed, it would be wrong of me to do so. Yours is lovely, by the way."

She holds the bouquet, larger than her head, to her nose like a blushing bride. "You're a darling to say so."

We both laugh, drawing the attention of the photographer away from Eliza. As he snaps our picture, she glares at us with petty malice. But before she can formulate some new plan of vindictiveness, one of the lords-in-waiting invites us to queue up before the doorway of the Throne Room.

My heart flutters against my chest as I take my place in line. Beneath my elbow-length white gloves, my palms are damp—partly from holding the weight of my nine-foot train over my left arm. My mind chooses this exact moment to regale me with images of myself tripping over said train and crashing to the floor in front of the entire Court.

Mama, lend me your grace, I think like a prayer. I close my eyes for a moment, and I can almost hear her voice, telling me, as she always did, that there was always strength within me if I would but reach for it.

The queue of debutantes moves forward until I stand at the threshold of the Throne Room. Royal guards in scarlet line one side of the room, prominent members of the Court on the other. At the end of the long room are the king and queen, seated upon their thrones, but I try not to focus on anything but the veil of the girl in front of me.

I take my first step into the room, my shoe bright white against the red of the carpet. The gold-leafed ceiling soars above me, brightly lit by seven enormous chandeliers. The room is designed to be awe-inspiring in majestic colors of gold and red, but I am too busy praying that I will remember the choreography of all I must do once I reach the throne.

A court attendant moves forward and indicates for me to drop my train. Shakily, I do so. With a golden wand, he spreads the heavy satin behind me until I can feel the weight of it pulling at my back.

Careful not to step on the train of the girl before me, I process forward. The name of the first debutante is announced, and after only a few moments, the next two names are called, until I stand alone before the king and queen.

"The Honorable Katherine Sinclair, daughter of Lord Edward Sinclair, Viscount of Bransfield," one of the court officials announces.

For one horrible moment, I freeze. Do I kneel or curtsy? Do I kiss the queen's hand, or do I only bow my head?

Something draws my gaze to the right of the king, and I lock eyes with the Earl of Thornewood. Gone is the characteristic look of arrogance. In its place is a warm smile. "Curtsy," he mouths to me with a nod.

I sink into a curtsy so low I'm almost kneeling before Queen Alexandra. She extends her hand to me, and I take it and kiss the back of it. Taking care not to step on my train, I move back toward the Throne Room entrance, curtsying to King Edward and again to each of his daughters in attendance, Princess Louise and Princess Victoria.

The court official with the wand replaces my train over my left arm, and with great relief, I am free to leave the Throne Room.

So much angst for so short an event. In the antechamber beyond the Throne Room, I duck into a dim hallway and lean against the wall, my ribs straining against my corset. An official will undoubtedly seek me out, but for now, I enjoy my brief respite.

"I am surprised, Miss Sinclair," Lord Thornewood says, appearing in the doorway like a specter. "I did not expect to find a newly presented debutante hiding in a darkened corridor like a wanton woman." I take a steadying breath. I cannot keep my hand from nervously smoothing my skirt, especially when his eyes trail over my dress.

To my chagrin, heat flushes across my cheeks. My eyes flick over his inky black velvet jacket and trousers. His ivory shirt and cravat are the only bright things on his body. I try to ignore how darkly handsome he is, how even the curve of his lips has my pulse jumping to life. "Is it a crime now to seek out a moment of peace?" I snap.

His grin only grows wider. "Such a tone I am greeted with, though I did my best to see you through your debut."

The warm smile he bestowed upon me in the Throne Room flashes through my mind and chips away at my defenses. "The awful truth is you're right. You did help me, and I am grateful."

He steps forward, so close if I but leaned toward him our lips would touch. "How grateful, Miss Sinclair?" I hold my breath as he reaches out and trails his fingers down the edge of my jaw. "Ah, but I shouldn't tease you. Tempting as you are, with your flushed cheeks, I am a man of honor . . ." A self-deprecating smile touches his lips. "Though the gossips may say otherwise."

Just as I am sure I will give in to my base desires and kiss the teasing grin from his face, a voice calls out from the room beyond, "Miss Sinclair?"

I jump away as though I have been burned and rush to the doorway. "Yes?" I say.

"There you are, my lady," a relieved-looking court official says. "Your carriage awaits you. Shall I show you the way?"

I flash a smile at the official. "Oh yes, of course. Thank you."

I glance back at the hallway, but there is no sign of Lord Thornewood—a small blessing, as I shudder to think of the repercussions if I were to be found alone with him in the palace, of all places.

There is no doubt in my mind: the man is a rake.

EIGHT

LATER in the evening, after my grandmother has allowed me to change into a soft blue evening gown, the carriage delivers us to a building with a façade that seems flat after the awe-inspiring architecture of the palace. The red brick is faded and devoid of any embellishments save for an iron fence and lampposts. Still, the very sight of it fills me with trepidation. Especially now I am to be escorted by the earl instead of Robert.

As Robert helps me out of the carriage, my eyes are immediately drawn to a dark figure leaning casually beside the door, his face a bored mask.

Even with such an unwelcoming expression, my heart races at the sight of him. "This cannot end well," I mutter, irritated once again by my traitorous body.

When Lord Thornewood notices us approach, he pushes himself away from the wall and walks toward us. "My dear Miss Sinclair, I am delighted to see you again so soon."

Robert raises his eyebrows slightly in question, but I ignore it.

Carefully I say, "Indeed, it was so lovely to see you at Court."

"You made it much more interesting, without a doubt."

Now Rob's interest is piqued as he glances between the two of us like a spectator at a tennis match. "You will be escorting my sister to this ball tonight, I understand?" he says, leveling his gaze at Lord Thornewood.

"I do have that honor, yes, though I am sorry to say I typically spend most of my time playing cards rather than dancing. She may have preferred a more attentive gentleman had she the choice."

Robert grins. "My sister has shown no preference for any type of gentleman as of yet."

"Robert," I hiss in warning.

The earl lifts his eyebrows. "I'm astonished. No country gentleman to pique your interest?"

My blush deepens, and I falter for words. I've never been so happy to see my grandmother approach.

"Lord Thornewood," she says with a gracious smile, "how kind it is for you to meet us here."

"The pleasure is mine," he says, his eyes shifting to mine. "The conversation so far has been fascinating, I assure you."

Grandmama's lips tighten slightly, but she maintains her smile. "I hope the rest of the evening will be just as entertaining."

"I intend to make it so, believe me," he says with a wicked grin.

"Shall we go in?" I interrupt before he manages to truly make my grandmother angry—an amusing pastime, no doubt, but one that will only make my life more difficult.

"Yes, I fear the rain will begin again soon," Grandmama says.

The earl offers me his arm. I hesitate only a moment before looping my hand through his crooked elbow. His arm is firm and unyielding, and I can feel the thick bands of muscle even with my light touch. I take a deep breath and will myself not to blush again. I refuse to be reduced to a simpering fool around him.

His face is in profile to me as I risk a glance. His sooty eyelashes frame even darker eyes, and I follow the straight line of his nose to his mouth, the edges of which are tipped up slightly in his characteristic aloof smile. I drop my gaze before he can catch me staring and focus instead on each step that brings me closer to the moment when I will have the attention of all in attendance.

In some ways, my debut in court before the king and queen was easier. There, I was one of many. I was expected to perform my perfectly choreographed series of curtsies and be on my way. Once I entered on the arm of the earl, my every word and action would be subject to censure.

"Are you always so tense?" he asks, his voice a quiet rumble above my ear.

I try without success to at least relax my shoulders. "No, my lord. Only when I'm forced to do something I very much do not want to do."

He glances down at me quickly, as if surprised. "You are not one of the hundreds of ladies in this assembly dying for the moment she will be welcomed into Society?"

"Perhaps if it didn't involve standing in front of everyone like horseflesh at an auction."

His body shakes with quiet laughter. "What an interesting comparison. I don't think I've ever heard it put in such a way."

I try to smile, but it comes out more as a grimace. Only a few debutantes separate us from the entrance to the ballroom where they will announce my name, followed immediately by the earl who escorts me. I picture the reaction of Eliza and girls like her and suppress a shudder.

"You truly are nervous," the earl says as if it is just occurring to him. I meet his stare, expecting to find teasing censure, but his expression is one of sympathy.

"I do not relish being the center of attention," I say quietly.

His left hand is warm on mine. "I will be with you the entire time. All you need do is smile. I promise it will be brief."

I feel my body soften at his words.

A footman dressed in crisp red and white livery holds the door for us. I tighten my hold on the earl's arm, and he glances down at me. "Just smile," he murmurs.

My lips curve upward, but I know this action does not banish the nervousness from my eyes. We enter the ballroom and pause at the top of a wide staircase, a sea of fashionably dressed ladies and gentlemen before us. So many people. Their whispers begin as soon as they catch sight of the earl beside me.

The earl stands quietly at my side, much closer than is strictly proper. Instead of making me uncomfortable, my tension eases as if the warmth radiating from him has a sedating effect. Just as it was in the Throne Room, my name is called, only this time, it is followed by the earl's. He gives me a gentle pull, and we descend the stairs into the main ballroom. I smile up at him.

He glances down at me, his eyes returning my smile. "You will find I am a man of my word," he says. "Was it not brief?"

"It was, my lord," I say. "I can only hope the rest of the evening will go as smoothly."

He pauses a few feet away from Robert and my grandmother. Taking both of my hands in his, he says, "It was a pleasure escorting you, Miss Sinclair. If you promise to save at least one dance for me, I will make sure your evening is very enjoyable indeed." His look turns rakish, and though his words are terribly arrogant, my breath catches in my throat. He leans down and kisses the back of my hand.

For once, I find myself incapable of responding as he walks away.

"So your coming out is complete," Robert says when we enter the main part of the ballroom. "I cannot tell you how relieved I am. I found the entire process tedious and agonizing."

I elbow him in the ribs, but a nervous giggle escapes from my mouth. "Yes, I'm sure riding through London in a coach only to arrive at a sumptuous ball with endless refreshments was sheer torture."

"Ah, but I have been with only Grandmama for company," he says in low tones and with a glance back at our grandmother.

"Indeed, you do have a point," I say as Grandmama joins us.

"This is a terrible crush," Grandmama says, but she is smiling so widely you'd think she was the one to make her debut. She steps closer to me. "We must make the most of our time before supper is served at midnight. But first, some things to keep in mind. Though you did well during your naming, you will find Duchess Cecily's ball is no country dance," she sniffs pretentiously, "there are rules." She is so serious that I must keep my eyes very still to prevent them from rolling back into my head. "Though Lord Thornewood has agreed to escort you to this ball, you must not cling to him through several dances. To do so is of extremely poor taste. I will seek out other suitable partners for you."

"Can I not simply cling to Robert instead?" I ask, and he snickers.

She levels a mean glare at us both. "You'd do well to take this seriously. May I remind you that not only is your reputation on the line, but your family's is as well."

I stifle a sigh. God forbid I lighten the mood in this stuffy place. "Yes, Grandmama."

"As I was saying, coquetry, excessive attention paid to one's dancing partner, and undue contact between one another is entirely inappropriate in dancing. Also, should you become overheated, you may go out onto the balcony, but never in the company of a gentleman." She gives us a look of extreme weariness. "Though in this case, I suppose, Robert is the exception."

"I should hope so," I say, quietly enough for her to ignore if she chooses, which she does.

She pauses to scan the room. "There, I see Lady Hasting. She promised to introduce us to an eligible cousin of the family."

We follow as she weaves her way through the elegantly dressed men and women. Lady Hasting is easy to spot since she has adorned another ridiculously opulent hat, this time with beads and lace surrounding a fully intact pheasant. She and a slender man I assume to be the eligible cousin face away from us.

"There's my Penelope," Lady Hasting says to the man. "Does she not dance beautifully?" She turns when she notices my grandmother. "Oh, Lady Sinclair, I'm so glad you sought me out. Here is the delightful cousin I spoke of, Lord Russell Clemens, Baron of Blackburn. Lord Blackburn, may I present Lady Lucille Sinclair, Dowager Viscountess and her grandchildren, the Honorable Robert and Katherine Sinclair."

If my grandmother were a sighthound, she could not be more alert. I can tell by the thinly masked surprise on her face she had no idea the cousin would be a baron—the lowest rank of the peerage, but a member nonetheless.

With a wide smile, he bows before us and I sink as gracefully as I can into a curtsy.

"I'm delighted to meet you all," he says, his voice as enthusiastic as his smile. His eyes are a pale blue, which, combined with his wavy dark blonde hair, makes him look much younger than I believe him to be. I can't help but compare his manner of greeting to my first encounter with the earl, and I have to say, I certainly appreciate the lack of sarcasm and arrogance.

"Lord Blackburn is newly in town after spending a few months in Scotland," Lady Hasting says, nodding her head, which causes the hat to tip precariously.

"But not for the reason you may think," he says and laughs.

He refers, no doubt, to Gretna Green in Scotland where young couples go to elope.

I return his smile. "I promise the thought didn't cross my mind. I hope you visited Edinburgh, though. I've heard it is a fascinating city."

"I did, actually, and I found myself quite enamored with it. The Society, too, was very enjoyable."

"What called you to Scotland?" Robert asks.

"Horse breeding. An acquaintance of mine has a particular bloodline of Thoroughbreds I have sought for many years."

"Interested in the sport of kings, eh?" Robert says with a grin.

Lord Blackburn smiles, and I notice laugh lines at the corners of his eyes. "I can thank my father for that. He bequeathed me several good mares and stallions, so I have made it my life's goal to expand our stables."

"My sister and I are avid equestrians ourselves. Is your stable nearby?"

"It is indeed. You are both welcome to visit. I would dearly love the chance to speak at length with fellow equestrians." He turns to me. "May I call on you later this week?"

"That would be lovely," I say with a genuine smile.

"Splendid," he says.

"Mr. Sinclair," Lady Hasting says, "I was just pointing out to Lord Blackburn how beautifully my daughter dances." She nods her head toward Penelope. Her gown is a lovely shade of blue and has so many ruffles that I can hear the *frou-frou* rustle from here. "See her there dancing with Mr. Young?"

"Yes, my lady," Robert says with a hesitant tone.

Lady Hasting launches into all the many talents of her daughter to my uncomfortable brother, and my eyes wander around the room. I'm looking for him again. I try and force myself to watch Lady Hasting instead, but my eyes refuse to obey me.

The dance ends, and the first few bars of another waltz begin. Lord Blackburn says, "Miss Sinclair, would you do me the honor of a dance?"

I drag my attention to his smiling face. "Oh, yes of course. Thank you."

We take our places on the gleaming dance floor, as he places one hand at the small of my back. When our hands join, he glances down, a curious look fleeting across his face. But in the time it takes me to blink, the look is gone, replaced by a contented smile. It makes me wonder if I imagined the whole exchange, since I sensed nothing unusual when we touched.

As we move through the elaborate steps of the dance, I take advantage of our central location on the dance floor to look for Eliza. I know she will only be too willing to make mention of Robert's faux pas.

I find her among the dancers. She catches me watching her and gives me a haughty little smile, so I glance away at the people on the outskirts of the dance floor. Again, I find myself searching the crowd for the earl, and this time I cannot resist. I focus on gentlemen who are taller than the others, and after a moment, I find him. His eyes lock on mine, and I give a little jerk of surprise at his glower.

My feet make the correct dance steps, and I tell myself to stop staring at the earl, but the more I tell myself, the more I sneak glances at him. Why is he frowning so intensely at me?

"You dance beautifully," Lord Blackburn says as we soar about the room. "Are you as graceful on a horse?"

I laugh. "Now how can I possibly answer such a question without sounding abominably conceited?"

"You must forgive me for putting you in such a precarious position. I think I can safely assume you are a skilled rider else your brother would not have recommended you."

"But how can you be so sure my brother was not playing a wicked joke?" I say with a teasing smile.

Though I'm tempted to check to see if Lord Thornewood is still frowning, I force myself to look upon Lord Blackburn's face instead. He is handsome; even his crooked bottom teeth are charming. With his lean frame and wan complexion, he seems almost fragile, as though his pale skin is actually porcelain. So different from the earl, whose presence could never be described as anything other than commanding.

"Another excellent point," he says. "I shall be forced to trust my instinct." He is quiet for a moment as we both catch our breath. "I look forward to being proven right when you visit my stables. I would love to have friends with whom I can share this obsession of mine."

His mention of the word *friends* relaxes muscles in my neck I didn't even realize were tense. "It would be our pleasure, believe me. We love anything to do with horses."

We spin in a circle again, and he leans toward me with a conspiratorial smile. "I say, do you have any idea who that gentleman is? The one who is even now staring daggers at us. I can't imagine what we have done to wrong him."

Still glowering then. My heart beats as if we've just danced a jig. "That is the Earl of Thornewood, my lord. But I cannot imagine why he is staring. Perhaps he is merely lost in thought."

We circle back to where we began our dance. I find myself facing the earl, so I keep my eyes on the lady in the pale pink dress to the right of him.

"Then his thoughts must be very dark indeed," Lord Blackburn says wryly. The waltz ends, and he bows to me. "Thank you for the dance, Miss Sinclair. Would you care for some refreshments? A glass of champagne perhaps? I'm sure you must be parched."

I smile gratefully. "That would be perfect, thank you."

He makes his way toward the refreshment table as Lord Thornewood approaches. "Miss Sinclair," he says and gives a short bow of his head. "You are quite the elegant dancer."

"I thank you, my lord. This is high praise indeed, especially from someone who was just a few moments ago glowering at me."

"I believe you must be mistaken. I was only watching the dance."

His tone has too much of a hint of irritation for my tastes, so I move toward Robert. "If you'll excuse me, I see my brother desires my attention."

His hand reaches out and touches my arm. "Miss Sinclair, wait."

I turn back, my eyebrows raised. "My lord?"

He hesitates. "Do you know Lord Blackburn well?"

"I only met him moments ago."

"I see." His eyes narrow as he glances in the direction of the refreshments table.

He is quiet so long I finally ask, "Are you well acquainted with Lord Blackburn?"

"No."

I blow out my breath in frustration. "Then why do you ask, my lord?"

His attention refocuses on my face. "Only a polite curiosity."

I'm aware he is not telling me the whole truth, but I am quite at a loss as to how to press him further. A rustle of silk draws my attention to the left, and I tense when I see the dress belongs to Eliza.

"Honestly," Eliza says with her characteristic mean smile. "I have yet to find the two of you on your own. I hope you won't mind my interruption, but I simply had to come and compliment you on your gown, Katherine. It's exquisite."

"Thank you, Eliza. The pale pink on your gown is lovely as well," I say cautiously.

"You are too kind," she says. "My lord, do not think I mean to slight you. Your coat is the very height of fashion."

"Thank you."

She frowns when he does not compliment her in turn, but Lord Blackburn returns with my champagne before she can say anything.

"Forgive me for taking so long," Lord Blackburn says as he hands me the small glass of champagne.

"No, it wasn't long at all," I say, my tone tense. I am so flustered I take a sip of champagne and nearly forget to make introductions. I do so, and Lord Blackburn smiles in welcome at Eliza and Lord Thornewood, but the earl doesn't return the gesture.

Eliza smiles sweetly at Lord Blackburn. "My lord, I have heard you are a horse enthusiast and have quite the reputation as one of the premier horse breeders in the kingdom."

He returns her smile, and his eyes brighten. "You have the first bit right, though as to the second, I can make no assertions either way."

She tilts her head, jewels winking at her throat. "Perhaps you have heard Miss Sinclair is also a very talented horsewoman?"

"Yes, so I've been told," he says with a grin in my direction. I make no move to return his attention since mine is entirely focused on Eliza. "I have invited both she and her brother to visit my stables."

Eliza's expression reminds me of the one our old tabby shows when she corners mice in our barn. "Oh, how delightful." She turns to me with mock concern on her face. "But Katherine, will you be able to handle such spirited horses with a sidesaddle? I know it is so very unfamiliar to you."

All I can hear is the pounding of my heart in my ears. This cannot be happening.

Lord Blackburn's eyebrows draw together. "Miss Sinclair does not ride sidesaddle?"

"On the contrary," the earl says, his expression firm. "She rides aside with great skill. Miss Gray refers to handling spirited horses, though in this, she is mistaken." His eyes hold Eliza's for many moments, as if issuing a silent challenge to contradict him.

She presses her full lips together. "Forgive me. I am indeed mistaken."

Lord Blackburn says something, but it doesn't even register in my mind. I cannot tear my eyes from Lord Thornewood. With very little effort, he has saved me from utter humiliation.

"We should enjoy the fair weather one day at Hyde Park," Lord Blackburn says, once I am paying attention to his comments again.

"Lord Thornewood and Miss Sinclair had quite the exciting afternoon just the other day there," Eliza says. She touches me ever so delicately on the arm, and I have to restrain myself from jerking it away like a toddler. "And it was a lucky thing you were both there since that little boy would have surely tumbled into the river."

"How terrible," Lord Blackburn says. "Were you instrumental in saving him, Miss Sinclair?"

I force my eyes not to dart to Eliza's face. "Not at all. Sadly, I could only watch from the other side of the bank."

Eliza turns to me. "I saw the whole thing," she says to Lord Blackburn, and my heart pounds in my throat. Surely if she saw anything she wouldn't say so here? "When they noticed the poor thing drawing too close to the water, Lord Thornewood rode to save him like a gallant knight." She puts her hand on her chest. "Really, it was too much."

I want to sag forward with relief, but I manage to stay upright. Still, the glint in Eliza's eyes keeps me on my guard.

"Very gallant indeed," Lord Blackburn says.

"I cannot say that it was since, ultimately, it was the muddy bank that prevented the boy from entering the water," Lord Thornewood says in his characteristically bored tone. His eyes meet mine. "But I can say in all certainty that the day was exciting nonetheless."

NINE

ONCE the conversation turns to more mundane affairs, I steal a glance at Lord Thornewood as I take a sip of wine. He watches the conversation with a disinterested look on his face, and then his gaze shifts to me. I look away and nervously bite the inside of my cheek. This will not be the last time Eliza will attempt to destroy my reputation. But I cannot help but think one thing, one I dare not hope for—that Lord Thornewood knows what she said was true and defended me anyway.

The conversation drops off abruptly, and I look up from my glass. Lady Spencer, one of the wealthiest and most influential ladies of Society, joins our group. Even Eliza is struck mute.

Despite her heavier size, Lady Spencer is intimidatingly elegant in a violet satin gown and more diamonds at her throat and wrists than even royalty can boast. She greets each of us by name as if she studied every member of the peerage. We manage to return her greeting, all except for Lord Thornewood, who looks as uninterested as he did the first night I met him.

"Lord Thornewood," Lady Spencer says, "I was surprised to see you here. I know you have looked down on dances in the past. Perhaps this fine ball has changed your mind?"

"Actually," the earl drawls, "I find this very dull."

Lady Spencer sucks in her breath in outrage.

"Perhaps if the dancing was livelier—the tango is taking hold in Paris, I understand."

Her eyes, already so close in appearance to a frog's, bulge. The tango is viewed as quite scandalous, even sinful, having come from the brothels of Argentina. No doubt Lord Thornewood knows this and is simply antagonizing her.

I glare at him. I can't help it. My debut is supposedly tied to his good opinion, but what good is his opinion if all he does is insult everyone? Especially one of the most well-known ladies of the peerage.

While Lady Spencer's mouth opens and closes like a fish, he turns to me. "Care to dance?"

He takes the glass from my hand, sets it down on a nearby table, and pulls me toward the dance floor before I can think of an excuse.

"My lord," I say through clenched teeth as I tug my hand free, "I didn't say yes."

"You didn't say no, either," he says and takes his position beside me.

Leaving him on the dance floor, though satisfying, would only cause a bigger scene. I sigh as I go through the steps of the waltz.

After a few minutes he says, "Your constant sighing is bothering me."

I narrow my eyes at him instead.

"I can't imagine what I did to deserve such censure," he says as he twirls me effortlessly.

"Can you not? Perhaps it has something to do with your rudeness."

He shrugs. "I see it more as candor."

The constant pauses in our conversation make me clench my teeth in frustration. "Lady Spencer will ask you to leave."

"If only."

I hesitate during one of the steps, and I bump into Lord Thornewood. He steadies me with his hand on my elbow for a moment, and my skin burns, even through the white satin of my gloves. He gives me a wry grin.

"I suppose your patronage of my debut was too much to ask for," I say.

"What a dramatic, overly emotional response," he says, still wearing his irritating grin. "And here I thought I'd found the perfect woman."

I ignore the way my heart beats faster when he calls me perfect and focus on the negative instead. "It may be dramatic to you, but your entire family isn't relying on your successful debut." My voice snaps like a whip, but he merely tilts his head to the side.

"How mad you are. You wear anger beautifully though. I've never seen a prettier flush."

I groan in frustration—both at my own body's joyful response at his words and the lack of appropriate response from him.

He leans closer to me on the next turn, and I feel my flush deepen. "Perhaps you would not be so annoyed if you could see Lady Spencer's face."

I glance up to find her watching us alongside Lady Villier, another influential dowager. Both have matching smiles as if they could not be more delighted to see us together.

"Why are they smiling?" I ask.

"Because I have intrigued them," he says. "They're not used to being treated in such a rude manner, and have decided I—and by extension, you—am the most interesting person this season."

"My lord, I—"

"What you don't realize about Society, Miss Sinclair, is it craves entertainment above everything else. Entertain them," he says with a dark smile, "and you can just about get away with murder."

We join hands for the finale, and as the skin of my palm burns from his touch, I turn his words over in my mind and wonder if maybe I shouldn't be so quick to judge the earl after all.

Supper is served promptly at midnight and, unused to eating at such a late hour, I fall upon the sumptuous buffet like I haven't eaten in days. I fill my small plate with canapés, lobster salad, medallions of foie gras, and salmon. I watch some of the other girls nibble at their canapés while I devour the contents of my plate and return for dessert.

"These late supper hours are torturous," I say to Robert, who is eating as voraciously as me.

"They are indeed," he says around a piece of cake. "Do you think we can raid Grandmama's kitchen when we return?"

The sound of Eliza's laughter interrupts our conversation. It has an edge to it, like the subject matter is not supposed to be funny. I turn and find her and another girl—Virginia something or other—with their heads close together.

"Can you believe how many ribbons she's wearing?" Eliza says, much louder than a whisper. "It's like she thinks she's a child."

I follow their line of sight to Penelope, who sits only a few feet away. Her face and ears are bright red, and I realize she can hear every word as well as I can.

"Or a pony—that dress is certainly big enough," Virginia says in a nasally voice.

When they laugh again, I put my plate down with a clink and march over to her.

"Penelope," I say with a huge smile, "there you are." She gives me a tentative smile, like she's afraid this is some horrible trick despite our camaraderie at Court, but I continue before she can respond. "I'm so sorry I didn't seek you out earlier. Would you mind joining my brother and me? I know he'd be grateful for the company, especially since he hasn't had the chance to dance with anyone all evening."

Her eyes brighten with understanding and she rises from her seat. "I would be happy to."

Eliza's glare digs into my back as I lead her intended victim away.

I'm prepared to give Robert a strong look to get him to play along, but I needn't have worried. As soon as we approach, he bows before Penelope like she's a princess.

"I believe we met earlier, Miss Hasting." He smiles his most charming smile—the one that makes his blue eyes look like they're lit from within. "My sister and I were just saying how lovely you look this evening."

Virginia lets out a huff and mutters something to Eliza, and they both stalk off like wolves that have lost their prey.

"Thank you," Penelope says with a shy smile, her voice as soft as her demeanor.

She reminds me so much of Lucy, I surprise her by looping my arm through hers. "You needn't thank us. We're glad to have the chance to talk with you."

"You're very kind." Her eyes flit to my brother's before darting back to my face.

I give her arm a little squeeze. "I will repeat the sage advice you gave me earlier today. You can't believe anything those girls say. It's their mission to make as many people as miserable as they are."

She plays with the edge of one of the pink ribbons. "That's true. But, I *am* wearing a lot of ribbons."

Robert nearly spits out his drink and laughs.

She smiles back at him. "It's my mother's fault, of course."

"Well," Robert says, "when you have a mother who wears hats like that, you can bloody well expect her daughter to be dressed in an abundance of fabric."

"Robert," I say with a warning tone. Apparently he needs a reminder he's not with his Oxford buddies.

He grins at us both impishly, and Penelope basks in his attention. I think even if Penelope were insulted, she'd forgive him anything.

"Would you honor me with a dance?" he asks in his most formal tone of voice.

Penelope tucks a piece of hair behind her ear and smiles at him. "I'd love to, thank you."

I finish the rest of my cake as I watch them move toward the dance floor.

"Katherine, the most wonderful news," Grandmama says as she joins me, her eyes bright with excitement. "Lord Blackburn has invited us to enjoy his box seats at the opera tomorrow."

For once, she brings good news. "How delightful. I've never been. Do you know what's playing?"

"What nonsense," Grandmama says with an exasperated tone of voice. "No one pays attention to the opera. We'll be too busy talking with Lord Blackburn."

Honestly, does no one take anything but the most frivolous things seriously? "Well, I will be watching the opera. I'll speak with him at the intermission."

"You will do no such thing. Lord Blackburn invited us there to be able to talk to you. It would be very rude indeed to ignore him."

I know I'm wearing a dumbfounded look, but really, what do I say to that? Her logic makes absolutely no sense. "I shall hang on his every word then," I say with mock seriousness.

"Good girl. Now when your brother finishes his dance, we'll take our leave. We can't be seen staying too long as if we have nowhere else to be."

I look up at the clock to see it is well after one in the morning. Oh yes, because we have *so* many other things to do at such an ungodly hour. But I give her a small smile and nod because I certainly won't argue when given the chance to leave.

My eyes fall back to the dance floor, and I realize Lord Thornewood is dancing, too. It takes me a moment to find who his partner is, but when I see her, my stomach tightens uncomfortably. Eliza wears a flirtatious smile, and her eyes stay locked on the earl's. Worse, he doesn't look as annoyed as he usually does with her. My stomach goes from feeling tight to making me wish I hadn't eaten so much cake.

"Lord Thornewood seems to be enjoying himself," my grandmother says with what I'm sure is the matching frown to my own. "That girl—Miss Grey, I believe—looks entirely too much like you."

My eyebrows raise. "You think she looks like me?" I can't decide if that's a compliment or not.

"From the back, especially. Lady Hasting just commented on it earlier." Grandmama's eyes scan my body critically. "She is more classically beautiful, but you have the same natural allure your mother had."

"Thank you," I murmur, my attention still riveted on the earl and Eliza. I tilt my head, considering. We are both tall, slender. I'm slender to the point where I think I can pass fairly well for a young man were I so inclined. Robert has mocked me endlessly about this ever since I first started wearing breeches. Our hair is blonde and our eyes are light, though the shades of both are very different. To be told I look like someone with such a hateful demeanor is disconcerting to say the least.

The dance ends, and Robert and Penelope join us. I want to immediately ask Robert if he agrees with Grandmama and Lady Hasting, but I manage to hold my tongue.

My eyes are drawn to Lord Thornewood again as Grandmama makes her good-byes, and I soon wish I didn't look. Eliza's gloved hand is on his arm as she leans close to him. He bends down to hear her better, and then his face breaks out into a grin. She smiles up at him, her button nose crinkling ever so slightly, and I feel a dark energy awake in me at the sight of it. Why am I so upset? Why should I care who the earl smiles at?

But as he offers her his arm, I wonder if maybe Grandmama was right about our similarities. Perhaps the earl finds us interchangeable.

TEN

I wake at a more respectable time since it was long after three before I went to sleep. I lie there for a moment, and the sickening sensation that something unpleasant happened the night before assails my mind. Eliza's hand on Lord Thornewood's arm, Lord Thornewood leaning in to speak to her, smiling at her, dancing with her . . . I can't make the torrent of memories stop. With a shake of my head, I dress myself without calling for Mary's assistance.

As has become my habit, I glance over at my mother's journal. The soft glow it emits could not come at a more welcome time. I open it eagerly.

> *My dearest Katherine,*
>
> *Though I am much older now, I will never forget the moment I first met your father. It was at a ball and yet not, for we met before I even set foot in the ballroom. I had only just come to this realm from my own. The Sylvani nobility required each son and daughter to go on tour in the human world once they reached maturity, so my knowledge of English Society was limited, to say the least.*
>
> *I was accompanied by a Sylvani guard, one who had much more knowledge of this world. Even with a fellow Sylvani posing as a wealthy*

Scottish noble, I remember being shaky with nerves, so much so that I stumbled on the manor's stairway. It is a true testament to my state of mind, for as you know, I never misstep. A strong arm prevented my fall, an arm belonging to the man with whom I would later fall in love. As soon as he touched me, I met his eyes, and the image of him holding an angelic baby with bright blue eyes filled my mind.

My gift of prophecy is imperfect, but once I saw that beautiful child—your brother—I knew I would do anything to make the image a reality. There is no such thing as love at first sight, but there is instant attraction. And for the Sylvani, we know when we have met the one for whom we were meant. It is the sole reason my mother fought for my chance to leave Sylvania.

Do you recall the song I always played for you? Though the beginning is mournful, it ends with great joy and hope. Our music always tells a story; that song told the story of my life. Leaving my spirit behind in Sylvania was heartbreaking, but in the end, I was blessed with an even greater joy: the three of you.

You are half-Sylvan and half-human. The best parts of both me and your father. You may not know the moment you meet the one for you, but you will, in time.

Never doubt yourself.

With much love,
Mama

I close my eyes as my mother's music plays in my mind. I knew it told a story, but I never guessed it was hers. Though I cannot say I am ever displeased to hear stories of my parents' past, this particular memory only dredges up a deep sadness. Mama knew my father was the one for her during their first meeting. Perhaps, then, the earl isn't the man I hope him to be. Perhaps his attention to Eliza is a sign I am meant for another—or, my deepest fear, that I am meant for no one. For how would Lord Thornewood react were he to know the truth about me? If he was to find out I am not even entirely human? A flash of my childhood friend Henry's reaction trickles into my consciousness, and I forcefully suppress it.

I close the journal. These self-pitying thoughts will not do. Maybe Lucy will help me realize how overly dramatic I'm being.

I look for her in the room where she usually studies with Miss Watts, but one of the servants tells me she has taken ill. Instead of eating breakfast, I go to her bedroom, worried she is suffering another of her headaches. She's had them ever since she was little. My mother would prepare a tea to take the pain away, and I remember her telling Lucy she was sorry—like she was somehow responsible for them.

"Luce?" I call softly as I push the door open gently. I try to make as little noise as possible as I go to the side of her bed. The heavy velvet drapes are pulled over both windows, pitching the room into darkness.

My sister is huddled on her side, one hand pressed on the ridge above her closed eye. "Morning," she says weakly.

"Morning indeed. You look as though you are in terrible pain. Is it another headache?"

She nods once.

"You should have sent for me, Luce," I scold gently. "Why suffer when I can help?"

"I didn't want to disturb you," she whispers, her eyes closed again. "I know how draining it is."

I wave her off. "Nonsense. Now lie back."

I have to give her a stern look for a few seconds, but she does as I tell her, lying back against the pillows and removing her hand from her forehead. I lay the palm of my hand over her forehead like I'm checking for a fever and close my eyes. Since we're indoors, I don't have much to draw on except for my own energy, so it's good I had enough rest—not that I'd admit that to Lucy.

I concentrate on the haze of red pain centered above her right eye and call my healing white light to the palm of my hand. A tingle shoots up my arm as a soft glow illuminates Lucy's face. Instead of the warm sunshine smell usually released with arcana, healing energy releases a scent like freshly tilled earth.

Lucy winces at first, the light bothering her sensitive eyes, but then she relaxes as my power erases her pain. I feel the drain on my body, and it's like a long night of dancing condensed into seconds. My energy ebbs, and I start to breathe faster.

Once the red haze of pain disappears and Lucy's entire body relaxes, I remove my hand. I flop down on the bed beside her, and she sits up.

"This is why I'm so reluctant for your help," she says, scolding me now. "I can't stand to see what it does to you."

"Well," I say between pants, "I can't stand seeing you in pain. In this, we're even."

She lets out an exasperated snort.

I force my breathing to slow, but I'm still fatigued enough to consider a nap. "I'll be fine after a little fresh air. You would do well to join me. A lack of it is probably to blame for your headache."

She watches me closely as I wobble a bit when I stand and her expression turns pensive. "What do you suppose would happen if you tried to heal something more serious than a headache?"

"Arcana always has a cost," I say, side-stepping her morbid question. The answer is I could drain all my energy, effectively ending my life. But I refuse to give in to my sister's worrying.

Her big eyes—so like my own—widen. "Promise me you'll never try."

"I won't do anything of the kind. If you or Robert or Papa ever needed my help, then I would give it to you without question." She gets a determined look on her face like she plans to continue this asinine debate, so I say, "Why are you so intent on this?"

"Because if I don't worry about you, who will?"

She has a point. I never give it a second thought. "Isn't that why we're here?" I bat my eyes at her and clutch my hands to my chest. "So I can find my Prince Charming, who will adore and worry about me every night?"

"I wish you would," she mutters, but a small smile peeks out before she can stop it.

"I'm doing my best, and believe me, so is Grandmama." I hold out my hand and help her to her feet. "Shall we walk down to the stables?"

"Just a moment," she says and walks to the vanity, which contains drawing materials instead of combs and perfumes. "It would be lovely to draw just for pleasure while we're there. I haven't had as much time of late with Grandmama's schedule."

"Yes, how foolish of us to think we'd have time for leisurely pursuits," I say with a teasing smile.

She gathers her materials in her arms, but suddenly turns toward me. "Oh, but Wren! In all that has happened this morning, I didn't ask you about your debut. You must tell me everything."

"It was . . . so much better than I had imagined," I say, a slow smile curving my lips as I think of Lord Thornewood's surprising chivalry. "But come, I'll tell you more on our way to the stables."

We make our way downstairs, careful to avoid any of the rooms Grandmama might occupy, for I'm certain such an outing is not on our tedious agendas for the day.

As we walk, I tell her in as much detail as I can remember what it was like to debut before the king and queen.

"So Lord Thornewood saved you?" Lucy says, a bit dreamily.

I laugh. "He saved me from embarrassment, yes. Although, I'm sure I would have eventually remembered to curtsy." My mind chooses that moment to play back our exchange in the dark palace corridor, and I feel a blush sneak up my neck.

"Describe the palace for me again. Was the throne room outrageously beautiful?"

I struggle to recall the minute details of the palace's design elements, though I am nowhere near as observant of such things as Lucy. As I describe them, she jots notes on her sketchpad. She is so gifted that I know my paltry descriptions will be later transformed into a perfect rendering of the palace.

"I simply can't wait to see the photographs," Lucy says as we reach the stables.

Warmth and the smell of hay greet us as soon as we enter. The grooms are hard at work mucking stalls at the other end of the stables, so we slip into Orion's stall.

"I didn't realize Papa sent Orion here," Lucy says, giving the stallion a pat on his neck.

"It was a surprise, I think," I say with a smile as I touch my forehead to Orion's. He snuffles into my hair, and I laugh. "We've come to visit with you," I tell him, "so make yourself comfortable."

In answer, he folds his legs under him and lies down on the newly changed straw. Lucy and I join him on the ground, leaning back against his warm side.

Lucy balances a small sketchpad on her lap and begins to draw. With the soft sounds of charcoal on paper beside me, I close my eyes and open myself to Orion's thoughts. As though I have suddenly submerged myself underwater, all other sounds and sights apart from those sensed by Orion become muffled and dim. He turns his head to look upon Lucy and me, our figures shining brightly with light.

I remember being frightened the first time my pony revealed how I appeared to him. Instead of the child's body I expected to see, my pony saw me as a girl-shaped being of golden light.

I ran to my mother with tears streaming down my cheeks. "Why do I look like that, Mama?"

She hugged me to her and stroked my hair. "Animals see us as we really are, darling. It's nothing to be frightened of."

"But why am I so bright?" I asked.

She pointed to the sun hidden behind a cloud. "Because the sun is bright. It's the sun's energy that lives inside us, giving us the power for our special abilities. The same ability that allowed you to communicate with your pony."

I splayed my hand over my navel, fascinated. "I have sunshine inside me?"

Mama laughed, the sound like the clear ringing of bells. "You do, my darling. My little ray of sunshine."

I smile as the memories play in my mind, mingling with Orion's thoughts. Lucy and I are almost too bright for him to look at; the energy within us flows into him like the warmth of the sun. His eyelids droop, and I absently rub his velvety nose.

I glance down at the sketchpad on Lucy's lap. Her drawing has taken shape: a stately ballroom with ladies lined up for a dance. She adds musical notes in the top corner and smudges them with her finger. When she catches me watching her, she says, "I've been experimenting with my arcana. May I show you?"

"Please do," I say.

She touches her finger to the smudged notes, and the sound of violins fills the air. Orion jerks his head in surprise. The music continues a lively Scottish tune, one we've danced to many times. The sound is so clear, it's hard to believe an orchestra isn't performing in Orion's stall.

"Luce, this is amazing," I say.

"Thank you," she says with a wide smile. She touches her finger to the notes again, and the music fades away.

"Truly, your ability in weaving arcana into your artwork is remarkable. Mama would be so proud."

She hugs the sketchpad to her. "Do you really think so?"

"I do," I say. "Her love for music was second only to her love for all of us."

The stall door rolls back, and one of the grooms takes a step back when he sees us curled up next to Orion. Lucy and I share a look, and I have to bite down on my lip to keep from laughing at the poor man's expression.

He gapes at us open-mouthed for a moment as all three of us stand. Lucy and I brush the straw from our skirts, and Orion shakes out his long mane.

"Beggin' your pardon, misses," he says, his bushy red eyebrows still raised. "I didn't realize Orion here had company."

Lucy giggles, and I smile. "He did indeed," I say, "but we were just leaving."

"I shouldn't saddle him up for you then?" he asks, his expressive brows now furrowing in confusion.

"That will not be necessary," I say. "We're already quite late for breakfast."

"Thank you though," Lucy adds.

We manage to nearly make it to the main house before dissolving into a fit of laughter. It's a freeing feeling not to be proper, well-behaved ladies. We haven't had the freedom to be ourselves in so long.

"The poor man didn't know what to make of us," Lucy says, sounding as though she will succumb to another fit as we climb the stairs.

"I'm sure he will assume we're both touched in the head," I say, and then our laughter begins anew.

Before we reach our rooms, Mary calls out to us with a letter in hand. "Do excuse me, misses, but the post just arrived."

When I see our father's name scrawled across the front, I smile. "Thank you, Mary. We'll just be a few more minutes before we come down to break our fast."

I turn to Lucy. "A letter from Papa." When she looks at me with eyebrows raised, I say, "Come, we can read it in your room."

Once in Lucy's cluttered room, with nearly every inch of space covered with drawing supplies, I climb onto her bed. She follows, pressing her shoulder into mine to get a better view of the letter.

My Darling Girls,

I hope Mother has been good to you so far. I miss you terribly, especially during mealtimes when I have only a book for company. Mr. Baxter has taken pity on me and now joins me for breakfast and luncheon, though he does so under protest since he insists it's most improper.

But enough of that. I write to you today to let you know we had to let one of the maids go—Clara. It has come to my attention that she has spread some of Margaret's story about town. I very much doubt it will affect your stay in London, as the story was treated as less than credible. I only tell you this because I could not bear it if the rumor somehow caught you unawares. The chances of someone hearing a fantastic tale from Gloucestershire are slim indeed.

I pray both of you are enjoying your stay. Be sure to insist Mother takes you somewhere other than a stuffy ballroom while you are there. If you cannot escape yet another ball, then I ask you to keep an eye on Mother. She tends to get carried away with her card games.

With much love,
Papa

"Papa," Lucy says in a happy sigh as I wonder at the strange mention of Grandmama's card games. "Oh, but this is distressing news. I cannot believe Clara would do such a thing. I always liked her."

I think of the young maid with her ringlet curls and sooty eyes, and the way she was often too flirtatious with the grooms.

"Well, she's certainly done plenty of damage," I say, my hand a tight fist in my lap. "I suspect Eliza may have heard the rumor."

Lucy's eyes widen. "But she only spoke of a rebellious girl from Gloucestershire—never a girl who could use arcana."

"Yes, but if she knows the first rumor, why not the other?"

Lucy takes the letter from me. Her eyes scan back and forth as if Papa would offer advice. "What should we do?"

"The same as we have been: be on our guard against her. And pray she doesn't get it into her head to spread the rumor here."

ELEVEN

ROBERT is able to attend the opera with us, and I squeeze his arm with excitement as we enter the Royal Opera House's lobby. Red velvet opulence awash in soft lighting surrounds us along with men dressed all in black and women dressed in silks and satins of every color, glittering tiaras atop their heads. The crowd herds us along toward the main entrance to the theatre, with the box seats above. We follow our grandmother to the spot where we agreed to meet Lord Blackburn.

The chattering of so many people creates a constant cacophony of sound, but it only contributes to my own excitement. The title of the opera is scrolled in bold black letters as we walk through one of the doorways that will lead us to our seats: *Don Giovanni* by Wolfgang Mozart.

"Dowager Lady Sinclair?" a liveried servant asks as we approach the box. She nods, and he sweeps the thick velvet curtain aside. "Right this way, my lady."

Lord Blackburn stands when we enter, dressed in an elegant tailcoat and trousers. He does a sweeping bow, and a smile lights up his blue eyes. "Welcome to you all. I am so glad you could accept my invitation."

While my grandmother proceeds to give him effusive praise of his box seats, I curtsy a greeting and go immediately to the railing. Before long, he is beside me.

"By the excitement in your eyes, I'm assuming this is your first time," he says.

"It's amazing," I say, almost breathlessly.

I have trouble deciding what to look at first. Our box floats high above the stage with ten enormous crystal chandeliers hanging even higher. The conductor leads the orchestra with strong but controlled movements, and just watching the bows of the violins is hypnotizing. Fluttery red curtains are drawn across the stage, which is lit by enormous candelabras.

"It's impressive for a building with such a cursed history, isn't it?"

I'm quiet for a moment, embarrassed to have no idea what he's talking about. But my curiosity wins out. "Has there been much misfortune here?"

To my relief, he doesn't shame me for not knowing, just nods sadly. "Indeed. It has been rebuilt three times. It burned to the ground twice, which is why it was rebuilt the last time about fifty years ago."

I shake my head, my eyes still riveted by the orchestra. "How awful."

"A maudlin bit of trivia, but I am fascinated by the history of places and people. The more unusual, the better."

Gradually, the crowd gets quieter, and I realize the opera must be about to start. I glance at Lord Blackburn and find he has been watching me with as much interest as I have given to my surroundings. I smile tentatively, but he shows no shame at having been caught staring.

"You must forgive me," he murmurs, "but watching you is like seeing the opera for the first time."

Unsure of what to say, I keep my eyes glued to the conductor's baton.

"I've been to countless operas," he says, "so it's refreshing to see it with someone who is so obviously enjoying it."

His clarification melts some of the tension from my shoulders, and I give him a more sincere smile. "Thank you for inviting me, because it's true, I'm enjoying myself very much."

"Excellent," he says. "But come, you must sit. I can't have you standing the entire opera." He gestures toward the chairs behind us. As he does, a ring on his right hand catches my eye. The design is similar to a cross but with a loop at the top. I tilt my head to the side. The symbol is unfamiliar to me. A smattering of diamonds gives it a subtle sparkle, but the band is wide enough to still remain masculine.

He catches me staring, and I smile. "I just noticed your ring. It's unusual. Is it a family heirloom?"

He glances down at his finger as if just remembering he wore a ring. "Oh, indeed. It was my father's, and I've always had a penchant for simplistic designs."

"Well, it's lovely," I say slowly. Despite his casual response, there is something about the ring that causes the fine hairs on the nape of my neck to rise.

The lights in the theatre dim, and I am once again distracted by the splendor of the opera. I take my seat but sit on the very edge, afraid to miss anything. Robert sits to my right, a drink in hand and a tired expression on his face. Grandmama, for once, is quiet. She has donned opera glasses, though, so she is no doubt busy in her scan of the crowd.

Lord Blackburn sits to my left, and as he takes his seat, the dramatic music calms and the curtains open on a haggard servant sitting alone.

As soon as he begins to sing, his voice a deep bass, I am sucked into the story. Though I know my grandmother wanted me to talk to Lord Blackburn and not pay the show any attention, I can't tear my eyes away from the stage. And when the female lead takes the stage, her voice a clear, powerful soprano, goosebumps erupt over my skin.

I envy her. I would love to use my voice to provide for myself, answering to no one but me and my talent. What would that be like? How freeing it must be, how self-reliant.

Lord Blackburn sits quietly beside me as I all but ignore him. A few side glances reveal him to be just as interested as me. Too soon, the curtain falls and the lights go up for the intermission.

He looks at me with a wide grin. "I don't think I need to ask you if you're enjoying it."

"I love it," I gush. "The music, the costumes, the singing. All of it. Thank you so much for inviting us."

He stands and offers me his hand. "It was nothing, truly. Shall we go have some refreshments?"

I take his hand and join him. "Only if we can return in time. I wouldn't want to miss anything."

I turn to Robert and Grandmama to see if they want to join us and find Robert asleep, his arms crossed over his chest. If Grandmama cares, she shows no sign of it.

"Bring your brother with you," she says, when she sees me looking in her direction. "I'm off to find Lady Hasting."

I poke him not too gently in the arm, and he wakes with a snort. "How could you sleep through that?" I demand.

"I wasn't asleep," he says, his voice groggy.

"Very well," I say, "then what's it about?"

He shrugs. "It's in Italian."

I let out a huff. "Well, Lord Blackburn and I are going to the lobby for refreshments. You're welcome to join—if you can manage to wake up."

He stands and stretches—probably just to annoy me. "I'm awake."

"This way to the lobby," Lord Blackburn says, his voice betraying a hint of a laugh. He holds the curtain aside for us.

"You can go fetch me some tea," I tell Robert. "It'll help you wake up." A teasing grin slips out, and Robert returns it.

"Very well."

Lord Blackburn offers me his arm as we stroll down to the lobby. His arm seems much thinner than the earl's, and I blush when I realize I'm comparing how muscular they are. He smiles down at me, his eyes focused on my face for just a shade too long, and a wave of awkwardness washes over me. Inwardly, I admonish myself for the feeling. We've been getting along so well it doesn't seem fair to be uncomfortable.

But as my eyes search the lobby for a crop of dark hair, I know why I feel this way. Because of *him*.

Instead of the earl, I see Penelope standing against the wall, her dress a bright peacock blue. When she sees me, her eyes brighten, and she gives a little wave.

"There's Penelope," I say. "I should go say hello."

"Indeed, and I should do the same with Lady Hasting." He nods his head in the direction of the lady in question, for once not wearing a hat.

"Oh yes," I say with a grin. "I almost didn't recognize her."

He chuckles as he walks away.

"Penelope," I say when I reach her side, "it's so good to see you here. Are you enjoying the opera?"

She gives a sigh in appreciation. "It's wonderful. I absolutely adore Donna Anna. Her voice is gorgeous."

I'd forgotten Penelope is a music enthusiast as well, and I probably surprise her with my own enthusiasm. "It's divine! I couldn't tear my eyes from the stage, and it took everything in me not to beg the director to let me join." I laugh a little to let her know I'm joking; though, it's partly true.

"I know what you mean," she says. "It would be such a dream to be able to sing and play music all day every day."

"What? And miss out on the balls? The husband hunts? Never," I say teasingly and she laughs.

Abruptly her smile disappears, and I turn to see what has caught her eye.

"Miss Sinclair," Lord Thornewood says gruffly, "might I have a word with you?" He is dressed, as usual, all in black. I'm bewildered by his tone, and even more bewildered by his presence here, though perhaps I shouldn't be. Nearly everyone in Society is present here tonight.

I raise my eyebrows at Penelope slightly—to cover up the way my heart is now beating furiously in my chest. "Certainly," I say. "Penelope, will you excuse us for a moment?"

She nods, and I follow the earl as he walks away, his back stiff. He leads us to an alcove just off the lobby, and the sudden quiet is unnerving after the loud din of so many people.

He turns on me, his brows drawn low over his eyes. "Was that Lord Blackburn's box I saw you in earlier?"

I'm sure my expression is the picture of confusion. With effort, I smooth out the wrinkles in my forehead. "You know it was."

"And your grandmother approves of this?"

His tone is so condescending I instantly prickle. "Of course she approves. It was her idea—not that it's any of your concern."

"Then your grandmother is misinformed about Lord Blackburn's character," he says with a sneer on the last word. "I have it on good authority that not only is he a gambling rake, but he is so indebted he must find a nice fat dowry if he ever hopes to settle his accounts."

My eyes go round, and I take a step back. Surely my grandmother would have found out as much as she could about Lord Blackburn. She was friends with his aunt for one thing. And Lord Blackburn has been nothing but kind to me. I think of the way Eliza whispered in Lord Thornewood's ear while they were dancing, and of his answering smile. If this is his source, I have nothing to fear. And yet . . . the whisper of caution within me is difficult to ignore.

Lord Thornewood's expression turns smug, and anger burns inside me. What right has he to warn me when he keeps company with Eliza? "I wouldn't trust gossipmongers if I were you, my lord. It just so happens I was also told *you* were an infamous rake."

The expression melts from his face. He leans in closer to me, and my breath catches in my throat. We are safe from prying eyes here in this alcove, but it doesn't make me feel any less exposed. Perhaps he does have the gift of arcana after all. "This is your response then?" he says.

I think about him flirting with Eliza on the dance floor and straighten my spine. "It is."

His eyebrows crease the skin between his eyes, darkening his nearly-black eyes. "Very well. Forgive me for intruding. Believe me, it was kindly meant."

Before I can respond, he turns on his heel and disappears into the crowd.

I wish I can say my little tête-à-tête with Lord Thornewood doesn't prevent me from enjoying the opera. And to an extent, it doesn't. But I have to fight to stay immersed in the beautiful music and the costumes and the drama of it all where before it was effortless.

Hateful man. Just because he heard a rumor at his club—no doubt in the midst of gambling himself—he has to burden me with it. Lord Blackburn has been a gentleman since the moment we met.

We give a standing ovation at the end of the opera, and Lord Blackburn grins down at me, his face softened by the dim lighting. I smile back, all the while searching his face for some indication he has bad intentions. Guilt twists through my stomach. Do I truly feel apprehension toward Lord Blackburn? Or are Lord Thornewood's words clouding my opinion of him?

"I know we didn't get to speak much," he says, "but I truly enjoyed watching this with you."

His words are so sweet the knife of guilt causes another stab of pain. "You were a superb opera-watching partner."

"Wasn't this your first opera?" he asks teasingly.

I smile wryly. "Yes, but anyone who enjoys it as much as I do and who can sit in companionable silence with me must be the best."

"Perhaps I sat in silence because I have nothing of interest to say."

"For shame, Lord Blackburn. That is not true at all."

"You are too kind," he says, his expression more serious—except for his eyes, which still maintain that sparkle of good humor.

"I must thank you again for inviting us," I say as Robert joins my side, looking very much ready to go. He barely stifles a yawn, and I shoot him a look.

"Believe me, it was my pleasure."

My grandmother repeats my thanks as profusely as she did when we first arrived, as if mine wasn't good enough. I turn away from her and roll my eyes at Robert. He chuckles softly.

"I hope that invitation to your stables still stands," Robert interrupts my grandmother, and Lord Blackburn turns. "I'll be returning to Oxford on Saturday."

"Ah," Lord Blackburn says with a nod. "Of course. You are both welcome to come tomorrow if it suits you. Though I must add Lady Hasting has invited a few others there—mostly family, but also Miss Uppington and Miss Gray, I believe."

I have to stifle a groan. Can I not do *anything* without Eliza showing up, too? I'm surprised I haven't run into her here.

"Such a large party," Grandmama says, her tone almost gleeful. "You honor us with an invitation."

"No, I'm thankful you expressed interest. I only hope I don't bore you with my endless talk of the horses."

"Not as long as we can ride," Robert says wryly. "That should negate any time wasted on conversation."

Before Grandmama can admonish Robert for speaking so candidly, Lord Blackburn lets out a loud laugh. "Not one for idle conversation, I see. That's good. I will certainly make riding the priority then."

Robert claps him on the back. "Good man."

Grandmama looks as though she may strangle my brother, so for his own good, I say, "Shall we return to the lobby?"

"Forgive me," Lord Blackburn says. "I hadn't noticed how late it is. You must be exhausted." He offers me his arm, and I take it, soothing my grandmother's wrath.

As we stroll through the lobby, my skirts swishing pleasantly against my legs, I feel a tingle of awareness on the back of my neck. I turn my head, and my eyes instantly land on Lord Thornewood. He leans casually against one of the lobby's columns, one hand in the pocket of his black trousers. His expression is at once dark and unreadable. My stomach flutters, and I turn away.

Lord Blackburn helps us into our carriage when it's pulled 'round, and when it's my turn, he meets my gaze and kisses the back of my hand. My eyes lock on his, and I am acutely aware of one thing: my skin has erupted in goosebumps.

I stare up at the lace canopy of my bed. Lord Thornewood's warnings resound in my mind despite my best efforts to ignore them. My body's reaction to Lord Blackburn suggests there is something about him that encourages caution, though he has been nothing but kind.

A soft glow catches my eye, and I turn toward my mother's journal. I clutch the little book to my chest briefly and whisper a thank-you to my mother. Surely her words will bring me comfort. The book falls open and words scrawl across the page as if my mother wrote them in great anxiety.

> *My dearest Katherine,*
>
> *By now you must be firmly ensconced in London Society. Forgive me, but I ask you to indulge a mother's gentle reminders. Your grandmother will no doubt be rushing you from ball to ball, even so, you cannot forget our reliance on the sun's energy. You must make time for your sister and yourself to be outside of the confines of London town. With the potential threat from the Order of the Eternal Sun, you cannot afford to be in a weakened state.*
>
> *With sufficient power, you will be able to protect yourself. I only wish I could be there to guide you, as I know you've never learned defensive arcana. As Sylvani, we are gifted with instinctual power, power that will come to our aid when we most need it. However, I fear you will be caught unawares at a time when the sun's energy cannot help you.*
>
> *Be vigilant, my daughter. And do not despair; you are more powerful than you know.*
>
> *All my love,*
> *Mama*

I close the little book. My hand shakes as I place it gently back on the side table. Tingles of unease race up and down my spine. Two warnings in one night cannot be coincidence.

I shake my head as a deep disappointment fills me. Lord Blackburn has been so charismatic and kind, even appearing frail at times. Is it a charade on his part? But no, surely he does not know the truth about me. I have done nothing to draw attention to myself. Then again, to ignore both my own apprehension and Mama's warning would be folly.

I must waste no more time in uncovering Lord Blackburn's intentions.

TWELVE

As soon as our carriage arrives at Lord Blackburn's estate, my initial doubts of his debt problems seem justified. The grounds are elegant and well-tended; the house itself is much larger than my father's—which has six bedrooms—and the stables look as though they can hold at least fifteen horses.

"His lordship has requested all guests join him at the stables," the footman says, his tone bland.

"Thank you," Grandmama says. Her eyes are busy taking in the grounds, no doubt calculating their value. "Will you show us the way?"

He does as he's asked, though he looks rather put-out about it. Probably because it isn't hard to see how to get there.

One of the horses snorts as we approach, and I find we are the last to arrive. Three small pavilions have been set up under the shade of an enormous old oak tree. The pavilions' soft chiffon fabric flutters softly in the breeze, providing additional protection from the sun. Card tables have been set up under each one, and I see many of the Society matrons in attendance here are already playing a game of bridge.

I stifle a groan when I notice Eliza, strolling arm-in-arm with Amelia. No doubt their casual promenade is to showcase themselves to the best advantage. Aside from Lord Blackburn, there are two other gentlemen in attendance whom I've never met.

Soft talk from the ladies drifts back to us on the breeze while Lord Blackburn gestures animatedly toward the horses. Five Thoroughbreds are lined up, a groom at each of their heads. Two bays, two chestnuts, and a gray.

Lord Blackburn and Penelope turn to me with welcoming smiles, but it's barely enough to overcome Eliza's venomous glare. I widen my eyes at her innocently, and she looks away. If I were to use her irrational logic, I should be irritated with her, since Lord Blackburn invited Robert and me first.

Penelope stands apart from the others, and she latches onto my arm as soon as I join her. "I'm so glad you're here." She looks as though she'd like to say more, but her mother moves within earshot.

"You'll have to fill me in on what I missed," I say with a pointed look in Eliza's direction.

"Nothing out of the ordinary," she says wryly. "Oh, but my cousin has been filling us in about the horses—that's rather interesting."

I suck in my breath. "That's right. You and Lord Blackburn are cousins."

She nods—confused, I'm sure, by my sudden enthusiasm. "Yes."

I lean in close and lower my voice. "Have you heard any rumors about him?"

She screws up her face in thought. "Maybe the odd scandal abroad— nothing too important, though." When my expression turns to one of relief, she hastens to add, "But we aren't very close. We're distant cousins actually, and my family rarely sees him."

My excitement dwindles. Just when I thought I had proof Lord Thorne-wood was mistaken. . . . Though, of course, it does nothing to explain my instinctual reaction to him. I watch as Lord Blackburn and Grandmama move away from the others, both speaking animatedly. From the pinched expression on my grandmother's face, and the rapid gestures Lord Black-burn makes, it seems as though they are arguing. But how can that be so when we've only just arrived? For once, I wish my grandmother and I had the type of relationship where I could ask her about the exchange later.

"Why? Have you heard any?" she asks.

I hesitate before shaking my head. "Someone mentioned something in passing, but I won't give it credence by repeating it."

"I hope it wasn't anything too far-fetched."

"Not particularly."

Lord Blackburn finally escapes from my grandmother and greets me again with a wide smile and an outstretched hand. If he is still bothered by his conversation with her, then he makes no show of it. "Come, you must see Destrier—one of my best-producing sires. Twelve of his foals have gone on to be champions."

He leads me over to a blood-red bay stallion that is taller and more muscular than the other horses in the line. He stands calmly enough, but the constant swivel of his ears tells me he's anxious.

"He's beautiful," I say and reach out to put my hand on his velvety nose. I infuse a feeling of calmness through our brief touch, and his muscles relax.

"You're the first of our party here to touch him," Lord Blackburn says approvingly. "Everyone else has kept their distance. Though they may just be more interested in observing than interacting."

I glance back at Eliza, Amelia, and the others. More likely, they're just here for a chance to observe not the horses but Lord Blackburn's estate.

Robert walks up next to me and pats Destrier, completely unintimidated by the horse's size. "This is a fine-looking animal. Is he fast?"

"He *was* fast," Lord Blackburn corrects. "He's now ten years old and only used for breeding."

Robert gives him a sly smile. "How fast?"

"English Triple Crown winner fast," Lord Blackburn says.

"This must be Destrier then."

Lord Blackburn grins, and I can tell by the puff of his chest he's thrilled. "You know your horse racing."

I must admit my mind wanders after that, for they both launch into every aspect of racing and I lose interest. So it must have taken Lord Blackburn several attempts to get my attention because his voice is loud in my ear when he asks, "Would you like to watch them run?"

I look around in surprise; all the horses have been taken away by the grooms. I have always been skilled at escaping from reality. My father used to tease I had wandered off to frolic with the faeries. Sometimes, like right now, it's embarrassing. I blush and try to look excessively interested.

"I have a grass track behind the stables," he says. "The horses should be saddled and ready to go."

I have never been to a horse race, but I could watch horses galloping for hours. "You must be able to read our minds and find what we'd like to see most," I say.

His smile is genuine as he leads us to the track, which is impressive enough in its own right. I had expected a down-trodden field for some reason, but instead, a very tidy area has been created with white fencing. One of the grooms trots a long-legged filly that reminds me of Robert's mare, Serenity. Her coat is even the same reddish shade of chestnut, though that's not uncommon. Most horses are either chestnut or bay in color.

"This is our most promising filly this year—Gifted out of Destrier. The colt," he indicates with a tilt of his head toward a tall bay, "is Ovation out of Destrier."

"Brother and sister then?" I ask with a glance at my own brother. I wonder if the horses are as competitive as we are.

"Only half, but yes."

Eliza joins us at the rail, her cheeks flushed from the wind. "You've prepared such an exciting day for us, my lord. Perhaps we should even place bets on who is the fastest." She puts her hand on his arm and leans in. "Though of course *you* couldn't join in the fun."

I wait for the little sting of jealousy like I had when I saw her dancing with Lord Thornewood, but it never comes. This makes me irritated enough to snap, "I'll take that bet."

Her eyebrows arch. "Katherine, I'm surprised. I didn't think you were the type."

I ignore her asinine remark. "What is your wager?"

Her expression turns more serious as she looks over both horses. The filly looks as though she will have speed on her side, but as I look over the track, I see the grass is rather long. This will slow her down. The colt is well-muscled, brawny where the filly is lithe, but I think he will have the advantage on this track. The grass won't be able to hold him back, and he'll have the endurance to make it to the end.

"Ten pounds on the filly," she says, and I hide my glee.

"Such a large sum," Lord Blackburn says. I search his face to see if there is any telltale sign of a man addicted to gambling, but his expression is unreadable.

"Then I will place the same on the colt," I say, and Penelope looks at me with wide eyes, her fingers worrying the ribbons on her hat. When Robert doesn't say anything, I know I made the right choice.

"Anyone else care to place a bet?" Lord Blackburn asks, but keeps his voice pitched low so Lady Hasting and Grandmama, who are standing a few feet away and deep in conversation, don't hear.

Penelope and Robert shake their heads.

Lord Blackburn nods to his grooms, and they line up the horses. The filly dances to the left, shying away from some unseen thing—probably the wind. I feel even more justified in my choice, until they take off.

The filly becomes focused as soon as she sees her half-brother racing beside her. She tries to pull ahead, but the jockey is smart; he keeps her in check. He means to save her speed for the end, and with a sinking feeling in my stomach, I realize I didn't take the riders' skill into account.

The colt's hooves strike through the grass like shovels, divots flying in his wake. He is in the lead, but I can see from here he's not really trying. When the jockey finally gives the filly her head, she'll pass him as if he was standing still.

I chew the inside of my lip. Ten pounds is quite a sum. I shouldn't have let Eliza goad me into such an agreement. I picture the way her face will look when she wins, the catty grin. I can't stomach it.

The horses are rounding the corner, about to start the homestretch, and the filly's jockey lets her make her move. She surges forward, quickly closing the distance between her and the colt.

Up ahead of them, I notice a rope dangling from the fence. I think of the way the filly shied at nothing in the beginning of the race. I wish I can say I don't do exactly what I am thinking, but once the image of Eliza's gloating face fills my mind, I can't let it go.

I concentrate on the breeze. It's been playing with us today, like a kitten with a ball of yarn, batting at our clothes and disappearing, only to pounce on us again. I close my eyes and summon that breeze to me once again. It hovers over me, questioningly, pulling baby fine hairs from my chignon. Out of the corner of my eye, I notice Lord Blackburn watching me. His expression is strange, his brows furrowed as if trying to puzzle out a difficult equation. It distracts me for a moment, and I almost lose my hold on the arcana. Just before it fades away, I form the image of what I want in my mind, and the breeze obeys.

When the filly passes the rope, it flies up, spooking her. She contorts her body away from it, eyes wide. Her gait falters, and the colt gallops past her. He crosses the finish line before the jockey can get the filly's attention back to the race.

The triumphant smile melts from Eliza's face, and though part of me is gloating, another part tells me misusing arcana was wrong, wrong, wrong. My brother looks in the direction of the rope and then back to me with a single eyebrow raised. Guilt flails inside of me like an earthworm wriggling in the sun.

"Well done," Lord Blackburn enthuses, looking more proud of me than of the horses. Something is off with his reaction, and goosebumps once again spread over my skin. Surely he couldn't have known what I was doing. I've never known anyone who could sense arcana, other than my family. Though isn't that exactly what my mother warned me about?

"Yes," Eliza says with a smile that doesn't reach her eyes, "well done. A nice piece of luck. I'll have the money sent to your townhome."

A few heartbeats pass while I struggle internally with myself. Here's a chance for me to redeem myself—sort of. Good Katherine wins out, and I say, "Oh, don't trouble yourself, Eliza. It was more fun just to watch the race."

Lord Blackburn looks horrified and angrier than he has any right to be. "Katherine, a bet is a bet. Reneging wouldn't be fair to either of you." His tone is sharper than I've ever heard it, and it puts me on edge. I don't care a fig for the bet anymore, and I grit my teeth. Why did he have to get in the way of my redemption? Eliza now has no choice but to hold to her end of the bargain.

"You'll get your money," she says and walks off with Amelia, no doubt as annoyed with Lord Blackburn as I am.

"Now that everything's settled," Lord Blackburn says, his mood switching to happy-go-lucky again, "anyone up for a tour of the house?"

Robert's face falls, and I belatedly remember Lord Blackburn's promise to take us riding—the only thing Robert ever really wants to do.

"We won't have a chance to ride?" I ask.

He narrows his eyes at my contradiction. "Not everyone would be able to participate," he says with a nod toward Grandmama and Lady Hasting.

I shoot Robert a sympathetic look, and he shrugs.

"Ah, forgive me," Lord Blackburn says after watching our exchange. "I'd quite forgotten my promise to you, Mr. Sinclair." He calls over one of the jockeys, the one who rode the colt. "Matthew, would you mind taking Mr. Sinclair on a tour of the stables? He's an accomplished horseman and would do well on Gifted."

"It would be my pleasure, my lord," Matthew says.

Robert's face relaxes into an easy grin, and a smile replaces my earlier tense expression. "This is more than I could have hoped for," Robert says. "I thank you."

"Good, good," Lord Blackburn says. "Now if you'll both excuse me for just a moment, I wish to inform the others of the tour."

When Lord Blackburn walks away, my grandmother pulls me to the side. I didn't realize she was so close, but judging by her serious expression, she must have heard the entire exchange.

"Don't cause any more problems for Lord Blackburn," she says, her voice an angry whisper. "This is his estate, and if he wants you to tour his home—his family *crypt*—you will do so."

"It may be his estate," I say, "but that doesn't mean I have to cater to his every wish—especially if it goes against an earlier promise."

"That's *exactly* what it means." Her grip on my arm tightens almost painfully. "Now don't ruin this."

She walks away in a huff, and I rub my arm while I glare at her retreating back.

Lord Blackburn returns with the others. Eliza and Amelia are both chattering animatedly, probably excited to see the inside of his grand manor. I glance in the direction of the stables and wish I could beg to join Robert. Honestly I'd rather see the horses than the inside of some stuffy house.

Penelope loops her arm through mine, and I smile at her gratefully. "We must take note of every piece of fine china and crystal," she says in a serious tone. "The number of chandeliers and paintings is also extremely important."

I nod seriously. "Yes, we must also be aware of the height of the windows in the sitting room, for I could not live anywhere that didn't have floor-to-ceiling windows."

She laughs and glances over at her mother and my grandmother behind us. "I swear they're having an identical conversation—only they aren't joking."

"Oh, I can practically guarantee it."

Lord Blackburn holds up his hand to get our attention. "If everyone will follow me, we'll walk through the garden first."

He strides away, and I lean toward Penelope as we follow. "The garden must have at least three fountains or it won't be worth our time."

"Yes, but our real concern should be whether the statues are Greek or Roman."

I laugh quietly, feeling only marginally guilty to be amusing ourselves at my grandmother and her mother's expense. But then I think of Grandmama's earlier censure, and the marginal guilt disappears.

The gardens, though, are nothing to scoff at. Amidst rectangles of perfectly manicured lawns are brightly-blooming azaleas, purple butterfly bushes, and a sweeping stone railing to contain it all. Penelope nudges me as we pass a weathered stone fountain, complete with a Greek goddess statue pouring the water.

The stormy gray house looms behind the garden, and Lord Blackburn brings us around to the front. His servants open the door with a flourish, and we enter into a marble foyer with a large crystal chandelier. I think again of the rumor Lord Thornewood told me and shake my head. He must be mistaken. No one living in such opulence could be indebted. Though, of course, Lord Blackburn's financial status no longer interests me. What I *am* interested in is whether he is one of the men of whom my mother warned.

When we enter the drawing room, Eliza touches the gilded frame of what appears to be a family portrait. "Such a beautiful family, my lord," she says. "Is this you as a child?"

A small, tow-headed boy with rosy cheeks clutches a wooden toy beside a regal-looking couple. Lord Blackburn smiles at the image. "It is indeed."

"Penelope," Lady Hasting says, "come see this painting of your grandparents. It's a lovely rendering."

"Coming, Mama," Penelope says with a quiet sigh.

The dark walls are covered with paintings of Lord Blackburn in his youth, his horses, and various noblemen and ladies. While the others view each one, Lord Blackburn touches my arm with a feather-light touch. "What think you of the grounds and the horses?"

I don't have to fake any sincerity when I say, "It's all beautiful. A lovely escape. I would never want to come to town."

". . . if you lived here?" Lord Blackburn adds to the end of my sentence. His expression is hard to read—serious? Hopeful?

"If I was mistress of a champion racing stable? No, I would never want to leave." My tone is light. I don't want him to read into my statement too much, as flirting is not my intention. I don't want it to be his either.

"Believe me, you and your brother are welcome to come back anytime." He glances over his shoulder at Eliza and Amelia. "Miss Gray, Miss Uppington, that invitation includes you as well."

Eliza smiles widely, showcasing her straight white teeth. "I will have to take you up on your offer, for I haven't seen such a beautiful home and grounds in ages."

"I am so glad you are all enjoying yourselves—this is a real treat for me, too," he says.

Now that he is distracted by Eliza, I glance around for Penelope. I would rather not give Lord Blackburn the chance to focus his attention upon me again. I frown when I realize she and her mother are no longer in the room.

"Is there something wrong?" Lord Blackburn asks.

"No," I answer, a trace of annoyance in my tone. Now I shall never be rid of him. "Only, do you know where Penelope has gone?"

"Actually, I believe she and her mother walked in the direction of my library. I have many unusual artifacts I've collected over time, and I'm rather proud of it." He offers me his arm. "Shall I show you the way?"

I think of the odd way he has behaved today. Perhaps it would be better if I did not follow him to some distant corner of his house. "Is it very far?"

He gives me a curious look. "Not at all. It's adjacent to this room, in fact."

I nod then and take his arm. He wouldn't dare try anything with so many others present, and when will I ever have the chance to be in his home again?

He leads me down a richly carpeted hallway and into a large library, only there aren't any books.

I look around, both eyebrows raised. "My lord, this is amazing."

Instead of books on the shelves, there are artifacts from all over the world. Enormous jade vases from Asia, carved ivory statues from India, glittering gemstones bigger than my fist, swords and armor from another era. But the most amazing things are the ones not on the shelves at all.

Lord Blackburn places his hand on the sarcophagus of an ancient Egyptian pharaoh. "This is perhaps one of my rarest acquisitions."

"Wherever did you get such a thing?"

A slow grin crosses his face. "Ah, that's my little secret. I have connections all over the world—other collectors who, like me, are searching for rare wonders." He takes a step toward me and runs a finger down my cheek.

"How fascinating," I say and take a step back. "It seems Penelope is not here; shall we return to the others?"

His eyebrows shoot up before falling down into a frown. "Perhaps an ancient mummy is of little interest to you." He gestures toward the shining gemstones behind him. "You would rather peruse the jewelry?"

I hesitate. I think of the strange ring I noticed at the opera. "Do you have anything like that?" I ask, nodding at the ring on his finger.

He holds it up to the light. "It's so interesting you noticed this. The symbol is an ancient one. An Egyptian ankh that represents eternal life."

"A powerful symbol indeed," I murmur. There is something about the seemingly innocuous shape that sends a shiver of apprehension racing up my spine.

"And considering what happened earlier during the race," a humorless smile fills his face, "I think you are more than worthy of knowing about the ring's origins."

He knows. My eyes widen as he steps toward me. I move back until the corner of a bookcase presses against my shoulders. "My Lord, I wouldn't want to pry. Clearly the ring is important to you—I only meant to say it was beautiful."

"As beautiful as you," he says. His eyes drop to the low neckline of my gown, and my lip curled in response. "Tell me, Miss Sinclair, would you like to know more about me? I could show you . . . so many things."

My heart is pounding a furious warning. I feel trapped pressed so close to the bookcase. Anger vies with fear within me. I've been a fool; I should have never trusted him. There is no mistaking the feeling that one wrong move will ensnare me as quickly as a snake could catch a mouse. I glance at the open doorway. "We should go back," I say firmly. "The others will be asking where we've gone."

A look of fury flashes across his face before he buries it again. His eyes search mine as if he expects me to change my mind. After a moment, he smiles, the gesture deceptively relaxed. I can tell by the stiff carriage of his back and the tightness of his jaw he is loath to relent. "Very well. You're right, of course. There's a proper way to do these things."

I sidestep around him and stride toward the door. When he does nothing to physically stop me, I let out a breath in relief. That was much too close, and I am lucky to have escaped unscathed, for one thing is clear: he knows the truth about me.

THIRTEEN

THE next week is a monotonous copy of the week before. Having some-where to be each night makes me long for the comfortable schedule at home. Though, as I think these things, I know the real reason this week is so much more tedious than the last: I've hardly seen Lord Thornewood. And when he does attend, it's only for such a short time that I barely lay eyes on him before he is gone again.

Lord Blackburn, on the other hand, has been almost impossible to avoid. Thanks to my grandmother, I have been forced into more than one dance with him.

In the beginning, I tried to explain to Grandmama how perfectly loathsome he is to me, but she would hear none of it. I couldn't very well explain what had happened at his estate, so I am forced to rely on my own ingenuity in avoiding him. Unfortunately, I am almost always hindered by the stifling social laws I must abide by while in town. Those very same laws, though, make it nearly impossible for him to get me alone. For this I'm grateful.

On the way to this particular ball, however, my stomach is a writhing mass of nerves. If for no reason other than it's the last ball of the week, so both Lord Blackburn and Grandmama will be at their most persistent.

I grasp my reticule tighter to my chest. Inside I've concealed a wickedly sharp letter opener—the best weapon I could find in Grandmama's townhome. I've brought it to every ball, and though Lord Blackburn has never done anything overtly threatening, I feel safer with it. Even if using it would almost guarantee my disgrace.

"Remember," she says to me in the carriage, "let Lord Blackburn have the first dance. There's been talk of his growing interest in you, though any fool with eyes can see."

I have long since given up arguing with her, so I just nod. The next few days—as far as I know—are free. Surely I can survive this one last evening.

"Mention his horses, too," she adds after a moment as if the thought just popped into her head. "You know he talks of nothing else."

This isn't entirely true, to be fair. But I'm not in the most charitable mood, so I just stare out the window with a mean smile on my face.

My grandmother leans over and pinches my cheeks. I suck in a breath with a hiss. "What was that for?"

"Oh hush, child," she snaps. "It's only to give you a little color."

"I don't need any," I say and then press my lips together. Even I can hear the childish note in my voice.

My irritable mood clings to me like wet sand as we enter the ballroom. When I see Penelope in the far corner of the room, a small smile touches my lips. No sooner do I move in her direction than Lord Blackburn approaches me.

"Miss Sinclair," he says with a dip of his head, "I was hoping to see you here tonight. How beautiful you look."

I manage a wan smile when I want to cringe. Damn the etiquette that requires me to stay and speak to him rather than go to my friend. "You are very kind."

"Would you save the next dance for me?"

He already feels much too close. I can detect not only his cologne, but also the soap he used to wash himself. Dancing will require us to get that much closer. "Absolutely," I mumble. "If you'll excuse me for the moment, though, I must go say hello to Penelope."

He bows, a scowl on his face as I scurry away from him; even my skirts feel clingy against my legs.

"You look as though you're running away from someone," Penelope observes when I reach her side, my expression no doubt harried.

"Oh, just from Lord Blackburn. I've promised him the first dance," I say, turning my back on his direction so I won't be forced to look at him any longer than I have to.

Penelope nods gravely. "And I fear your night may be about to become more trying." She points to the ballroom's entrance. "Lord Thornewood has arrived."

My eyes shoot to the doorway and drink in the sight of him. He seems taller, darker—more aloof than usual. His bored look is in place, his clothes midnight black. I shouldn't let myself revel in that happy-bubbly feeling, especially since every other time, he left after only a few minutes. But as he makes his way toward me, his strides long and sure, the bubbly feeling reaches my face and I can't hold back a smile.

Penelope and I sink into curtsies when he reaches us. He gives a short bow back. "Miss Sinclair, I am shocked to find you without your shadow for once."

My smile disappears. "Oh? I'm sure I don't know who you mean."

He jerks his chin toward Lord Blackburn, who stands not far away—but not at risk of overhearing, thankfully. "I see you were quick to take my advice," he says in a sarcastic tone.

If only he knew. He was right to warn me away from Lord Blackburn, only his reasons for doing so were slightly off-target.

I glance at Penelope to see what she makes of the conversation. Her eyebrows are drawn in concentration, and she is shifting from foot to foot in a way that suggests she's nervous.

"I'm taken aback you're talking to me. You haven't spent more than a few minutes at any event I've been at this entire week."

"And I'm surprised you noticed."

I cross my arms over my chest, and then realize it makes me look defensive and drop them back to my sides. Penelope coughs quietly.

Lord Thornewood shoves his hand in his hair as if he's frustrated. Since I've never seen him anything but aloof or cavalier, I arch my eyebrows at him in surprise. "Have you a partner for the next dance?" His voice is gruff and abrupt.

"I—"

"Sorry, old chap," Lord Blackburn's harsh voice interjects, with—horrors—a pat on Lord Thornewood's broad back. "The lady promised that dance to me."

Lord Thornewood turns to Lord Blackburn with such a cold look I'm afraid for half a second he intends to hit him. I wish he would. I wish *I* could. Instead, he inclines his head slightly. "I see."

Lord Blackburn offers me his arm with an expression that's trying, but failing, to appear not to gloat. For the second time that night, I curse etiquette. I want to tell Lord Thornewood I'd much rather dance with him, that I hope he will dance the next set with me, but I know it would only make things worse. I say nothing as I follow Lord Blackburn to the dance floor.

We take our places, and I reluctantly look back at where Penelope and Lord Thornewood stand. I thought he would just leave like he's done every other night, but he watches us, unreadable mask in place.

"Distracted tonight?" Lord Blackburn's voice jars me from my thoughts.

I force my attention back to the dance. "Forgive me, yes."

"No need to apologize. I was merely making an observation."

The dance continues, and I make all the movements without thinking or bothering to add any elegance. My reticule dangles from a satin ribbon around my wrist. I take comfort in the fact there is a weapon so close at hand.

Once my mind is easily a thousand miles away on another continent, Lord Blackburn says in quiet tones easily drowned out by the other dancers, "I'm not the marrying type." My eyes leap to his. He has my full attention now. "But I cannot deny the attraction I have for you."

My stomach sinks. He'd alluded to that at some of the other balls, but never in so direct a manner. The dance ends before he can finish, and I seriously contemplate bolting. Unfortunately, he guides me off the floor to a section of wall no one currently occupies.

"My lord—"

"I believe you to be my match in every way." He is much too close again, the smell of soap and cologne cloying. "We have chemistry, you and me. We could see how compatible we really are." He lowers his voice to an intimate level. "You could show me all the things you can *do*." His expression is intense as his gaze travels the length of me. I feel naked, exposed. Etiquette be damned—I'm leaving.

I try to walk away, but he touches my arm. "Come to my townhome tonight."

"You are too forward, sir," I snap. "I will do no such thing. Never say that again."

I avoid looking in Penelope and Lord Thornewood's direction and head straight for the terrace. My breathing comes in huffed gasps. I feel as though my lungs are being held in a vise, as if every breath is a struggle. I grip the rail of the balcony, taking deep, cleansing breaths of the fresh night air. The moon is bright overhead, allowing me to catch a glimpse of a row of perfectly trimmed hedges, a fountain, and rose bushes. I wander down amongst the vegetation, my muscles relaxing now I'm away from the crush of people—and Lord Blackburn.

I have no choice now but to tell him outright I never wish to have contact with him again. If that risks a scandal, then so be it. I cannot continue this fear of every ball. For some time after the library debacle, he remained over-attentive but still polite. Tonight, he seems to have grown much bolder, insulting me with his disgusting proposal.

There is still the very real threat he is one of the members of the Order of the Eternal Sun. My fingers seem to seek the comfort of the makeshift weapon in my reticule on their own, for before I know it, I've pulled it free. The pearl handle shimmers dully in the moonlight.

A crunch of gravel behind me alerts me to someone's presence, and I spin around, clutching my letter opener to my side.

"My dear Miss Sinclair," Lord Blackburn says, reaching a hand out to steady me, "I didn't mean to frighten you."

"No, my lord. Not frighten—just startled me is all." My tone is wary. There's something about his energy—something that raises the hairs on the back of my neck.

He arches an eyebrow. "Enough of this 'my lord' talk. Come, we know each other better now. Call me Russell." He smiles, but I'm not sure I like the look in his eyes—it reminds me of a hound that has spotted its rabbit. "And I hope I may call you Katherine."

I murmur something in the affirmative and glance back at the house. Can I make a run for it? Or will he grab me as I run by?

"Have you seen Lady Drake's rose bushes?" He puts his hand on my elbow. "Come, I'll show you. They're breathtaking."

"I'd rather return—"

"Come, I insist."

His hand on my elbow is firm, and I long to jerk away and dash back to the house. I keep the hand holding the letter opener pressed against my skirts. He hasn't noticed yet, so I have the advantage. My instincts are screaming to be cautious, that he is like a predator that loves the thrill of the chase. I try to borrow energy from the moon, but it's much weaker than the sun. Whereas a slice of sunshine on my arm can partly replenish me, it would take prolonged exposure to the moon's gentle brightness to do the same. It's no help that my mind is a jumble of worry, and my lack of concentration prevents me from storing up anything useful.

I know I can use my weapon if I have to, but I hate to think of the repercussions.

Before I can summon an excuse, he leads me farther into the shadows, the smell of the roses almost as overpowering as the soap and cologne on his skin.

"You were very clever to come out here," he says in a low voice. "I take it you agree to my offer?"

I take a step back as a cold sickness settles in my stomach. "You think I would agree to be intimate with you?" My cheeks flush with anger, and my palm itches to slap the lascivious look off his face.

He smiles again, but the dangerous look in his eye hasn't lessened. "Why else would you come out here alone?"

"To find a moment's peace, nothing more."

His smile drops away as quickly as it appeared. "You are saying no to my offer?"

"That's absolutely what I'm saying. You've given me no choice but to be blunt. Not only do I have no romantic interest in you, I want nothing to do with you." I turn on my heel to return to the house, but his hand darts out and grabs my arm. I raise my eyebrows. "Unhand me at once."

His grip tightens, and his mouth forms a close-lipped smile.

The whispers of worry increase in decibel until they're all but shouting in my mind. I try to gather energy to me but every time the moon grants me its power, my emotions swirl it away like a tornado. Concentration is needed to channel arcana, and a calm state of mind is something I do not have at the moment.

He pulls me against his chest and shoves me roughly against the wooden fence. My heart is beating so hard I'm afraid it'll burst free from my chest. If we're caught, I'll be ruined. My father will be forced to make this horrid man marry me—which Lord Blackburn might actually do for my dowry alone—and I'll be trapped with this monster until the day I die.

He leans in close. His breath is on my cheek. "I know what you are. I'd suspected before, but after that day in my library, I *knew*."

A shiver of fear racks my body. He breathes in deeply as if savoring a delicious aroma before taking hold of both my shoulders. I feel the slight tug in the core of me—the one I only feel when I use arcana.

True terror licks at my insides like flames. My mother was right to fear I would be caught at a time when the sun's energy could not help me. My thoughts are as rapid as my breathing, and I lose all hope of calming myself when he presses his lips to mine. I struggle, clamping my mouth shut and twisting this way and that, but his grip is tight, bruising. The tug on my abdomen is stronger as more of my power is taken from me. Sour nausea churns inside of me. He is *forcing* the energy away from my body; violating me. My limbs become heavier as more power leaves me. I try to hold on to it, grasping fleetingly with my mind as a child may try to catch the string of a kite before it flies away.

I try to bring my knee up to kick him, hurt him, but he has me flush against the fence. The wood digs into my back and my bare arms.

I manage to free one arm and bring the letter opener toward him. Everything is in slow motion. I feel as though I'm moving underwater. He grabs my hand with a sneer, squeezing my wrist until I cry out. He slams my hand against the fence until my grip loosens and the letter opener falls to the ground.

A shout rings out, and I struggle harder. With a mighty wrench, I manage to free my arm and shove Lord Blackburn with all my strength. He goes flying backward, and I stumble to the side.

Did I shove him that hard?

And then I see him.

Lord Thornewood.

Lord Blackburn whirls on him like an angry dog, even takes a swing at him, but Lord Thornewood dodges it. He watches Lord Blackburn with a look of contempt.

"How dare you interrupt us!" Lord Blackburn shouts. His pale eyes convey such malice, I flinch. Curiously, his previous fragility seems to have disappeared. No longer does his skin remind me of porcelain. The lean wolf appearance of his face and body has been replaced by a complexion almost glowing with vitality.

Lord Thornewood appears calm, but his jaw is tight and his right hand is curled in a fist at his side. "The lady didn't seem to be enjoying your company."

Lord Blackburn must realize his attempts at intimidation have no effect because he wears a conspiratory grin. "Come now, Lord Thornewood. We've all heard the rumors about you. You know how these elegant ladies can be. They like to play at being hard to get."

Lord Thornewood narrows his eyes. His face is murderous, and a muscle in his jaw twitches. He takes a menacing step forward. The tension between them is so taut, I'm afraid they will start a row amongst the rose bushes. But Lord Thornewood must shove his fury down where he stores all his emotions because all he says is, "Enough of this. We're leaving. Come, Miss Sinclair." I move to his side on shaky, newborn foal legs, and his arm wraps protectively around me. To Lord Blackburn, he says, "You are to never speak to Miss Sinclair again. Is that clear?"

Lord Blackburn tilts his head and raises his chin slightly. "Or what, precisely?"

"Or I ruin you." The threat is delivered so smoothly, without any further explanation, and I watch Lord Blackburn's Adam's apple bob as he takes in Lord Thornewood's meaning. With his influence, a mere word from him will end Lord Blackburn's reputation forever. He will be barred from every club in London, uninvited to every elegant ball, blacklisted by every member of Society.

We start back to the house, but Lord Blackburn calls out to Lord Thornewood. "And what if the lady welcomes my touch?"

Without even turning, Lord Thornewood says, "If you touch her again, I will kill you."

FOURTEEN

AFTER we enter the ballroom, Lord Thornewood guides me to a quiet corner of the room. His movements are stiff and his jaw is tight as he blocks most of my body from view of the others.

"Did he harm you?" he asks, his voice pitched low enough I hope no one around can hear.

I think about being thrown roughly against the fence, and I tense. Emotions crash inside me. I feel as violated as I would have if Lord Blackburn stripped me naked. He touched a part of me so intimate, so much a part of who I am. Anger flares as brightly as the sun within me. I want to hurt him. I want to search among all the artifacts of this room and find something sharp to inflict the same amount of pain and fear he caused in me.

Suppressing this loathsome feeling, I inwardly inspect the damage. I feel perhaps a little fatigued, much like I do when I use a bit of arcana— like making the rope fly up during the horse race. The difference is that he took it from me; I didn't expend it. And it isn't hard to imagine what might happen if he was able to continue—if he took it all.

Anger and disbelief crash over me again and again. My back aches, but it's nothing I cannot heal later. I wish I could tell Lord Thornewood everything, but I don't dare. "I'm fine, my lord, thank you."

He shakes his head once, brusquely. "We may forgo such formalities. Please, call me Colin. Now, did he touch you?"

I know he means more than the forced kiss. I drop my eyes and shake my head once. Lord Thornewood—for there is no way I can think of him by his given name—lets out a breath as his wide shoulders relax.

I want to reach out and take his hand, but I cannot—already our private conversation in the corner has drawn attention. "Thank you for . . . just, thank you."

"Think nothing of it. May I get you something to drink? A glass of wine, perhaps?"

I smile gratefully. "Yes, thank you."

I watch him weave deftly through the crowd, brushing off all attempts to waylay him. He returns with a small glass, and I take it from him with a shaky hand.

After a sip of the thin wine, I ask, "I do wonder, though, how did you know to come to my assistance?"

He glances away, an almost sheepish look crossing his face. "I watched you leave after the last dance, and I saw he followed not long after."

I manage a wry smile to cover my surprise. "I hadn't realized you monitored my movements so closely."

His self-conscious look disappears into one of naked admiration. "I do, and I have since the moment we met."

For once, I have nothing to say in return, only a wide smile upon my face. But lest I actually get a chance to bask in this glowing feeling, Eliza and Amelia approach us.

"Lord Thornewood," Eliza says with a slow smile I'm sure she means to be coy, "you cannot think to spend the remainder of the ball in this corner."

He drags his eyes from my face to hers. "No, of course not."

I stiffen and shrink back into myself. How could I have forgotten? I think of them flirting with each other on the dance floor and take a gulp of wine.

"I'm very glad to hear it because I have a cousin who is eager to speak with you. The two of you knew each other at Oxford." She points out a man in a beautifully tailored coat talking animatedly to our hostess.

"Edward," Lord Thornewood says with a nod. "I hadn't realized he was in town."

Eliza takes a step toward her cousin. "Come, I'll help you get reacquainted."

"Will you excuse me, Kath—Miss Sinclair?" Lord Thornewood asks, and I watch Eliza's eyes narrow at his slip.

Backed into a corner, I cannot say no without appearing both desperate and rude. "By all means."

The waltz that has been danced the entire time I've been speaking with Lord Thornewood ends, and Penelope joins me. I'm relieved to see her. There is nothing quite like distraction to cope with something traumatic.

"I saw Eliza steal Lord Thornewood from you a moment ago," she says, a look of disdain on her face as she glances in their direction.

"She resented not being able to eavesdrop." I frown. "I am surprised he went so willingly."

Penelope puts a gloved hand on my arm. "Too much attention from a suitor is scandalous to Society, dear, you know that. I'm sure he was trying to spare you from their censure."

I let out a breath of disgust. "Such stupid rules! How can anyone ever follow them?"

"You and Lord Thornewood must get along famously. You both care so little for Society."

"Yes, it's what tends to happen when you haven't been forced into the thick of it as you have." I glance at her mother who is even now hanging on every word of a potential suitor for Penelope.

Penelope lets out a little groan. "Not Sir Bondsworth, Mother. He's old enough to be my father."

"Oh, Penelope," I say in a fair imitation of her mother's brush tone, "he is very rich, and that's all that matters."

She laughs—probably to keep from crying. "So what were you and Lord Thornewood talking about so intently? I thought you found him disagreeable."

I take a sip of my wine to stall for time. Should I tell Penelope what happened? She has become a very dear friend these past few weeks. If we are overheard, though, the results could be disastrous. And though she and Lord Blackburn are distant cousins, I am still reluctant to reveal everything I know about him. I decide I will tell her a portion of the truth, but not here. Not where we could possibly be overheard.

I smile, and it turns even brighter when Lord Thornewood catches my eye from across the room. "I find he is growing on me."

I seek out my grandmother and beg her to leave early, but my pleas go ignored. Worse, she keeps asking me where Lord Blackburn has gone and what I have done to upset him. So by the time Lord Thornewood returns, I am in a foul mood and a tad tipsy.

"Oh-ho, so *now* you've deemed it a good time to seek me out," I say.

Annoyingly, he seems unperturbed by my acidic tone. "I came for that dance I requested of you earlier."

I *harrumph* and glance around, my vision just a little swimmy.

He pulls the wineglass from my hand. "You've had enough of this, I think." He leans toward my ear and murmurs, "But I don't blame you."

He holds out his arm to me, and tears pool in my eyes. Horrified, I blink rapidly until they evaporate unshed. Before he can lead me to the dance floor, I put pressure on his arm. "Wait. Can we—can we just stay here?"

He must sense how shaky I am because he guides me to one of the strategically placed chairs—the ones for elderly ladies to sit and rest. I don't even care. I sit with a luxurious sigh.

"Should I find your grandmother and tell her you're ready to leave?"

I let out an unladylike snort. "Be my guest. Maybe she'll actually listen to you."

He arches an eyebrow. "I can do better than that. I'll take you home myself."

I glance over at my grandmother, who is deep in conversation with Lady Hasting, as usual. She will be furious when she finds out. The wine has guaranteed I don't care.

I stand. "Yes, I think that would be wonderful."

It isn't until we're standing at the top of the stairs while the driver pulls 'round Lord Thornewood's carriage that it hits me: Lord Thornewood and I will be entirely alone. In the dark. In a very small space. In spite of the trauma I have just survived with Lord Blackburn, I do not fear the same from Lord Thornewood. I know he would never harm me.

No, it is not fear of him that makes me hesitate. It's fear of what *I* might do.

The footman tries to hold the door open for us, but Lord Thornewood waves him away and helps me into the carriage himself. I settle into the seat, and the carriage dips a bit as he takes the seat on the other side. He raps on the ceiling and we roll forward.

I arrange and rearrange my skirts. Our legs are inches away from each other, and I can feel the wine-induced flush spreading.

Lord Thornewood clears his throat. "Do I remember correctly that you have a sister?"

I nod, not trusting my voice.

"Will she be at home?"

I glance up sharply. "Yes."

"I only ask because I don't feel comfortable leaving you there alone—even with a house full of servants."

"Surely you don't think I'm in any danger?" The thought had not occurred to me, and a cold, sharp fear grips me. I will be sure to bar my door tonight.

He lets out his breath in a rush, the polite indifference he wears so well slipping enough for me to see the torment underneath. "I don't know what to think," he says in a voice that is more like a growl. "When I found him—his hands all over you—it was all I could do not to demand satisfaction."

"I can't think of anything more horrible than someone dueling over me." I lean forward and touch his arm, my eyes intent on his. "Swear you would never do that." He lets out some sort of grunt in affirmation, and I sigh. "I have to admit I'm a little surprised," I say. "It's not like you've gone out of your way to be around me this week."

His eyes search my face like he can't tell if I'm serious. When he determines I am, he frowns. "I can't imagine what I've done to make you think that."

The wine loosens my tongue even more than usual. "Well, you'd leave only moments after arriving at every ball and event I attended."

"I see. Is that all?"

"No. You favor Eliza over me." The words are out before I can stop myself. I wrap a cloak of righteousness about me so I can't feel the embarrassment.

His sharp bark of laughter makes me jump. "Eliza! How could you think that?"

"At Duchess Cecily's, you were hanging on her every word as you danced. And just this evening, you jumped at the chance to leave with her."

His laughter dies away, but his eyes still hold some of the mirth. "Are you so naive you don't realize how much Eliza dislikes you?" I avert my eyes briefly. It's rather obvious—probably to most everyone—how she feels about me. "You do? Well, then, you might see the things I did in a different light. That night at the Duchess's, if you'll recall, your own brother had just given her some serious fuel for gossip. And tonight, she'd seen you with Lord Blackburn—not outside, no one saw that, I made sure of it—no, she saw how much attention he gave you. As embarrassingly conceited as it sounds, favoring her with my attention provides the perfect distraction and keeps her from doing too much damage."

I stare at him, dumbfounded.

"The reason I left early during all those events is much harder to admit, but it has to do with our lascivious mutual acquaintance."

I think about his snide comment about Lord Blackburn being my shadow. I clear my throat and say quietly, "Because I was with Lord Blackburn?"

His jaw tightens. "It makes me sick I let my pride and jealousy get in the way. Thank God I stayed tonight."

I don't even want to think about that scenario. "It seems I completely misunderstood your intentions, my lord. Then again, that isn't unusual for me apparently."

"I won't have you blame yourself," Lord Thornewood says sharply.

I shrug and look out the window. I don't blame myself—though I was warned by Lord Thornewood about Lord Blackburn's character. *Blame* isn't the right word—it's more disgust than anything.

The carriage comes to a stop, and we stare at each other. His eyes are on me, an intense expression on his face. I pause, mesmerized by it. He leans forward and cups my cheek, and I freeze, afraid to break the spell.

The kiss is achingly gentle—so different from the horrible forced one with Lord Blackburn. But everything changes when I respond. He groans and tugs me onto his lap. I rearrange my skirts until I am draped across him and then we are pressed so tightly together we become one heartbeat, one breath.

His hands leave trails of fire wherever they touch. When his lips leave mine to kiss my jaw, my throat, and lower—the tops of my breasts—my breathing changes to quick pants. His eyes seem to devour me with one sweep, and I writhe on his lap . . . needing something I cannot yet name.

"I've wanted to do this for so long," he says, his lips at my throat.

I grasp the collar of his shirt and give a little tug until our mouths connect once again. Our tongues tangle, and I press closer to him, eliciting a groan. He pulls back, pressing gentle kisses on my temple and cheekbone. The reduction in pleasurable intensity only makes me squirm more. A teasing smile crosses his face for a moment before he continues his onslaught on my mouth. His tongue gently rakes over my bottom lip, and I let out a shuddering sigh.

Warm, strong hands caress the curves of my spine. Fingers plunge into my hair, freeing it from its chignon.

We kiss until I can barely think of my own name. Until Lord Blackburn's face is obliterated from my mind.

"Please tell me to stop," he says between kisses. His hands grip my waist tightly before sweeping gently over my ribs and up to my breasts.

I gasp—both from surprise and pleasure.

He slides his hands back to my waist and leans forward to press a gentle kiss on the side of my neck. "Forgive me, my darling. I had all the intentions of playing the gentleman this evening."

"There is nothing to forgive," I say. "You are mistaken if you think I was innocent in this." I touch my still-tingling lips. "I wanted this just as much as you."

He drops his gaze to my lips, an almost hungry look flaring in his eyes. "I'll walk you to your door," he says, his voice deep and husky.

The footman helps me down, and I avoid his gaze, a blush flaring over my skin. I hope he hasn't seen anything—I hope the door blocked his view.

"Will you be at Hyde Park tomorrow?" Lord Thornewood asks.

I smile widely. "I can be."

He trails his fingertips down my cheek, and my legs suddenly feel as though they will no longer support my body. "I very much hope you are. There's something I would like to speak to you about."

"How intriguing," I murmur, my eyes still riveted on his. "Where should we meet?"

"Near the river, of course," he says, a hint of teasing laughter in his eyes. "Perhaps under the small copse of trees?"

I nod. "I know the place." We're quiet for a moment, and I look away before I fantasize about kissing him again. "Thank you for bringing me home."

"It was my pleasure." He raises his hand to knock on the door, but stops himself and turns back to me. "I implore you to call me if you need any further assistance. I would be more than happy to carry out my threats to Lord Blackburn."

"Thank you, my lord," I say, warmth spreading throughout my body.

"I'm quite serious," he says. "It would be my pleasure."

I smile. "Be assured I will call if I need you."

He touches my cheek before knocking lightly on the door. It's opened after a moment by a sleepy-eyed servant. It makes me grateful I didn't give in to my urge to kiss him again—the servants would all know about it by morning.

"Good night, Miss Sinclair."

"Good night, my lord."

I rush up the stairs before the butler can become awake enough to notice my mussed hair and lips.

FIFTEEN

THE next morning, I am so lost in the recesses of my own mind I can scarcely carry on an intelligent conversation. On the one hand, Lord Blackburn's attack causes me to jump at every noise. Every time I think of his hands and mouth on me, my stomach threatens to empty itself. I want to believe Lord Thornewood's threats will keep him at bay, but I cannot be sure. Especially since he has tasted my power. A shudder racks my body, and I rub my arms.

In the end, I always return to the same question: what am I to do? How can I guarantee he will never violate me in such a way again? Though my mother was the one with the gift of prophecy, I can still say with relative certainty he will not give up so easily.

But then my mind turns to thoughts of Lord Thornewood. Where before thoughts of him were intrusive, I find these thoughts very welcome indeed. I blush. Am I so brazen, then? That a shared kiss with a gentleman changes my opinion of him? But no, I know it isn't the only thing. I think of the times he stood up for me against Eliza—even when I didn't realize he was doing so.

I can't stop touching my lips, and my cheeks seem to have a permanent blush as I remember how close we were. I could feel every inch of his body—a body that was much more muscular and hard than one would expect of an aristocrat.

Of course I cannot simply bury what happened with Lord Blackburn—much as I'd like to. Perhaps I should send for Robert? But no, I wouldn't want to keep him from his studies. And I refuse to send a letter to my father begging him to let me come home; I've surprised myself in realizing I'm not ready to give up on London just yet, especially with Lord Thornewood and my relationship becoming so much more . . . intimate.

Intimate, and yet, he does not know the truth about me. Would he be so interested if he knew I was only half human? That Lord Blackburn had attacked me as much for my body as for my power?

I glance at the clock on the mantle. Another hour until I am to meet him in Hyde Park. I pick up my mother's journal, almost too afraid to see what other warnings it may reveal. I open the book and watch as words appear on the creamy pages.

My dearest Katherine,

Though my gift of prophecy has certainly proved useful in many instances, it often only leaves me frustrated. I see so many lovely things for you in your future, but also great hardship. Because I can never know which future will come to pass, I am left only giving you vague warnings.

Long ago, when I was young and naive, I thought my gift gave me power over the future. During my first visit to this world, on the estate in which I stayed, I met a young farmhand. He was so kind to me, though I know he must have thought I was touched in the head. I knew very little of the ways of the world, you see, and even the cows he milked were strange to me.

My vision of his death came to me during my second visit with him. I can still remember the sweet smell of the hay we sat upon. I saw him thrashing in the middle of the pond, and, later, lying on the ground with soaking wet clothes. His face was gray. The vision brought tears to my eyes, for even in knowing him just a short time, I knew he was a beautiful soul. I asked him if he knew how to swim, and he told me he'd always been afraid of the water. I took it upon myself to teach him, and soon, he could dive to the very bottom effortlessly. We celebrated with a feast of freshly baked bread and cheese, talking and laughing well into the evening.

He nearly died the next day. I had succeeded in changing his future: he did not die by drowning. Instead, a sudden gust of wind caused him to fall from the roof of the barn he loved so much. He was barely breathing when I found him, and in my arrogance, I believed I was powerful enough to heal him without consequence. I was able to steal him from Death, but the cost was great for me. I lay unconscious and lifeless for several days; it was as if Death wanted to take me instead. When I finally recovered, I vowed I would never fall victim to my own arrogance again. I held true to this vow until I faced a vision I would do anything to prevent from coming true. The cost of this decision was, ultimately, my life.

So now you see, my darling Katherine, why this gift is also my greatest burden.

All my love,
Mama

I think of saving Robert from a terrible fall; would I not have done anything to save him? I cannot imagine what my mother must have gone through in seeing the futures of those around her, unable to change them. But what vision did she see that led her to endanger her own life?

I start to close the journal, but then I see it. Another rune. It's been so long since one appeared, I almost gave up hope of seeing another. This one is by far the simplest, only a series of three parallel lines.

With a deep breath, I press my finger to the lines. Instantly, a map appears before me. No village names, no cities, no countries. Only a dark, meandering line, and the words: The Great North Road.

The vision of her realm, the rock formation, and The Great North Road. Mama has given me the keys to finding the entrance to her realm, I'm sure of it.

A loud rap on my door causes my whole body to jerk as if I've been stung. My grandmother's voice calls out in an angry tone, "Katherine, open this door at once."

My stomach sinks with the horrible realization I haven't spoken to her since last night, when I left without her permission.

I open the door, and she bursts into my room. Her expression is so angry I wince. How could I think I'd escape her censure?

"So you *are* here," she says, her voice as ominous as a black sky.

"Lord Thornewood was kind enough to bring me home." I'm not sure if this would help or hurt my case since she'd either think it was wonderful—or scandalous.

"I'm not sure how you managed that," she says snidely, "since every effort I've made to throw you into the path of a suitor has been ruined. Lord Blackburn was said to be quite put-out at the end of the night." She paces about the room. "And how do you think I felt when I discovered my granddaughter wasn't even there anymore? Humiliated doesn't begin to describe it."

True to character, she wasn't worried or concerned for my safety or possible whereabouts. Her only concern was for herself.

"I'm very sorry for inconveniencing you," I say, my tone stiff. "As for Lord Blackburn, I care not a whit for his state of mind."

"Hateful girl! How could you say such a thing? A gentleman—a *baron*, no less—has shown great interest in you and may have even offered for your hand in marriage."

I fight down the panic at the thought of marrying such a man. "I'll not have him."

My grandmother draws herself up and raises her hand as if to slap me, but she stops herself at the last second. I flinch despite myself.

"Lord Thornewood has also shown interest in me," I say, inwardly cringing as I dangle Lord Thornewood's noble status before my grandmother as though he means no more to me than bait on a hook. "Surely you can agree that an earl is a far better catch."

Her eyes narrow. "Has he proposed?"

"Well, no—"

"Then do not speak to me about his superior title until he has." She turns on her heel and leaves in a huff, but stops at the entrance to my room. "I trust you know you won't be allowed to leave this house until I say otherwise."

"Grandmama, please," I say, swallowing my pride. "I sincerely apologize for leaving without your knowing last night. It was—wrong of me." I don't bother with an explanation. I can't bring myself to tell her of what transpired between Lord Blackburn and me. In truth, I'm afraid of her reaction.

She pauses. "Why should I forgive you? You've made a terrible mess of things, and now I am left to clean it up."

"Because no one but Lord Thornewood knows I went home unchaperoned. And because he asked me to meet him at Hyde Park this morning. I still have a chance to redeem myself."

She tilts her head, considering. Several moments pass before she says, "Your apology is accepted but I cannot chaperone you today. I have business I must attend to."

She turns as if to leave, and I have to think fast. "Lucy can come with me—she's been desperate for some fresh air."

Her pause seems to take years. "I suppose that would be alright." Her gaze falls sharply on my dress. "The green velvet riding habit would be a better choice."

She leaves, and I rush to Lucy's room.

"Luce," I say, and her eyes meet mine in the mirror. Her lady's maid gives me a smile and a bob of her head as she continues to style my sister's hair. "You must come with me to Hyde Park."

"Must I?" she teases.

"Lord Thornewood has asked me to meet him there this morning, but Grandmama refuses to chaperone me."

"And she will allow me to substitute?"

"Yes—I told her how badly you wanted to get out of the house. You know how she lives to make you happy."

"Of course I'll come. But can we take the phaeton?"

I nod. "It's of no consequence to me, but it's been ages since I've driven."

Her smile is sly. "I'm sure you'll be able to control the horses."

"Hm," I say, my mind already miles away at the park, "we'll see. I'm going to go ask the grooms to pull it 'round." Nervous energy quickens my pace as I think of laying eyes on Lord Thornewood again.

"Thank you for accompanying me, Luce," I say as I carefully guide the horses through London's narrow streets. "In truth, I have ulterior motives."

Lucy smiles teasingly. "Of course. You needed someone to come with you to meet Lord Thornewood."

"Well, yes, but I also discovered another rune."

She lets out a little sound of excitement. "Another? What did this one look like?"

"Three parallel lines, one on top of the other. It showed me a vision of The Great North Road on a map."

"I know this one, too! It means 'the way.'"

"I believe Mama wants me to know how to enter her realm," I say. I sneak a glance at Lucy. It was harder than I thought to admit that aloud.

"It does seem like it," she says slowly. "Oh, but Wren, we must be careful. If Mama could never return, how do you think they'd react if one of us went through?"

My shoulders drop a bit. "You're right, of course. It's just . . ." I let my words fall away, since it's so difficult to express this *need* I have to see our mother's realm.

Lucy puts her hand on mine. "I feel it, too, you know. That longing. But then I think of Papa, or you and Robert, or what Mama always said, and it disappears. We can never miss what we've never had, right?"

"Then why show me at all?"

Lucy has no answer for me, and I didn't expect her to.

When we arrive at the park, it's as crowded as ever. I keep the horses close to the edge of the road so others can pass without jostling us. I steer toward the little copse of trees near the river, scanning for signs of Lord Thornewood.

"Are you ready to tell me why you're so excited to meet Lord Thornewood? I thought you didn't care for him."

I give her a sly smile. "Well, perhaps things have changed."

She grins like a five-year-old who's been handed a new toy. "I knew it. Have you finally admitted to yourself you care for him?"

"You could say that." My mind drifts to the night before, to our kiss, and the feel of his body pressed against mine.

"You didn't tell me I'd be burdensome when you invited me."

I shake free of my thoughts and glance at my sister. "You will *never* be a burden. I can't think of anyone I'd rather spend the day with—Lord Thornewood included."

"We have been rather busy lately. Grandmama seems to only be happy if everyone has their entire day filled to the brim." She turns to me. "Oh, but that reminds me, I heard Grandmama say something about Lord Blackburn to her steward before we left."

My hands tense on the reins. "What did she say?"

"I'm not sure. She was talking in a low voice, so I only caught his name. Why? Does that upset you?"

"He's a horrible man," I say vehemently, and she raises her eyebrows. I try not to think of the night before, but the thoughts come anyway. His disgusting proposition, his failed attempt at a kiss, and the way he threw me against the fence. The way he took my power from me.

Lucy's curious expression changes to one of concern. "Did something happen?"

I hesitate. A part of me wants to tell her—badly. The other part wants to protect my younger sister. In the end, though, she has the gift of arcana, too. She could become a target. "He is one of the men our mother warned us of."

Her mouth falls open in shock. "How do you know?"

"He assaulted me in the garden and siphoned away my arcana." My words are blunt, and my jaw tightens as the echoes of the anger and helplessness reverberate over me.

Lucy throws her arms around me. "Wren, I'm so sorry. Are you all right? Have you recovered?"

I feel some of my tension melt away at her touch. "I'm fine now."

Her head jerks up as she suddenly meets my gaze. "Oh, but what of Lord Thornewood? Is he—"

"No, not at all. Lord Thornewood is the opposite. He's much kinder than he first appeared."

She grins widely. "I knew it. Kind enough to marry?"

A surprising surge of hopefulness rises within me, and I dampen it. "I wouldn't go that far."

"And how will you avoid Lord Blackburn? Do you think if we told Grandmama—"

I shake my head. "Grandmama would never help. I'll have to think of something myself."

I guide the horses off the path and onto the thick grass until we reach a copse of trees. A low branch provides me with a place to secure their reins. I rub each of their velvety noses, glad for once my grandmother only keeps well-mannered horses.

"It feels so wonderful to be able to walk around without Grandmama watching our every move," Lucy says. She points to a bench surrounded by flowers. "Would you mind if I sit on that bench for a while and draw? It's so lovely here."

"Please do. Here, I'll walk with you."

I pace around behind Lucy when she settles on the bench. What if Lord Thornewood changed his mind? What if he thought of the kiss as a mistake? Maybe he thought I was too forward as well. I happen to glance up, and that's when I see him emerge from a small group of trees. He catches sight of us immediately and strides over, an uncharacteristic grin on his face.

"You came," he says.

"I could say the same to you," I say, trying unsuccessfully to suppress a grin of my own.

"Your doubts wound me as usual." He turns to Lucy and bows smartly. "Good morning to you, Miss Sinclair."

"Good morning, my lord." She dips her head shyly.

He tilts his head for a better view of the drawing in her hand. "Those are quite good," he says, and her eyes dart to his. "Even in black and white, it's a perfect rendering of the area."

As he continues to help my sister open up with casual talk of drawing, I have to restrain myself from pulling him aside and pressing my lips to his. Every time he glances at me, it's as though I can no longer control my thoughts.

"We must be boring your sister," Lord Thornewood says after a moment.

"Not at all," I protest. "On the contrary, I was deeply contemplating everything you said."

"Hm," he says and turns to Lucy, "should we quiz her then?"

To my surprise, Lucy laughs as though he is an old friend instead of an intimidating earl. "No, that would be cruel."

I shake my head. "When did you become co-conspirators against me?"

Lord Thornewood ignores my comment, as usual. He holds out his arm. "Shall we walk for a spell? I think we've distracted your sister from her drawing long enough."

I glance at her, but she only makes shooing motions at me. "Go," she says, "I'll be fine."

I take his arm, and we walk deeper in the woods. We're still within sight of my sister, but just barely.

After a moment, he says, "There's been something I've been meaning to ask you. I've been considering it for a while now." My heart thumps an unsteady rhythm against my rib cage. "Would you—and your family—like to join me at my country estate?"

I'm so shocked, I do nothing but stare at the fine veins of the nearby leaves for so long he finally adds, "Others will be invited, too. My brother James will be home from Oxford and has requested a house full of guests and a ball to greet him."

"I'd forgotten you had a brother," I say, and then realize I've completely ignored his main point. "I would love to visit your home."

He smiles, his carefully maintained mask disappearing for a whole two or three seconds. "Excellent. Your grandmother will not mind leaving town for a few days?"

I didn't think about Grandmama's reaction. It will be difficult to get her permission, but I am willing to do just about anything to get what I want. "Oh, I'm sure she'd love the chance. She so rarely leaves town after all."

"That reminds me," he says and steers me in the shade of a wide oak. "Was your grandmother terribly angry I brought you home last night?"

His voice is low, and he's close enough that if I just leaned forward an inch or two, our noses would touch.

"Not terribly, no," I murmur.

He reaches out and brushes a lock of hair from my neck, his fingers lingering just a moment too long. My breath hitches in my throat. "Good. Because I've only agreed to this party as a way to get you to my home." He grins wickedly.

We both hear the hooves approaching and jump apart. Well, I jump away from him. He holds his ground, looking around with a disinterested expression. Two ladies I don't know pass by, smiling in greeting.

A vein in my neck is throbbing as I meet his intense gaze. "You wish me to see your home?"

"I wish you to see a great many things, but yes, my estate is at the top of the list."

If I was the flirtatious type, now would be the time to say something clever and provocative. For once, my wit fails me. "Then I very much look forward to it."

He smiles as if I've said something much more intriguing. "I'm afraid our meeting today must be short in anticipation of your visit, as I must return home and prepare to depart London on the morrow." He offers his arm again. "Shall we return to your sister?"

Just before we are within hearing range of Lucy, I ask, "Who else will be invited?"

He winces. "Ah, that. I'd hoped to avoid telling you."

"It's that bad?"

"Miss Gray overheard me discussing my plan last night at the ball. I'm afraid an invitation was unavoidable."

I resist the urge to hang my head in defeat. Does Eliza have spies employed to watch Lord Thornewood's every move? "Very well."

Lord Thornewood gives me a half-grin. "There'll be many others there. Perhaps she won't even seek you out."

"It'll be the first thing she does, actually. But I thank you for attempting to comfort me. I know it was kindly meant."

He halts our progress and takes both my gloved hands in his. "Don't let her ruin your stay. Know this: I planned this frivolous ball with only you in mind. I care nothing for dancing, even less for socializing. But I find I'd do just about anything to have even the slimmest chance to be with you."

A quip jumps to the tip of the tongue, but instead I say, "I'm finding I'd do the same."

We stare at each other until I begin to think he might kiss me right here in front of everyone, but instead, he bows over my hand and presses a kiss to the back of it. My sister grins at us like it's our wedding day.

"I'll send word and a formal invitation first thing in the morning," he says. "Oh, and Miss Sinclair? Tell your servants to prepare your luggage but not to load your carriage. I will send my own vehicle to transport you."

With a smile and another kind word about Lucy's drawing, he leaves us.

"So," Lucy says as we both watch him walk away. "I take it we'll be seeing more of Lord Thornewood."

"Oh yes," I say, "a lot more."

SIXTEEN

WE arrive home in time for tea, and for once, I might even be able to tolerate my grandmother's presence. The smile has not left my face since my meeting with Lord Thornewood. Thrills of excitement dance inside me every time I call to mind our frustratingly brief conversation. My grandmother's dreadfully boring discussion of the various aspects of Society may be just the thing to calm me.

While Lucy resumes her studies with Miss Watts, I make my way to the parlor alone. Before I reach the door, a bevy of voices escapes from within. I pause, surprised to find my grandmother engaged in anything but her usual dull routine.

"Well then, Lady Sinclair, what stakes are we to play for today?" one of the voices asks.

"I would like the chance to win back my carriage," Grandmama says. "Though I wouldn't mind playing for two of your lovely riding horses, Lady Hasting."

"Those are high stakes indeed," another voice adds.

I am of a mind to agree with the last voice. Gambling is not such a surprising thing; most members of Society indulge themselves, even ladies. But I'm quite certain most ladies gamble for negligible amounts of money—not horses and carriages. Suddenly, I think of the missing barouche the night of my debut. I knew my grandmother to be cold but not reckless. Was this what Papa warned us of? Just how serious is her penchant for cards? This newfound aspect of her character sends a chill of apprehension up my spine. The talk of horses especially unnerves me. What is to stop her from gambling away one of the horses Robert brought back for me?

"If I am to put up two of my horses," Lady Hasting says, "then you must do the same."

Before my grandmother can answer, I rush through the door. Four ladies including Grandmama sit in pairs playing the illegal game of baccarat. I recognize Lady Hasting, an elaborate crimson hat upon her head. The other two ladies are dressed in an abundance of satin and jewels, but their names, like so many others introduced to me by my grandmother, escape me.

Grandmama greets me with an aggravated look. "Katherine, it is abominably rude to interrupt us in such an abrupt manner."

"Please forgive me for interrupting you," I say with mock sincerity, "but I couldn't help but overhear you about to gamble away the contents of your stables. As two of my horses are currently residing there, I came to be sure you would not include them in your ridiculous stakes."

"Really, Katherine," Lady Hasting says, the feathers of her hat quivering with her words, "this is most irregular."

Grandmama shares a long-suffering look with Lady Hasting. "You must all forgive my granddaughter. She lost her mother at such a young age, and she has not had the benefit of knowing when to hold her tongue."

One of the ladies makes a soft sound of sympathy and nods. "Such a terrible thing." Her soft look melts into one of calculation as she meets my gaze. "If you are concerned about the loss of your horses, dear, then why don't you join us for a game?"

"As I am unskilled at most card games, I must decline," I say, anger sharpening my tone. Baccarat may be the favorite game of the king, but I'd rather not risk participating.

"Alas, Katherine has many letters to write. Isn't that right, dear?" Grandmama says calmly, as if I am merely a child throwing a temper tantrum. When I obstinately remain standing in my spot, she sighs and says, "It wouldn't very well be honorable for me to gamble away something that does not belong to me, now would it?"

"Those are the rules," Lady Hasting adds when she sees me wavering.

"Very well," I say. "I'm sorry to have interrupted." Though I'm not sorry for much else. I have no doubt my grandmother would have done just as she pleased, whatever the consequences. As I return to my room, I am struck once again by how uncharacteristic gambling is for my grandmother. All the times she chided me for acting less than proper, and she treats her own parlor as though it were one of the gaming hells. I know but a few of the rules of gambling, only the ones Robert has seen fit to tell me, but I do know all debts must be settled immediately.

Worry makes its bed in the pit of my stomach as I keep watch on the stables from my window. It isn't until later, when the three ladies leave without any of the horses, that I finally allow myself to breathe a sigh of relief.

The next morning, the invitation arrives as promised. It's delivered by a liveried servant who refuses to hand off the creamy envelope to anyone but me. My name is scrolled in a bold hand across the front. On the back is Lord Thornewood's crest stamped in red wax. I clutch it to my chest and race up to my room to open it free from distraction.

The invitation is straightforward enough, containing all the information he told me at the park. It's the personal note to me that makes my breaths come a little faster. In the same bold handwriting, Lord Thornewood has written:

> *Dearest Katherine,*
> *I enjoyed our brief outing in the park, but I look forward to you setting foot at Thornewood. There I hope we will be able to steal a moment or two of privacy—perhaps like those shared in my carriage.*
> *Yours,*
> *C.*

I read and reread the note. So he *does* think about our kiss. His note all but implies he'd like the chance to do it again. A rush of excitement fills me at the thought that I'm not the only one who cannot stop thinking about that night.

I fold the letter and hide it in my reticule. I should probably dispose of it to avoid the risk of anyone ever finding it, but I can't bear the thought.

Now for the hard part. Convincing Grandmama. After my confront-ation with her only yesterday, she has been even chillier toward me than usual. But as I cannot walk myself to Lord Thornewood's estate, I must gain her permission.

I push open the door to her sitting room, my hand more tremulous on the handle than I would like. "Grandmama?" I call.

She looks up from her mahogany writing desk. "Yes?"

"May I come in?"

She covers whatever she was writing with a blank sheet of paper. I try not to feel offended—or suspicious. "I suppose. What is it?"

"This invitation arrived this afternoon from Lord Thornewood." I hand it to her, hoping it'll do the talking for me.

"Hm. This is quite the opportunity. But we'd have to leave on the morrow."

"It's only for a couple days, though, so we won't need much luggage. Lord Thornewood also said he will send transportation for us."

Her eyes scan the invitation again, and I hold my breath. She looks at me. "And you wouldn't mind staying at his estate?"

I shake my head. "On the contrary, I think it'd be a lovely change of scenery." When I see some of the tension leave her, I add, "Penelope and Lady Hasting have already assured Lord Thornewood they'll be there."

Grandmama lets out a breathy sound that sounds suspiciously like a snort. "Yes, she informed me yesterday. It comes as no surprise. Lady Hasting jumps at any opportunity to parade her daughter in front of potential suitors."

"He personally invited Lucy, too," I say, grasping for my only other leverage.

"Oh? And what did your sister say?"

"She was eager to go."

Grandmama sighs. "Very well. Call my steward to me at once. We mustn't waste a moment if we are to leave in so short a time. Earls are unbe-lievable in this regard. No care given to the convenience of anyone else."

She's still ranting as I run to find Mr. Bancroft. Let her rant all she wants. I'm just grateful it was easier convincing her than I thought.

True to his word, Lord Thornewood sends a vehicle to bring us to his estate. Only it isn't the carriage we expected. In its place is a gleaming motor car, its chauffeur impeccably dressed in black.

"I am Jasper," he says with a short bow. "Please allow me to escort you to Thornewood estate as his lordship requested."

"Well this is quite the surprise," Grandmama says, almost grudgingly.

Lucy turns to me with excitement shining in her eyes. "Oh, Wren, is this not amazing? Not even Papa has a motor car!"

I can only stare at the beautiful machine, a thrill racing through me at the thought of being driven in it.

Jasper helps the servants load our luggage, and then assists us into the back, the black leather seats buttery soft.

"Thank you, Jasper," I say. "Lord Thornewood had informed us he would be sending transportation, but we never guessed it would be something quite as modern as this."

Jasper smiles. "His lordship wants you there as soon as possible, milady. This will cut your travel time down to only two hours."

With a short bow, he closes the door and walks around to the front of the motor car. The engine starts with a rumble, and with a little jolt, we are on our way.

Grandmama sits across from Lucy and me in the motor car, preventing all meaningful conversation, but with the scenery racing by faster than I have ever seen, I am content to look out the window.

Everything looks so green after being in the cold city. Now we're outside of London, the countryside is rich farmland with rolling hills shaded by tall, leafy trees. Homesickness stabs low in my chest as I think of my father's estate. The Season has been more interesting than I could have hoped, but I still desperately miss home.

I let my mind wander and even nap for a while, until the motor car turns off the main road and onto a long, curving path. I sit up straighter in the seat, eager to catch the first glimpse of Thornewood. A large lake shimmers in the sun, reflecting the enormous oak trees that tower over it.

Lucy sucks in her breath as we go around the final curve. "Oh, my. I don't believe I've ever seen such a thing in England."

I just stare at the house—if it can even be called such a common name. I cannot believe Lord Thornewood didn't breathe a word of warning. Glimmering white in the afternoon sun, its Persian architecture all graceful lines and rounded arches, like a miniature Taj Mahal, stands the Thornewood manor. Lucy's right. I've never seen such a thing in all of England and am surprised I hadn't heard of it before. There are many aristocrats fascinated by all things Eastern, especially Indian, but never to the point their home is a replication of one of the great wonders of the world.

Even Grandmama's mouth hangs open in shock. "What in the world?" she says.

The chauffeur takes us right to the front steps, and instead of the liveried servants one would expect of an earl's household, lithe Indian men with copper skin and jet black hair emerge to take our luggage. My hands shake as I take the footman's proffered hand. It's like I've stepped into the words of a storybook. The front door opens again, and Lord Thornewood jogs down the steps to meet us.

His smile is wide and welcoming. "Kath—Miss Sinclair," he corrects himself with a glance at my grandmother, "I trust your trip was uneventful."

"Very," I say, acutely aware of how my knees now feel like jelly. "Well, until we drove up the path to Thornewood, of course."

Lucy joins me, and he bows. "Miss Lucy, I'm so happy your governess could spare you."

"I am, too," she says, without a hint of her usual shyness. "I wouldn't have wanted to miss this. Your estate is breathtaking."

For once, his confidence falters, replaced by an almost boyish hesitancy. "I know it must be a terrible shock. I find it's often better just to see it with your own eyes, which is why I so cruelly didn't prepare you."

"It's beautiful," I say, my wide eyes still taking in this exotic piece of India transplanted to English soil.

Some of the tension leaves his face as if he had been waiting for some sign of my approval. "I cannot take credit for it, of course. My father was enamored with the story of the great Taj Mahal. He spent much of his time in India, actually."

"I would love to visit India," I say, watching the servants carry in our luggage, their silken clothes fluttering in the breeze. "So I thank you for giving us the opportunity."

He smiles. "Of course. Ah, Lady Sinclair," he says when my grandmother joins us, "it's an honor to have you and your granddaughters at my home."

"Your home indeed," she says. "A home like no other in England. No, the pleasure is ours, my lord. I know both my girls have grown restless in London. This will be a welcome retreat."

"I'm glad to hear it. Come, then. I'll show you to your rooms."

We follow, and I try not to stare at his wide back, which I know from experience is knotted with muscle. It certainly doesn't help he's casually dressed, in only a light linen shirt, riding breeches, and tall boots.

When we enter the house, his boots ring out over the marble floors. I have to force my mouth closed, as I am tempted to stare at the soaring ceilings and enormous crystal chandelier. Everything is marble. Marble and ornate Persian rugs threaded with gold. Wide columns in the entryway give the impression we're inside an emperor's Eastern palace. He leads us up a sweeping staircase lined by beautiful paintings—the kind you can get lost in. Lucy gazes at them with naked admiration.

"This will be your room, Lady Sinclair," Lord Thornewood says, standing to one side of the doorway. Grandmama breezes through, much less humble and appreciative than she should be.

"This is a well thought out room," she says, gazing around her. Despite the marble floors, the room could be like any other found in a grand English estate. Perfect for my grandmother. I lean in to see what view she has from her window—it's of a quaint English-style garden. "This will do nicely. I thank you."

"Absolutely," Lord Thornewood says. He turns back to Lucy and me. "Shall we continue?"

"Did you choose each room we'd stay in?" I ask.

"Naturally." He leads us to another room, five doors down from my grandmother's. "I chose this one with you in mind, Lucy."

A wide smile brightens her face. "This is perfect, my lord, thank you."

The room is dainty and feminine, and colorful paintings adorn every wall. The rounded archways continue here, and exotic leafy foliage makes it feel as though we truly have left England for the weekend. His obvious love for my sister makes my heart swell.

"Your maid will be here shortly." He reaches out and tucks my hand under his elbow, and his grin is mischievous. "Now for your room."

"My room?" I ask, my brows furrowed. "I'm not staying with Lucy?"

He looks at me askance. "Why would I have you share when I have twenty-three guest rooms?"

His question is so characteristically arrogant I can't help but smile. "Very well. Lead on."

We walk down the hallway and pass many rooms. I try to count how far away I am from Lucy, but I lose track. "Are you trying to get me lost?" I ask.

"Not at all," he says as we turn the corner. "You won't sound nearly so irritated when you see your view."

As soon as I walk into the room, I stop and stare. The entire wall opposite me is windows. Floor-to-ceiling length windows. The doors to the balcony are thrown open, pale curtains waving in the soft breeze. The smell of flowers fills the room, both from the number of bouquets in golden vases and from the garden beyond. The view is of the shimmering lake and gardens. In fact, from this room, it seems I can see the whole of his estate—at least the part of it that spreads from the front of the house.

But it's the marble tub in the middle of the room that gives me pause. It's perfectly round and set up on a dais, appearing as if it grew out of the marble floor beneath it. It's big enough for two people to bathe comfortably. I have never seen the like in all my life. The only bathtub I've ever enjoyed has been made of hammered copper.

It takes me a moment to realize my hand is still attached to his arm. "Does this please you?" he asks, his voice rumbling in my ear.

"Very much so," I say, my eyes still on the sweeping view from my windows. The bed is even situated in such a way I will be able to watch the sun rise above the trees while propped against pillows. It'll be like sleeping outside—something I haven't done since I was very small.

He runs his hand along the edge of the tub. "What think you of this?"

Still in shock, I answer him completely uncensored. "I think it's big enough for two." The blush spreads up my neck as nervous flutters release in my abdomen.

His eyes darken. "Truly, Katherine, I believe you'll be the death of me. I dare not even ask if that was an invitation."

I give him the coy smile I've been suppressing since the moment we met. Its impact is lessened, I'm sure, by my furious blush.

He must take pity on me because he changes the subject. "I know you are probably tired from your trip, but would you care to walk with me?"

"I would—especially if we are to walk in one of the gardens. Truly your groundskeeper must be very talented."

"Does this mean you approve of Thornewood?" All hints of his teasing smile are gone.

I meet his gaze. "It's more beautiful than I could have imagined."

A look of relief passes across his face. "It's been a long time since I cared what someone would think of my home—if I ever have."

His words are simple, but the underlying meaning speeds my heart and sends warmth traveling through my chest. "I can't think how to thank you properly for such a beautiful room."

A slow grin spreads on his face. "You could kiss me."

He's teasing, but his intense gaze tells me he's also serious. Do I dare? My eyes drop to his mouth. It must have been enough of acquiescence because he takes one determined stride toward me and wraps me in his arms.

I hold my breath as his mouth descends upon mine.

Before my mind even fully comprehends the feeling of his full lips, my body responds as if we've kissed every day of our lives. Could it possibly be like this for everyone? This all-consuming need for another person?

I press into him, my body melding against the hard contours of his. He groans, deepening the kiss. He draws the tip of his tongue across my bottom lip, slowly, teasingly, and warmth floods me. My hands reach up to touch his hair, and it's as thick as I imagined it to be but surprisingly soft. He trails kisses on my jaw and down my neck, and I arch back brazenly to give him better access.

His hands skim the sides of my body, strong but gentle, and I wish I was wearing a tea-gown with no corset instead of the heavier satin traveling dress. Desire pools low in my abdomen, a primitive craving for him to touch my bare skin. As if he hears my thoughts, his fingers skim the side of my neck down to my décolletage, teasing the tops of my breasts.

I want to feel him, to revel in the differences between our bodies. I trail my hands down from his hair to his wide shoulders and lower still, to the unyielding muscles of his back.

He smiles into my lips. "Your tentative touch is driving me mad."

"And you've been teasing me for the past few minutes," I say between kisses.

"Only because I don't want to push you too far," he says, pulling away to meet my heavy gaze. "I swear to you it isn't my intention to kiss you so soundly, but you make it bloody hard not to when you respond to me like that."

A surprised laugh escapes me. It's a heady realization to know I can affect him just as much as he affects me. "Shall we promise to be good for the rest of the afternoon then? Perhaps go on that walk you mentioned earlier?"

"Yes, a walk sounds safe. We'll even invite your sister to make it that much more proper. Maybe then I will be able to keep my hands off you."

The hall is quiet as we walk, and I try to compose myself. I'm more than a little self-conscious about the contact, but only because I'm afraid of either Grandmama or another guest seeing us—not that I'd seen anyone else.

"Have the others arrived?" I ask, with another paranoid glance around.

"Everyone else will arrive on the morrow."

I raise my eyebrows. "Even your brother?"

He smiles. "No, you'll meet James soon enough."

He's back to being cryptic, so I try to relax for once and not try to control the situation. He stops at the room I think is Lucy's and knocks.

"Care to join us for a walk?" Lord Thornewood asks when Lucy answers the door, his expression all innocence.

"Oh, I'd love to," Lucy says. "Would you mind waiting for a moment while I get my drawing materials?"

"Not at all."

She rushes back inside her room, and I keep my eyes focused on one of the paintings on the wall. I will *not* review the previous ten minutes in my mind. I will *not* think of the way his soft lips felt against mine.

"You're blushing," Lord Thornewood says quietly, a self-satisfied grin on his face.

"Ready," Lucy calls, clutching her drawing paper and charcoal to her chest as if it was a beloved child.

I thought Lord Thornewood would release my hand when Lucy joined us, but he keeps it tucked under his elbow as if it is the most natural thing in the world. To my sister's credit, she doesn't even give me a questioning look.

He leads us out a side door and into a garden blossoming with hydrangea, peonies, and ivy. The garden is controlled chaos, with blooms exploding over one another and atop trellises. Lucy makes a happy little squeak, her eyes darting around for the best vantage spot.

I lean over to smell one of the peonies' sweet fragrance. What would it be like to live in such a place? To feel every day as if I've stepped into a story from *Arabian Nights*? I haven't even seen the stable yet, but I'm sure it's as amazing as the rest of his estate. When I glance back at Lord Thornewood, he's looking at me in that intense way that makes my body come alive.

A loud bark startles me, and I turn around just in time to see a massive wolfhound barreling toward us. His tongue is lolling out, so despite his considerable size, I don't worry he plans to attack.

"James," Lord Thornewood shouts, "come get your bloody hound before it knocks one of these ladies over."

James strolls toward us, completely unconcerned by his brother's obvious anger. His resemblance to Lord Thornewood is uncanny, though he is much more lean and lanky. He has the same hair, the same strong jaw, but his eyes must have come from the other parent as they are much lighter.

"To me, Bear," James says with an impish half-grin. The wolfhound goes immediately to his side, calm and obedient. I stifle a laugh as I wonder if he sent the dog ahead just to rile Lord Thornewood.

Lord Thornewood pinches the bridge of his nose and gestures for his brother to join us. "You've made your entrance. Now come meet our guests."

His grin still in place, he executes a short bow as Lord Thornewood makes the introductions. Lucy keeps her eyes everywhere but James, her momentary air of ease all but disappeared.

"James, the Sinclairs are daughters of Robert Sinclair, Father's dear friend."

James nods. "I know. And you've been asked to make the elder Miss Sinclair the talk of London." He turns to me and arches his eyebrows. "Well? Has my brother been successful?"

Lord Thornewood groans. "You don't have to answer that. In fact, you don't have to answer any of his questions."

James laughs. "You're just afraid of what she'll say. My brother has the advantage of being a wealthy earl, but his personality can be somewhat lacking."

"I recognize sibling banter when I hear it," I say, "so I think I will take Lord Thornewood's advice and decline to respond."

"No fun at all," James says. He turns to Lucy. "And what of you, Miss Lucy? Do you believe my brother has been any help to your sister?"

"Leave her be, James," Lord Thornewood says. "If I'm lacking, then you are overbearing. The girl is too well-bred to respond to any of your taunts."

James shrugs and takes a seat on one of the benches. The wolfhound stays stuck to his side. "Since you won't even let me talk to either of these beautiful ladies, I hope you have invited other guests for the ball tomorrow."

"Yes."

"So a round of cricket in the early afternoon and a ball in the evening?"

"If you wish."

"My brother is a sphinx," James says to me, and I swallow a laugh. "He *is* capable of holding longer conversations, but he has to be passionate about something." He glances at me again. "Or someone."

"Enough," Lord Thornewood says. "Come, my brother has taken over the garden with his hound and his running commentary."

I laugh. "My lord, it's fine. Your brother is not as bothersome to us as he is to you. Trust me, I have a brother, too. They only have the power to annoy their siblings."

James holds up his hands. "I'll go. I need to settle in anyway." He bows again toward Lucy and me. "It was truly a pleasure to meet you."

"And you, my lord," I say.

He smiles, his eyes crinkling at the corners. "This will be a fun party indeed."

SEVENTEEN

THE morning is refreshingly peaceful without the constant noise of London's streets. Rays of sunlight glint off the lake, turning the water into liquid crystal as I sit at the mahogany vanity.

Devi, the maid Lord Thornewood provided for me, runs a brush through my hair and smiles at me in the mirror. She wears the traditional Indian sari, a lovely rose color that looks so rich against her jet-black hair. "You have lovely hair, my lady."

"I thank you, but I'm afraid I can never do anything with it. If it was left to me, I'd look more banshee than lady."

There's a kindness in her eyes as she laughs. "No indeed. Hair like this won't take me long at all."

"You're more talented than me then," I say, sorting through my jewelry for something simple to wear. I point over my shoulder at the gown I've removed from my trunk. "Do you think that will be suitable for what my lord has planned?"

She turns to look. "Perhaps a wrap, too, for warmth."

I nod as I watch her smooth my hair. It makes me think of my own maid at home. "Devi," I say after a moment, and she meets my eyes in the mirror, "have you always been a lady's maid?"

She bobs her head. "Yes, my lady. Since I was sixteen."

I watch her fingers gain control of my thick hair, deftly weaving it into a soft chignon. "How do you remain so skilled when there are no ladies to wait on here?"

Her smile is wistful. "My fingers haven't forgotten what to do. But you're right, it's been a long time since I've had the pleasure of serving in the position I was originally brought here for."

"Were you Lady Thornewood's maid?" I ask.

"Yes, and I miss her terribly. It was such a tragedy to die so young, leaving those boys without a mother."

I suspected Lord Thornewood's mother was no longer living, since he made no mention of her. Now I know for sure. "He and I have that in common, then."

Her hands pause in the act of smoothing my hair. "I am sorry to hear that, my lady." She resumes her work with a shake of her head. "My lord was much too young when he began caring for his younger brother. He's always taken on too many responsibilities."

He had lost his father, too, I know. My own had attended the funeral, though I can no longer recall when it was. "When did Lord Thornewood's father die?"

"Not terribly long ago. Two years. But he was never as involved with his family as Lady Thornewood. And there's no replacing a mother."

I think of my own kind father, of the way Robert and I had helped raise Lucy. What would it have been like if it was only Lucy and me? Without the benefit of Papa's wisdom or Robert's wit? If I had to shoulder the entire burden of the responsibility?

"Lord Thornewood must be a very kind brother."

"Oh, the kindest, my lady," she says with great enthusiasm. "I've never had a more generous employer. All the servants know we can go to him with anything, and we will be heard."

Such a different picture than the one I formed of Lord Thornewood when I first met him. I wonder, though, if he's generous and kind enough to accept even my true identity. I frown and look down at my hands. The closer I grow to him, the more I am afraid of my secret ruining everything.

"There," Devi says, patting the last few stray hairs in place. "Is it to your liking?"

I drag myself back to the present moment and hide my worries with a smile. "It's lovely, thank you."

"Anything else you need, my lady?"

"No, nothing, Devi. Thank you."

She smiles and bobs her head, closing the door behind her. As I fasten a gold cross around my neck, my father's words return to me unbidden. *It never prevented me from marrying your mother.* Papa knew about Mama, but he married her for love. Still, I struggle with the idea there are two such men in the world. Can Lord Thornewood possibly be as open-minded?

I shake my head and stand. It's no use staying in my room fretting. Better to face the day.

I find him in the library, sitting in front of the fireplace. The fire crackles and licks at the logs, and I watch its flames for a moment, suddenly unsure of myself. His face is in profile to me as he reads a thick leather-bound book of some kind. The firelight glints off his dark hair. My skirts rustle as I take another step forward and he glances up.

"You're up early," he says as he stands.

"I'd be up this early every day if Grandmama would let me. It's much more peaceful when only the birds and servants are awake."

His eyes take on a teasing glint. "Is that a hint you'd rather explore the library alone?"

"Even if I did, I very much doubt you'd do anything other than exactly what you wanted."

"You're right about that," he says unapologetically. "Since you're joining me, shall I ring for another cup of tea?"

My stomach rumbles, and I press my hand over my abdomen to stifle the noise. I smile sheepishly. "Yes, if you don't mind."

He pulls a velvet rope hung amongst the draperies. "Won't you sit?" He gestures to the settee across from his wingback chair. "Or would you rather hover there amongst the bookcases?"

I cast him a withering look to mask how nervous I feel.

"I trust you slept well last night?" he asks when I sit.

"Yes," I say with a sigh of pleasure, "it was so lovely to escape the London street noise. I'd all but forgotten how peaceful it is in the country."

"London is one of the most miserable places on Earth. I much prefer it here."

My lips part in surprise. "Truly? I thought you to be a connoisseur of all London had to offer." When his brows draw in concern, I hastily add, "That is, things of a . . . proper nature." I look away, wishing desperately for the cup of tea, or at least a servant to interrupt.

He leans back in his chair, appraising. "You believe the rumors then. That I'm a terrible rake?"

"I . . . had not—" I glance at the door, willing someone to enter. "Not really," I finish lamely. The truth is I've learned so much about Lord Thornewood in the past few days, I'm not sure *what* to think.

"Hm," he says and stands. "Does it bother you that you are very much alone with a man rumored to be a rake?" He walks to my chair, leans down so we are eye-level. "Alone in that man's home?"

His voice is husky, and his dark eyes hold mine captive. What game is he playing? My chest rises and falls rapidly, but an answer comes to my mind. One I've already realized to be the absolute truth. "It doesn't bother me at all. I trust you."

The intensity in his eyes melts into relief. "I thank you for your trust," he says quietly. "Perhaps you'll trust me enough to let me steal another kiss?"

This time, I reach for him instead of the other way around. This kiss is rougher than before. I kiss him, savoring the way he caresses not only my lips, but my neck and hair as well. He hauls me to my feet, his hands sliding down from around my waist to my hips. He pulls me close until we are pressed together wantonly.

My hands rove over his firm chest. A brief smile touches my lips as I feel his heart pounding a furious rhythm to match my own. I am aware our behavior has long since passed from merely improper to scandalous—something I never would have thought I'd succumb to—and yet I willingly fan the flames within my own body. I want him. I want him, and I'm beginning not to care a whit for the consequences.

"Why do you taste so good?" he asks in almost a groan. He covers my mouth with his before I can answer.

His hands explore my body more boldly this time, cupping my breasts over my bodice. He rubs his thumbs over my nipples until they are straining against the fabric.

"Please," I say breathlessly, not even comprehending what I'm pleading for.

When his hand slips between my bare breast and the fabric, I nearly cry out. He continues to kiss me thoroughly all the while massaging first one nipple and then the other.

"God, you feel beautiful in my hands," he says, his voice husky against my throat.

I whimper in response. I'm becoming a quivering mass of nothing but primitive feeling again, nearly drunk on his deep kisses and firm touch.

Thank God the footman knocks before entering and we have time to jump apart.

"You called, my lord?" the young man asks. To his credit, he doesn't seem affected in the least by the palpable tension in the room.

I turn away from the door, touching my fingertips to my lips. I know even without a mirror my cheeks are flushed and my lips are red as blood.

"Tea," Lord Thornewood practically growls. "Thank you, Rama," he adds in a softer tone.

"Right away, my lord."

Lord Thornewood rakes his hand through his hair, a gesture I've quickly learned to recognize as frustration. "You must forgive me, Katherine," he says firmly. "I'm treating you abominably. You deserve so much better than to be seduced in a library."

"Then you will have to strive to do better," I say, still flushed from being thoroughly kissed.

He half-laughs, half-groans and strides over to the library door. "I'm leaving it open," he says, "before I give in to temptation."

I smooth my skirts and walk over to the bookcases to hide my smile. Running my fingers along the leather spines, I sigh. The whole room reminds me of Papa so much a stab of homesickness hits me in the stomach.

"Take any book you'd like," Lord Thornewood says behind me.

"There are so many. It'd take my entire stay to peruse your shelves." He has everything from the *Aeneid* to medical texts.

"Then you'll have to stay until you've read the title on every spine."

I smile and return my eyes to the books, suddenly nervous again. Would he kiss me as fervently if he knew what I am?

"Forgive me for interrupting again, my lord," Rama says from the doorway, "but I've brought your tea."

"Very good, Rama."

Rama sets the tea service down on the low side table and pours the steaming hot liquid into dainty blue and white cups. I take it from him gratefully and add two sugar cubes and a splash of milk. Lord Thornewood, I notice, drinks his straight—just as my father does.

"Mrs. White sent up some scones to tide you over until breakfast is served," Rama says, and I could kiss whoever this Mrs. White is. I'm half-starved, and I know it's only a matter of time before my stomach outs me again.

Before I have a chance to sit down and enjoy my tea and scone, Lord Thornewood's brother joins us.

"Oh, am I interrupting?" James asks from the doorway, his expression more mischievous than apologetic.

"Not at all," I say with a welcoming smile. "We were just enjoying some tea before breakfast."

He walks over to the tea service and smiles hugely. "And Mrs. White's scones. How delightful." He stuffs one into his mouth and sighs contentedly.

Lord Thornewood shakes his head. "Kindly pretend I raised you right— at least in front of Miss Sinclair."

"What?" he asks around a mouthful. I laugh behind my tea cup.

Lord Thornewood smiles despite himself. "You may delight in vexing me, but at least you're entertaining Miss Sinclair." He sits in the same wing-back chair. "Come and sit with us then. Tell us of Oxford."

"That's right," I say. "You've been away at Oxford. My brother attends there as well."

James grins. "Oh, I'm well acquainted with Robert. He and I have spent a lot of time . . . studying together."

Lord Thornewood snorts. "More like enjoying all the gaming clubs have to offer."

"Hm," I say, pursing my lips like a governess. "Is that so?"

"Now you've made her cross with me," James accuses his brother. "Robert does very well at Oxford, and he never gambles for more than a few pounds."

"How comforting," I say, imagining my brother gambling and drinking away in the gaming hells.

Before I can interrogate him on what exactly my brother has been up to at Oxford, a man wearing a rumpled suit—as though wrinkled from a long journey—strides into the room. He has the bearing of someone of a higher station than a servant, but from his manner of dress, I do not believe him to be a fellow peer. He is tall, with black hair and eyes, and could easily be Rama's brother save for a prominent Roman nose.

"My lord, forgive the intrusion," the man says, his tone serious and his bushy eyebrows drawn low, "but you said to seek you out as soon as I returned."

Lord Thornewood jumps to his feet, surprising both James and myself. "Yes, yes, of course, Tavi." He makes a short bow to me. "If you will excuse me for just a moment, Miss Sinclair. Tavi has been making some business inquiries for me and has only just returned."

"By all means," I say, though I am not entirely convinced business would produce such an anxious reaction.

When the door closes behind Lord Thornewood and Tavi, James turns to me with both eyebrows raised. "Well, that was unexpected. It must be something terribly important to produce that extreme a reaction in my apathetic brother." He leans in conspiratorially. "I have to admit, if you weren't here to provide witness to such bad behavior, I would follow them and eavesdrop."

I smile, secretly agreeing with him. "They did seem rather intense. But perhaps this was a particularly exciting business venture?"

James makes a noise of dismissal. I take a sip of tea, trying in vain to calm the growing suspicion and anxiety churning within me. When I look up again, I find James watching me with an appraising smile.

My hand flutters to my mouth. "I have crumbs on my lips, don't I?"

"Not that I can see. No, I am smiling because I think I have divined the true purpose of Tavi's errand."

"Ah," I say, trying and failing to mimic his nonchalance. "And what have you foreseen?"

"I don't want to ruin any of my beloved brother's plans, but I will say I shouldn't be at all surprised if he sent his most trusted man to acquire a certain piece of jewelry."

He only continues to grin at me like the Cheshire Cat while I furrow my brows at his cryptic pronouncement.

The door opens, and we both turn. Lord Thornewood strides into the library. "Forgive me for leaving you at the mercy of my brother," he says, any hint of his dealings with Tavi hidden behind his usual façade. "I hope he has managed to carry on a decent conversation with you."

"But of course, Colin. I am not the cretin you so desperately want me to be."

"He has been perfectly entertaining, I assure you," I say.

"We were discussing the merits of eavesdropping on secretive earls," James says, and I feel the heat of a blush spread across my cheeks. "Miss Sinclair was skeptical, but I assured her it was a delightful pastime."

Lord Thornewood only shakes his head. "You are welcome to eavesdrop on me any time. I have asked you many times to express more of an interest in our family estates and business ventures."

His response is so calmly rational that I realize how silly I've been—did I not just tell the man I trusted him? And how terribly egotistical of me to even suspect the conversation had anything to do with me.

"Oh, yes, a conversation on business," James says, with a little wink in my direction. My blush spreads to my neck.

The footman returns, saving me from any further teasing by Lord Thornewood's mischievous brother. "My lord, breakfast is served in the formal dining room."

"Thank you, Rama," Lord Thornewood says. "Have you informed our other guests?"

"Yes, my lord. Lady Sinclair has been waiting for you in the dining room since she came downstairs—she insisted," he adds when Lord Thornewood makes as if to protest. "She said she would be more comfortable there instead of the library. Miss Sinclair should be there shortly."

"Very good, Rama. Thank you."

He turns to me and offers his arm. "Shall we?"

I take it, ignoring the fluttery feeling in my stomach. I'm relieved to know it's beyond the power of human beings to read minds. Because I cannot stop imagining what it'd be like to have tea and breakfast with Lord Thornewood every morning.

EIGHTEEN

WHAT is on the agenda for today, my lord?" Grandmama asks when we are all seated for breakfast.

I let out a barely perceptible sigh. Her love of a schedule is beyond annoying. I could care less if we did nothing but wander the grounds all day.

Lord Thornewood places his glass down on the table and sits back in his chair as if in thought. "James suggested a game of cricket to entertain us before the ball this evening."

"Croquet would be better," Grandmama say with a dour nod of her head. "Though either way, I would be an observer only."

Then what does it matter? I think to myself, barely resisting the urge to say it aloud. I can't imagine why my grandmother is being so rude.

"I do hope you play in a space with plenty of shade," she adds, and I shoot Lucy an incredulous look. Lucy shakes her head, her cheeks lightly flushed.

But Lord Thornewood only smiles good-naturedly. "I will do my utmost to assure your comfort, madam."

"You're a gracious host," she says.

I take a bite of my toast, hoping she has nothing more to add. If she does, the butler's sudden appearance dissuades her.

"My lord," the heavyset butler says, "forgive the interruption, but some of your guests have arrived—early," he adds with an apologetic glance in our direction. He is the first English servant I've seen since we've arrived, but he almost seems out of place in this Indian-style paradise.

"Not a problem, Worthington," Lord Thornewood says, but I can see from the tightness of his mouth he's annoyed. When I hear the familiar high-pitched voice carry to us from the foyer, I understand why.

Rama holds open the door to the dining room, looking harried. "Miss Gray and Miss Uppington, my lord," he announces, Eliza and Amelia on his heels.

Lord Thornewood and his brother stand, and I plaster a tight-lipped smile on my face. After the usual pleasantries, Lord Thornewood says, "Worthington, would you mind having more places set for Miss Gray and Miss Uppington?" He turns his attention back to Eliza and Amelia. "Please join us," he says, and indicates the two seats next to Lucy.

I eye my unfinished eggs longingly, since etiquette dictates I cannot eat until Eliza and Amelia are served.

"Your estate is breathtaking, my lord," Eliza says, her eyes darting about the room, resting briefly on every piece of china, crystal, and silver, as if taking inventory. "Amelia and I were just saying we cannot wait to see our rooms."

"Actually," Lord Thornewood says, "I thought you'd be more comfortable sharing a room, as you're so close."

I glance down at my plate, suddenly nervous to see her reaction. Much as I love the fact I've one-upped her with a spectacular room of my own, I hate to see what she'll do when she finds out.

"Oh?" she says, her enthusiasm dampened.

"How lovely and thoughtful," Amelia interjects, a genuine smile on her face.

Eliza glances at my sister, who sits to her left. "I'm sure the room you have with Lucy is quite comfortable," she says to me.

With a wolfish grin, James speaks up for the first time. "Actually, Miss Sinclair has her own room, with an attractive view of the lake."

I want to kick him beneath the table.

Her eyes narrow. "Oh?" she repeats.

Lucy folds and unfolds her napkin as I glare at James. Grandmama, who seems to have no interest in the conversation whatsoever, continues to sip her tea.

Lord Thornewood, as unapologetic as ever, merely shrugs. "The lighting in the younger Miss Sinclair's room is more conducive for drawing whereas the elder Miss Sinclair has a fondness for nature."

Eliza affects a saccharine smile. "How thoughtful of you to think of such things. You are truly a superior host."

Lord Thornewood bows his head at the compliment just as the rest of the food arrives.

It isn't until well after luncheon that we are able to watch the gentleman play a game of cricket. Evidently at least eight players are needed, and the rest of the guests didn't arrive until noon.

Penelope sits by my side on a blanket beneath a wide oak as we watch James bowl to his brother at bat.

"Are they on opposite teams?" Penelope asks, tilting her head up so she can see from beneath her wide-brimmed hat.

"Yes," I say with a grin, "they're competitive that way."

Penelope gives me a little nudge with her shoulder. "You sound as if you know them well already."

"Well enough. Lord James seems to love nothing more than to annoy his brother. It's quite amusing." I pause as I think of how his little game at breakfast has set Eliza and me even more at odds. "Well, perhaps he does tease at the expense of others sometimes."

Penelope fans herself nervously. "Keep him away from me then. I've had enough teasing from Eliza—enough to last a lifetime. And your wonderful brother isn't here to shield me."

A cool breeze tugs at our clothes and hair, and I pull my emerald green wrap tighter around me. Lord Thornewood catches my eye as he bats, his grin arrogantly confident. I smile back.

Penelope gives me a little nudge. When I turn to look at her, she indicates I should look to my left. I stifle a groan as Eliza and Amelia approach us.

"You have such a nice vantage point here," Eliza says with a tight smile, "Amelia and I thought we'd join you."

"If it wouldn't be a bother," Amelia adds.

"Of course not," Eliza answers for us. "Penelope and Katherine are the epitome of graciousness. I've always said so."

"Please," I say with a sarcastic edge to my voice, "join us."

After seating herself on the blanket and arranging her skirts just so, Eliza touches Penelope's arm. "Penelope, dear, how do you like your room? I was amazed by how tasteful and elegant mine is."

Penelope sneaks a glance at me, as if unsure what to make of Eliza's question. I watch Eliza with tension in my neck and shoulders. "Aside from sharing it with Mama, it's very comfortable."

"Oh, I see. So you're sharing with your mother. Lord Thornewood was kind enough to arrange for Amelia and me to have a room together." She taps a nail against her chin. "But what's *so* interesting is Katherine was given her own room." She trills a fake laugh. "What could that mean, Penelope? What secret plans must Lord Thornewood have?"

Penelope flounders for words. A cold feeling churns inside me. Even Amelia shifts positions, as if uncomfortable.

"I'm sure he didn't give much thought to it," I say.

Eliza tilts her head. "No? I wonder, though. I wonder about a lot of things, really. That reminds me, dear Katherine. Have you heard any news from Gloucestershire?"

I stiffen and try not to answer her defensively. It's clear she's baiting me, and though I have proof Lord Blackburn is a member of the Order, I still have no reason to think Eliza is anything more than a gossipmonger. "Not lately, no," I say.

The sound of the cricket bat connecting with another ball causes us all to look up, and Eliza erupts in loud applause for Lord Thornewood. Though I haven't been watching with rapt attention, I can tell he's been doing rather well—especially since his brother has been wearing nothing but a glower on his face for the past ten minutes. I'm simply happy it served the purpose in distracting Eliza from her current game of torture.

Lord Thornewood turns, his eyes searching for a moment. When they land on me, he smiles widely.

"I *know* there's something odd about you," Eliza says, her voice low and much too close to my ear, "and I mean to find what it is. No rebellious country mouse could secure the interest from such a gentleman, of that I'm sure." Louder she says to Amelia, "Lord Thornewood and Lord James must feel neglected without us to watch and cheer them on. Shall we join them?"

Amelia nods eagerly. "Yes, let's."

Eliza and Amelia move closer to the field, and I am left with a cold feeling of doubt. What if Eliza were to make good on her promise?

"What did she say to you?" Penelope asks, the bridge of her nose wrinkled with concern.

"Oh, you know," I say lightly, "the usual thinly veiled threats."

She laughs. "Jealousy is such an ugly thing."

I agree with her there. Unfortunately, jealousy is also a destructive force when wielded by someone like Eliza. It would be different if I had nothing to hide.

It occurs to me I haven't seen Lucy for quite some time. I spot her still in Grandmama's clutches and wave her over. She shoots me a grateful look.

"I couldn't get away," she says. She folds her legs beneath her and joins us on the blanket. "She wouldn't stop complaining of the breeze, or of the sunshine, or of the lack of tables suitable for card games."

Penelope sighs. "I know how you feel. Mama probably isn't helping matters. At least you didn't have to endure Eliza's uncomfortable interrogations."

Lucy grimaces. "A continuation of breakfast?"

"Indeed," I say.

Lucy pats my hand. "I'm sorry she's being so horrible to you both. Perhaps we should talk of other things." She looks out toward the cricket field. "I haven't been able to watch the match. Who's winning?"

"You can't tell by Lord James's face?" I ask. "Lord Thornewood is most certainly winning."

"I'm torn as to whom I should cheer on, then," Lucy says. "I'm terribly fond of Lord Thornewood, but I do love an underdog."

"Oh dear," Penelope says, "don't let Lord James hear you call him the underdog."

I laugh, and Lord Thornewood turns in our direction. His eyes light upon my face, and he grins. "Miss Sinclair," he calls, "come join me for a moment."

I smooth my skirt as I stand. "Whatever for?" I call back.

He just continues to wave me over. I roll my eyes at Lucy and Penelope, though inside, my stomach is doing that vexing fluttery thing it does whenever I'm around him.

"Yes, my lord?" I ask when I reach his side.

He answers by handing me his bat. "We've all grown tired of the game, so I've decided you can settle it for us."

"What are you going on about?" James says, his arms crossed over his chest.

Lord Thornewood leans close to my ear, the whisper of his words tickling my cheek. "I must beg your aid in this. It's our chance to be the ones to frustrate my brother for once."

My heart beats faster at his nearness, but I nod. "Certainly. What would you have me do?"

"Miss Sinclair will bat next. However many runs she scores will be the deciding factor in the game. Do you agree, brother?"

James shrugs, grinning despite himself. "Have you ever played cricket before, Miss Sinclair?"

"No."

James laughs and holds his hand up. "Be my guest, then."

I take the bat from Lord Thornewood, and he stands behind me. I look back in surprise when he moves so close I can smell his crisp linen shirt and the slightly woodsy scent that is his own.

His hands touch both my arms. "You'll need to bend your elbows," he says, his voice deep and rich.

I nod, not trusting my voice.

He takes another step closer, so I can feel his chest rise against my back. I think of the way my hands roved over his muscular chest just this morning. Warmth pools inside me. He gently manipulates my arms into swinging the bat. "Smoothly. Like this."

After a few more practice swings, I nod again. "I've got it."

"He'll bowl the ball fast, so you'll need to swing right as it's arching toward you," he says.

I test the weight of the bat in my hands. James's smug look catches my eye. I truly didn't intend to use arcana to aid me, but I simply cannot resist the fun of surprising them all.

"I shan't take my eye from the ball, my lord."

"Good girl," he says. I feel him step away, the breeze cool against my now-exposed back.

"Ready?" James asks.

"I've trained her well," Lord Thornewood says, and his brother snorts. I narrow my eyes, eager to prove him right.

James reels back, throwing his whole body into the bowl. I open myself to my power. It flows around me like a warm afternoon breeze, and I channel it. With the sun so warm and bright on my skin, I barely feel the small loss of energy. Inwardly, I direct it to heighten all my senses, especially sight. One moment James is blurry around the edges. The next, I can see the eyelash that has fallen onto his cheek. I watch the ball, seeing every crack in the leather until I can practically feel it in my hands.

When he finally releases the ball, it flies through the air—just a blur really. It hits the ground about two feet away and arches back toward me. I channel my energy into the bat, and it connects with a satisfying *crack*. The ball flies away. Lucy and Penelope let out a cheer behind me, and James looks at me with mouth agape.

Lord Brashier, Lord Thornewood's friend, scores the last run needed. Lord Thornewood's team wins. I turn to him with a wide smile, and he lifts me in the air as if I weigh no more than the cricket bat and twirls me around.

"Put me down at once," I try to say amidst my own laughter.

He lowers me to the ground and keeps his arms around me much longer than is proper. Though with his eyes locked on mine, it's hard to worry about propriety.

"Well done, Miss Sinclair," James says with a genuine smile. He turns to his brother. "I must congratulate you on your choice of champion. She did extraordinarily well." He gives us both a sly look. "Are you sure this was your first time at bat?"

"Quite sure," I say with a wink.

"I know you will be dancing almost exclusively with my brother, but as the loser of this little game, I beg you will favor me with at least one dance tonight."

"You honor me, Lord James." I glance at Lord Thornewood. "And I'm sure Lord Thornewood will not be dancing as many dances as you say."

"Perhaps not," Lord Thornewood says, "but only if the younger Miss Sinclair and Miss Hasting will agree to dance with me."

"Very good," James says with a clap on Lord Thornewood's back. "Let us go freshen up then. I'm sure the ladies would like to rest before this evening."

We start back toward the house, but not before I see not only is Eliza glaring at me like I stole her favorite dress, but my own grandmother has her arms folded across her chest as if I've done something terribly improper.

"Lord help me," I mumble to myself. The evening should be exciting indeed.

NINETEEN

LUCY and I enter the ballroom arm-in-arm, the satin of our dresses making pleasant rustling sounds as we move.

"Oh, how beautiful," I say, drawing in a breath as soon as I get a good look at the room. Lit by three enormous crystal chandeliers and countless wall sconces, the soft lighting illuminates the floor-to-ceiling length windows facing the lake. From where we stand, the reflections of the colorful guests and the floral decorations shine back at us in the windows. But I see several spots that have been left dim or dark, as if inviting one to enjoy the view of the grounds.

"I wish I had my drawing pad," Lucy says, her wide eyes scanning the room.

"I wish you *would* paint this scene," I say wistfully. Just then I spot Eliza, dressed in a creamy gold gown scattered with pearls. She is accompanied by a rather handsome older couple—her parents, I assume. "Perhaps you could omit a few things, though."

Lucy follows my line of sight and laughs softly. "Indeed I can."

I continue scanning the grand room for any sign of Lord Thornewood, and I finally find him amidst a group of gentlemen. I sigh in disappointment, but for some reason, he looks up. He smiles, says something to Lord Brashier, and makes his way toward us. My heart thumps in rhythm to his footsteps in anticipation of the moment when he will take my hand and guide me to the dance floor.

When did I become so besotted with the man?

"Katherine," he says, his voice low, admiring. His eyes sweep over my body before returning to my face. "You look absolutely stunning tonight."

Lucy gives me a questioning glance at his familiar address of me, but I cannot drag my gaze from his for more than a few seconds. Perhaps he is truly the one with power.

"And you, Miss Lucy," he says with a sweet smile for my little sister. "Your sister and I will have to keep a close eye on you when you debut. We won't be able to hold off all the suitors."

"You are much too kind, my lord," Lucy says, her face glowing as it always does when Lord Thornewood is around.

I tuck away his casual mention of the future for later analysis. He has never made mention of the future with me, and I wonder if he meant it as a meaningless pleasantry or as something he's thought of before. I confess I've avoided thoughts of such things thus far, save when I imagined what it'd be like to see him every morning.

"Do you mind if I beg the first dance from your sister?" Lord Thornewood asks Lucy.

"Not at all," Lucy says. "I was on my way to the refreshments table."

When Lucy leaves, my smile is teasing as I turn to him. "You asked Lucy, but you didn't ask if *I* was ready to dance."

"My apologies. I must rectify this immediately." He takes my hand in his, and I wish I wasn't required to wear satin gloves. I long to feel his bare skin against my own. He bows low over my hand and presses a kiss to my palm. Little shivers of excitement race up my arm. "Katherine, will you do me the honor of dancing with me?"

"I would love to," I say truthfully.

"I hope you can tango," he says, a truly naughty grin upon his face.

"Of course I can . . ." I pause. "Did you say a tango?"

He grins. "I did. We're not in London anymore, my darling. We can dance any dance we choose—even if it's one those old biddies have deemed inappropriate."

I laugh. "How scandalous. Although, they say it's a favorite in France." I joke with him, but in truth, my limbs are jittery with nerves. As dancing the tango was never part of my lessons, I have never learned the steps, but I know it requires more intimacy and more lingering touches than I am used to.

We move onto the dance floor as the first low tones of the piano are played. He takes my hand and twirls me into his body, and my eyes seek his. I vaguely notice the other dancers. Lord James is there with Penelope, whose cheeks are a bright pink. She must be as flustered as I am. Then we take that first step, and everything but Lord Thornewood fades from my awareness.

He guides me with expert skill, until we are gliding through the steps. Every time his hand touches my hip, my hand, or runs down my arm, it leaves a trail of warmth.

"Katherine, you have no idea the power you hold over me," he says and my spine stiffens. Surely I haven't loosed enough arcana to enchant him?

I laugh nervously. "What do you mean?"

His eyes are clear and direct. "You are the only woman who has had the strength to challenge me—on everything," he adds with a grin. "I know I can sometimes come across as arrogant."

I make a sarcastic scoffing sound, and he twirls me a bit too vigorously. I smile back at him innocently, relieved he doesn't seem to be referring to my power.

"As I was saying, you've never seemed intimidated by my station or how intolerable I can be."

"I was as cold to you as you were proud. And you've always given me sound advice—I learned that the hard way."

He groans. "Do not remind me of that night. I still have nightmares."

"I just pretend it never happened," I say quietly.

"Katherine, you must know I'd do anything to protect you." His lips form a crooked smile. "On the rare occasions you actually need it."

"I'm glad you recognize I'm not a typical female member of London Society." But of course, he's unaware of how different I really am.

When he guides me in the next step, which brings us close together again, he leans in toward my ear. "There's something I would like to speak to you about—if you'll agree to meet with me. Tonight. In the library."

I think of the last time we were alone in the library, and my stomach tightens. "When exactly should I meet you?" I keep my voice quiet.

"After everyone else has gone to bed." We step apart for a moment, following the dance, and when we come back together he says, "Will you meet me?"

"I will."

As the last bars of the dramatic song end, he dips me low, his lips coming tantalizingly close to my décolletage.

He grins, and I smile back as the dance ends.

My knees are wobbly as I join Penelope and Lucy for a glass of lemonade. Footmen offer trays of white wine and champagne, but I'll need all my wits about me tonight.

"Lord, that was fun," Penelope says, fanning her face with her hand. "I don't think I've ever danced the tango in public."

"Was Lord James an accomplished partner?" I ask.

"He was indeed. Funny, too. You were right about him, Katherine. He truly is kind."

I arch my brows at her in jest. "Oh dear, does my brother have competition already?"

She blushes and swats at me. "Stop teasing me."

I'm about to say more when Lucy puts her hand on my arm. Our grandmother makes her way toward us for the first time tonight, and she's not alone.

"Katherine, I would like for you to meet Lord Hampton," she says, holding her hand out toward a man at least twenty years my senior. I hide my frown. She's introduced me to older men before, but I didn't think she would bother to throw me in the path of other potential suitors this weekend. I guess I naively thought I'd be given a brief reprieve.

I curtsy as formal introductions are made. The man is pleasant with a kind smile, though old enough to be my father.

"May I have the honor of the next dance?" he asks, his thick eyebrows raised expectantly.

Grandmama gives me a stern look as if she's afraid I'd be rude enough to turn him down. Obviously I cannot, so I smile. "I thank you, yes."

"Very good," he says. "If you'll excuse me for a moment."

"Grandmama, whatever could you be thinking?" I demand as soon as he is far enough away not to overhear.

"Did you not listen to my introduction, girl? Lord Hampton is a marquis with nearly as big an estate as this one."

"He's much too old for me."

"Age has nothing to do with whether a man is suitable," she says. She keeps her eyes on the dancers in front of us, a slight smile on her face, as if we are merely discussing fashion or the weather.

My jaw is tight as I clench down on my teeth. I have no reason to be so angry with her since this isn't exactly new behavior on her part. But I cannot escape the suspicion she's doing it just to keep me from enjoying more dances with Lord Thornewood. I just don't understand why.

The current dance ends, and Lord Hampton returns to escort me to the dance floor. He moves stiffly, as if one of his legs was injured in the past. His face is handsome, but his mustache reminds me of Papa. I force a smile. There's no reason to be unkind to this man simply because I'm frustrated with my grandmother.

"Your grandmother tells me you enjoy the country more than the city," he says when we have settled into our dancing rhythm.

"I do. I'm sure you find that rather strange."

"On the contrary, my wife always preferred the ease and space of the country." His eyes are wistful, and I realize he must have recently lost her.

Now I'm reminded even more of Papa, and I give his hand a little squeeze. "I'm sorry for your recent loss."

He smiles back, the gesture not quite reaching his eyes. "Am I being terribly obvious?"

"Not at all. I just recognize the signs."

"You are so kind to dance with an old man. I told your grandmother I didn't want to impose, but she insisted."

A flare of frustrated anger quickly pushes aside the feelings of guilt. I glance in Grandmama's direction, but there is no way to divine her intentions from her blank expression.

"You are not imposing, my lord. Tell me, did your wife enjoy riding?"

My question is all Lord Hampton needs to regale me with tales of his wife, some funny, some bittersweet. Above all, it is clear he is still very much in love with her. Even more shameful, then, that my grandmother was taking advantage of his situation to throw me in his path.

He bows low when the dance ends. "I thank you for the most pleasant dance I've had all evening. You've made my heart feel a little less heavy."

"I'm glad to have done you such a favor," I say.

"Enjoy the rest of your evening," he says with a kind smile.

When he leaves, I go directly to Grandmama, my hands in tight fists at my side. "Very poorly done," I say in almost a snarl. "You had no right to drag that poor man into your matchmaking machinations, if indeed that was even your intention."

"You would do well to curb your tone with me," she says, her voice quietly ominous. "I'll not stand to be dressed down by my own granddaughter."

Heat rises to my cheeks, but I don't back down. "Did you know he was a recent widower?"

She meets my stare. "Why else would I put you in his path?"

"Well, it was very wrong of you. Think of my father—how hard it was for him. For all of us."

She *tsks*. "Yes, and he would have been much happier if he had remarried. I always encouraged that, but he would not listen to me. Just look at how wild *you* became. Had you a proper mother, you'd be much better turned out."

Her barbs sting, and for a moment, I'm a lost little girl with no mother and a grandmother who despises her again. "You said I've done well in my debut—with my etiquette."

"I thought so—at first. But then you made such a muddle of things. It'll be a miracle if we get you married off at all."

I gape at her. How could she say such things when we've been personally invited to the Lord Thornewood's home? I say as much.

"Lord Thornewood is a rake. It's time you realized that. You'd do well to guard your heart around him."

I think of the man she believes to be a good match instead of Lord Thornewood, and I shake my head in exasperation. She will never believe the truth about Lord Blackburn, and even if she did, she would only blame me for it.

"I've had quite enough," I say, and stalk off. But though I am out of her sight and away from the conversation, her words linger in my mind.

TWENTY

I make my way to the refreshments table to find Lucy, my whole body tense. I'm angry at my meddling grandmother, but I'm also wary. Her judgment of the character of potential suitors is questionable at best.

"That's quite the dark look you're wearing," a wry voice calls out behind me. I turn to see James grinning at me. "Has my brother run you off so soon?"

"No, indeed. I was just looking for my sister."

He arches an eyebrow. "And the cross look you're wearing is because . . . ?"

I sigh and smile despite my mood. He reminds me too much of Robert. "Family squabbles. Failed matchmaking efforts." I wave my hand about flippantly. "You know, debutante problems."

"Ah. Well, perhaps a dance would cheer you up? I'm not my brother, but I'm sure I can manage to entertain you for a few minutes." He offers me his arm, and I take it.

"I think a dance would be just the thing," I say.

"Excellent."

He leads me onto the dance floor, his movements sure and confident. With each twirl, my body relaxes more, until I'm able to genuinely smile again.

"You were right," I say to James. "I feel much improved."

"I'm delighted I could be of assistance. Though, of course, it behooves me to be in your good graces."

"Whatever could you mean by that?"

His expression turns sly. "Don't think I haven't noticed how much my brother cares for you, Miss Sinclair. His secret meeting with Tavi aside, there have been other signs. He has even made mention of you in his weekly letter to me. 'I've met an intriguing woman who is frustratingly headstrong,'" he says in a deep voice that I suppose is meant to be an imitation of Lord Thornewood's. "'Her beauty is second only to her biting wit.'"

I'm blushing furiously. "I'm not sure I believe you, sir."

"I wouldn't lie about matters of the heart. Especially my brother's."

I repeat the lines from Lord Thornewood's letter to James over and over in my mind. It does sound like him, and I cannot deny the way my heart has swelled at the words. Another lady, perhaps, would not be so delighted with his commentary, but I love he sees me as headstrong. And even I cannot deny how deliciously thrilling it is to be called beautiful.

"I see I've given you plenty to think about," James says at the end of the dance. He bows low before me. "Thank you for the dance."

"No, it is I who should thank you." I smile and resist the urge to hug him as I would my brother.

James pulls out a gold pocket watch and checks the time. "Time for my announcement. If you'll excuse me, Miss Sinclair."

He grins and strides away toward the orchestra. He holds his hand in the air until everyone quiets and gives him their attention. What could he be up to? I glance around for Lord Thornewood and find him with a glass of wine in his hand next to Lucy. He shakes his head in a resigned sort of way.

"Ladies and gentlemen," James says, "if I could have your attention for just a few moments. I wanted to take this chance to thank you for coming this weekend. I hope you've enjoyed the ball. I know I have." His eyes seek out Penelope's and I raise my eyebrows in surprise at her shy smile. "Tomorrow we shall continue the fun with something rather unusual: a scavenger hunt."

My brows furrow, and I see several people glancing around at each other with curious expressions.

"It's delightfully fun, and very *en vogue* in Paris," he says and many nod their heads, tittering excitedly. Any mention of a Paris fad will garner a following—no matter if it's true. From the way James is grinning mischievously, I imagine he is fabricating most of this. "The rules are simple. Everyone will be given a list of things to find on the grounds of the estate, and you will each have a partner. The first team who finds everything on the list will be awarded the grand prize. I'll clarify everything tomorrow. For now, enjoy the rest of your evening."

Scattered laughter and applause rings out over the ballroom, and I watch as James joins Penelope with a wide smile.

Perhaps I am not the only one who finds the Thornewood men irresistible.

It's well after midnight when I make my way to the library. I took Devi into my confidence and asked her to inform me when the other guests went to bed. I told her a half-truth: I had difficulty sleeping and liked to read late at night. I also asked her to draw me a bath, since I feel I will need something to help me sleep after spending so stimulating an evening with Lord Thornewood. She didn't question me, but she did give me a knowing look. I chose to ignore it.

The halls are dimly lit by wall sconces, and the windows admit clear moonlight. I keep my footfalls soft and hold the hem of my nightgown so I won't trip. I couldn't dissuade Devi from helping me undress and prepare for bed, so my hair is in soft waves down my back and I'm probably the most improperly dressed I've ever been. *Good thing I'm used to such impropriety*, I think to myself with a grin.

I pull my wool shawl tighter around me when I reach the door to the library, and my brazen mood dims. What if he becomes as disappointed as my father in my state of dress? I pause with my hand on the doorknob. Dare I enter? Suddenly my mouth has gone dry. I am not completely ignorant of what is expected from a midnight rendezvous, but neither am I wholly prepared for the consequences.

With a deep breath, I open the door. A cheerful fire greets me, but it's the heat from Lord Thornewood's eyes that makes me feel as if I've stood too close to the flames. He stands with one arm resting on the mantle, the other cradling a snifter of brandy. I stare at the amber liquid swirling in the crystal.

Our eyes meet, and the evident desire in his causes a surge of heat in my body. "Come by the fire," he says after a moment. He puts his glass down with a clink. "You must be cold."

I move closer until I am facing the fireplace. The warmth from the flames is delightful but in no way calms my galloping heart. I give him a nervous half-smile. "Is that a comment on my manner of dress?" My eyes flit to his as I hold my hands out toward the fire.

The intensity is still there, but banked. "If it was, it certainly wouldn't be to complain," he says. He takes a step forward and runs his fingertips through my hair. "So beautiful."

The shaky feeling in my knees and stomach grows. The smell of fire and cedar wraps itself around me as he presses his lips to mine. Gently, while still holding on to the ends of my hair.

"Forgive me," he murmurs. "I swore to myself I would only speak with you, but I didn't prepare myself for how splendidly underdressed you'd be."

I blush, feeling desirable yet self-conscious at the same time. Does this mean I'm not here to be kissed senseless? Threads of disappointment weave themselves around my heart. "What did you wish to speak to me about?" I ask, my voice quiet.

"I wasn't able to make myself clear during the ball this evening—not with so many prying eyes and ears." He takes both my cold hands in his warm ones. "Katherine, I have known for some time now I am desperately in love with you." My mouth goes dry as a thrill races up my spine. "Though I cannot say it was at first sight, it was certainly soon thereafter. In fact, I believe I first felt my feelings toward marriage change when you asked me in the park if perhaps you should dumb down your conversation." He laughs. "Not only was it the most outrageous thing any lady has ever said to me, but I knew then I didn't want a wife who only talked of frivolous things."

"My lord, for once, I am quite at a loss of words."

"My intentions are to declare myself to you and ask for your permission to speak with your father."

I stand rooted in place. My heartbeat thrums loudly in my ears. So many emotions crash over one another until my mind is a tumult. Shock. Joy. Anxiety. Lord Thornewood loves me. He loves me, and he wants to ask my father's permission to marry me. But I realize I've never asked myself: do I love him? I think of all the moments spent with him and realize, like him, my heart changed a long time ago. A smile blooms briefly across my face, but it falters at the last moment when I remember.

He has no idea who I really am. I have never told anyone else, save one little boy. Will Lord Thornewood—for even with his declaration I still cannot think of him as simply Colin—react in the same way as Henry? Unbidden, my memories drag me back to that day. I can still see the smattering of freckles across the bridge of Henry's nose, the warm brown of his eyes, and then, the way his features twisted with disgust. There is nothing quite so painful as fear on a child's face, especially when I am the source of it. I cannot bear if Lord Thornewood looks at me in the same way. I cannot.

I blink rapidly to prevent the tears from falling. Lord Thornewood reaches out and cups my cheek. "Have I shocked you?" There is concern in his eyes.

"A little," I admit. I want to tell him; I do. But I cannot make my lips form the words. What if he pushes me away as Henry did? Worse, what if he never speaks to me again? Or betrays my confidence? Instead, I say what I know he wants to hear. "But only because I have hoped to hear you say it for so long."

He smiles as if relieved. "And . . . you return the sentiment?"

I let out a breathy laugh. In this, I need not lie. "With all my heart."

"You are not disappointed I did not formally propose? I have always respected your father, and I would like to speak to him before I go down on one knee before you."

"I understand perfectly, and I appreciate it more than you know."

"Then allow me to give you a small token in lieu of your engagement ring," he says, reaching for a black velvet box on the table beside us. He opens it to reveal a necklace nestled inside, with a cross of sapphires and diamonds.

"It's beautiful," I say, my breath catching in my throat. I think of James's cryptic comment about jewelry and wonder if he knew the truth all along.

He smiles a little sadly as he removes it from the box. "It was my mother's. She would have wanted you to have it. A small bauble for a future countess." His fingers send tingles of excitement racing over my skin as he brushes my hair to the side and fastens the delicate clasp.

I touch the gem-encrusted cross where it lies over my breasts.

"I have one other gift for you, but this one is of a more . . . practical nature." He retrieves a long slim box and hands it to me.

Inside is an ornate dagger. The blade is sharp, the metal glinting in the light. A single sapphire is set in the hilt amidst elegant filigree. I pick it up, feeling the weight in my hands. It is light enough for me to handle easily, but not so light it wouldn't be a dangerous weapon.

"After that horrible night, I wanted you to have something more formidable than a letter opener for your protection."

I shoot him a small smile. "You knew about that?"

"It was terribly clever of you." He frowns. "But it only shows how you must have already had reason to fear him."

I glance down at the shiny dagger. "He was . . . inappropriate with me when we went to visit his estate." When his face darkens, I hasten to add, "Not in the same way as that night, but enough to make me question his character."

He takes a deep breath, opens his mouth as though about to say something of importance, but then seems to think better of it. "I encourage you to question his character. Lord Blackburn is . . . a man who cannot be trusted," he says finally. "Promise me you'll carry this with you anytime I'm not with you."

"I promise." When his mood continues to stay serious, I smile and nudge his arm. "Thank you for such a unique gift. I do believe I'm the first who has been given both a cross and a dagger at the same time—aside from a vampire hunter."

He smiles back and pulls me into his arms, so close I can feel his heartbeat beneath his thin, linen shirt. "You are very welcome. I know I promised to keep my hands to myself tonight, but I cannot resist a few moments of celebration with my soon-to-be betrothed."

Desperate to escape my memories and the whisper of worry inside me, I kiss him back fervently. He shoves both hands into my hair as we press even closer to each other. Gradually, we move toward the fainting couch until the backs of my knees bump into the velvet fabric. I sit, and he follows me down, supporting the majority of his weight on one arm. I stare at his arm—the fine smattering of dark hair, the strong muscles and sinews.

He trails burning kisses down my throat and atop my collarbone. The muscles on his back jerk as I run my fingertips over them. He is all hard planes and firm, unyielding flesh. I know he will pull back soon, so I cling to him. I wish he could read my mind. I wish he could tell me everything will be alright and he will love me still.

When his hands reach the curve of my breasts, a soft moan escapes from my lips, begging him not to stop. His tongue continues the teasing assault on my mouth as he frees my breasts from the bodice of my gown.

He lowers his head to them, tongue swirling around each nipple, and I nearly cry out. His fingers replace his tongue as his mouth takes mine once again. His kisses are deep, almost desperate in their intensity. I plunge my fingers into his thick hair, my bare breasts flush against his chest. I want him to know I desire this every bit as much as he does. If this makes me wanton, I cannot bring myself to care.

When I tentatively graze my teeth over his bottom lip, he groans and murmurs, "The death of me."

Our lips meet again, as his hips press against mine. The thin fabric of my nightgown allows me to feel everything, and I suck in a breath in wonder. Our bodies fit perfectly together, despite our height difference, and tears sting my eyes. If only this were proof we are meant to be.

I'm a coward. A terrible coward for not telling him the truth, but in this moment, when he is kissing me as if I'm the most beautiful woman in the world, I cannot bear to do anything that may jeopardize this one instant of perfect happiness.

With hooded eyes, and one last kiss, he draws away. "Katherine," he says, his voice gruff, "I lose all my good sense when I'm around you." In one smooth movement, he stands and tugs me to my feet.

I turn my back to him and readjust my clothing. "I quite enjoy you senseless," I say.

He laughs. "Do you now? Well, you shall have your fill of it, believe me." His self-assured grin is back in place. "Now allow me to escort you back to your room. James will never forgive me if you are too tired in the morning to participate in his scavenger hunt."

I hesitate. My body is still throbbing, and I know this may be the only night we have. Once he finds out the truth about me, he may never find me desirable again.

He strokes a finger down my cheek. "Is something wrong?"

"You said you'd escort me to my room," I say quietly. "Devi has drawn me a bath." I take a deep breath. I can do this. We're practically betrothed, but once I reveal the truth of who I am, I cannot be sure I will ever have a wedding night. The only certainty is that we have this night, and I must take full advantage of it. "Will you join me?"

The fiery desire in his eyes flares, and he lets out his breath in a rush. "Good God, Katherine. How could I say no?"

I stand staring at the tub. Gentle steam rises from it invitingly, but my legs shake beneath my skirt.

Lord Thornewood moves closer to me from behind and wraps his arms around me. "We don't have to do anything you aren't ready for," he whispers in my ear. "I cannot deny my desire for more time spent pleasuring you, but only say the word, and I will leave you with a chaste kiss on the cheek."

I close my eyes and shake my head. That's the last thing I want. And yet . . . giving myself totally to him without vows being exchanged is a social and moral law I cannot overcome. "I . . . I would rather keep my virginity."

He kisses the side of my neck. "I find I much prefer it if we saved something for the wedding night."

I turn in his arms, and he takes possession of my mouth once again. His tongue is gentle, stroking, awakening a fire within me. I sigh into him.

He moves his hand down to the ribbons on the front of my nightgown and looks at me, a question in his eyes.

"Yes," I say, the blood pounding in my ears.

His fingers deftly undo the ties and skim the thin fabric off my shoulders. The nightgown becomes a puddle of cotton and lace on the floor, and I stand before him, completely naked. Though most ladies would be blushing with embarrassment, I watch the mounting desire in his eyes with a sort of feminine pride. My mother never adhered to Society's bashfulness over the body. She reveled in the beauty of the human form, and indeed, was never shy about bathing or even swimming in the pond at Bransfield. *We should never be ashamed of our bodies*, she would tell me, *each one is a work of art.*

"Exquisite," he murmurs, reaching out to cup my breasts in his hands. They fill his wide hands, and I arch back as he returns his attention to my neck and throat.

He pulls away for a moment and hurriedly removes his shirt. I stare at the rippling muscles of his chest and abdomen. His skin is smooth, like satin over granite. A work of art, indeed. I believe I have found what my mother was referring to.

I cannot resist reaching out and running my hands over his broad chest. He smiles and cradles my cheek with his hand. "Why do you look so perplexed?" he asks. "Is my form so foreign to you?"

I smile. "I am not so naive that I have never seen a man's chest before. No, I am only surprised it is so well-formed. Most aristocrats are rather soft."

He laughs quietly. "Perhaps I do not spend time reclining as so many other gentleman do." He holds his hand out toward the tub. "Now come, I'll help you in while the water is still hot."

The water envelopes me in warmth, the exotic scent of some unidentifiable oil wafting up amidst the steam. Watching me, he removes his trousers until he stands completely exposed to my virgin eyes.

Warmth rushes up my neck to my cheeks as my heart beats furiously in my chest. He enters the tub behind me, his legs stretched out on either side of mine. "My body must be very frightening to put such a look in your eyes."

Though there were parts which were certainly . . . intimidating, to say the least, I could never say I was afraid of him. "I find you beautiful," I say with another blush.

He reaches out and pulls me forward, until I am nestled against him, reclining against his broad chest. "Your skin is lovely when you blush," he says. He bends his head down and presses a kiss to my neck. "And dear God, why do you always smell of roses?" His fingers gently run up and down my arm. When I turn to look up at him, he lowers his mouth to mine.

His tongue is gentle at first, then more demanding, urging the desire inside me to take over. His hand moves from my arm down the side of my breasts, and still lower, until he is stroking my bare thigh. He returns his attention to my breasts, cupping them before teasing the nipples until they ache for more of his touch. His hand skims lower, and I whimper into his mouth.

"Say the word and I'll stop," he says, his fingers stroking just below my navel.

"Please," I say, my breaths coming faster.

"Please stop?"

I shake my head. "Please don't stop."

His hand moves lower, and I cry out before his mouth descends on mine again.

TWENTY-ONE

I awake to the morning sun's weak rays peeking over the tops of the trees. As soon as the previous night's memories come rushing back to me, I smile and cover my face with a pillow. Never before have I experienced such pleasure, but it's almost bittersweet. Now that I have been so intimate with him, I cannot imagine losing him. I roll over fitfully, and a glowing light catches my eye. My mother's journal.

I pick up the book gently, my hand shaky on the soft leather. Every other time, her words were predictions. What would she say now? I almost cannot bear to look. Especially since Lord Thornewood's declaration is so fresh and with no official proposal.

I let the book fall open.

My dearest Katherine,

I thought long and hard over what my greatest piece of advice would be to you on matters of love. I was so lucky to have found your father. It was so easy for us—so effortless. But even at the tender age of five years old, you always resisted the idea of marriage. I am sorry this world's Society expects it of you. I can only hope love finds you first. We are often the only things standing in our own way, especially in our beliefs. Sometimes the thing our head is telling us is a lie, but our heart knows the truth. I know you find that silly, but we are largely ruled by emotions. Think of your love for music, and I know you will find it difficult to argue.

The man who will be your husband should be like the most beautiful piece of music: complex, provocative, but makes your heart soar.

This man should also be one who knows how to protect you from yourself. With our gifts, we are often faced with difficult choices. I was in such a position, and I am at peace with my choice. Your father, however, is not.

When I became ill, it was because I used arcana beyond my abilities. My sweet, innocent Lucy was born with a disease I knew would ultimately take her life. The physicians, of course, could do nothing. But I could. Much like resurrection arcana, I removed the hateful disease from her body. It came at a cost, as all arcana does, and I am so terribly sorry it took me from the rest of you. Though Lucy still has headaches, she will never have to fear death will come too soon.

The future will present you with hard decisions, Katherine.

Trust yourself. I always have.

Love,
Mama

Our mother sacrificed herself for Lucy. This, then, must be the vision her earlier journal entry referred to. I roll the thought around in my mind for a moment, my chest tight. Papa must have known the truth. How tortured he must have been to know his wife was slowly dying to save their child. Tears sting my eyes as I think of all the times she treated Lucy's headaches. I only ever knew Mama was sick, never the cause. I think of the power I loosed to save Robert, and I know my mother did the right thing. Still, I cannot contain the sob wrenched from deep inside me.

Lucy can never know the truth. She would never survive the guilt, of this I'm certain. I clutch the journal to my chest as tears roll down my cheeks.

If I am ever faced with giving my life for one of my siblings, I will do it without hesitation. Even knowing the truth about my mother. From the beginning of her letter, she must hope there is someone who can protect me from my own recklessness. "Yes, but what will he say when he knows the truth?" I whisper to the pages. How can love exist when one person has such a terrible secret?

I lie in bed with the intention of only sleeping until Devi comes to fetch me for breakfast, but she must have had pity on me because the sun is much higher when I wake again. I'm groggy without a full night's rest, but I force myself out of bed and ring for Devi.

"There's a nip in the air, so I think you'll be most comfortable in the wool riding habit," Devi says as she helps me dress quickly.

While she does my hair, I eat a small meal of biscuits and tea. "Am I terribly late?" I ask.

"No, my lady. You'll be right on time as breakfast ended not long ago. The other guests are preparing to join Lord Thornewood and Lord James outside."

A soft knock at the door, and then Lucy calls out, "Katherine? May I come in?"

"Yes, do," I say.

She knits her brows. "Are you alright? You never came down for breakfast."

"I'm well. I'm sorry to have worried you." I smile when she looks unconvinced. "I only overslept. I had trouble falling asleep last night—probably from the excitement of the evening." Not a lie, just not the whole truth. I itch to tell her, but I cannot say anything in front of Devi.

Her face relaxes into a smile. "That's a relief, but it's unfortunate you didn't get enough rest. I don't blame you, though—the ball was wonderful."

"It was, and I suppose this scavenger hunt of Lord James's will be fun as well. Did he mention anything about it?"

She shakes her head. "Only for us to meet him by the stables. Evidently we can either ride or go on foot—whichever we're more comfortable with."

"I suppose that's in a misguided attempt to include our grandmother and Lady Hasting."

She giggles. "They would never do something so free-spirited."

"All done, my lady," Devi says. "Do you need anything else?"

"Thank you, Devi. No."

She smiles and bobs a curtsy before exiting the room.

Lucy loops her arm through mine. "Shall we go?"

I look down at her smiling face, and I almost tell her. Something stops me though. Maybe it's because it hardly feels real.

I nod. "Yes, let's."

There will always be time to tell her later.

Everyone save my grandmother and Lady Hasting is outside the stables when Lucy and I join them. Lord Thornewood catches my eye, and I smile at him and lift a hand in greeting. I let my breath out in a rush when he returns my smile. I must have been anxious for his reaction without realizing it.

Lord James moves among the small crowd, handing out pieces of parchment. "On these pieces of paper is written a list of items. You are to find these items before anyone else, and in so doing, win the prize."

"Ribbon? A bird's egg?" Lady Alford, one of the guests who arrived yesterday, says with a frown. "However are we to find such small things on all this land?"

James grins. "You didn't expect this to be easy, did you?"

"What's the prize?" Lord Brashier asks.

James sighs loudly; but from his wide grin, I can tell he's enjoying every second of this. "Do you really want to know?"

"Yes," several of the other guests say.

"If you insist." He clears his throat and speaks in a loud voice. "The grand prize shall be: a trip to Bath in Lord Thornewood's own motorcar and a stay at his luxurious home there."

I hear appreciative murmurs from those around me, and I must say, I join them in thinking this is a lovely prize. I've never been to Bath. I glance over at Lord Thornewood and wonder with a secret smile if he is also included in the package.

"You will each have a partner, so that should make it easier to find these things," James continues.

"Can we choose our partner?" Eliza asks. When James nods, she continues with a calculating smile, "then I choose Lord Thornewood."

"Oh, I'm sorry," Lord James says. "I forgot to mention all teams must be same-sex. Also, my brother will not be able to participate as he has an unfair advantage."

Her face falls comically, but before I can revel in her disappointment, Lord James calls out with a mischievous grin, "But I'm sure the elder Miss Sinclair would make a superb partner."

I open and close my mouth a few times. Lord Thornewood glares at his brother, whispering to him in what I'm sure are harsh words. Lord James has clearly decided to stir up as much strife as he can. Worse, neither of us can refuse without seeming abominably rude.

I smile as if I don't mind when she takes her place beside me. Penelope and Lucy choose each other as partners, casting me sympathetic glances as they read over the list.

We are able to choose our mounts, and Eliza makes the mistake of choosing the same feisty mare Lord Thornewood brought for me to ride all those weeks ago. I go with a calm, bright-eyed gray gelding. I'm in no mood to manage both a temperamental horse and Eliza.

The air buzzes with excited chatter, but Eliza and I are quiet. She shoots me a glare. "You could have at least worn a different color."

I look down at my black riding habit. Eliza is wearing a nearly identical outfit. I roll my eyes. "As if I can help it."

She makes an irritating huffing sound and yanks the reins of her poor horse. "Let's get this over with then."

"Good luck, everyone," James calls. Everyone else rides away with bright expressions, happy banter in their wake.

I follow Eliza silently, letting her take the lead as she canters away toward the lake. The gelding has a smooth gait, and I try my best to enjoy it. When we arrive, my eyes scan the list of items: ribbon, bird's egg, honey, statue, ball, fishing net, peony, and gloves.

"What do you expect to find here?" I ask. "I know where we can find the peonies, but none of the others."

"A fishing net would be used in water," she answers in a biting tone. "Do you see water anywhere else?"

I don't deign to answer her, just watch with a bored expression on my face as she dismounts and searches the water's edge. After a few moments of pushing aside tall vegetation, she snaps, "You could assist me you know."

"Very well," I say and dismount. I examine the shoreline, searching for anything that resembles a net. Then I notice the narrow wooden pier. A sign with a pile of nets sits at the very end. My boots make hollow sounds as I walk over to the nets and retrieve one from the top of the pile.

I dangle the net from one hand and smirk. "I suppose this won't be so hard after all."

Eliza marches over and snatches it from me. "Only because I determined where to go in the first place."

I grit my teeth. "Shall we go to the garden next?"

She doesn't answer at first, just glances in the direction of the copse of trees behind the lake. In the distance, I see Lord Thornewood and his brother, talking and laughing in the shade. "No," she says, "I believe we'll search for the bird's egg next."

"The peony would be easier," I say.

She waves her hand in the air flippantly and mounts her horse. "Do as you wish."

I would like nothing more than to go my separate way, but I know if I do, she'll seek the attention of Lord Thornewood. An ugly streak of jealousy twists inside me. "I'd rather help you," I say sweetly.

She shoots me a nasty look and mutters something under her breath.

We ride around the lake, Eliza sawing on the horse's bit. I grit my teeth as Eliza delivers another pointless smack with her riding crop to the mare's side. It reminds me of when I was younger and got in a terrible row with Robert. He took my favorite doll and hid it from me, and we ended up in a wrestling match. When I went riding with Mama later, I was still sore at my brother for not only taking my doll, but beating me at wrestling. I pouted the entire time, and my pony responded by being as stubborn as a donkey. I never stooped to treating him badly as Eliza is now, but it was one of the only times I saw my mother angry. She told me that my pony could feel every bad emotion I was feeling, but unlike me, he could do nothing about it. Save throw me off. Which is probably exactly what Eliza's mount would like to do.

I watch the mare's tail swish angrily back and forth. She prances in place as a warning, but Eliza only gives her another smack with the crop.

My stomach twists in response. Even from a few feet away, I can sense the mare is only moments away from her breaking point. I open my mouth to say something to Eliza just as the mare tosses her head. Eliza jerks hard on the reins; but when the mare tosses her head again, she wrenches the reins out of Eliza's hands. Eliza makes a dive for the fallen reins, nearly unseating herself in the process.

Spooked by Eliza's sudden movement, the mare takes off as though baying hounds chase her. I suck in my breath as Eliza pitches forward and clings to the horse's neck. She has absolutely no control of her now.

There is a horrible moment where I shame myself by thinking: *this is only what she deserves.* But then Eliza's scream carries back to me on the wind.

Her panicked horse heads straight for the woods—no doubt the fastest way back to the stables and, therefore, safety—but also full of thick oak trees and thorny underbrush. Galloping through the woods can be dangerous even for a skilled rider, but for a rider who has lost all control, it's practically a guaranteed way to get one's neck broken.

I may hate Eliza, but that does not mean I would see her dead.

I urge my horse into a gallop after them until we reach the entrance to the woods. I cannot risk my horse getting tangled in the underbrush, so I jump from his back and race ahead on foot.

Out of my peripheral vision, I see Lord Thornewood and Lord James in a flurry of activity, but my focus is on the runaway horse and rider.

Branches and thorns tear at my face and clothing. I leap over fallen logs and debris, following the sound of thrashing hooves and fearful screams.

I reach them just as the mare tosses Eliza from her back. Eliza flies through the air, her arms flailing uselessly. With a crash, she lands in a heap in the hedges. The horse is blowing hard, her eyes wide. I take hold of her reins and put my hand on her nose, and she drops her head and relaxes her body.

"Eliza?" I call, and she answers me with a strangled sob.

I lean down to help her to her feet, and that's when I see the blood spread from a wound in her side. With a shaky hand, I pull her cloak away to reveal a sharp branch protruding from her chest. Blood bubbles from her lips, and I realize it has punctured her lung.

TWENTY-TWO

"HELP me," Eliza says, nearly choking on her own words. Her eyes are wide with panic. "*Please.*"

I can fix this. Lord knows she doesn't deserve it, but I cannot leave her here to die when I possess the power to heal her. I have only seconds to make up my mind. The cost will be high for me—this arcana is akin to stealing her from the jaws of death. I think of the little kitten in the stables and of Henry's devastating revulsion afterward. I think of my mother. In truth, I'm not sure I'm strong enough.

"Please," she says again, her lips red with blood.

But I have to try.

I crouch beside her and close my eyes, calling my power to me. Channeling this much energy has a different pull on my body than my normal arcana. The tug inside me is painful, and I suck in my breath. I grip the branch in both hands and take a deep breath.

I meet her eyes. "I'm sorry," I say and pull.

Eliza's scream of agony reverberates through me.

The branch comes free, bringing a torrent of blood with it, and I immediately switch to healing arcana. I hold both palms over her battered body.

A breeze tickles my neck, and my palms begin to glow with a bright, golden light. The light churns around us, humming with ancient power. The smell of rich earth permeates the air. The smell of healing.

The dappled sunlight fuels some of the energy but the majority comes from my own stores. The effects are near instant. I can feel my own life flowing into her, bleeding out of me like a mortal wound.

"Katherine," a voice calls—panicked, insistent. "Katherine, where are you? Answer me!"

It's Lord Thornewood's voice, but I cannot stop now. Eliza is bathed in the light, and her body is slowly mending itself. I watch her muscles knit back together as the blood finally slows to a trickle.

"Katherine, thank God. I thought—"

This time, the voice is right behind me. I don't even turn around. What's done is done. Though I only halfway believe it.

My heartbeat weakens, flutters. Sweat pours down my face as a terrible pain radiates out from my chest. Tingles of numbness run down my arm. My heart is failing me.

From behind one of the towering trees, a snowy white fox appears. Its gaze pierces mine in the same way it did when I first saw it in my vision. Images of my mother gently scolding me the day I brought the kitten back to life fill my mind.

"Resurrection arcana has too great a price," she said, her gaze meeting mine as intensely as the fox does now. "You must never attempt it again."

The fox takes another small step forward. *Let go*, it says in my mind.

I cut the flow of power as one would snip a loose thread.

Another moment, another heartbeat, and Eliza sits up, her hand on her newly healed side. Eliza's eyes are wide as she stares at me. "You healed me," she says, her voice filled with incredulity.

I glance at Lord Thornewood, but he stands motionlessly. My eyes swing back to Eliza's. "Yes," I say. Where her face should be, I see only black spots. I'm so cold, as though my body no longer has the strength to produce any heat. Eliza's chest is heaving. I'm still connected to her, so I know fear drives her rapid breathing. I should be terrified of her reaction. I should be feeling so many things, but I feel nothing. I am numb.

"How is this possible?" she asks, probing the spot in her side that was once a gaping wound.

As her question seems to be more rhetorical than anything, I concentrate on staying conscious. My body begs me to lie down, to give in to the dark edges of my vision.

Eliza's wide, panic-stricken eyes finally take in Lord Thornewood. Like a flash of lightning, her demeanor changes. "Lord Thornewood, you must help me. She *did* something to me." Her voice is desperate, insistent.

"I only healed you, Eliza." My voice sounds like I've aged sixty years.

"Only? *Only?* I *knew* there was something wrong with you! What are you?" she asks as she scrambles to her feet.

"I'm a girl, just as you are."

"You're not. I knew those outrageous rumors were true." She turns back to Lord Thornewood, her whole body shaking. "I'll tell you what she is. She's a witch," she says, her voice as accusatory as Henry's.

But rather than appear fearful, her eyes have a glint in them, as though this may be the very thing she has hoped for all along: that I will have made such a disastrous mistake all of Society will shun me. Before Lord Thornewood can even respond, she races away. A line from my mother's letter pops into my mind: *There is no greater scandal than the one fueled by fear.*

Lord Thornewood steps forward and places a warm hand on my shoulder. I look up into his dark eyes and see concern swirling in their depths—concern, and something else. Determination?

"You are uninjured?" he says, and his voice sounds hoarse. His eyes sweep over my person.

"I am well enough," I say weakly.

He helps me stand. I sway on my feet, and then I see nothing at all.

I awake to disembodied voices just outside my room.

"Her heartbeat seemed stronger this time?" Lord Thornewood asks, his voice strained.

"Absolutely, my lord," another man answers. "You should get some rest yourself. Miss Sinclair will fully recover."

"I'll rest when she wakes up and tells me herself she's better." The sound of booted heels on marble ring out and then soften as they approach the bed where I lie.

I try to force my eyes open, but they feel weighted. After a moment, Lord Thornewood sighs and moves away. I hear him settle into a nearby chair, and I relax. I'm having trouble remembering exactly what happened and where I am, but I'm sure it'll come to me—probably much too soon.

At last, I manage to get one eye open. A view of the lake at Thornewood greets me. A fire crackles in the marble fireplace to the left of the bed. Blankets are piled all around me, and as I concentrate on other areas of my body, I find the mattress is exceptionally plush.

In a rush, my mind reminds me of how I came to be here. I nearly drained myself healing Eliza. Worse, I remember Lord Thornewood discovering us. I writhe my head around in the agony of the memory.

"You're awake," Lord Thornewood practically shouts as he comes immediately to my side. "How are you feeling? Can I get you anything?"

"Yes," I say, my voice sounding dusty from disuse. "A glass of water, please?"

He pours a glass from a crystal decanter at my bedside. The glass tremors slightly when he hands it to me.

I meet his intense stare. "I'm so sorry to have worried you."

He shakes his head. "Think nothing of it. I'm just glad you're awake."

"How long has it been?"

"Two days," he says, deep frown lines etched into his forehead and the sides of his mouth.

I let my breath out in a rush. Two days. I've never been unconscious for so long. This, then, is the price I paid for practicing arcana I didn't have the strength for. I think of the snowy white fox. Did it stop me before I drained all my energy? Or was it only a hallucination of someone close to death?

"Oh," I say and try to sit up, "my sister—she must be so worried about me."

He lays a hand on my shoulder, gently restraining me. "Don't strain yourself. Your sister has been here and only just left. I insisted she get some rest."

I relax against the pillows. "That was good of you." He continues to watch me, his expression tense. Now my most pressing concern is addressed, a feeling of unease settles over me. Just how much did Lord Thornewood see? What conclusions has he come to? Does he think I am a witch?

He must realize the change in mood because he clears his throat. "That day . . . I was witness to so much, and yet I still question what it was I saw. Eliza was injured, perhaps gravely so, but you . . . healed her. Is this the truth of it?"

The weight of his question feels like an elephant sits upon my chest. I don't know what to say, so I go with the truth. "Yes."

He raises his eyebrows like he's surprised I admitted this. "And then what happened?"

"I lost consciousness." There—the easiest fact first.

"That's one thing I was sure of. But what *caused* you to faint?"

"What I did to Eliza."

"Have you always been this good at interrogations?" he asks, the corner of his mouth tipping up slightly.

I move my gaze to the ceiling. "In healing Eliza, I used too much of my own energy and nearly stopped my heart."

"Good God, Katherine. Why would you risk such a thing?"

"Would you rather I left her to die?"

He opens his mouth, shuts it again. "No, I—no, of course not." His hand is warm on mine, his eyes intense. "But neither would I want you to die in her place."

"I've been given the power to heal, so I had to help her."

He's quiet for so long I risk a glance at his face. The frown lines are back. The tension in the air mounts and fear of his poor opinion of me causes my stomach to churn. "And what Eliza said—is that true, too?"

"No, I'm not a witch."

He waits again, obviously wanting me to tell him without prompting. It's my most guarded secret, though, and I have no experience with explaining it to other people. Curiosity must win out because he says, "But you're not human?"

"Yes, I'm human," I snap, prickly and insulted despite myself. "Mostly. Well, half. My father is. My mother is—was—Sylvan."

"Sylvan," he repeats as if testing the word. "And this allows you to . . . heal other people?"

"Among other things," I say wearily. "We derive our power from the sun."

My hand is shaking as I pull up the covers higher. My eyes grow heavy again, and I blink slowly.

"Forgive me," he murmurs. "I've pushed you too hard and you're not yet recovered. Are you hungry, should I send for one of the servants?"

"No, I just need to rest. Forgive me," I whisper.

Everything goes black again.

TWENTY-THREE

WHEN I wake again, the sun has set, and the fire casts long shadows on the wall. I turn toward the chair Lord Thornewood occupied earlier. My sister is there instead, engrossed in sewing a floral needlepoint. Guilt eats at me when I see the shadows beneath her eyes. Even the way she sits is tired, with her shoulders hunched forward.

She must sense me watching her because she looks up and widens her eyes. "Wren," she cries, tossing her needlepoint to the side, "are you feeling better?"

"I am, actually." Upon careful inspection, the terrible weakness I struggled with for the past few days has dissipated.

I push myself into a sitting position, and Lucy throws her arms around my neck. "Oh, I'm so relieved," she says with a watery smile. "You must be terribly hungry. Would you like for me to call for something to eat?"

"That would be divine. Some tea as well—if it's not too much trouble."

"Not at all, let me just ring for one of the servants." She pulls the velvet rope hidden on the other side of my end table. She gestures to the space next to me in the big bed and asks in a small voice, "May I join you?"

I pull the covers back to make room for her. She smiles at me just as she used to do when she was little and sought comfort from a nightmare. Her slim arms wrap around me as she snuggles close. "I was so frightened for you," she says.

I rest my chin on the top of her head. "I'm sorry to have worried you. I'm much improved, though, I promise."

"I have so many questions. Lord Thornewood has refused to tell us anything other than you had a terrible fall while riding. But I know that can't be true."

"No, it's not the truth. But it was very clever of him to say so."

"Does it have to do with Eliza?"

The pit of my stomach feels like a gaping hole. I pull back, and she turns around to look at me. "How do you know she was involved? What have you heard?"

Lucy chews her bottom lip, something she only does when she'd rather not tell me. I stare at her until she gives in. "After we all discovered you had been hurt and returned to the house," she says in a quiet voice, "Eliza was there, ranting you'd done something to her."

"And?"

"She said you used witchcraft. But no one believed her," she hastens to add.

I fall back against the pillow, tears stinging my eyes. "I am ruined."

Lucy touches my arm. "Don't say that. Lord Thornewood told everyone she'd also suffered a bad fall and was confused."

"He'll never marry me now," I whisper.

"Marry you? What do you mean?"

I tell her everything. From the night he saved me from Lord Blackburn, the stolen kiss, the declaration, and finally, what really happened with Eliza.

Lucy shakes her head. "Even so, Lord Thornewood cares for you—I know it. He was the one who sat by your side when we first thought . . ." she trails off and wraps her arms around herself.

"You thought I wouldn't wake up?" I ask gently.

She nods and dabs at her eyes with a handkerchief. "He never gave up hope, and he has the best doctor attending you. He even carried you out to rest on a lounge chair in the sun—against the doctor's orders, of course—just because I asked him to."

I wince as I think of him carrying my unconscious form. What must he have thought? "Yes, but where is he now?"

She avoids my look for a moment. "He said he had urgent business in London. But he waited until we were sure you were better!"

I smile sadly. No doubt he has fled just as Henry did long ago. "In any case, I appreciate the care he's given me."

"He did so because he loves you. You must see that."

"The only thing I see is an honorable man who took care of a house guest when she needed it."

One of the servants arrives with our tea and my late supper, but she quickly leaves as if sensing the tension in the room. Lucy returns to her chair by the fire, and I eat my food mechanically, the clink of metal on china loud in the quiet room.

Another knock on the door causes us both to startle, and I spill a drop of amber tea on the pale sheets. I watch it soak in, unable and unwilling to look up.

"Yes, come in," Lucy says.

The same maid returns, her expression reluctant. "Forgive me for intruding, but Miss Lucy, your grandmother is asking for you."

Lucy puts her tea cup down on my side table and squeezes my shoulder. "I'll be back in a moment."

I nod, swallowing the last bit of food. I can't even say what it was I just ate.

Lucy follows the maid out and closes the door with a firm click. I put my tray to the side and get shakily to my feet. Mama's journal is hidden in my trunk.

After retrieving it, I clasp it to my chest. "Please, Mama," I whisper.

I open the journal.

I stare until my eyes burn. The words never appear.

Does my own mother judge me for what I did? For using forbidden arcana? For outing myself to all of Society? I sway on my feet. The weakness assailing my limbs makes me feel as though I am walking underwater. I return to bed and curl my body around the journal as if it can bring me the same comfort I would get from my mother. A sob escapes, and I press my fist to my mouth. But it isn't until I think of everything I've probably lost that the tears start to flow in earnest.

Because losing Lord Thornewood would be far more devastating than losing Henry was.

I haven't cried myself to sleep since my mother died. My eyes are puffy and difficult to open, gritty as they are from salty tears.

A sharp knock rings out, and I force myself to sit up, sweeping tangled hair from my face. "Come in," I say.

Grandmama marches in, her gaze direct. "Good. You're awake. I understand from Lucy you are feeling much better."

"I am."

"It's only a matter of time before Eliza reveals to everyone what really happened." Her lip curls in disgust. "Now you've shown your true nature."

I lower my eyes to the sheets.

"You've ruined everything—just as I thought you would. I only pray I can salvage what's left of your reputation for Lucy's sake." Her words tear into me, and I wrap my arms around myself. "We shall not trespass on Lord Thornewood's hospitality any longer. Once you are dressed, we will return to London posthaste."

I flounder for an excuse, my mouth opening and closing several times. Then I realize I shouldn't bother. Lord Thornewood is no longer here, and I have no further claim to a room in his lovely estate. I probably never will again.

"Yes, I think that's best," I tell Grandmama. Her eyebrows lift slightly at my acquiescence, but she recovers quickly enough.

"I'll notify Devi you will need assistance getting dressed."

"Could you also ask her to prepare a bath?"

"Very well, but be quick about it. Lord Thornewood is not the only one who has business to attend to in London." She leaves without another word—not that I expected any concern. Not from her.

London greets us with cacophonous noise, dirty streets, and dreary rain. It matches my mood beautifully, though, so I cannot bring myself to be cross with it. The rain is cold as we walk up the few stairs to Grandmama's townhome.

"I will not be joining you for tea," Grandmama says once we're inside. "I have much to attend to, so please excuse my absence."

This is all said mostly to Lucy, but I nod as well. She gives Lucy an apologetic smile, which wanes as she glances at me. I save her the potential awkwardness of being kind to me and walk away. Tea sounds like a lovely diversion. Anything to hide from the damage Eliza could be doing at this very moment.

One of the maids has set out steaming hot tea by the time I enter the parlor, and I settle into one of the more comfortable chairs with a cup.

"You must send him a note," Lucy says, closing the door behind her.

I sigh and close my eyes. She began this nagging argument before we left. Since any meaningful conversation in the carriage with Grandmama is impossible, she has probably been dying to continue it.

I can feel her watching me as she stirs sugar and milk into her tea. The spoon clinks pleasantly against the sides of the china. "He must know you are no longer in the country. I know he'll come to call if he has word you are here."

"And allow him the chance to tell me that not only is my reputation in tatters, but he could never marry someone who isn't entirely human?" I scoff and take a sip of tea, unsuccessfully hiding the bitter poison spewing from me. "You may call me a coward if you wish, but I cannot face him at the moment."

Lucy paces in front of me. "Then when? You cannot remain in this horrible limbo of not knowing forever."

"Better that than knowing for sure I've lost my chance with him forever."

Lucy slams her tea cup down on the table. "Are you listening to yourself, Wren? It doesn't even sound like you!"

My eyes widen at her tone. Her cheeks are flushed with the intensity of her feeling. Immediately my self-righteous attitude deflates. A sob is struggling its way out of my throat, but I swallow it down. Tears fill my eyes anyway. "Because I love him too much to hear the truth," I say in a tortured voice.

Her anger disappears as quickly as it came. She wraps her arms around me. "Forgive me. I shouldn't have raised my voice at you. You've been through so much."

I shake my head, tears still making tracks down my cheeks. "No, I needed to hear it."

She pulls back and stares into my eyes. "We could have a compromise. You could think on it tonight and send word to him in the morning."

I hesitate because, truthfully, even tomorrow is too soon. "I can agree to that."

"Good." She grins. "Because if you don't, I will."

Mary interrupts us with a bob of her head in apology. "Pardon me, mum, but a Miss Eliza Gray has come to call on you. Shall I . . . show her in?" she asks hesitantly when I do nothing but stare at her.

"I suppose," I say finally.

"Are you sure, miss?"

I glance at Lucy. "Yes, it's fine. She can . . . join us for tea."

"Are you mad?" Lucy asks in an angry hiss as soon as the door closes behind Mary. "You should have turned her away!"

"No, I will hear her out." I'm sure I will only regret it, but I must know how much damage has been done.

Mary returns with Eliza, who is dressed in a lavender striped satin gown. She looks regal in it, and I glance down at my casual white blouse and dark skirt with a frown. Already she has made me feel inadequate, and she hasn't said a word.

Despite her noble appearance, my sister and I still outrank her, so we keep our seats. "Hello, Eliza," I say, and Lucy mumbles a half-hearted greeting. I hold out a hand toward the pale pink chair across from us. "Won't you sit?"

"I cannot stay long," she says as if we were the ones to invite her. Her eyes sweep around the room as she sits on the very edge of the chair.

"Tea?" I ask.

She barely hides the upward curl of her lip. "No, thank you."

When she continues to look around the room, I sigh. "What brings you here? Last we spoke, you ran away screaming."

"I came to be sure what you *did*," her emphasis on the last word is like a verbal sneer, "doesn't have any lasting effects."

Lucy stiffens beside me, and I put a hand on her arm. "What I did? You mean, saving your life? Should I have left you with the branch protruding from your lung then?"

"How do I know you didn't bewitch that horse in the first place?"

Anger explodes inside me. "Believe me, if I had any wish to harm you, I wouldn't have suffered through your odious company for so long."

Her eyes narrow. "I knew it. You are capable of harming someone. I hope they lock you up in Bedlam."

Being imprisoned in an insane asylum would be a worse fate than death, and for a moment, the possibility strikes me mute. I think of the conversation I once stumbled upon at a country dance in Gloucestershire. How the asylum treated its inmates with the utmost cruelty and inhumane treatment. How it had a dark history of allowing the public to view the inmates and mock their unstable mental states.

My greatest fear has been my family's good name being ruined because of my mistakes, but Bedlam would be so much worse—for us all.

"You are being most unkind," Lucy says, her fingers gripping her tea cup tightly. She turns to me. "I think she should leave, Wren."

"I don't take threats of Bedlam lightly," I say, my expression hardening. "I have never done the least bit of harm to you, and from the moment you met me, you have treated me as the worst sort of criminal. Against my better judgment, I let you into this room. But I see you have nothing but vitriol to spew, as usual."

She stands, her chin arrogantly held aloft. "I treated you the way you should have been treated by everyone who met you. To think, a rebellious little outsider from Gloucestershire could attract the attention of Lord Thornewood! As if that wasn't enough, you had the ability to enchant him with your witchcraft. You probably even went so far as to bewitch that poor little boy into running toward the river!"

"That's enough," I say and stand so I am at eye-level with her. "Your accusations are groundless."

"I know what you are now," she says, "and I've already told as many people as I could. All of London knows Lord Thornewood abandoned you as soon as he saw you for what you were. You're in disgrace, Katherine Sinclair, just as you should have been the moment you set foot in London."

My voice shakes with anger. "Leave. Now."

She smiles meanly and walks toward the door. "You'll never have him now," she says over her shoulder. "I will make certain of that."

The door closes behind her, and I have to bite back the tears. Because I know she's right. Lord Thornewood will never have me now.

Later in the afternoon, with Eliza's threats still fresh in my mind, I sit down to write a note to Lord Thornewood. I cannot let Eliza prevent me from at least trying to reach out to him. Not when the love I feel for him threatens to break me if it is not returned. After mentally crumpling numerous sheets of paper, I pen a note to him.

Dear Colin,

Grandmama insisted we return to London, and I was loath to trespass on your kindness any longer. I appreciate all the care given to me while I was at your home. I hope your schedule will permit you to come to call in the afternoon.

Yours,

K

I struggled with the closing more than the actual words. Would he think I was being too forward in using the word "yours"? But then, it's the truth. I am his, though I am no longer sure he is mine—if ever he was.

I hand Mary the carefully folded note when she comes to help me dress for bed. "Will you be so kind as to put this note in the morning's post?"

She glances down at Lord Thornewood's name printed carefully on the front. "Yes, mum."

I close my eyes in relief. "Thank you so much."

I'm able to relax as she brushes the braids out of my hair and ties it back loosely with a satin ribbon. For better or worse, I will have a response from Lord Thornewood on the morrow.

TWENTY-FOUR

DAYS go by with no word from Lord Thornewood. At the end of the first day, disappointment and despair threatened to consume me. But now I have cocooned myself in a sort of numb apathy.

By the fourth day, Lucy is desperate to bolster my spirits.

"We could go for a ride in the park," she says with a forced smile. "Anything to escape the confines of this house, right?"

I stab the needle through the rose I'm embroidering. "It's a tad too warm for riding today."

Lucy releases a tortured sigh. "And yesterday it was too humid. The day before was too sunny."

"I cannot help it if the weather is uncooperative," I say without looking up from my embroidery.

"It is you who is being uncooperative," Lucy says, her tone full of exasperation. "All I want is my sister back."

"Then concentrate on your studies and leave me to wallow in the pain of being right."

She's quiet for so long I almost believe she's given up. "There must be some explanation," she whispers. She sounds so lost I finally look up.

"There is, but you won't hear of it."

She wraps her arms around herself. "I just cannot believe he would do such a thing."

"Not everyone can handle knowing the truth about our kind," I say gently.

"Papa can. He cannot be the only one."

I return to my embroidery. "It certainly appears that way."

"And why hasn't Grandmama required you to attend any balls? It's odd, don't you think?"

"Not at all. I'm sure she cannot bear the censure we're sure to meet. I've destroyed any hope of a successful debut, remember?" I stab the needle through again and end up pricking my finger. I watch the blood well at the tip. Because of my recklessness, I have ruined not only my chance for a happy marriage, but Lucy's and Robert's as well.

I should have left Eliza to her games when I had the chance. She would have flirted shamelessly with Lord Thornewood for awhile, but it would have been like a soothing balm for her anger. I let my own pride and jealousy get in the way, and it cost me everything. So far, no one from Bedlam has come for me, but I freeze in terror every time one of the servants enters the room. I'm sure Eliza has done as she promised in every other regard, however, and my reputation is in tatters.

Lucy sits beside me on the settee. "I have a confession," she says, and I pause in my sewing and drop the blood-stained embroidery to my lap. "Before we even left Lord Thornewood's, I told Grandmama I wanted to send word to Robert. I penned a short note we needed to see him, but I haven't heard back. For awhile I thought he'd simply appear, but there's been no sign of him."

"I was wondering why he did not come," I say, a little embarrassed to admit I wanted the same. It was better for him to take sanctuary at Oxford for as long as he could.

"I was about to send a telegram to Papa as well, but then you woke, and well, here we are."

"I'm afraid my ability to process abstract concepts has left me of late," I say, my voice a tired reflection of the way I feel. "You'll have to be more precise explaining your thoughts."

"I'm worried my note was intercepted. And if the one to Robert was, then perhaps the one to Lord Thornewood was as well."

The smallest bud of hope stirs inside me, but I push it down. "What would Grandmama have to gain in such an endeavor?" But even as I ask it, I think of her unusual behavior of late. The suspicious letter, the rude treatment of Lord Thornewood, her apparent disinterest in our developing relationship.

"I know it isn't much to go on, but I cannot escape this feeling."

"We must think on this further," I say. "We don't have all the facts, and we are restricted by our lack of independence. We cannot even leave the house without Grandmama knowing."

Lucy is quiet for a time, worrying the skirt of her dress as she thinks. She finally says in a hushed voice, "Not if we leave at night."

I turn to her with shock warring against amusement. What had become of my well-mannered little sister? "And go where?"

"To Lord Thornewood's."

I cannot help but smile at the determination in her eyes. "I dare not argue with you when you are in this mood, but I feel I must point out we have no idea where his townhome is located."

Her face falls for a moment. "Then we shall walk the streets until we find it."

I shake my head. "Absolutely not. It's much too dangerous, and my power has not returned to the same level it was before."

"We cannot stop trying. Let's ask Grandmama about going to the park. If we go every day, we may run into Lord Thornewood."

"Very well," I say, getting to my feet.

Before I can walk to the door, the footman enters. "Miss Sinclair, there's a gentleman here to see you. Shall I show him in?"

I glance back at Lucy, whose face is awash with excitement and hope. "Please do."

"Very good, miss," he says and leaves to retrieve him.

Lucy jumps to her feet. "It's Lord Thornewood! It has to be. He must have sought you out after he didn't hear from you."

A smile is spreading slowly over my face. Could Lucy have been right all along?

The door opens again, and we turn to greet our visitor.

But instead of Lord Thornewood's characteristic dark form, the meticulously dressed Lord Blackburn stands in the doorway.

I stand gaping, all trace of my welcoming smile long gone. My heartbeat thuds in my ears, though I wonder how my heart continues to beat at all. I almost wish it was someone from Bedlam. I think they would be more of a welcome sight than the man who attacked and threatened me. Lucy looks confused, then apprehensive, lines forming between her arched brows.

"How did you get in here?" I demand finally.

He raises his eyebrows in mock surprise. "Why, the butler let me in, of course."

I straighten my spine. "You must leave at once. You are not welcome here."

"On the contrary, I have every right to be here." He strides forward, and I move in front of my sister. With a mocking smile, he reclines in one of the chairs as if it is a throne.

I grab Lucy's hand. "Then we have the right to return to our rooms. Let's go, Luce."

"Not so hasty, if you please. We have business to discuss. In fact, your grandmother will join us any moment."

His comment stops us. Icy fear splashes inside my stomach. I think we are on the verge of discovering just what Grandmama has been up to, and it won't be something pleasant.

"I thought it was understood you would no longer seek me out," I say, still gripping Lucy's hand tightly.

He smirks. "You are referring to Lord Thornewood's barbaric threats, no doubt? Well, I believe we can all agree he no longer has an interest in your affairs. Not after the scandalous events of this weekend."

I swallow down my questions. I desperately want to know what he has heard, but I refuse to give him the satisfaction. "I thought I made myself perfectly clear. Even without Lord Thornewood's intervention."

Lucy keeps looking back and forth between us, her eyes wide with fear.

"That was then," he says. "Things have changed for you now. Without Lord Thornewood to hide behind, I'm free to press my suit. You see, I still want you for my wife."

Lucy stiffens beside me. I try not to picture being married to him, but I'm overcome by an ill feeling anyway. I narrow my eyes. "Because of your insurmountable gaming debt?"

His loud bark of laughter jars me. "My what? Wherever did you hear that?"

"From a reputable source," I say between gritted teeth. "Do you deny it?"

In answer, he laughs again. "Ask your grandmother," he says, his eyes glittering with laughter . . . and something darker.

As if on cue, she joins us, a tight smile on her face. "Lord Blackburn," she says without so much as a glance in my or Lucy's direction, "how delightful to see you again."

The lines on my grandmother's face are more pronounced, especially by her mouth and eyes, as if she's been under a lot of strain. Again, apprehension sneaks its fingers up my spine.

"Your granddaughter said the most amusing thing," he says, his eyes humorless. "She accused *me* of being in debt. For gambling no less."

She pales. "I cannot imagine where she'd hear such a thing."

He shrugs. "Idle gossip, perhaps."

"Perhaps," Grandmama says warily.

"In any case, I'd just declared my intentions to Katherine. As my future wife, she has every right to inquire about my financial stability."

"Grandmama, I will not marry him. There is no love between us, and you do not understand the sort of man he is."

"I understand plenty. Unfortunately, the decision is not yours to make."

Anger crackles over my skin. "Without a doubt it is. It's my life."

"It may be your life, but your father sent you here under my guidance. This is the best match for you." She leans toward me. "The *only* match."

I turn back to Lord Blackburn, my hands in fists at my side. "Why would you even want me as your wife? You said yourself you know of the events of this weekend."

He smirks. "I know all about them, thanks to your grandmother. As a member of the Order of the Eternal Sun, however, a beautiful lady with abilities such as yourself is beyond desirable—even one who has publicly disgraced herself. You see, there is no one quite so rare as you. There have been others, of course, other members of your race our esteemed Order has uncovered . . ." he pauses as both Lucy and I share a look of reluctant surprise. "Oh yes, there are others, but they are so few and far between—the last we found living in India. None have been as powerful as you, though. In this, you are quite unique. And as you might remember from visiting my library, I'm an avid collector of the rare and exotic."

Dark rage stirs in my stomach. "I am not some Egyptian sarcophagus you can put on display. Grandmama, you cannot expect me to accept such an offer. Though Society expects marriage from me, I'm no longer in good standing with Society anyway."

Her expression is unmoved.

Desperate, I blurt out, "He tried to take advantage of me. In the garden. The night of Lady Drake's ball."

Her expression only turns to one of disgust. "I'm sure you did something to encourage such improper behavior. You may feel free to throw your life away, but I won't let you drag your sister down with you."

I tense, my anger giving way to true fear. She pinpointed the one thing I cannot argue against.

"It doesn't matter," Lucy says, her voice shaky. "You cannot bring me into this." She turns to me with wide eyes. "You cannot marry him, Wren."

"She is resisting our arrangement, Lucille," Lord Blackburn. "Perhaps we should explain to her just how important it is she complies."

Grandmama pales.

He chuckles. "Truly, I think you may find it almost comical. At the very least, you'll find it ironic. You see, when you accused me of being the one in debt, you were close. Unfortunately, your information was skewed."

He shifts his gaze from Lucy and me to Grandmama. Lucy lets out her breath in surprise. "Your grandmother is the one with a gambling problem. In fact, it seems to have reached the point of an addiction. Not unusual in our set, but what *is* unusual is what she likes to play for."

I think of the game of high-stakes baccarat I found Grandmama engaged in, and of the missing barouche. My chest tightens.

He stands, moves much too close to me. Lucy shrinks back, but I force myself to stand unflinching before him. "Luck has always favored me, and your grandmother made the tremendous mistake of agreeing to play baccarat with me. She lost, of course." He turns to Grandmama. "Tell her the stakes, Lucille."

My grandmother stands ram-rod straight before us, her wan face and tightly pressed lips the only signs of distress. "We played for your hand in marriage."

Lord Blackburn's smirk disappears. "And I always collect on a debt."

TWENTY-FIVE

THE blood pounds in my ears, muffling Lucy's anguished cry. Her hand tightens on my arm. "Grandmama, how *could* you?"

Suddenly, everything falls into place. The way Grandmama practically forced me to dance with him every dance, the argument with Lord Blackburn at his estate, the intensity of her anger when she believed me to be disagreeing with him. I think of the day after that terrible night Lord Blackburn attacked me, when I interrupted her writing a letter. Of course she wasn't encouraging my relationship with Lord Thornewood, not when she'd promised me to Lord Blackburn.

"And why," I say, my eyes narrowing as I stare at my grandmother, "should I agree to honor such an arrangement?"

A slow, humorless grin spreads across his face. "You are a rarity, Katherine, it's true, but you are not the only one with arcana." When his gaze falls on Lucy, my hands curl into fists.

"No," I say, my tone low with warning.

"If you will not agree to marry me, then I will take your sister as payment instead."

"I will tell our father the truth—you cannot force either one of us to marry you," I say.

Lord Blackburn glances at Grandmama. "Your grandmother is prepared to spread a rumor that will be Lucy's ruin if you refuse."

Behind me, Lucy sucks in her breath in disbelief.

"Lucy will be blacklisted from every ball, every party," he continues. "Even her dowry won't be enough to tempt a suitor. With your own considerable scandal to shame the family name, Robert will have to search for a bride in the lower rungs of Society, but even then, families of any worth will refuse to have him as a suitor. If you refuse to honor the agreement, Katherine, and if I cannot take Lucy as substitute payment, then all three of the Sinclair siblings' lives will be ruined."

Desperation builds in me, and like a trapped animal, I whirl on our grandmother. "You lost more to him than just my hand in marriage. What hold does he have over you?"

"Witnesses," Lord Blackburn says with a self-congratulatory smile that begs to be smacked from his face. "I have witnesses to your grandmother not only participating in an illegal card game, but gambling away her granddaughter's hand in marriage."

"Men under his pay and control," Grandmama says weakly.

"Can you imagine the scandal?" Lord Blackburn says.

I feel the way a moth must when it realizes it will never escape from the spider's web. His words succeed in their goal. True fear claws at my insides, and for the first time in my life, I have no idea how to get myself out of the muddle I'm in. A horrified silence descends upon Lucy and me. I glance at my younger sister; I would do anything to keep her from this monster. "When are we to be married?"

"Wren, *no*," Lucy says, dissolving into quiet sobs.

"No posh London wedding for you, I'm afraid," Lord Blackburn says. "We will elope. No waiting days for the reading of the banns, no permission needed from protective fathers." He walks over and cups my cheek in a mockery of a loving touch. "Do we have an understanding?"

I wrench my face away from his hand. "How long do I have?"

He smiles. "I'll give you a full day to prepare."

I pull Lucy with me as I leave the room, slamming the door behind us. I want to bring the house down on Grandmama and Lord Blackburn both, but I haven't the strength.

She's quiet until we're safely behind my closed bedroom door. With panic in her voice, she grips my hands. "You cannot marry him. I won't let you." Her eyes plead with me. "Tell me you have a plan."

My throat feels clogged with the need to cry—mostly out of frustration. I pull away gently and pace in front of my bed. If I don't stay in motion, I know I will dissolve into frantic tears.

"Not a plan exactly—not yet," I say. Her eyes fill with tears, and I have to look away so she won't see the devastated expression on my face.

"What is it? What can we do?"

"I think we can safely assume Grandmama will intercept any note we write—to Papa, to Robert, or even to . . . Lord Thornewood."

She nods sadly. "I think there's very little she would not do."

"Lord Blackburn said it himself: I no longer have Lord Thornewood to hide behind. He's afraid of what the earl can do—socially, and . . ." I pause as I think of Lord Thornewood's clearly uttered threat. "Physically."

"Yes, of course," Lucy says, hope renewing in her eyes. "Lord Thornewood will gladly come to your aid; I am so happy you finally see reason."

I cannot bear to dampen her spirits, but the truth is Lord Thornewood is an honorable man who hates Lord Blackburn. He would come to anyone's aid in this situation, and he seems to truly care for Lucy. We would be united in not wanting such a terrible fate to befall her. His social pull is such that one word could destroy Lord Blackburn, just as he threatened.

"Oh, but how will we send him word?" Lucy asks. "Grandmama will surely intercept any note."

"We will write to Penelope in secret," I say. I grab Mama's journal on my nightstand and hand it to Lucy. "Mama thought of a way."

Lucy runs her fingers over the front of the book, her brows furrowed. "How?"

"I'm going to attempt to copy her arcana," I say, little quivers of nervousness fluttering through me. I'm not sure I can pull this off. But I have to.

Lucy gives me a skeptical look. "Do you know the way?"

"I have no choice. With this arcana, I can pen a frivolous note to Penelope, only to have it change to our real message once she opens it."

A slow smile spreads across her face, and I return it. "That might actually work."

"It has to," I say. I stride to my vanity and pull out a piece of paper and pen. "Help me write it."

She joins me at my vanity and leans over my shoulder. "Which one should go first?"

"The real message. With any luck, I'll make it disappear and hide it with the other."

My pen scratches across the paper, my normally neat handwriting as shaky as I feel. When I finish, we stare at the words.

"They're not disappearing," Lucy whispers.

A nervous giggle escapes me. "I haven't done anything yet."

"Oh. Well—"

"I'm thinking. I've never tried to make anything disappear before." I glare at the paper like the force of my desperation will make the ink fade before our eyes. I think of all the arcana I've ever worked. Of healing Eliza, influencing animals, taking Lucy's headaches away. I gasp. "It's just like your headaches," I say.

"What?"

"Your headaches. I make them disappear," I say, an enthusiastic grin appearing on my face. "It might work with the words."

She leans forward, her eyes wide with excitement. I hold shaky hands over the paper, pretend it's my sister's forehead instead. My eyelids flutter closed.

It's so much harder than taking away the pain. With her headaches, it is a real, pulsing thing. These words are nothing but ink on paper. I clench my teeth and *concentrate*. Nothing. I say the words I've written in my mind. I repeat them like a mantra.

And then, I see them. They float behind my eyes like dandelion seeds. Painstakingly, I erase each one with healing light. Sweat trickles down my face, and my breath comes in pants. When I reach my initial scrawled at the bottom of the page, I sit back with a loud exhalation.

Lucy's face is etched with concern. "Are you alright? You look ill."

I nod, unable to speak. Instead, I take in great gulping breaths of air. I'm still so frustratingly weak. "I'm fine," I say after a moment. I glance down at the now blank piece of paper, reassuring myself it worked.

I grab the pen and scratch out a note to Penelope.

"Pen, I hope you are well," Lucy reads aloud as I write. "I hope you can forgive me—that we can still be friends. Write to me, and I will explain everything that happened. Yours, K."

"Will it pass inspection?" I ask, and Lucy nods.

I stare at the paper again. I'm not entirely sure how to make it so the real message will reveal itself. I bite the inside of my cheek, as fear of failure flays my insides.

Lucy stares at it as well, her head tilted to one side. She straightens. "I can do it."

I glance at her. "Do what, Luce?"

"Switch the notes once Penelope touches the paper. I know I can do it."

I give her my full attention. "How?"

"It's like one of my drawings," she says, running the tip of her finger over the paper. "I often paint hidden messages or objects. It's my own arcana."

I think of her landscape paintings, of the creatures of fantasy hidden in the flowers, or the Shakespearean quotes that appear when one stares hard enough at the clouds. "Of course," I murmur.

"Let me see the pen," she says. In ornate calligraphy, she writes Penelope's name at the top. She runs her finger over it, but instead of the ink smearing, the name disappears. "Now the paper will recognize her." Again, she runs her finger over the paper, this time over the words of my short note. I watch her lips move as she does so.

When she leans back with a relieved smile on her face, I ask, "What words did you recite?"

"The words from the other note. Now, when it comes in contact with Penelope, the words from this note will fade and the others will appear."

"Then let us hope she has a strong constitution. I'm sure she'll think she has lost her mind."

"They'll blur first. With any luck, she'll blame it on a trick of the eyes."

I hug Lucy in a firm embrace. "Thank you so much, Lucy. This might actually work."

She hugs me back. "It will. I refuse to believe we will be denied our happy ending."

"Grandmama?" I say, entering the parlor cautiously. When I find her there alone, I let out my breath. Lord Blackburn must have already left. The loathing I feel for her is almost palpable, but I keep it carefully hidden. "May I ask a favor of you?"

She looks at me with tired eyes. The lines of her face are even more pronounced, but I do not pity her. "Yes, what is it?"

I hold up the carefully folded note. The one steeped in power. My only hope. "Will you make sure this note is sent to Penelope? You may read it beforehand."

"Why are you bothering me with such a trivial thing?" she demands. "Have the footman add it to the morning post."

"Because I know you've been intercepting my letters," I say, anger stiffening every muscle in my body. A hopeful little voice whispers that perhaps even incoming mail, particularly from Lord Thornewood, may have been hidden from me as well.

She lets out her breath in a huff. "Very well, let me see it."

I march over and hand her the note. My nerves fray like old rope as her eyes scan the contents. "I only seek to renew our friendship," I say.

"I'm not sure what good it will do," she says, "but you may send your letter."

"Will you call your footman in now and tell him?"

She gives me a look of utter exasperation. "William!"

The young footman with unfortunate pockmarked skin opens the door. "My lady?"

"Take this note and have it sent to the Hasting's immediately. It's to be hand-delivered to Miss Penelope."

"Right away, my lady."

She turns to me. "There. Does that satisfy you?"

"Yes, thank you." I follow the footman out and watch from the top of the stairs until he leaves the house, my note clutched in his hand. Only then do I allow myself a tiny smile to celebrate my first victory.

TWENTY-SIX

THE sun sets on my "full day to prepare" without an answer from Penelope or a visit from Lord Thornewood. I sit on my bed the following morning, staring in numb horror at my packed trunk. Lord Blackburn will be here within the hour.

Lord Thornewood's face appears in my mind again, and I swallow a sob. Why has he not shown? Is what I am so disgusting, so impossible to love?

All night long, one thought has taken over my mind: Lord Blackburn does not want me as a wife, he wants to use me as an endless source of arcana. He has made it clear he will use any means necessary, and I know he will never stop coming for my family.

My hands shake, and the beautiful dagger Lord Thornewood gave me, the one I clutch desperately, glints in the light. Mama spoke of defensive arcana, and I hope it will aid me when the time comes. I take a shaky breath.

I will never allow him to steal from me again, but there is only one way to stop Lord Blackburn.

The door creaks open, and I quickly hide the dagger in my reticule.

"Wren?" Lucy calls, her face as drawn and wan as mine must be.

I pat the bed beside me. "Come sit." When she does, I take her hand in mine. "I think it's time to admit this may actually occur," I say quietly.

Inside, I am crumbling, but I must be strong for Lucy, and for what I must do.

Lucy shakes her head, tears tracking down her face. "We must think of other options."

But there are no other options, at least none that result in a happy ending for all of us. Lucy and Robert are my everything. I won't see their lives ruined because of me. Especially since I have lost my chance at love and a happy marriage. Lord Blackburn and Grandmama are right. Who will want me now?

Lucy rummages through my things until she finds Mama's journal. She hands it to me, her eyes so wide and full of hope it pains me. "Perhaps Mama will know what to do."

I have opened the journal every day since the moment I regained consciousness. Always it remains blank. As though even my mother has abandoned me.

To appease my sister, I open it, the flower of hope inside me withering as soon as I see the page without a single word.

I squeeze my sister's hand. "Luce, I have to tell you my real plan." Her eyes jump to mine, but the hope in them dies almost instantly when she sees the grim resignation reflected there. "Lord Blackburn wants me—or you, if I were to escape—for our arcana. It is clear that Lord Thornewood isn't coming to our aid—" I grit my teeth as the pain of his rejection grips me once again.

"He may still come," Lucy says, but her weak tone suggests even she has doubts.

"He may, and no one would be more relieved than I, because it would prevent me from having to do the one thing that will keep Lord Blackburn away from our family." My hands begin shaking violently again, and I clutch my skirt to prevent Lucy from seeing. How can I tell her what I mean to do, when I can barely think of it?

Lucy's voice is so low I barely hear it. "You mean to . . . kill him then?"

"Yes," I say, forcing myself to admit it aloud, to truly acknowledge what I have decided to become. A murderess. "It's the only way we will ever be free from him. My only chance will be in the carriage as we travel to Scotland."

"But the carriage driver will know . . . will you have to . . ." She grows even paler, her unspoken words hanging between us.

I shake my head. "I am unsure whether I'm capable of bringing Lord Blackburn to justice, much less an innocent. Which is why once I have done such a thing, I cannot remain here."

Lucy begins crying in earnest. "Where will you go?"

I wrap my arms around her, swallowing a sob of my own. I thought I had cried myself dry the night before, when I realized that I must leave my family behind and possibly never return. "I will go to Mama's realm."

Her head jerks up. "Wren, you can't! Why do you think Mama never returned? She never mentioned her family—there has to have been a reason. Who knows what awaits you there!"

"I have to, Lucy. What other choice do I have? Think of all the signs Mama left. She would never let any harm come to us, so this has to be what she had in mind. She foresaw this disaster, and she knew this would be the only way."

"But you *can't* . . . I just . . . what will we do without you?"

My eyes fill with tears, and I press my fingers against them to make them stop. I haven't long now, and I don't want to scare my sister.

"You don't have to do this," Lucy says. "We'll think of something . . . perhaps Papa can—"

"There is no other way," I say quietly but firmly. "Papa hasn't the social pull or the assets to stop Lord Blackburn. I will stop him myself and escape to Sylvania. I can't let him take arcana again from me, Luce."

Lucy's eyes refill with tears. "And I would never want such a thing to happen to you again, but *God* . . . how I will miss you!"

"I cannot even think of how much I will miss you." I hug her tightly. "It's my hope that once some time has passed, I will be able to return. There is still a chance this will not be a permanent exile."

Lucy's eyes refill with tears. "Do you really think so?"

"I will do everything I can," I say, but in truth, I haven't the faintest idea.

She nods, a little calmer, her sobs turn to mere hiccups. I am in no danger of crying. Not anymore. I only feel deadened inside. Like every hope I ever had has been ripped from me.

We both startle when Mary knocks on the door. "May I come in?" she asks.

I kiss the tear falling down Lucy's cheek. "It will be alright," I whisper. Louder I say, "Yes, come in."

Mary bustles in, nervously smoothing her skirt when she sees how distraught Lucy is. "You are wanted downstairs, Miss. Lord Blackburn is here for you."

"Will someone collect my trunk?"

She nods. "Yes, mum. I'll have one of the footmen bring it down to the carriage right away."

"Thank you. You may let Lord Blackburn know I will be down shortly."

She bobs a quick curtsy, seemingly in a hurry to leave.

I turn to Lucy. "As soon as you can, go home to Papa. Never return to this house again. But in the meantime, play your part."

She squeezes me as tightly as she used to do when she was little. "I love you, Wren."

"I love you, too, Luce. With all my heart." I tip her chin up so I can look into her eyes. "*None* of this is your fault, and there was nothing you could have done differently." She shifts her gaze to the side, and I know I've pinpointed her true feelings. I give her a gentle shake. "None of it, is that clear?"

"Yes."

I kiss the top of her head and back away, so many emotions churning inside me I'm afraid I'll burst. Despair bleeds into fear engulfed by a simmering rage. I take one step at a time toward the stairs. I can see the top of Lord Blackburn's head. I loathe the sight of it. But as I gaze upon his light-colored hair, my mother's words haunt me. *Two gentlemen will present themselves to you as potential suitors. They will be two sides of the same coin, one dark, one light. Only you will be able to discern which is which, and this will be your greatest challenge.*

Her premonition came true, but though I managed to determine which one was my enemy, I'm still trapped.

"I hope I have not kept you waiting long," I say, my voice thick with sarcasm.

He smiles charmingly, ignoring my tone. "Not at all." He offers me his arm. "Shall we go?"

I long to slap his arm away, but if I am to be successful in my plan, I must have the element of surprise on my side. I firmly avoid any thoughts of how long I will have to maintain this façade. "Yes." I wrench my cheeks upward into a semblance of a smile.

With a patronizing pat on my hand, he says, "I hope you will find my carriage comfortable."

"Oh, I'm quite sure I will." I glance back at the stairs where Lucy watches from the top. She has stifled her tears and glares at Lord Blackburn with open malice. Her solidarity gives me strength. "How long before we reach the nearest inn?"

"Only a few hours." He grins. "Why? Are you so eager to spend the night with me then?"

His laughter causes my teeth to grind against each other. I will have a few hours, then. Precious little time when we are alone on the road, and I must determine if I can truly do such a terrible and permanent act. "I only wanted to know what to expect, my lord," I say tightly.

As he leads me from Grandmama's townhome, I pause and look back. I will my legs not to carry me back inside, back to my sister. When will I ever see her again?

"Did you forget something?" he asks, his tone inching toward irritation.

I continue on without answering. Once inside the carriage, I squeeze as close to the window as I can. Lord Blackburn sits across from me, and I tuck my legs flush against the seat to minimize any chance of our legs touching. He casts an amused look my way, but makes no comment.

With a rap of his fist on the roof of the carriage, we roll forward. I hold my breath, hoping, praying Lord Thornewood will appear and stop this horrible event from happening.

But he does not show.

An hour outside of London, Lord Blackburn moves onto the seat next to me. I have pressed myself so closely to the window that every muscle screams in protest.

"I cannot help but notice how nervous you are, Katherine," he says, a mocking smile on his face.

Despite my fear, I find my ire rising. My cheeks flush. "Indeed? What gave you such an impression?"

He chuckles, which only makes my angry flush deepen. "Come now, let's not quarrel. We are to be married soon, after all."

I touch the side of my reticule, the dagger safely hidden within. "Why this insistence on making me your wife?"

"I believe I answered you before."

"No, you gave me only part of the answer before. I am demanding the truth now. You owe me that much at least."

He sighs as though I am nothing but a petulant child. "Very well." His eyes bore into mine. "I want your power. As my wife, I will have constant access to a wealth of it. And, through me, so will the rest of the Order."

I swallow down the nausea churning in my stomach. I already figured out as much for myself, but hearing him admit to it disgusts me. "What is the goal of your brotherhood? Do you hunt others like me?"

"We have many interests, I suppose you could say," he says with a mean smile. "Some of us delve in the dark arts and alchemy, but we are all avid collectors of the exceedingly rare. There are many objects that house large amounts of energy—nothing like your own, of course—and we mean to harness that power. For I'm sure you've come to realize that those who hold the most power are the ones who rule the world."

This reminds me of my mother's story of her arranged marriage to the Sylvani male who could level whole cities with his power, and I swallow hard. "Who else is in the Order? Do they know about me? What about my family?"

"Katherine, my darling, calm yourself," Lord Blackburn says in a voice steeped in condescension. "Others may suspect, but I haven't confirmed anything yet. For now, I want your power to myself."

This relieves some of my fear for now. I cannot let anyone get word of the truth of my family. "And what is it you do with this power?"

"Have you ever come across tales of the Fountain of Youth?"

"Yes, of course," I snap, tired of his belittlement. "What of it?"

Bright excitement glitters in his eyes. "You *are* our Fountain. Your energy extends our life spans, keeps us youthful in appearance, and protects us from plague and disease."

I feel the color drain from my face. I think of the way Lord Blackburn appeared after stealing power from me—the way he seemed renewed, even glowing with vitality. Suddenly, I feel very light-headed. If I fail, my energy will be used to prolong the life of a madman.

His eyes scan the length of me, and I press myself closer to the carriage window.

I was foolish to think it'd keep him from touching me.

He trails his finger down the side of my face, and the glimmer from his diamond ring catches my eye. *An Egyptian ankh that represents eternal life.* I understand why the Order chose such a symbol now. Cold fingers of warning trail down my back.

He notices me looking at the ring and holds it up. "You once asked me about this," he says, glancing down at it with an odd sort of pride reflected in his eyes. "If only you had known such a ring is a sign of a member of the Order." He smiles when my eyes widen. "And it's astounding, isn't it? I can drain your power away and siphon it directly into this ring. Once filled, it becomes the wearer's own Fountain of Youth."

"Then why do you need me?" I ask. "Why not take enough arcana to fill the ring and be done with me?"

"Oh, but I couldn't do that. You see, the ring will be worth a fortune to those who know its true value. With such an object in my possession, I will become one of the highest-ranking members of the Order." He twists the hateful thing around on his finger and looks at me. "Shall I give you a demonstration?"

Before I can remove the dagger from my bag, he is on top of me, his hands pinning my shoulders against the seat. I panic and try to shove him away. But he has the advantage, both in height and weight. His awkward position on top of me guarantees I will have limited motion, limited ability to fight back.

My rising desperation gives me strength, and I manage to wrench one arm free. I thrust my hand into the bag. The sharp blade cuts my finger, and I yelp.

With a vicious slash, I arc it toward his face. He bellows, cradling his cheek.

"You little bitch," he says in a snarl. "I'll drain you until you're too weak to even move."

He lunges toward me again. This time, when I try to stab him, he grabs my wrist. The other hand wraps around my throat, squeezing until I can no longer draw breath. When the tug in my abdomen turns into a painful ache, I struggle wildly against his hold.

The look in his eyes is murderous. I must end this before I am too weak to fight back.

The energy inside of me is chaos, just as my mind is a mess of panic. Fear steals away every thought in my head until I am as lost as a raft caught in an ocean storm. My body continues to flail in a desperate attempt to save itself. More and more power leaves me, sucked away by whatever strange power Lord Blackburn has. The changes it has on him are instantaneous; his cheeks are rosy as if just having come in from a walk in the sun, and the bands of muscle in his arm become like iron.

I must gain control of my mind. I cannot let him win—not like this. I sink inside my own consciousness and let the rush of power wash over me like a river. I've channeled it before, but never with the intention to hurt someone. Never in defense of my own life.

I gather it to me, closing it off from him. I steal away energy from him before he can take hold, and it almost feels as though I'm being torn in half. Energy builds at the core of me, swirling inside as though a million butterflies beat their wings in desperation. The pressure mounts until my whole body shakes.

I think of the helplessness I felt when he attacked me in Lady Drake's garden; the horror of being the subject of his machinations; the fear of never escaping him. Rage builds, its darkness all I feel.

I grit my teeth while inside I'm screaming in agony. I give into the whirlwind of power inside, the energy continuing to build until I am so full I may shatter into a thousand fragments. Instead, I focus it entirely on Lord Blackburn.

"No!" I scream. I shove against him with all the force I've stored. An explosion of light hits him square in the chest. With a *crack* as loud as thunder, he is catapulted into the other seat. The force buffets me like the strongest wind as the roof of the carriage collapses around him.

Panting, I shove at the door and stumble to the ground. My legs threaten to not hold my weight, and I steady myself with one hand on the carriage. With a shaky feeling of horror in my stomach, I assess the damage. Though my side is untouched, the carriage looks as though a cannon ball shot clear through it, the explosion collapsing even the driver's seat. The driver himself is on the ground, unmoving.

A sob catches in my throat. Did my arcana bring death to this innocent bystander?

Slowly, his chest rises and falls. I let out my breath and relax my shoulders. Thank God. There was no way I could have helped him. I'm completely depleted of energy.

As I watch, his eyes slowly open and focus on my face. "My lady?" he calls weakly.

A strange feeling within me grows when I realize he is not only alive but conscious. Shame causes my breath to hitch as I give name to the feeling: disappointment. I have left a witness to my fatal power.

A frightened whinny calls my attention to the horses. The lead horses are rearing and plunging unsuccessfully against their harnesses. One of the wheels of the carriage has cracked, preventing it from rolling forward. They appear uninjured, and for this, I am grateful. I hold my hands up to calm them. Once their eyes stop rolling back in their heads, I return to the side of the carriage to retrieve my dagger and reticule. My mother's journal is inside, and I will not leave it behind.

Tentatively, I reach inside, my eyes never leaving the unmoving form of Lord Blackburn. Unlike the driver, his chest remains still. I watch for several moments, until I am sure he is lifeless. Relief hits me so strongly I stumble.

As deftly as I can, I free one of the lead horses from the straps that connect it to the trace. I'm forced to saw through the reins with my dagger as I no longer have enough energy inside me to guide them without a bridle. Once the reins are shortened, I haul myself astride.

I cluck encouragingly to the stately black gelding to walk on, and I can tell from his hesitant gait he is unused to having a rider. Still, he will get me to where I need to go.

Fatigue threatens to overtake me, and I know I will never make it far. I am far too weak to attempt to cross over to Mama's realm. The waning sunlight on my back is restorative—it is keeping me seated upon the horse, at least—but I know I will need rest.

The only choice is to stop at a roadside inn. The anonymity there should be enough to keep me safe tonight, but I must leave first thing in the morning.

I'm sure I won't have much time until the carriage driver is found and confesses what he has seen.

Because I cannot very well ride up to the entrance of the inn riding a carriage horse, I dismount when I see the building in the distance. On foot, I lead the black gelding, who seems relieved to have me on the ground again.

I stare at the wooden sign of the inn, the words THE HORSE AND HOUND emblazoned in black while silhouettes of a horse and dog are prominent beneath them. A young, dusty groom approaches me with a concerned look on his face, and I inwardly rehearse the tale I've concocted to explain my situation.

"My lady, are you in need of assistance?" he asks. "Are you injured in any way?"

I affect a harried smile. "I thank you for your concern, but I am uninjured. I do, however, require stabling for my horse."

"Of course, right away." Confusion draws his reddish blonde eyebrows inward. "But, if I may ask, where is your carriage?"

I let my breath out in a rush. "We had trouble on the road—a broken axle—so my driver stayed with the carriage and my luggage. I went on ahead because I am concerned about my horse's hoof. I fear it may be bruised. Would you be so kind as to examine him?"

"I'm so sorry for your trouble," he says, looking so sympathetic I almost feel guilty for my deception. "I'll be sure to look over your horse as you've asked. Should I also send one of the footmen to meet your driver?"

"Oh no, that is quite unnecessary, thank you. He assured me he'd take care of everything," I say with a flippant wave of my hand. "Now, please excuse me, but I really must see if I can secure a room for the night." I flash him a tired smile and head toward the inn.

The main floor of the inn is a pub, cool inside with dim lighting. I draw my shoulders back and march inside like I belong there. As though I am not an unaccompanied single lady who has no business traveling alone.

An elderly gentleman with a shock of white hair and matching white muttonchops comes out from behind the bar counter when he notices my approach. "My lady, what can I do for you?"

I smile as brightly as I can muster as I've found smiling can often cause people to overlook a bold-faced lie. "Sir, I am Mrs. Blackstone," I say, providing a name I hope will cause him to assume I'm a widow. "I'd like a meal and lodgings for the night."

He returns my smile, and I relax a bit. "Right away, Mrs. Blackstone," he says. "Has my groom already taken care of your horse and carriage? Do you need assistance with your luggage?"

"He has, and unfortunately, I encountered trouble on the road with my carriage. As of now, I will not be able to retrieve my luggage."

"How very unfortunate indeed," he says, his deep blue eyes conveying genuine sympathy. "Please let me know if there is anything we can assist you with."

"There is one other thing, if you could be so kind," I say. "My uncle, Lord Edward Sinclair, will be covering all my expenses."

"Of course, madam."

Another cause for relief. I have a few coins in my reticule but not enough to cover my stay.

"Supper will be served shortly if you'd like to sit and rest while I have your room prepared," he says.

"That would be lovely. Thank you."

He guides me to one of the tables in the far back corner of the room and holds out a chair. "Anything else I can do for you?"

I shake my head. "No, you've been perfectly accommodating. Thank you."

"My pleasure, madam."

When he walks away, I finally allow myself to relax and take note of my surroundings.

An older couple sits at the next table over, enjoying wine and a roast. My stomach doesn't even respond to the presence of the meat, though it smells delicious. Another gentleman dressed in plain but expensive clothing drinks a flagon of beer by the fire, while one of the barmaids refills his cup.

I look down at the whorls in the wood of the table. Flashes of the way it felt to have my power sucked out of me threaten to come to the forefront of my mind, but I won't let them. I would rather not relive the moment when I used my arcana to do harm instead of good, but I cannot deny that I am reveling in the fact that I managed to hurt him as he hurt me. As soon as I can walk farther than a few feet, I must search for the gateway.

When a red-cheeked barmaid arrives with a glass of wine and the same roast the older couple to my right are enjoying, I try to force myself to at least eat a little. I know I will need my strength.

I chew and drink mechanically, the adrenaline that got me this far abandoning me all at once. My eyelids grow heavy, and when the barmaid returns to clear my plate, I practically slur out my request to take me to my room.

She leads me up the stairs and to a warm, quaint room with sparse furnishings. The bed beckons to me, but in a flash of cognizance, I turn to her. "I wonder if I might have pen and paper for a letter?"

"Of course, m'lady. Anything else I can get you?"

"No, I think I shall be quite comfortable. Thank you."

With a bob of her head, she closes the door behind her. My eyes continually droop closed, but I force myself to remain standing until she returns with my writing supplies.

"If I write this letter quickly, will you be able to post it in the morning?" I ask when she places a few sheets of writing paper and a pen on the small desk in my room.

"Yes, mum. Just call for me when you are finished. My name is Sarah, and I'll busy myself in the hall until you're ready."

The paper is rougher than I'm used to, and the ink smears in several places, but it serves its purpose. Now that my grandmother can no longer intercept them, I am free to write letters to my father and brother.

Sarah is waiting for me in the hall, just as she promised, and I hand over the letters.

"I'll be sure to post it first thing, mum," she says, her wide eyes earnest.

I thank her and shortly after collapse in bed fully dressed. Before I give in to the sleep I desperately need, I open my mother's journal and pray she will advise me in what I must do next.

When the words appear, finally, after so many weeks without them, a muffled sob escapes me.

My dearest Katherine,

There are times in our life when it seems all hope is lost and despair threatens to overtake us. These times are like eclipses of the sun. They are fleeting, and they will not last. We make our own future, Sylvan and human alike, through our decisions and, most of all, through a powerful hope that there is meaning even in suffering.

With our powerful gifts, we are held to an even higher standard. It is a cruel truth that our mistakes often cause permanent ramifications. And yet . . . there is hope still. When we are in our weakest moments, logic can fail us. The thing we think would be the best choice may, in fact, be the most destructive.

These are the times we must forsake the guidance of our minds and follow instinct instead. It may lead you to the one thing you need most of all.

With much love,
Mama

Tears well in my eyes, but I'm too exhausted to release them. If ever there's a time when I felt lost and despairing, this is it. I press the tips of my fingers to my forehead until I'm sure I make indentations in my skin. I know my mother is trying to convey an important truth in this entry. But what does my logic tell me is the best course? I thought escaping to her realm was the only answer, but perhaps this is the wrong choice? I cry out in frustration and shove the journal to the side. How can I be expected to puzzle through this when I can hardly keep my eyes open? I can only hope the light of day will bring answers I can never hope to find in this dark night.

I awake to a stabbing pain. Rolling to my side, I cradle my stomach, tears springing to my eyes. It takes me a moment to remember the horrible events of the day before. But when I do, I force myself out of bed.

The first time Lord Blackburn took my power from me by force, he was interrupted. Yesterday, he nearly succeeded, and my body has still not recovered. Only the sun on my skin can help me now.

I stumble to the window, but the view outside only causes a dejected moan to escape from my mouth. It is before dawn, the sky a dismal gray-black.

But before I can truly give in to the cloud of dark self-pity hovering just above me, the brush of something soft against my leg startles me, and I look down. A white fox, more silver in the dim light really, gazes up at me.

Katherine, the fox says in my mind.

"Are you really here?" I ask. Perhaps I'm so weak now that I'm hallucinating.

In spirit, it answers. *I served your mother once. A piece of me will always be bound to her will. In this case, my consciousness was stored in her runes.*

Spirit. The visions of this creature finally make sense. "You were my mother's spirit animal." Waves of awe crash over me when I think of the true scope of my mother's abilities.

It regards me with a deep loss reflected in its eyes. *Long ago, yes. I am no longer what I once was.*

Tears burn my eyes as an intense longing just to hear my mother's voice again grips me. "You've come to lead me to her realm then?"

I have come to show you Sylvania.

Its answer seems to be subtly different from what I asked, but the fox has already proven itself as mysterious as my mother. Interrogation will get me exactly nowhere.

It pads silently to a full-length mirror I had previously paid little attention to—an unusual enough object in such a Spartan room. *Your spirit must enter the mirror. Your body, in its current state, cannot make the journey.*

I give a little jerk of my limbs. Separating one's soul from one's body seems to be a rather intensely dangerous sort of arcana. "Will I ever be able to return?"

Once you have seen what I have been sent to show you.

The fox's words do nothing to reassure me, but its eyes, so reminiscent of my mother's, do. Coupled with the fact that I have very little to lose, I take a shaky step forward. "You must tell me what to do," I say, "for I confess I have not had the occasion to separate my soul from my body."

Something close to a display of amusement—the barest hint of a chuckle, perhaps?—flashes through my mind. *This mirror will serve as our portal. You need only step through as I do. Your spirit will pass through.*

"And my . . . body? What will happen when I cross?"

Your body will remain here, unconscious.

A prickle of fear chased with a glimmer of excitement rushes across my skin. I hesitate only a moment before going to the rough wooden door of my room and assure myself it is barred from the inside. I imagine it would be something of a shock for the poor maid to find me in a heap upon the floor.

I join the fox before the mirror, our reflections ghostly pale. The bruises on my throat are a garish purple, shaped like Lord Blackburn's hands. I close my eyes against the anger that rises in response. *Dead*, I remind myself. *He is dead.*

The fox glances up at me, nods once, and we both step through the cold glass.

TWENTY-SEVEN

RATHER than the rush of air I expected, our journey through the mirror is more like a submersion in a still pool of water. The glass turns to liquid around me, sounds are muffled, and though my eyes are clenched tightly closed, I have the impression of being surrounded by darkness. All these strange sensations last only a moment before soft light and the musical sound of birds replace them.

I am only spirit, and therefore cannot draw my breath in exclamation of my awe, but I make the gesture anyway when I open my eyes. The brief glimpses of Sylvania I had seen before through my mother's runes were nothing compared to the actual sight before me. The fox and I stand on a precipice that looks out upon a mountainous wood of such beauty, I suddenly wish for Lucy's ability to recreate scenes on canvas.

The trunks of the trees are similar to birch in that they are of a snow white color, but the leaves are so ethereal there is no doubt they are from another world entirely. Most are of the same shimmery silver color I first saw in one of Mama's visions, but many are the pinks and lavenders of a sunset. They remind me of wisteria, but the tree trunks are so wide, they must be ancient.

Massive waterfalls plummet from rocky outcroppings, and rising from the valley is a city of such majesty, it would put all of London to shame. The buildings themselves are as white as those found in a Mediterranean village, their architecture at once organic and ornate with intricate scrollwork and columns, which seem to be wrought from the rock itself. Even more awe-inspiring is the fact that many have been built directly on top of a waterfall, so that the water cascades from beneath the stony foundations.

This is the city of Cascadia. Your grandfather is king here.

Surprise shoots through me. "King?"

The fox gives me no time to process this before continuing down a stone pathway, winding toward the city proper. I follow in my ghostly form, somewhat bewildered by my own gliding movements. It is unsettling to say the least not to be able to feel the stones beneath my feet, though I know they must be smooth and cool to the touch, nor the breeze I can hear moving through the leaves. Of my senses, only vision and hearing remain.

The fox continues on at a rapid pace. Above me, the trees murmur in a language I feel I can almost understand—if I could only stop for a moment and listen. When I reach the bottom of the stone path, the landscape around me changes. If it weren't for the conviction I hold that I truly left my body behind and followed my mother's spirit fox to another realm, I would be tempted to believe this is merely a dream. For just as a dream deposits the dreamer from one surreal vision to another without warning, I suddenly find myself in the entrance of a great hall.

Ceilings of a polished white stone soar far above us, calling to mind the gothic architecture of Italian Cathedrals. A grand staircase with bannisters made of tree branches winds its way on either side of a massive, ornately carved throne. The hall is quiet as a tomb, but brightly lit—the sun reflecting off the white stone with a nearly blinding quality of light.

The fox halts beside a column seemingly constructed of the ethereal white trees, runes like the ones found in Mama's journal carved into the sides. I lean closer to inspect them, once again wishing for Lucy.

The soft echo of footsteps rings out over the polished stone floors, and I flatten against the column, my eyes searching for the source of the sound. Nine men in gray tunics and tall boots march past me. They are accompanied by wolves with silvery-white pelts, padding silently at their sides.

They cannot see you, the fox thinks into my mind when I let out an unintentional sound of distress. *You are only spirit.*

Satisfied I am not to be discovered, I return my attention to the men and the wolves beside them. The wolves behave neither as the feral creatures I am familiar with nor as trained beasts. As with the fox beside me, there is an innate intelligence in their countenance, a dignity in their carriage. It is clear, then, that these are the spirit animals of the nine Sylvani men.

The men themselves bring to mind guardsmen or soldiers. They have a military air about them—something in their bearing, perhaps. The features of their faces all share a similarity to my mother's, with leanly muscular bodies, almond-shaped eyes, and a beauty that has long been copied in the great Grecian statues. There is an otherness in the sheer perfection of their features, as though they are truly statues come to life.

At the other end of the hall, they form two rows on either side of the throne. They stand at attention, tall and silent.

I turn toward the entrance of the hall, searching for the source of their anticipation. "What are they waiting for?" I whisper to the fox.

A bell tolls, somber and eerie throughout the quiet hall. Beside me, the fox stiffens as if preparing for a blow.

A gentleman enters—he is of such regal bearing that I almost fall into one of the ridiculous curtsies I executed at the Royal Palace in London. His hair is long and as black as ink, and a diadem of silver branches sits atop his head. Beside him is a white stag, silver leaves sprouting from its antlers. A jolt of recognition strikes me as I realize it is the same I first saw in my mother's vision. The gentleman strides toward the throne and settles himself upon it as the Sylvani soldiers remain stiffly at attention. His face, though beautiful, has a fierce quality to it, as though he does not often smile.

"The Court may enter," he says, his voice deep but melodic.

Another bell sounds, this time much less somberly, and the doors to the great hall fling open. A crush of beautifully dressed Sylvani nobles enter, dressed in richly brocaded and colorful gowns and evening attire—clothing so lavishly adorned with silver and gemstones even the Crown Jewels would be hard-pressed to contend with. These ethereal creatures are strangely quiet as they take their places on either side of the hall. No inane conversations, no tittering from ladies; even the shoes upon their feet make little to no sound. This lends the whole proceeding a solemn formality, one that sends a chill of apprehension through me. Even more curious is the absence of spirit animals.

"Where are their animals?" I ask the fox, and it shakes its head.

Only King Brannor, the royal family, and the king's guardsmen are permitted to have their spirit animals present at Court.

"Bring forth Isidora," the king says from his throne.

"Isidora?" I say to the fox, turning in shock toward the entrance of the hall. "But surely he does not mean . . ."

The doors to the great hall open, and a girl with hair as pale as my own is brought forth, flanked on either side by Sylvani guardsmen and their wolves. Her head is held high, her mouth tight in an expression of displeasure I know so well.

"Mama," I cry, my voice choked with a sudden torrent of emotion. I turn to the fox. "How can this be?"

The rattle of chains draws my attention back to the unbelievable scene before me, and with a slowly dawning horror, I realize my mother is being brought before the king—her father—in chains. Following at a distance is a snowy white fox, and the fox beside me hangs his head in sorrow.

Across the room, the king comes to his feet. "Isidora," he says, his voice somehow carrying though he does not seem to speak in a loud tone, "it pains me to see you brought before me thus."

"If it brings you so much displeasure, Lord Father, then you need only remove my chains and your pain shall be alleviated." Her tone is calm but with a defiant edge to it that makes my chest swell with pride.

His face seems to darken. "I have been forced to call the Cascadian Court to bear witness to my sentencing. You have openly defied me, but if you will only recant your declaration to leave the Sylvan realm for the human one, then all will be forgiven."

There is a pause so great it feels as though everyone present is holding their breath.

"And if I do not?" my mother asks, almost too quietly to hear.

"Then you will be kept locked away until your wedding ceremony with Lord Elric. I have no doubt he, with all the power he has been blessed with, will be able to bring you to heel."

Anger, sharp and bitter, strikes through me on behalf of my mother. The words of her journal entry spring to mind: *my marriage was arranged without my consent.* Through some powerful arcana I have yet to understand, Mama's spirit fox has brought me to the moment when she chose to leave the Sylvan realm.

"I have seen what the future holds for me, and Lord Elric is not part of it."

A loud crack like thunder splits through the room as my grandfather bashes his fist against his throne. "Such insolence!"

All at once, the room darkens. The crowd of Sylvani nobles shift nervously, their eyes casting first about the room and then up at the ceiling. Black, ominous clouds hover over the great hall, as a threatening rumble of thunder sounds above us. The sudden storm is quite obviously unnatural. Aside from the fact that it is occurring indoors, every fiber of my ghostly being senses the arcana behind it. From the equally dark expression on my grandfather's face, I can only assume the storm is his doing.

My mother stands unflinching in the face of such power, the tension mounting until I am sure lightning will strike her down.

"My Lord Husband," a new voice calls from behind us, the tone harshly scolding. I turn to watch a grand lady stride toward us. She wears a flowing dress so celestially white it appears to be made from starlight. She is the image of my mother, only her hair is the color of a fiery sunset. "Enough of this!" She waves her hand imperiously at the thunderstorm above us. "Even your fellow nobles are cowed in the face of such temper. It shall not be borne."

As she passes Mama, her fingertips just barely brush my mother's arm, a pained expression flashing across her face before being quickly replaced by one of censure.

"Arria," the king says, a reluctant scowl upon his face. As quickly as they appeared, the clouds dissipate. "I was told you were at sea."

"And you thought I'd hold no objection to your sentencing our only daughter without my presence? What's more," she says, her voice shaking as though overcome with anger, "you have brought her before the Court bound in chains?"

"Our daughter is powerful."

"We are *all* powerful," Arria's voice snaps through the great hall. She shimmers brighter and brighter, her gown becoming almost iridescent in the face of such radiance. If King Brannor's anger took the form of darkness, then Queen Arria's became a light more blinding than the sun. She stalks toward the guardsmen on either side of my mother. "Take the chains from her at once."

The guardsmen scramble to do as she commanded. When the last chain drops to the floor, Mama's spirit fox presses against her side as though relieved. I smile down at the spirit fox at my own side, but its expression continues to look solemn.

"What would you have me do, my queen?" the king asks from his throne. It seems that he alone can look at her while she is shining so brightly. Everyone else in the Court has averted their eyes.

"Do you deny our daughter has been blessed with the gift of prophecy? Many times you have called upon her to divine some political strategy or another."

"I do not deny it."

"And yet you think you can thwart the most important of all prophecies? A vision of future children? Children this realm, with so few births and much war, can ill afford to lose."

Thunder growls through the hall again, but no darkness appears. "Children who will be half-mortal."

The queen bows her head in acquiescence. "They will still be of our blood."

"I do not choose this path lightly, Lord Father," my mother says, glancing down at her spirit fox. "I understand the consequences. I know what I must leave behind."

"You cannot possibly," the king says. "List them for her, Arria. If you are to support this madness, then I, and the entire Cascadian Court, must bear witness to Isidora making an informed decision."

The queen straightens. "Isidora, if you choose the mortal realm over Sylvania, then you must know all portals to our realm will be closed to you. Spending more than a short amount of time in the mortal realm will change you irreparably, and you will never be able to return. Separated from your spirit animal, you will be forced to seek another source of power. Only the sun of that realm will have the strength to provide your arcana with the energy it needs, and as you know, the mortal sun is a fickle thing. It is only present during a short part of any day." The queen pauses and meets her daughter's eyes. "But because you are full-blooded Sylvani, you will adapt."

Mama remains silent throughout her mother's speech, one hand upon the head of her spirit fox.

"Your future children will be gifted with the abilities of our race, but they will face unique challenges. Half-Sylvani, they will be born without a spirit animal and forced to draw on the sun as a source of energy. Always they will long for the realm of their ancestors. The portals will call to them, but should they cross, their power will rapidly desert them. Our realm is not their realm, and even the sun's rays shine differently here. At best, they will live a half-life, never truly belonging in either realm."

The king's eyes search his daughter's. "This is what you'd wish upon your future children?"

"Your dire warnings have been heard," Mama says, "but I vow before all, I will do everything in my power to make sure my children are never affected thus."

The barest hint of a smile appears on the mouth of the queen.

"I commend you for your selfless conviction," the king says, "however, there is one last thing you will lose should you leave this realm. Arria, if you will continue?"

A murmur of distress works its way through the Court, placing a heavy weight upon my chest. Mama glances down at the spirit fox, her eyes shining as though full of unshed tears. The fox gazes back at her and nods once.

Though I do not yet understand this exchange, a dark sorrow descends upon me.

"In leaving this realm and losing your immortality, your spirit animal will be cast aside, forced to remain here—" the queen pauses and takes a shaky breath, "separated from you for the rest of eternity." Everyone in the great hall flinches as though the queen cracked a whip above their heads. Mama, though, remains steadfastly silent.

"I understand the consequences," Mama says in a steady voice, though tears stream unchecked down her cheeks. Again she glances down at the fox. It presses against her as though urging her on. "I choose the mortal realm."

The queen gazes at Mama with sorrowful understanding upon her face, but the king's face darkens once again. "So be it," he says. "You have made an informed choice before the Cascadian Court. I will grant you permission to leave this realm, but you leave now."

Mama's head whips up, and the queen makes a move toward her daughter, but a powerful wind blasts through the hall. Everyone is thrown to the outer walls; several nobles passing through my unsubstantial body.

The queen and Mama are screaming, but I cannot make out their words. The wind is surely more terrible than even those in Hell. Mama and her spirit fox are lifted into the air, held aloft by some unseen force. Mama's arms are outstretched, and the queen reaches for her. Mama struggles high above us, but the wind holds her captive.

Then, with a sound like a limb being torn forcibly from someone's body, the wind rips the fox free from Mama.

Her soul-shattering scream is the last thing I hear before I am pulled away from the horrific memory.

TWENTY-EIGHT

THE return to my body after being nothing but spirit is so painful and disorienting, I can do nothing but lie in a broken heap upon the floor.

"Why would you show me such a thing?" I ask the fox, tears streaming unchecked down my face. "I cannot imagine the pain you must have gone through . . . what Mama . . ." I choke on a sob.

Above all other memories, your mother chose this one. It was one of the most traumatic of both our lives, and yet, it was not such a singular event. As much power as each Sylvani possesses, that power is checked only by the harsh rulings of its leaders.

It was the longest speech the little fox had given me, and my mind struggled to muddle through its meaning. "The king's cruelty toward his own *daughter* . . . surely that wasn't a common thing?"

He is king because he shows no mercy—even to those of his own blood. You have always seen Sylvania as a utopia, a place where arcana thrives without fear of recrimination from mortals. But it is bound by its own set of laws, its own customs—ones that will seem harsh to you.

A utopia. I think of the many stories I heard of Sylvania growing up, of the way I so desperately wanted to see it for myself, to see unicorns and dragons and all the mythical creatures in the flesh. In the fox's words, I hear my mother. She said as much in one of her entries: *And yet, the rules of English Society pale in comparison to those of Sylvania.* I cradle my head in my hands. I was so sure she was leading me to escape to her realm, but now . . .

"Then what am I to do?" I ask—though whether I am asking my mother or the fox at my side, I cannot say.

Your mother left that memory as a means of communicating exactly what hardships you may face in Sylvania, but it still stands as a possible refuge should this mortal realm prove ruinous for you. The queen, your grandmother, would welcome you.

I force myself to my feet, swaying as nausea and the stabbing pain in my abdomen nearly knock me down again.

"Then Mama did intend for me to cross over?" I press my hand to my forehead as if to keep my poor brain from escaping. I have never been so confused, nor so indecisive. I think of the carriage driver, lying witness to what I had done. He may not have understood how the explosion came about, but he will find Lord Blackburn's body and remember that I walked away unscathed. Imprisonment is likely my only other option.

I will lead you to the gateway. You must choose whether you will cross.

I can only sigh in resignation at this unhelpful response. "Lead on, then," I say, and open the door for the fox. After securing my reticule to my wrist, I limp down the stairs like an old woman, avoiding eye contact with the few people already in the pub so soon after sunrise. Since no one so much as glances our way, I can only assume the fox is visible only to me in the same way that we were hidden from the Sylvani in the other realm.

I make it to the back of the inn before I lose the contents of my stomach. I lean against the rough wooden beams like a drunken wastrel. The fox waits patiently, sympathy clear in its large eyes. Breathing hard, I continue a short ways down the road, far enough not to have to worry about any of the kind inn staff finding me. When the inn is far enough in the distance, we leave the road and walk laboriously to the top of a small hill. With my face tilted up to the sun, I close my eyes. The sun penetrates my skin, its healing light chasing away some of the pain until I can almost breathe normally.

Lord Blackburn must have done more damage than I'd thought, and tingles of apprehension race through me.

It is not far now. The fox lopes away, and I follow at a much slower pace.

We stay close to the Great North Road, just as the map showed—not far from Lord Blackburn's wreck of a carriage. When the rock formation once again looms before me, just as in my vision, the fox stops. I glance back at the inn, still within sight. I cannot believe how close I've been this whole time.

Only your blood will open the gate.

I step forward and touch the rock, the surface rough and cool against my palm. A thrum of energy seems to awaken the longer I touch it. My reticule still dangles from my wrist, and from within it, I withdraw the dagger Lord Thornewood gave me. A sad smile touches my lips as I see my reflection in the blade. I'm sure drawing my own blood wasn't what he had in mind.

I press the tip of the dagger to my wrist. A single bead of blood wells up before running down my skin onto the rock.

Above me, the gateway awakens. Energy cascades over the rock like water, while the air under the bridge shimmers. Still, it isn't enough. I know more blood is required. My family's faces rise up in my mind to torture me one by one. Can I really do this?

The soft sound of a boot on grass alerts me to someone's approach. I turn, my heart racing in my chest.

"Hello, Katherine," Lord Blackburn says. His clothes are rumpled and torn, his hair standing up in patches. But it's the look on his face that really clues one in on the fact he is unhinged.

"Lord Blackburn," I say, the realization that he is truly alive and standing dawns on me slowly. "But how—"

"How did I survive?" He holds up the accursed ring. "You gave me the power."

I nearly sink to my knees in defeat. "The ring had the power to heal you?"

He sneers at me. "Are you devastated, my love? If it brings you comfort, you did succeed, but not for long." He steps forward and grabs hold of my arm. "Come, there's an inn nearby where we can hire a coach. Despite your best efforts, we will be continuing on our journey."

With my hands curled into tight fists, more blood from my self-inflicted wound falls upon the rock. A steady hum begins, and an indistinct doorway faintly shimmers.

Lord Blackburn stills. His expression is perplexed at first but rapidly moves to excitement. "I don't believe it," he says. "This is the gateway, isn't it? The portal to the Sylvani realm." He looks at me with manic excitement shining in his eyes. "I knew having you for my own would be life-altering for me, but I never imagined you'd lead me to the portal."

Not only have I failed to free my family and myself from this monster, but I have led him to more of my kind. The fox catches my eye, then, still undetected by Lord Blackburn, and I think of the display of power I saw there. I almost smile when I think of Lord Blackburn facing my grandfather's awesome ability.

He touches the rock reverently. "I have only to step through this doorway, and all the wonders of the Sylvani realm will be before me."

"And you plan to go there alone? I wish you good luck then, for you are mad."

"The Order of the Eternal Sun stands behind me on this. I have only to inform them I've found the gateway, and I will have their assistance. As you have seen for yourself, you and your kind are weak when it comes to those like me. And if you, who are only half-Sylvani, can provide such a burst of power, imagine what those beyond this portal can do."

An ice cold sensation washes over me. As he has been my only threat, I have forgotten there are others like him. "I'll never let you through."

"And how will you stop me? Your stores of energy must be nearly depleted. In truth, I had no idea you had the power to not only resist my energy drain, but also to cause such a massive explosion. Had it not been for the residual power left in my system, I never would have survived. As it happens, my driver was not so lucky."

I suck in my breath in disbelief. "He was breathing when I left."

"Was he? Impressive, that. Well, he was very much dead when I found him."

The guilt flays my insides until I clutch my abdomen in much the same way I did earlier. I killed an innocent man. I didn't even stay long enough to be sure he would recover. A sob catches in my throat.

Lord Blackburn tilts his head in mock sympathy. "How terrible to take a human life. I can't imagine the shame you must feel."

I shake my head as tears fill my eyes. Never before have I used arcana to harm someone. My pain is so all-consuming I don't even pull away when Lord Blackburn's fingers wrap around my arm.

"With so much energy expended," he says into my ear, "I doubt you have much left. So tell me, Katherine, this portal requires your blood to open, yes? Then we must be sure to feed it plenty."

My eyes snap to his. A cruel darkness swirls in their depths, but I will not give in. I shove him as hard as I can and hold my dagger at the ready.

He sneers at me, the slash across his face I gave him earlier red and jagged in the sunlight. "You won't have the chance to use that this time."

"Perhaps not," I say, "but you cannot expect me to stand here docilely and let you bleed me dry."

A determined look replaces his sneer, and I balance on the balls of my feet, prepared to leap out of his path. He charges me, but without my full energy, I'm as slow as any human and hampered by the full skirts of my dress. I yelp as his hand grabs my arm, his fingers digging into my flesh like talons. He grasps hold of my hand holding the dagger and squeezes until I fear the bones of my fingers may break. The dagger falls to ground. He pulls me close, and I struggle so violently his fingernails draw blood from my arms.

The thunder of horse hooves causes us both to jump. Though I stand in full view of the road, I cannot trust my eyes. Surely the man riding toward us is not who I think it is.

But I'd know that devastatingly tall, muscular frame anywhere.

Lord Thornewood.

Riding with him is Tavi, the man who had brought him news at Thornewood.

His eyes waste no time in seeking me out. The dark anger there blazes when he takes in the scene. He jumps down from his horse and stalks over to us, every muscle in his face tight. Tavi dismounts as well and takes hold of both horses. I take advantage of Lord Blackburn's momentary distraction and wrench away from his grasp. I run to Lord Thornewood and with a gentle touch, he pulls me close to his side. Only then does he seem to relax—marginally.

"Katherine," he says, his voice rough, "thank God I found you. Are you well?"

"Well enough," I say truthfully.

"Has he hurt you?" he asks. I hesitate, and his jaw muscle twitches as he takes in both Lord Blackburn's slashed cheek and the bruises on my throat.

Before I can answer, his hand snaps forward and yanks Lord Blackburn by the cravat until they are eye to eye.

"Unhand me at once," Lord Blackburn says. Despite his tone, his face is contorted in fear. He struggles against Lord Thornewood's hold as uselessly as I struggled against his in the carriage.

"I warned you what would happen if you touched her," Lord Thornewood says, every muscle in his body taut.

"None of this involves you, Thornewood."

"It does when you steal my betrothed away like a thief in the night."

Lord Blackburn scoffs, but his expression is wary. "You expect me to believe that? Neither Katherine nor her grandmother said a word."

"I've only just returned from her father's house. Imagine our surprise when we came to London and found her missing."

"You spoke to Papa?" I ask, my voice high-pitched with incredulity.

His face softens as he looks at me. "Did I not tell you I would do so? I am a man of my word, after all."

Lord Blackburn takes advantage of Lord Thornewood's momentary distraction and shoves him away. He draws himself up to his full height, which is unfortunately a head shorter than Lord Thornewood. "Well your *betrothed* and I are eloping." He turns to me and narrows his eyes. "Isn't that right, Katherine?"

My heart pounds loudly in my ears. I open my mouth to pronounce the truth but am interrupted.

"Only because she was forced," Lord Thornewood says, his voice deeper with anger.

I close my eyes and whisper a quick prayer of thanks. Penelope must have contacted him after all.

"This changes nothing," Lord Blackburn says in a hiss, his eyes burning on mine. "You *will* do this."

"I will never open the gateway for you."

Lord Thornewood's gaze shifts to the rocks behind us. I can see his quick mind putting the pieces together. "The gateway . . . to the Sylvani?" he asks, and the absence of fear or disgust in his eyes brings a rush of relief.

"My mother's realm lies beyond these rocks," I say.

"If you refuse," Lord Blackburn says, "then Lucy will pay the price instead."

Lord Thornewood takes a menacing step forward. "You dare threaten her?"

Lord Blackburn smirks. "It is Katherine who is the dangerous one here. She let out a blast of energy so powerful it destroyed my carriage and killed the driver. She—"

"The driver may have been injured," Lord Thornewood interrupts, "but he was very much alive last I saw him."

I jerk in surprise. How could I have let myself be taken in by Lord Blackburn yet again? My relief that the driver still lives is nearly palpable.

"What does it matter?" Lord Blackburn demands. "Her power is so monstrous that she nearly succeeded in killing the both of us!"

I swallow, my mouth suddenly dry. "He gave me little choice. He is a member of a brotherhood that can pose a danger to my family and me."

"I know what you are," Lord Thornewood says to Lord Blackburn, his eyes narrowed dangerously, "and I know Katherine. In truth, I'm sorry she didn't succeed."

My gaze jumps to Lord Thornewood's.

"I am well aware of this . . . Order of the Eternal Sun," Lord Thornewood says with a look of disgust. When Lord Blackburn shoots him a look of surprise, he smiles darkly. "My man of business here has been making inquiries on my behalf. I knew there was something wrong about you, I just didn't know what. You hid your involvement well, but not well enough for a man of Tavi's talents. So talented, in fact, that he was able to track you. But what we have not been able to determine is whether you are one of the monstrous beings who drains the energy from your victims."

Lord Blackburn pales, no doubt disturbed by how much information Lord Thornewood has uncovered.

"Then you must have also discovered that I am not without my own abilities," Lord Blackburn says. "She and I have an agreement. I want what was promised to me."

"What was *promised* to you was I'd ruin you if you ever pursued Katherine again. I mean to make good on my word."

Lord Blackburn laughs humorlessly. "Ruin? Why should I fear ruin from a dead man?"

His statement hovers in the air, igniting the tension like the strike of a match.

Lord Blackburn pulls a pistol from beneath his jacket and aims it straight at Lord Thornewood's chest. Tavi drops the reins of the horses to come to his employer's aid, but I know he will never make it in time.

Despite my depleted energy, I call every drop of power left inside me to stop the pistol from discharging. A sharp cramp nearly doubles me over as a blast of white light shoots from my palm. The weapon and Lord Blackburn's hand are frozen in place.

Lord Thornewood lunges forward. His fist hits Lord Blackburn square on the jaw, knocking his head back. Before Lord Blackburn can react, he hits him again—an uppercut just under his chin. Lord Blackburn swings back, and his movement frees him from my weak hold on the pistol. Tavi circles them, searching for an opening. Before he can act, Lord Thornewood barrels into Lord Blackburn. They crash to the ground, and a scream bursts from my mouth as they wrestle for control of the weapon.

A dark desperation burns within me. I will not stand aside weakly, hoping for a favorable outcome. I force my uncooperative limbs forward.

The fox, forgotten until now, appears at my side. Its clear eyes stare up at me, waiting.

"Help me," I say, my voice so twisted with anguish I barely recognize it.

It steps forward and bows its head. As if I have done it a thousand times before, I touch my hand to its soft forehead.

A surge of pure energy fills me, and a blinding light emanates from my skin, noticeable now even to my own eyes. I think of my grandmother, the queen, shining as brightly as the sun. This power makes me feel as though I can bend even the elements to my will. I move as though gravity has no hold over me, flashing to the wrestling men's sides. My entire being is focused on stopping Lord Blackburn.

I thrust myself between the two of them and grab hold of Lord Blackburn's arms with such force that he loses his grip on the pistol. Lord Thornewood and Tavi race to retrieve it, but my attention shifts to the hateful ring on Lord Blackburn's finger. I wrench it free and use some of the power pulsing through me to crush it in my fist.

"Katherine—" Lord Blackburn cuts himself off shakily. He cannot even look at me, but shields his eyes as though he gazes up at the sun.

Every threat, every moment of fear he inflicted upon me tears through my mind. No amount of blackmail will keep this man from looming in the background, continuing his threats against my family until we are forced to constantly look over our shoulders, waiting for the day when the Order of the Eternal Sun finds us and opens the portal to the other realm—or worse.

I think of Lucy and Robert, my father, of myself and Lord Thornewood. I think of the destruction this one man could reap in our lives—has *already* brought upon us.

My fingers encircle Lord Blackburn's wrists, squeezing until he grits his teeth. "Katherine, *please.*"

I feel his own power just under the surface of his skin, racing like an erratic pulse. It buffets against my own energy, testing the invisible walls this immense power has erected around itself. The power within me is like a hurricane compared to the tame breeze contained within Lord Blackburn. And then I realize what I must do.

I close my eyes.

The energy surges within me, desperate for release, and I let it.

Lord Blackburn smiles in surprise and triumph as his innate ability greedily sucks up my released energy. But his expression rapidly turns to panic as his body fills with more raw power than it could ever contain.

For a moment, he shines as brightly as my grandmother did in the Sylvani hall.

I let go as he falls to the ground in convulsions as though he is being electrocuted, crying out for help in a strangled voice.

I watch unblinking as he gasps his last breath. The cruel darkness leaves his eyes until they are as lifeless as glass.

A warm hand touches my shoulder, and I turn reluctantly toward Lord Thornewood. If he didn't revile me before, then what must he think after I used my power to take a life before him? But his face holds no hint of censure, only relief.

He pulls me into his arms. "Katherine," he says, his voice rumbling beneath my ear, "he left you with little choice, and if you had not killed him—" he tilts my chin up to meet his eyes, "I would have."

I glance down at the body at our feet, nausea churning inside me. I shiver as if in shock. I cannot believe Lord Blackburn is dead. I cannot believe that I—

"It's over," he says. "I haven't the faintest idea how you did what you did, but it was necessary.'"

"I used his own power against him," I say quietly. "I filled him with so much energy it stopped his heart."

Lord Thornewood looks down at Lord Blackburn's still form grimly. "He would have never stopped coming after you or your sister. What happened here was nothing other than self-defense, Katherine. His actions sealed his fate long before you entered the fray." He turns to Tavi, waiting silently nearby. Despite his exotic coloring, he has the ability to disappear from notice, and yet, when he so chooses, he can be rather intimidating. "Tavi, would you be so good as to fetch the innkeeper? Tell him we witnessed Lord Blackburn collapse with convulsions."

Tavi bows. "Right away, my lord."

I watch him go. "He can be trusted? He won't . . . tell anyone what he has really seen?"

"And tell them . . . what exactly? You touched Lord Blackburn and he fell to the ground with convulsions? It sounds as if the man had a terrible medical condition." When I fail to appear relieved, Lord Thornewood says, "Tavi is my most trusted and loyal servant. I employ his entire family. He would never betray me."

"I believe you."

He offers me his arm. "Come, there is no reason we should continue to stand here, agonizing over what has already happened. Tavi will fetch the innkeeper, who will in turn contact the proper authorities."

"Yes, you're right," I say, but something calls my attention back to the portal. It shimmers like mist in between the rocks, just a hint of the world that lays beyond visible.

The fox appears again, hovering near the rocks.

The gateway will close, his voice whispers in my mind.

I glance up at Lord Thornewood, but though he faces the fox, he makes no sign of awareness. In spite of the terrible memory I witnessed in Sylvania, there is still the part of me that longs for the beauty of that realm, for those who are like me.

Lord Thornewood touches my hand upon his arm, his own hand warm and strong. And I know. I can never leave now; I'm as bound to him as my mother was bound to my father.

The fox bows his head and disappears through the portal. A sense of loss threatens to rise up and engulf me, but I stamp it back down.

Lord Thornewood glances down at me as though sensing my hesitation. "Are you ready to go home?" he asks, his voice quiet.

"Where is home, my lord?" Not to my grandmother's, surely.

"I swore to your father I'd bring you home to Bransfield," he says, and I can hear the smile in his voice. "It was the condition he set when I refused to let him accompany me."

"I can go home?" I ask, wistfully. I'm still in shock I won't have to leave this world behind.

He laughs softly. "You may." He tips my chin up to meet his stare. "To one of your homes, at least."

I draw in a breath as I remember my sister. "Oh, but what of Lucy? We cannot leave her at Grandmama's. We must go back to London immediately."

"Your sister is safe. She and your brother are on their way to Bransfield as we speak."

My head drops in relief. "I cannot thank you enough, my lord. For everything. But how in the world was Tavi able to find me?"

A muscle in his jaw twitches, his face tormented. "We received word that he had eloped with you just yesterday, and we knew he would avoid the trains. The Great North Road was his only option, and Tavi and I rode all night until we came across the destroyed carriage. It wasn't long after that we discovered you by the road."

Mama. Logic told me to go, to give up on this world entirely, but just as her last journal entry said, instinct led me to the hillside—where Lord Thornewood found me. "And I cannot tell you how happy I am you did."

He smiles and gives a gentle squeeze of my hand. "Come, we have a long carriage ride ahead of us. I am glad Tavi had the forethought to order my coach sent to the inn to await us."

I walk beside him, a dark cloud eclipsing some of the happiness. "Is it wrong to feel relieved over the death of someone?"

"Not when it's over a man who would have never stopped trying to hurt you or the ones you love."

I glance back at the field where Lord Blackburn still lay. "Still, I fear this guilt will only grow in time."

Lord Thornewood stops and turns to me. "Katherine, you did what you had to do, what I would have done in your position. Let him not continue to have a hold over you, else what you did will be for nothing. Lord Blackburn would have killed either one of us given the chance. Perhaps I should feel regret for the end of his miserable existence, but I find I cannot." He touches my cheek. "I would never be able to live with myself if anything happened to you."

I lean into his hand, blinking back tears.

"So please," he says, his face serious, "tell me, has he told any others in the Order about you? About your family?"

"He assured me he never alerted them to the truth about me. I believe him—if only because he wanted me, and access to my mother's realm, all to himself." I deliberately omit the fact there may be others who suspect. I cannot bring myself to burden Lord Thornewood—not yet. Not after he has done so much for me already.

Some of the tension leaves his face, and he continues toward the inn again. "It's a relief to hear I won't have to keep you under lock and key," he says with a teasing grin.

I scoff, a small smile playing across my lips. "As if you could."

He only smiles and leads me toward a black coach with the Thornewood crest emblazoned on the side parked a short distance away. His hand is warm on the small of my back as he helps me in, and it lingers there for a moment longer than necessary. Suddenly, I feel much too warm.

He boosts himself up and takes the seat across from me, lounging comfortably so his legs touch mine. With a word from him, the carriage takes off—much more smoothly than Lord Blackburn's.

"You have questions," he says, a relaxed half-grin on his face.

"I have a plethora of questions, my lord," I say with a smile. Though, with his leg touching mine, and the closeness of the carriage, I have difficulty thinking of a single one.

We stare at each other for a moment or two. "Perhaps you will allow me to ask a single question?" he says.

I wave my hand in a vague "go ahead" gesture.

His easy smile disappears. "Why did you leave Thornewood?"

I glance down at my lap. "I thought it rather obvious."

"Not to me," he says. "Were you unhappy with your care?"

"No, of course—"

"Were you unhappy with me?"

My eyebrows draw low over my eyes. "That's more than one question."

"Well, what was I supposed to think, Katherine? I declare myself to you, promise to ask for your hand in marriage, watch you nearly die, and then as soon as you are better, you leave without a word?"

I stare at him, rather dumbfounded. I never thought of it in such a way. "I did not think—"

"You're absolutely right. You did not think. And if we are to have a successful marriage, we must both get in the habit of thinking of the other person."

"We might also have a better marriage if you would kindly stop interrupting me," I snap.

He grins. "God, you're a handful."

"And you're incorrigible."

He tilts his head. "So I've been told."

Memories of the past few days, of the anguish I felt not knowing if I would ever see him again, pushed aside all happy thoughts of our reunion. "I must know something," I say, my voice tight.

He nods seriously. "Anything."

"Where were you?" I ask, my voice breaking. Tears fill my eyes against my will. "Where were you when I was forced back to London with my grandmother? When I couldn't leave her house? When Lord Blackburn blackmailed me into eloping?"

A rustle of movement, and then the seat sinks as he sits beside me. "It seems we both have been operating under misunderstandings. I never wanted to leave you, Katherine. You must believe me." He moves his hand down to my lap to grip mine. "But I could not let Eliza destroy your reputation—your family's reputation. More importantly, as soon as I discovered the truth about your abilities, I was certain that was the reason Lord Blackburn had been singling you out."

My lips part in surprise. "You knew the truth about the Order when I was there at Thornewood?"

"Only just. Tavi arrived with confirmation that Lord Blackburn was a member of such a nefarious brotherhood the morning of your accident."

Suddenly, Lord Thornewood's apparent anxiety at the arrival of his man of business all those days ago made sense. "And you knew Eliza would do everything she could to make sure all of Society knew the truth about me," I say, finally piecing everything together. I think back to what Lucy said when I'd first woken up. That Lord Thornewood lied for me and insisted Eliza was confused.

"It did seem to be her goal," Lord Thornewood says, "but I was also terrified it would confirm the truth about you to Lord Blackburn. You needn't concern yourself over Eliza, though." He retrieves *The Examiner* from the seat across from me and turns to the gossip section. "Read it," he says with a nod when I look at him questioningly.

My eyes scan the page.

London was a-twitter this morning with news of a distressing nature. Though the play for a certain earl's heart has been well-known, it would seem the jealousy of a certain lady with the initials of E.G. has boiled over. In a shocking display at Lady Bellemont's ball just yesterday evening, E.G. insisted her rival, K.S., was involved in none other than witchcraft. The young lady would hear no dissuasion on the matter, despite the fact that witchcraft has not been seen nor heard of for ages. The earl in question was heard to say that poor Miss E.G. had suffered quite a blow—both to her pride and to her pretty head—and, as such, her allegations cannot be believed. As it was discovered at the earl's now infamous country ball which lady would be his future countess, it is this humble author's opinion that poor Miss E.G.'s words are nothing but lies born out of jealousy. Perhaps she would do well to return home for the Season, as this author is quite certain none of you gentle readers would allow such pitiable madness into your homes.

"Good Lord, this article will ban Eliza from every ball in London," I say. Truly a fate worse than death for her. "I must say, though, I'm quite at a loss. If Society has turned on her, then why am I in disgrace?"

This time it is his eyebrows that furrow in confusion. "Where did you hear such a thing?"

"From Grandmama and Lord Blackburn." I realize my mistake as soon as he asks. "They were lying."

"They were indeed," he says, his eyes sympathetic. "As for my continued absence, when I learned you'd left Thornewood without a word, I knew I had to seek out your father without delay. I wanted you under my protection as soon as possible. Once I gained his permission to ask for your hand in marriage, I returned to London. Mere hours after I returned, Penelope arrived with grave news." His expression darkens. "And here we are."

I lean back in relief. "Penelope came to our rescue after all." At his questioning look, I elaborate. "Grandmama was intercepting all our letters. We were unable to contact Robert or Papa, or . . . you."

"Nor receive any from me," he says. "It's as I thought. Or, rather, hoped. But how were you able to send word to Miss Hasting?"

I swallow and look out the window again. "We used arcana."

"Arcana? I assume you refer to the power you have?" I force myself to look at him again, but I see no censure in his eyes. He leans down and presses a kiss to my hand. "I love *you*," he says. "Even if that means you come with . . . unexpected but certainly useful abilities." He grins.

A surprised laugh escapes me. "I've never heard it put in such a way."

"But you must promise never to use it in such a way that it nearly takes you from me. Not ever again." His expression turns intense, almost pained. "I don't think I could endure another agonizing night of not knowing whether you'd ever wake up."

"I can only promise to try never to be in the same situation again. As I've told Robert and Lucy many times, I won't hesitate to save someone I love—no matter the cost."

"Then I must make sure you are never in that position."

I squeeze his hand gently in answer.

"Have I answered all your questions to your satisfaction, my lady?"

I did have one more. "You still wish to marry me . . . after everything that happened?" I ask, gripping my seat with the hand not in his until it turns white.

"You think I am in the habit of making promises I never intend to keep?"

I turn my head toward the window to hide my hurt. "So this is only about your honor?"

His hand cups my cheek, and I turn toward it, craving his touch even though he is the source of my pain. His fingers gently turn my head toward him. My lips part as I meet his hooded gaze. "I don't blame you for being cross with me. After all, you never received a formal proposal."

His fingers leave my chin and search inside his coat. When he pulls out a ring, it becomes difficult to draw a breath. The carriage shifts as he drops one knee to the floor.

"My darling Katherine, I find I cannot live another moment without your wit and beauty in my life. Will you do me the exquisite honor of becoming my wife?"

I pull him back onto the seat with me and press my lips to his. "Yes," I say between kisses. "I would like nothing more."

TWENTY-NINE

I stare at the star sapphire on my finger. Slivers of moonlight reflect off it, making it appear to glow. I gaze up at Lord Thornewood—no, *Colin*—who brushes my loose hair from my neck with a self-satisfied smile. I will have to restore my hair to some semblance of decency before we arrive to Bransfield, but for now, I can only stare at my fiancé with an embarrassing degree of adoration.

"We should arrive at Bransfield in less than an hour," he says, his hand drawing lazy circles across my abdomen. As each muscle twitches in response, I wonder if this is what it feels like to be tortured.

I make a noise somewhere between an acknowledgment and a sigh of pleasure.

"I only point this out as I want you to know . . ." he pauses to kiss the side of my neck, which he has figured out makes me completely unable to think, ". . . this will be our last chance to be alone before the wedding."

"And when will that be, my lord?" I ask, a hint of teasing in my voice.

"As soon as I can damn well arrange it," he says gruffly.

When he pulls me onto his lap, a nervous giggle escapes me as desire licks at my insides like flames. "Try not to destroy my dress. I'll never be able to face my father."

Colin laughs. "Kindly refrain from mentioning your father when I'm trying to kiss you senseless. It has a terrible effect on the mood."

My answering laugh dies in my throat. His hands leave a path of shivery heat as he runs them over my breasts and down the sides of my bodice. We kiss each other desperately, until both our chests are heaving.

"This is the village," I say, when we pause for air. "We have only minutes left."

His eyes devour mine. "Then we'd best make the most of them."

ACKNOWLEDGMENTS

FAIR warning: I am Southern, and I become eaten alive by guilt if I don't properly thank everyone. This may be lengthy.

First and foremost, I would like to thank God, from whom all good things come.

Thank you to my loving and supportive husband, Sam. Not only do you have an awesome career that allows me to stay home and write, but you also never hesitate to entertain the kids when Mommy has a deadline! I love you.

A huge thank you to my parents, Ann and Larry, who have always believed in me and encouraged me. To my mom, especially, who has read *Arcana* in about a thousand different versions, helped me every step of the way, and should probably be paid as a second publicist for how much she marketed this book.

I must thank my cousin, Kelsey Sandy, because if it weren't for sleepovers where we made up ridiculous stories about Ben Affleck and Josh Hartnett, my love for telling a good romantic story may never fully developed. It was you who first started writing those stories down, and you will forever inspire me with your gorgeous prose! Thank you for all your love and support.

Thank you to my fantastic critique partners: Mandie Baxter and Jamie Manning. You read nearly as many versions of *Arcana* as my mom and never once complained. Mandie, I'm so glad we found each other! You're my other writing half. All our texts and emails keep me sane, and I can't thank you enough for all your support. Working/writing Mama, you are my hero. Jamie, your eagle eyes were essential, and your own books are an inspiration to me. Thank you for all your help!

I have the most incredible family and friends, all of whom have been so encouraging and supportive throughout this whole process. My grandmother, especially, has been looking forward to the moment she can walk into a bookstore and pick up my book. The time has finally come, Grandmom!

To my amazing agent, Brianne Johnson: thank you for pulling this story from the slush! It was truly the best Christmas present ever. Thank you, also, for your persistence. It's because of you that *Arcana* found such a wonderful home in Skyhorse Publishing. On a related note, thank you to the Writers House readers, who snatched my story out of the slush for Bri to read and cheered for its success. Thank you especially to Bakara Wintner, who gave some truly phenomenal editorial feedback.

To my editors, Nicole Frail and Constance Renfrow: thank you for falling in love with this book. It's been an absolute pleasure working with you!

For all the wonderful writers, readers, and authors who beta'd *Arcana* for me: Claire Gillian, Julie Reece, Susanna Hearn, and Amy Boyles. Thank you for all your helpful thoughts and feedback.

To my fellow debut TeamTalos author, Karina Sumner-Smith: I'm so glad we united during our debut angst. Your funny and brilliant emails were a large part of how I was able to keep calm.

To all the Skyhorse Publishing staff, especially Jason Snair. My cover is breathtaking; I can't thank you enough.

For everyone who has helped spread the word about *Arcana*, especially my in-laws, Mike and Carol, and all my friends and family in Greenville: thank you so much for your support!

And to you, dear reader: I am so grateful.